A special collection of three heart-warming stories where three loving couples receive the most precious gift of all!

Precious Gifts

When baby's delivered just in time for Christmas!

Marion Lennox

Josie Metcalfe

Kate Hardy

Marion Lennox is country girl, born on a south-east Australian dairy farm. Married to a 'very special doctor', Marion writes for Medical Romance™ as well as Tender Romance™, where she used to write as Trisha David for a while. In her non-writing life, Marion cares for kids, cats, dogs, chooks and goldfish. After an early bout with breast cancer she's also reprioritised her life, figured out what's important and discovered the joys of deep baths, romance and chocolate. Preferably all at the same time!

Josie Metcalfe lives in Cornwall now with her long suffering husband, four children and two horses, but as an army brat frequently on the move, books became the only friends that came with her wherever she went. Now that she writes them herself she is making new friends, and hates saying goodbye at the end of a book – but there are always more characters in her head clamouring for attention until she can't wait to tell their stories.

Kate Hardy lives on the outskirts of Norwich with her husband, two small children, two lazy spaniels – and too many books to count! She wrote her first book at age six when her parents gave her a typewriter for her birthday. She's wanted to write for Mills & Boon® since she was twelve – and says it really is the best of both worlds – especially as she gets to meet a new gorgeous hero every time... Kate is always delighted to hear from readers – do drop in to her website at www.katehardy.com

Precious Gifts

Marion Lennox
Josie Metcalfe
Kate Hardy

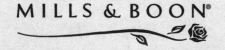

MILLS & BOON®

First published in Great Britain 2005
Harlequin Mills & Boon Limited,
Eton House, 18-24 Paradise Road, Richmond, Surrey, TW9 1SR

PRECIOUS GIFTS © Harlequin Enterprises II B.V. 2005

Dr Blake's Angel, Instant Father Christmas and *A Baby of Her Own*
were first published in Great Britain by Harlequin Mills & Boon
Limited in separate, single volumes.

Dr Blake's Angel © Marion Lennox 2002
Instant Father Christmas © Josie Metcalfe 1998
A Baby of Her Own © Pamela Brooks 2002

ISBN 0 263 84953 8

108-1205

Printed and bound in Spain
by Litografía Rosés S.A., Barcelona

Dr Blake's Angel

by

Marion Lennox

CHAPTER ONE

'I'M NOT a patient. I'm your Christmas present.'

Right...

The woman had glossy, copper-red hair. She was wearing purple patchwork overalls, a pink T-shirt and pink flowery sandals. She was also heavily pregnant.

Dr Blake Sutherland still had urgent house calls to do. He'd promised Grace Mayne he'd visit her tonight and the elderly fisherwoman was already waiting. He'd been up since dawn, he was exhausted and now he had a nutcase on his hands.

'Excuse me?'

'I bet you've never had a Christmas present like me.' The woman's bright smile exuded happiness.

Who on earth was she? Blake didn't have a clue. She'd arrived an hour ago, settled to wait for his last afternoon appointment and had been placidly reading old copies of *Rich and Famous* until he'd found time to see her.

His Christmas present...

On reflection, he decided to ignore what she'd said and try again. 'You're pregnant.' He sat back and did a slow assessment. She was at least seven months, he guessed, or maybe more. She was glowing with the health most women found in late stages of pregnancy, and she looked...lovely?

Lovely was as good a way as any to describe her, he decided as he took in her startling appearance. Her riot of copper curls was close cropped but not enough to stop the rioting. Her freckled face was enhanced by huge green eyes, and she had the most gorgeous smile...

Oh, for heaven's sake! Ignore the smile. She also had a problem or she wouldn't be here.

5

'Yes, I'm pregnant. Great work for noticing.' She chuckled. It was a nice, throaty chuckle that went beautifully with her eyes. 'Em said you were a brilliant doctor, and you've just proved it. Pregnant, hey?' She patted her tummy. 'Well, well. Who'd have guessed it?'

He had the grace to smile. 'I'm sorry, but—'

'I guess since I'm pregnant you have two gifts for the price of one—but maybe the outer package is the only useful bit. That's me.'

She was a nutcase! But she *was* pregnant and she may well have medical needs. He needed to step warily. The worst medical mistakes were made when doctors were tired, and he didn't intend to toss her out unchecked because she was a bit unbalanced.

'Have you come to see me about your pregnancy?' He glanced at her naked ring finger and took a punt. 'Miss...' Another glance to the card his receptionist had given him. 'Miss McKenzie.'

'It's Dr McKenzie,' she told him. 'Or Nell if you prefer.' Her smile deepened and she held out her hand in greeting. Dazed, he took it. 'Nell's better. Dr McKenzie always makes me feel like someone's talking to my grandfather.'

Her hand was warm and firm. His hand was shaken and released and that was how he felt. Shaken.

This conversation was way out of line, he decided. He didn't have a clue what was going on. 'Miss... Doctor...'

'Hey, you *are* exhausted,' she said, on a note of discovery. 'Emily and Jonas told me you were. They said you really, really needed me, and after an hour in your waiting room I'm starting to see that they're right.'

'Look, Miss—'

'Doctor,' she reminded him, and she smiled again. It was *some* smile. It was a smile that lit parts of the room he hadn't even known were dark.

He sat back and let his tired eyes assess her. She really was wearing the most amazing outfit. She looked exceedingly cute, he decided. And her red hair gleamed. Actually, all of her gleamed! She sort of beamed all over...

'Doctor, then.' He continued his visual assessment but his mind was working overtime.

She was right, he thought. He was exhausted. This town had far too much work for one doctor and the weeks before Christmas had seen things go haywire. It was the start of the silly season, and whatever happened in the town, the consequences usually ended up here. In his surgery.

That included barmy pregnant ladies who said they were doctors...

'Can I ask—?'

'I think you should.' She rested her hands lightly on her very pregnant tummy. 'Ask away. Or I can explain by myself if you'd rather.'

'Go ahead,' he said faintly, and her smile deepened.

'You promise not to rope me into a strait-jacket?'

'I promise no such thing.' Her smile was infectious. Somehow he found the corners of his mouth twitching in response. 'But I'll listen.'

That was better! Nell settled further back into her chair and relaxed. He seemed nice, she thought. And he was younger than she'd expected. Jonas and Emily had described him as best they could but it had hardly been a comprehensive description.

'Blake's in his mid-thirties,' Em had told her. 'He's got the most gorgeous gold-brown hair and smily brown eyes. Creasy eyes, if you know what I mean. Nice. They're tired creased as well as laughter creased but I guess you'd expect that after what he's gone through. And what he's going through. His life's all medicine. Work, work and more work. Except his marathon running—though how he finds the time to fit that in is anyone's guess.'

Emily had sighed as she'd described him. 'You'll like him, Nell. You must. Anyone would. It's a damned shame...' She'd hauled herself back on track. 'No matter.

But what else? Oh, he's tall. Over six feet. He's taller than Jonas.'

'Oh, for heaven's sake…' Jonas had interrupted then, cutting across his wife with good humour. 'Nell wants a medical description—not the sort of description you'd find in the lonely hearts column.' Jonas had grimaced his disgust, and Nell had grinned.

'OK, Jonas. What would you tell me about him?'

'He's a great guy. He likes beer.'

'Gee, that's useful,' Nell retorted, and both the women had chuckled.

'Well, he's a really talented surgeon,' Jonas told her, in a valiant attempt to fill in the bits his wife had left out. 'His training is in vascular as well as general surgery, so Sandy Ridge is lucky to have him. He's one caring doctor, with far more skills than the normal country doctor possesses. But Em's right. He drives himself into the ground.'

'Which is where you come in,' Em had added.

Which was where Nell came in. She'd gone to visit her friends and she'd ended up here.

So now Nell faced Blake Sutherland across the desk and she knew what she had to say. 'It's as I told you,' she said blandly. 'I'm your Christmas present. Take me or leave me, but I'm here, to use as you will.'

Blake Sutherland was not often flummoxed, but he was flummoxed now. And he was also so tired that he was having trouble understanding what was in front of him.

Sandy Ridge was an isolated medical community. Thirty miles to the north, the marriage of Jonas Lunn and Emily Mainwaring had given Bay Beach good medical cover, and his two friends gave him his only time off, but it wasn't enough.

That was the way he liked it, he'd told himself over and over through the two years he'd been here. He liked being a country doctor, and he liked being on his own. It was just every so often that he felt snowed under.

Like now. Like when he had the Christmas rush and a crazy pregnant stranger to cope with, and too many house calls after that.

'You'd better explain a bit more,' he managed, and Nell's smile softened into sympathy.

'Can I get you a cup of tea while I do?'

A cup of tea? She'd booked in as his patient and *she* was offering *him* cups of tea?

'Thank you, but no.'

'You look like you need it.'

What he needed was to get out of here. He needed to do his house calls, see Grace Mayne and then he needed to sleep—for about a hundred years!

'Can you just tell me what the problem is, and let me get on with my day?' he said wearily. 'Have you filled in a new patient summary?' He lifted a form and held it up without hope. Marion should have insisted she fill it out. He had no idea why she hadn't.

'Fill out a form when I could read ancient copies of *Rich and Famous* magazine?' Nell grinned. 'Why would I do that? I've been learning all about Madonna's love life, and very interesting it is, too. Much more gripping than anything I could write on a stupid form. And I'm not a new patient.'

'Then would you mind telling me what the heck you are?'

'I'm trying,' she complained. 'But you keep interrupting. I'm your Christmas present.'

'My Christmas present.'

'Yes.'

Blake sat back and gazed at this extraordinary purple and pink vision and he had trouble convincing himself he wasn't hallucinating.

'You're not gift-wrapped,' he said cautiously, and received a grin for his pains.

'That's the trouble with being so pregnant. It's hard to find enough wrapping paper.' She hesitated. 'You don't think we could find a pub where we could talk about this, do you?'

'Why do we need a pub?'

'It's just… Maybe we need a Christmas tree and some mistletoe and a bit more atmosphere.'

'Just explain.' It was a growl but he was at the end of his tether.

And she realised it. Nell spread her hands and she smiled across the desk at him—her very nicest smile.

'It's simple,' she told him. 'Your friends, Jonas and Emily, the doctors at Bay Beach…'

'I know who Jonas and Emily are.'

'Then you'll also know that they're very grateful to you for giving them time off when they need it. But you won't reciprocate, and with the sudden popularity of Sandy Ridge as a tourist destination your workload's become huge. So now…'

'So now?'

'They're repaying the favour. They're giving you a holiday. Four weeks, to be precise. Jonas was hoping to come himself but, with Robby recovering from his latest skin graft and another baby on the way, they don't want to leave each other over Christmas. When I said I was coming here…'

'You were coming here?' He was clutching at straws.

'Sandy Ridge is my home,' she told him. His look of incredulity seemed to annoy her. 'I might not have lived here for ten years, but I own the house out on the bluff. It's my home now. Or it will be soon. I intend to do it up and live in it.'

'But—'

'Yeah, there's the but,' she acknowledged. 'The place is a mess. I need to put a landmine under it to clear out the junk, and I need a base while I do it. That's where you come in. I'm only seven months pregnant so I'm good for at least another four weeks' work. Em said you needed someone now, so she and Jonas organised with your hospital board to pay me locum wages for four weeks. That means you, Dr Sutherland, can take yourself off for a Christmas holiday, and leave me with your responsibilities. All of them.'

To say he was flabbergasted would be an understatement. To walk away for four weeks...

No.

'The thing's impossible. I don't know what Jonas and Emily are thinking of.'

'They're thinking of you.'

'I can't go away.'

'Why not?' She smiled at him and her wide eyes were innocent. 'I'm very well qualified. Ring Sydney Central and they'll tell you. I worked with Jonas before he was married—that's how we met.' She arched her eyebrows, knowing before she said it that her next statement was hardly likely to be believed. 'In fact, I'm a very responsible doctor. Until last week I was in charge of Sydney Central Emergency.'

This was crazier and crazier. 'So why aren't you now?'

'In case you hadn't noticed, I'm a little bit pregnant.' She was talking to him as if he was stupid, and that was how he felt. 'I'm moving on. The new registrar can start work now, and Jonas said you needed me.' She smiled. 'So I came. If I'd left it much longer I could have dropped my bundle on your doorstep, and I wouldn't be much use to you with a baby in arms. Or not for a while.'

Blake took a deep breath. 'So let me get this straight. You've quit your job early specifically so you can give me four weeks' leave?'

'That's right.'

'And you're just going to walk in here and take over?'

'That's the plan.'

He shook his head in disbelief. 'I can't just walk out.'

'I expect it'll take a day or two to hand over.'

'You couldn't do it.'

'Don't be ridiculous,' she retorted. 'If you can cope with the medical needs of the town, I don't see why I can't.'

'Hell!'

'Why is it hell?' It was a polite enquiry—nothing more.

'You don't know anybody.'

She had an answer to that, too. 'That's where you're wrong. I lived here for the first seventeen years of my life so I imagine I know more people in the district than you do.'

He shook his head again, trying to clear the fog of weariness and confusion. 'Jonas and Em have paid you?' It came out an incredulous croak and she smiled.

'And the hospital board. Yes, indeed. An obscene amount.' She chuckled. 'No more than I'm worth, of course, but an obscene amount for all that.' She made her lips prim. 'I expect you'll have to write them a very nice thank-you note.'

He stared at her, baffled. 'You have it all sorted.'

'Of course.'

'The fact that you're pregnant didn't enter your calculations as something that needs to be factored in?'

'I'm a very fit pregnant doctor,' she told him.

Silence.

'The idea's stupid,' he said at last, and she shook her head.

'It's not stupid at all. Your hospital board have approved it. They're the ones who employ me—not you. I don't see you have much choice.'

He thought it through. On the surface it seemed fine. Only... 'Do you have any idea how many patients I see in a day?'

'I guess...a lot?'

'I've seen fifty today.'

'Fifty.' For the first time, her confidence ebbed a little. 'Fifty!'

'That's not including hospital rounds, and not including house calls. It's peak holiday season and I'm snowed under.

I started at six this morning, I don't expect to be finished before eleven and if I'm unlucky—and I'm nearly always unlucky—there'll be calls out during the night.'

'Good grief!'

'If you took it on—'

'I must.' She might be dismayed but she was still game. 'I made a bargain.'

'If you took it on you'd drive your blood pressure sky high. You'd give yourself eclampsia and I'd have a dead baby—and maybe even a dead mother on my hands. You think I want that?'

'Hey, that's a bit extreme.'

'Go home, Dr McKenzie,' Blake said wearily. He raked his hand through his hair. It verged on being too long, Nell thought inconsequentially, but, then, why shouldn't it be long? He had the loveliest hair. It was sort of sun-bleached brown with streaks of frost, and it was thick and curling. His strongly boned face, his tanned skin and deep brown eyes made him almost stunningly good-looking.

Oh, for heaven's sake! What was she thinking of? Get a grip! she told herself. Focus on what's important.

'Home's here,' she said softly, and watched as his startled gaze met hers.

'What do you mean?'

'I mean I've moved here. For ever. I want to have my baby here.'

'You want to deliver your baby in Sandy Ridge?' The idea was ridiculous. People didn't come to Sandy Ridge to have their babies. They left Sandy Ridge to have babies. With only one doctor, maternity was frankly dangerous.

He was shocked into saying the first thing that came into his head, and as soon as he said it he knew it wasn't wise, but it came out anyway. 'And the baby's father? What does he think of you moving here?'

She glared at that. Then her eyes fell to his hand. To a gold band on his ring finger.

'And your wife?' She used the same tone he'd used on

her, and it was frankly accusing. Their eyes locked across the desk, anger meeting anger. 'What does your wife think of you working yourself into the ground? Or isn't your personal life any of my business? OK, Dr Sutherland.' Her glare grew angrier. 'You tell me yours and I'll tell you mine.'

His gaze fell first. '*Touché*,' he said lightly, but she knew the word wasn't meant lightly at all. He'd been touched on the raw.

As had she. Damn, she wasn't going to feel sorry for the man. Or for herself. She was here to take over his responsibilities for a month and then get out of his life. But...

'How many patients a day did you say?' she asked faintly, and his mouth curved into the beginnings of a smile.

'Fifty.'

It gave her pause. 'I don't think I can—'

'I don't think you can either.' He rose. 'So it was a very nice idea, from you and from Jonas and Emily and the hospital board. But it's impractical and impossible. I'll ring them and thank them—as I thank you—but I think we should leave it at that. Don't you?'

'No.'

'No?'

'I told Jonas and Emily that I'd give you a decent Christmas.'

'And I've said it's impossible. You can't take over my Christmas.'

'No,' she said slowly, and her chin jutted into a look of sheer stubbornness. 'OK. Maybe I can't. But maybe I can share it.'

'What?'

'Maybe somehow we could have a Christmas to remember. Together.'

Nell wouldn't be budged. No matter how many arguments he raised, she countered them.

'You need a rest. You know you do.'

'Yes, but—'

'You know very well that a tired doctor is a dangerous doctor.'

'I can—'

'You can't. No one can. When you're tired, your judgement's impaired. That's why Jonas and Emily are worried about you.'

'Did they say my judgement was impaired?'

'Not yet. But it will be.'

'For heaven's sake, this is ridiculous.'

'What's ridiculous,' she said serenely, 'is you continuing to argue with me.'

'I don't even know you,' he threw at her, goaded. 'You walk in here like some outlandish—'

And that had been the wrong thing to say!

'You don't like my overalls?' She stood up, her eyes flashing fire. 'You don't like my gorgeous patchwork overalls? And you're judging me on them? How dare you? Of all the intolerant, prejudiced, male chauvinist—'

'I didn't say anything about your overalls,' he said weakly, but she stalked around the desk and advanced on him.

'Outlandish! What about me is outlandish except for my overalls?'

'Your temper?' he tried.

That brought her up short. She stopped a foot away from Blake and she glared.

'You *meant* my overalls.'

'They're…they're wonderful.'

'I made them myself.'

'Like I said—'

'They're wonderful,' she agreed, her eyes narrowing. 'Not outlandish.'

'I…not outlandish.'

'You're not colour prejudiced?'

'I like pink. And purple…'

'That's enough. There's no reason to go overboard.' Nell glared some more. 'Do we have a deal, Dr Sutherland, or do I go to the medical board and say you won't employ me because of stupid prejudices about pregnancy and patchwork pants?'

'I'm not employing you.'

'No. The hospital board is. And they already have. So if I'm now unemployed then I've been sacked and you're the one that's doing it. So I'm right. Prejudice...'

'I'm not prejudiced.'

'You want a quiet Christmas?'

'Yes.' How would he get a quiet Christmas if this virago was in town?

'Then do what we want. Let me share your load. Let me take on as much as I can, while you enjoy mince pies and mistletoe to the max.'

'I can't.' He took a deep breath. 'Look. Miss McKenzie—'

'Doctor!' It was an angry snap. 'Think it through. Think of what you're refusing.'

He took another breath, but still she glared at him. Her anger gave him pause. It made him stop and count to ten...

And counting to ten helped. It did give him time to think.

'Um...' he said, and she homed right in on it.

'Yes?'

She was deadly serious, he saw. She really was intending to live in the place. 'Maybe you could just do morning clinics for a bit,' he said weakly. That might get her out of his hair.

And maybe it'd even be a good idea.

It was a generous offer Jonas and Em had made. So maybe he should accept. If this woman could take on his morning work then he'd have only a normal day's work left to do himself.

She considered what he'd said and her anger faded. A little. 'It's a start,' she said grudgingly, sinking back into her chair and watching him across the desk. 'But I've been paid to work.' She brightened. 'I can take every second night's house calls.'

He bit his lip. 'You can't. The emergency calls are switched through to my house. It'd be too much trouble to change the system just for a month.'

'We wouldn't need to change the system.'

'Why not?'

'Because Em told me the situation here is the same as the one at Bay Beach,' she said sweetly. 'The hospital has the doctor's residence attached and it has four bedrooms. They were built at the same optimistic time—when hospital boards imagined doctors might *like* becoming country practitioners in remote areas. So, that's a bedroom for you, there's one for me, there's one for Ernest and there's one left for whoever wants to drop in.'

Ernest? Who was Ernest? Another child? A partner?

Blake didn't want to know. It was irrelevant. 'You can't stay with me.'

'Why ever not?' Her eyes widened in enquiry. 'The doctors' residence is supposed to be for doctors—isn't it? It's designed for up to four doctors. There's two here. Me and you.'

'Yes, but—'

'And my house is unlivable. That's one of the reasons I agreed to do this locum.'

'Miss McKenzie—'

'It's Dr McKenzie,' she said sweetly. 'And the board has already given me permission to move in with you. You know, you're going to have to get used to it. And…you really don't want to refuse.'

He looked across the desk and met her eyes. She'd calmed down, he realised. The laughter and temper and over-the-top threats had died. What was left was understanding. And sympathy.

And something more?

Something he didn't understand.

But he didn't want this woman in his house. He didn't want *anyone* in his house.

He didn't want anyone in his life!

And who was Ernest?

He was saved by the waiting-room bell. Marion, his receptionist, had ushered Nell into his surgery but with the last patient safely with Blake, she'd felt free to leave, so there was no one out there to see what the problem was.

'I need to see who this is.'

She glowered. 'There's no need to sound pleased. We haven't come to an arrangement.'

'Afterwards,' he told her, and opened the door with real relief.

CHAPTER TWO

As a rescuing angel, Ethel Norris didn't quite make the grade.

She was a massive woman, weighing close to twenty stone. Normally well groomed and cheerful, she was anything but well groomed now. Her clothes were soiled. Her mass of grey curls looked as if it hadn't been brushed since she'd climbed out of bed this morning and her cheeks were grubby with tearstains. She looked up as Blake entered the reception area, and the look she gave him said it was the end of her world.

'Oh, Dr Sutherland. Dr Sutherland...' She put her face in her hands and sobbed as if her heart were breaking.

'Hey...Ethel.' He guided her to a chair and pushed her into it, then knelt before her and pulled her hands away from her face. 'What is it?' His eyes were on hers. He was totally focussed on her distress, unaware that Nell had followed him to the door and was watching.

'I can't... I couldn't...'

'You couldn't what?'

'I broke.' She took a ragged gasp. 'And I've been doing so well. I've lost four stone and you were so pleased with me. My clothes have been getting looser and looser, and then all of a sudden I couldn't go on. I dunno. I sort of snapped. I went out and bought everything I could find. Ice cream. Biscuits...' She took a searing gulp. 'Not just one. Tubs and tubs of ice cream. Packets and packets of biscuits. I've stuffed myself stupid, and I've been sick but not sick enough. I'll have put all my weight back on and I can't bear it.'

'Ethel, you can't have put it all back on.'

19

'I have.' It was a wail of agony.

'How long have you been dieting?' Nell's voice cut across both of them.

Blake flashed her a look of annoyance but Nell seemed unconcerned. In fact, she appeared not to even notice.

'You must have been dieting for ever to lose four stone,' she said in a voice of awe. 'That's fantastic.'

Ethel looked up at her, her attention caught. Well, how could it not be caught by purple patchwork?

'Don't mind me. I'm just another doctor,' Nell told her blithely. 'I'm Dr Sutherland's new associate. But losing four stone. Wow!'

'I haven't—'

'How long have you been dieting?'

'Six months.'

'And this is the first time you've cracked?' Nell's voice remained awed. 'Six months of solid dieting! I never heard of such a thing. That's fantastic.'

'But now I've ruined it.'

'How have you ruined it?' Nell's eyes took in the vast-ness of the woman's figure, and her sharp intelligence was working overtime. Ethel must have had a serious eating disorder over many years to account for so much weight. 'It's my guess that eating a few tubs of ice cream wasn't a rare occurrence before you started dieting,' she said softly. 'You did it often—right?'

'Yes. But—'

'But now you've had a day off your diet.'

'I wasn't just off my diet.' The woman wailed. 'I binged.'

'Well, I don't blame you,' Nell said stoutly. 'If I'd lost four stone in six months then I'd binge, too.'

'Dr McKenzie.' Blake was glaring at her. This was his patient. She had no business butting in.

'Yes, Dr Sutherland?' She gave him her sweetest smile. 'Am I saying what you were about to say? I'm sure I am.

I understand all about diets. I've been on 'em ever since I was a kid.'

'You?' the woman whispered, and Nell chuckled.

'Yeah, well, I'm not on one now. As you see, I'm a bit pregnant and it'd be bad for baby. But as soon as I stop breastfeeding I'll be back to dieting. I just have to look at a tub of ice cream and I gain a midriff.'

'But nothing like me.'

'But not like you,' Nell agreed. 'I'd imagine you and Dr Sutherland have talked about the underlying problems—why you got so big in the first place.'

'Yes, but—'

'But nothing.' Nell crossed to Blake's side. She stooped and elbowed him aside. 'Dr Sutherland, this is women's business.'

He glowered. 'How can it be women's business?'

'Have you ever dieted?' She looked up and down at his long, lean frame. 'Marathon man.'

He was taken aback. 'No.'

'There you go, then.' Another sweet smile. Then she turned back to Ethel. 'You know, losing the amount of weight you need to lose to be healthy is going to take a couple of years.'

'I know that. That's why it's so terrible…'

'That you broke? No. That's why it's understandable. And there's no way you'll have gained four stone in a one-day binge. You won't have come close.' Nell smiled. 'You know, I'm watching my weight while I'm pregnant, but I can't do it all the time. I'd go stark staring mad. So I give myself days off.'

'Days off?'

'Like Christmas.' Nell's voice was totally serious now. She had eye contact with Ethel and she wasn't letting go. Woman to woman. 'Christmas is in two weeks. I can last until then, but I intend to eat way too much on Christmas Day. Far too much. Then on Boxing Day I'll think how much I enjoyed it and get on with being sensible.'

'But—'

'But there's lots more time to go before you hit an ideal weight,' Nell agreed. 'More so for you than for me, but eating sensibly is a lifetime thing for all of us. So I won't make it impossible for myself again. I'll promise myself a day off from being sensible on New Year's Day. Then January fourteenth is my cocker spaniel's birthday so that's a day off, too. Because how can he celebrate alone? After that... Well, no one can diet on January twenty-sixth. That's Australia Day, and it wouldn't be patriotic! And in February... I'll think of something to celebrate. There's bound to be a reason if I put my mind to it.'

The woman caught her breath. Her tears had been arrested. Nell had her fascinated, and Ethel gazed at her purple midriff in awe. 'You might...you might have your baby. In February, I mean.'

'So I might,' Nell said with aplomb, appearing exceedingly pleased. 'There you go, then. There's no need to circle the calendar for that one. It's a ready-made celebration.'

'It sounds crazy.'

Nell shook her head. 'No. It sounds logical. You need to see some light at the end of the tunnel. You can't keep losing weight for years without breaks, and those breaks need to be planned well ahead or you'll crack again.'

'But Dr Sutherland says—'

'Does Dr Sutherland disagree?' She swung around to face him, and the look she gave him was determined. 'Surely not? Do you, Dr Sutherland?'

He managed to rise to the occasion. Somehow. 'Days off seem a very good idea to me,' he said, and she grinned.

'See? We have consensus.' She turned back to Ethel. 'OK, what are you planning for Christmas dinner?'

'I hadn't thought about it. Maybe a fillet of fish.'

'A lone fish fillet for Christmas dinner?' Nell sounded appalled. 'Oh, you poor dear, no wonder you binged. You're absolutely forgiven and then some. Isn't she, Dr Sutherland?'

Blake could only gaze at her in astonishment. And agree. There was nowhere else to go. 'Um…yes.'

'You need turkey and roast potatoes and cranberry sauce and pudding,' Nell said solidly. 'With brandy cream. Not brandy butter. Trust me. I'm an expert on this one. You can't get enough brandy into brandy butter. I know this fantastic recipe for brandy cream, where's it's so alcoholic no one ends up knowing who's pulled which end of the cracker. I'll write it out for you if you like.'

'But—'

'No buts. I'm sick of buts. You're ordered to eat as much as you like on Christmas Day.' Nell's smile softened. 'And I'll bet that, having given yourself permission to eat as much as you like, and with no guilt attached, you won't eat yourself sick. You'll just enjoy your food very much indeed. Then, at the end of the day you give the remains of your pudding to an elderly aunt or the town drunk—or even a very appreciative dog. My cocker spaniel will volunteer if no one else comes forward. You drink the rest of your brandy cream as a nightcap, you wish yourself a merry goodnight—and then you go back to dieting the next day. How easy's that? It'll work. No sweat.'

Ethel looked wildly at Blake. 'Will it?'

But Blake was smiling. 'I don't see why not,' he told her. He took a deep breath. It took a big man to admit he was wrong but maybe… 'Maybe the diet sheet we put you on was a bit harsh long term,' he told her. 'Maybe Dr McKenzie is right.'

'Record this for posterity,' Nell said, mock-stunned, and Ethel even managed a chuckle.

She looked at the pair of them, and she smiled. 'You…you will give me that recipe for brandy cream?'

'Hand over a prescription form,' Nell ordered Blake. 'The lady needs urgent medication. I'll write it up for her now. And, Ethel…'

'Yes?'

'If you love cooking and you want to cook more than

you and your family can eat, then think about offering treats to the nursing home or to the hospital. Or even me!' She chuckled. 'Just don't give this prescription to the pharmacist. He'll think Dr Sutherland's barmy.'

'I think you're both barmy,' Ethel said softly, and for the first time her face relaxed. 'You've made me feel so much better.'

'Punishing yourself is the pits,' Nell said strongly. 'Heck, Ethel, the outside world criticises enough—there's no good to be gained by criticising yourself. And if you've lost four stone you have so much to be proud of.'

'Thank you.' Ethel sighed and rose ponderously to her feet. She looked Nell up and down, really seeing her for the first time. Then she cast an uncertain glance at Blake, and another at Nell. 'Do I know you?'

'I'm Nell McKenzie. My grandparents owned the place out on the bluff.'

'Nell McKenzie!' The woman seemed stunned. 'Well, I never. You've changed so much. And... Did you say you were Dr Sutherland's new associate?'

'That's right.' Nell beamed at Blake, defying him to deny it.

But Ethel was off on the next track. 'They're amazing overalls you're wearing.'

'They are, aren't they?'

'They look as if they're made from a quilt.'

'Funny you should say that,' Nell told her. 'They are. From a king-sized quilt.'

'You cut up a quilt to make overalls?' Ethel's voice took on a horror that said she was a patchworker from way back and Nell had just committed a crime somewhere up there with murder. 'You're joking!'

'No.'

'But why on earth?'

'I needed overalls much more than I needed a king-sized quilt,' Nell said in a tone which stated that no more questions were welcome on this score. 'Enough of that. OK? Let's get this prescription written and get Christmas on the road.'

Blake left her writing her brandy-cream script and made a fast phone call. Was she really who she said she was?

She said she'd come from Emily and Jonas but he didn't want to ring his friends yet. He knew the surgical registrar at Sydney Central. It took five minutes to page Daniel, but he came through with the goods straight away.

'Nell McKenzie? Of course I know her. She's the best damned doctor we've had in Emergency for a long time and we're going to miss her badly. There's been pressure on her to put her baby in child care here and keep on working.'

'Why doesn't she?'

'Who knows?' Daniel hesitated. 'But it'd be a hard job. Emergency's relentless, and who knows how much support she has? She's kept her private life very much to herself. She's such a mousy little thing that—'

'*Mousy little thing!*' Blake sat back in his chair at that, and frowned. 'We must have the wrong woman.'

'Five four-ish high, freckles, red hair hauled back like she's ashamed of it?'

'There are similarities, but—'

'Oh, she's not mousy around patients,' Daniel told him. 'She's extremely competent and decisive and very, very kind. The patients love her. But…you know…she's sort of self-effacing. We didn't even know she had a boyfriend or a husband, and we were stunned when she announced she was pregnant. The nurses had a running joke about immaculate conception.'

'Good grief.'

'But if she's turned up at Sandy Ridge… Hell, Blake, don't look a gift horse in the mouth. If you have Nell McKenzie wanting to work with you, then you hang onto her with everything you have. She's worth her weight in gold.'

* * *

A real little work horse. Blake came back out to Reception as Nell waved goodbye to Ethel and gazed at her incredulously. Anything less like a work horse he had yet to meet.

But she was here. She was another doctor and he really was overworked.

Who was Ernest?

It couldn't matter.

'All right,' he managed. 'All right.'

'All right what?'

'All right, you can stay.'

Her smile flashed back into her eyes. 'Gee, that's nice of you—and so gracious.'

He glowered. She had him unnerved. 'I can cope on my own.'

'I'm sure you can.' she told him. 'But you'll crack eventually. You can't go on working at this pace for ever.'

'I have for two years.'

'And it's getting to you.'

'It's *not* getting to me.'

'OK, it's not getting to you,' she agreed blithely, and grinned again. 'You're coping magnificently. All's well with the world and I'm doomed to spend four weeks being a pest. But that's my fate, Dr Sutherland. I know my place in life. Pest *extraordinaire*. So can we get on with it?'

He was having trouble keeping up with her. 'What—now?'

'Take me to where I'm going to live,' she told him, smiling sweetly. 'Take me to the doctors' quarters and then we'll get on with me being your Christmas present.'

The doctors' quarters were not to Nell McKenzie's liking. She took one step through the door and stopped short.

'How long did you say you've been living here?' she asked in stunned amazement, and Blake gazed around defensively.

'Two years. It's not so bad.'

'It's awful.'

'Gee, thanks. If I go into your home, would you be happy if I said it was awful?'

'I'd hope someone would point it out if it was this bad.'

'It's not *this bad*.'

'It's worse.' She stared around the starkly furnished apartment in distaste.

OK, it wasn't very good, Blake admitted. The last doctor at Sandy Ridge—Chris Maitland—had lived offsite. When Blake had taken over from Chris two years ago, the doctors' quarters had contained a stark laminex table with four vinyl chairs, a vinyl couch and a plain bedstead in each room. Oh, and one black and white television. There had been nothing more, and Blake had never had the time or the inclination to turn the place into something else.

'You can't live here all the time,' Nell breathed, and Blake found himself getting more and more annoyed.

'Of course I do. Where else would I go?'

'Oh, for heaven's sake...' She stalked over and hauled open the bedroom doors one after the other. The only difference between his bedroom and the others was that Blake's bed was made up and there was a pile of medical journals on the floor. 'Very cosy,' she retorted. She swivelled back to face him. 'Where's your Christmas tree?'

'Why would I need a Christmas tree?'

Why indeed? They gazed at each other, eyes locked, and her gaze was accusatory. Like he'd personally shot Santa Claus!

This time he was saved by his beeper. He looked at the little screen and he sighed. He was needed. It was more work—of course—but his sigh was a sigh of relief.

'I need to go.'

'Of course you need to go,' Nell said cordially. 'I would too if I stayed in this dump.'

'You asked to live here.'

'Nobody lives here. People *stay* here. There's a difference. You don't *live* on torn green vinyl dining chairs and ugly grey linoleum. You exist.'

'I'm leaving,' he told her. 'I have a patient in hospital who has heart problems, and then I have house calls to make. Make yourself comfortable.'

'Comfortable? Humph! Ernest will hate this place.'

Who the hell was Ernest? He didn't have time to find out. 'Well, ring Jonas and Em and complain about your working conditions,' he said with asperity. 'I'm sure the three of you can work it out. You're all so good at organising.'

'We are at that.'

He cast her a last, long, dubious look. There were schemes going on behind those sea-green eyes. He could feel their vibes from where he was.

Who was Ernest?

'Don't do anything. Just unpack.'

'And I'll make myself comfortable,' she said. 'It's what all guests do.'

'Don't!'

'Go, Dr Sutherland,' she said cheerfully. 'Go and doctor to those who need doctoring. Leave me to my own devices.'

He didn't have a choice. He left.

By the time Blake reached Casualty, Harriet Walsingham's heart had decided to behave.

'Though it gave me quite a scare, Doctor,' she said, sitting up and crossing her ankles primly on the ambulance trolley. 'I came over all funny, I did.'

'Then you can lie straight down again in case you come over all funny again,' he told her, pressing her gently back on the pillows and moving his stethoscope into position. 'What exactly happened?'

'She was out cold on the kitchen floor,' one of the ambulance officers told him, and Blake looked a question at the younger of the two men. If something was grey, Henry painted it black.

'Bob?'

'She wasn't unconscious,' Bob told him truthfully. 'She was just gasping like a fish out of water and she'd managed to grab the phone and call us.'

'It's got to be angina pectoris,' Henry told him triumphantly. 'Like I told you when we called. That's what it'll be. Won't it, Doc?'

'Possibly.' Not for the first time Blake thought longingly of big cities and fully trained paramedics. Henry was the local postman and Bob ran the menswear store. For them, a call for the ambulance meant major excitement in otherwise humdrum lives.

If only they wouldn't act like would-be doctors, he thought. Half the patients who arrived at the hospital via ambulance had been given an amateur diagnosis on the way, and sometimes it scared the pants off them.

'What's angina pectoris?' Luckily, Harriet wasn't one to let big words scare her. She was just like the ambulance officers—seemingly grateful for such an interesting event to disrupt her mundane existence. She gave a delicious shiver. 'Is it dangerous?' She really was feeling better.

'It's when your heart muscle is starved for oxygen,' Blake told her. 'But by itself it's not dangerous. Shush for a minute while I listen.'

They all shushed. For about ten seconds. Then...

'Can I have our new Dr McKenzie look after me?' Harriet enquired. 'No offence, Dr Blake, but I've always fancied a lady doctor, and she sounds lovely. I remember her when she was a teenager. She was such a sweet little thing, but so quiet.'

Our new Dr McKenzie... 'How did you know about Nell?'

'It's all over town,' Harriet told him. 'It's so exciting. Lorna is on the hospital board and she told me in strictest confidence. She said no one was allowed to say anything until today because they wanted to surprise you. You must be so pleased. Isn't it the best Christmas present?'

He took a deep breath. Was the whole town in on this? 'Harriet, be quiet.'

'But it *is* exciting.'

'I'll sedate you if you don't shut up,' he told her. Angina might be a minor problem, but it could also be a symptom of something major. 'Let's get you admitted and get an ECG done.' He glanced up at the ambulancemen. 'Thanks, boys.'

'Think nothing of it.' The men moved reluctantly off and then stopped. There was clearly something bothering them. 'How are we going to get to meet our new doctor, then?' Bob asked. He hesitated. 'Shouldn't there be some sort of function to welcome her back? So she can get to know people like us? Except for her grandma's funeral it's been over ten years since she was home. We'd hardly recognise her.'

'She's only here for four weeks.'

Bob shook his head. 'Lorna says it might be for longer. If the town's nice to her—for a change—and if she settles here after the bub's born, then she might stay.'

'And if she likes you, Dr Blake.' Harriet giggled. 'Not that she couldn't.'

Blake took a deep breath. This was getting out of hand. A welcome party? 'We're hardly likely to find any comers for a welcome party in the weeks before Christmas.'

'But it's Nell McKenzie,' Bob said, as if that made everything different.

'You'll have to explain.'

'The town feels bad about Nell McKenzie,' Harriet told him. 'And in a way maybe we should. No one ever did anything.'

'We couldn't,' Henry retorted. 'We weren't allowed to.'

'No, but she was such a little thing. And they were so awful.'

'Who were so awful?'

'Her grandparents, of course.' Then Harriet clutched her chest and her colour faded. 'Ooh… I think it's starting again.'

'Let's get you through to Intensive Care,' Blake snapped, annoyed with himself for being diverted. He motioned to the nurse at the head of the trolley. 'Now.'

Blake refused point-blank to think about Nell for the rest of the evening. Not once. Or not once very much.

Harriet refused to be transferred to Blairglen. Well, why should she leave Sandy Ridge? She was sure Dr Blake would look after her beautifully, just as well as any of the clever doctors at Blairglen, and she thought she was paying Blake a compliment by staying put.

As did all the locals. They refused to take themselves to the major hospital, supremely confident that Dr Blake would look after them.

Dr Blake and whose army? he thought wearily for what must be the thousandth time since he'd taken over here.

But… 'We don't need another doctor,' he found himself telling Grace Mayne as he finally had a cup of tea with the old fisherwoman. Grace's husband had died just a couple of months ago and she was desperately lonely. Her only son had drowned when he'd been little more than a teenager, and now she had no one.

Blake had liked Grace at first sight. She was tough, wiry, belligerent, and as huge-hearted a woman as he'd ever met. The weeks since her husband's death had cast her into deep depression, so Blake had found himself dropping in frequently—just to see her. Tonight the last thing he wanted was to socialise, but he forced himself to pause, take a seat at the old lady's kitchen table and accept her hospitality.

The alternative might be worse, he thought. He'd watched Grace's face as they'd buried her husband, and he found himself increasingly concerned as to her welfare. There'd been one tragedy after another in the old lady's life. This last death had left her feeling desolate—so desolate that he wondered how she could keep going. He watched her take her fishing boat out through the heads, and each time he saw the little boat make the run he wondered whether she'd come back.

And if she didn't, he'd feel dreadful. So he made time to call and chat, even though a million other things were pressing. Tonight the most obvious thing to talk about was Nell. After all, the rest of the town was talking about her. Why not Blake?

And Grace was definitely interested. 'Nell McKenzie...' The woman's sea-bleached eyes narrowed. 'You mean the lass who was brought up here with Doc and Mrs McKenzie?'

'That's the one.'

'I remember when Nell left for university,' she said slowly. 'Haven't seen her since.'

'No one has. But it seems she wants to come back here to live.'

Grace thought it through and shook her head in disbelief. 'I don't know why. The town made life miserable for her.'

'Did it?' Blake was pleased. He'd caused a spark of interest, which was more than the old lady had shown for a long time.

'Yeah. Or her grandparents did and we didn't object.' Grace stared reflectively into her nearly empty teacup and, to Blake's astonishment, something akin to a smile played around her mouth. 'Nell McKenzie. Well, well.'

'Well, well.' Blake cast a curious glance across the table. 'You sound like you know her fairly well.'

'No. No one does. No one was allowed to know her.'

'Why not?'

But Grace wasn't answering. She was staring into the dregs of her tea like she was staring into the past, but the smile remained on her face.

At least she wasn't suicidal tonight, Blake thought thankfully, rising to leave. He'd given her something to think about, even though he didn't understand why she was so interested.

But at least she *was* interested, and for that Blake could only be thankful.

It was after midnight when Blake drove home from the last house call and it was all he could do to keep himself awake. He opened the car windows wide, he turned the radio up full blast, but he knew he was still in danger of going to sleep at the wheel.

Back at the hospital he checked on Harriet who was sleeping soundly, hooked up to the heart monitor. If he could keep her quiet she might well stay that way until morning.

It seemed there was a block of some kind, he thought as he examined the results of his tests. There was no evidence of heart-muscle injury on the cardiograph or in the blood tests, but she had a very slow pulse.

She needs a cardiologist, Blake thought, and maybe a pacemaker and he knew it'd take him hours the next morning to convince her that he couldn't fit her with a pacemaker on his own. She'd have to go to Blairglen.

Finally, almost asleep on his feet, he pushed open the door between the hospital and his living quarters. And he stopped dead.

Nell was waiting for him.

'You've been ages,' she told him. 'I knew you'd be late but this is ridiculous.'

'What?' He was so exhausted he was having trouble taking it all in.

First of all, Nell had been transformed. No longer in purple overalls, she was now dressed in a bright crimson, floor-length bathrobe. It had rich burgundy lining, it was big enough to wrap around her twice, and she was curled up on the sofa with her bare toes poking out, looking like...

Looking like he didn't know what.

And what on earth was she sitting on? Where was his horrible settee? Where was his dining setting?

The sofa Nell was sitting on was enormous. It was ancient, a great mass of soft velvet cushions. Like her amazing dressing-gown, it was vivid crimson. It was the sort of sofa you just wanted to sink in and...

And nothing!

'What have you done to my house?' he managed, and if his voice came out strangled who could blame him?

'It's *our* house,' she reminded him gently. 'As an employed doctor in the town I have just as many rights to this place as you do. Don't you like it?' She gazed up at him, a picture of injured innocence. 'I've gone to so much trouble. And do you like my dressing-gown?' She beamed down at her splendid self. 'This belonged to Grandpa. Such a waste.'

'But—'

'I've been so busy...'

'I can see that.' He was still taking everything in. What was new?

Everything was new.

The vinyl furniture had disappeared completely. There was now the amazing sofa and a couple of great squishy armchairs. There was a new dining table—or rather an old one—an oak affair that looked as if it had been polished for generations. There were matching dining chairs with scatter cushions. And rugs...three vast Turkish rugs covering almost every available piece of floor space.

There were even pictures on the walls!

'Did this all come out of your suitcase?' he enquired, and she chuckled.

'I just waved my magic wand.'

He glanced at his watch. He'd been away for exactly five hours.

'You just nipped out to the shops, then. Or called in a decorator?'

'Well, no.'

'So would you like to explain?'

'I went exploring and caught Bob and Henry before they left the hospital.'

He thought that one through. Bob and Henry. He only knew the one Bob and Henry pair. 'The ambulance drivers?'

'I know them both from way back,' she told 'him. 'They weren't ambulance drivers in my day. In fact, I went to school with Bob, and when I showed him the conditions we were expected to live in he was shocked. Both of them were.'

'He's given you this stuff?' Blake's voice was unbelieving, and Nell giggled.

'No, silly. It's from my house.'

'Your house.'

'I told you,' she said patiently. 'I own a house out on the bluff. It's ancient, it hasn't been used for years but it's full of extremely good stuff. Like this.' She patted her sofa fondly. 'I knew it'd be comfortable. I was never allowed to sit on it when I was a kid but, oh, how I wanted to.'

He was distracted—almost—but there were burning questions. 'How the hell did you get this stuff back here?'

'The ambulance, of course,' she said blithely. 'How else?'

'You used the ambulance to transport furniture?' He was gearing himself up to explode.

'If I hadn't then I'd have needed the ambulance tomorrow to cart me away for major back repair.' Her tone was innocence personified. 'It was a case of preventative medicine, and I'm really good at that. I was determined to get it here, and my little sedan only has a very tiny roof-rack. Anyway, once I explained the situation to Henry and Bob they were only too pleased to help.' She smiled up at Blake. 'So we took the stretchers out of the ambulance and went for it. It took us five trips and we've only just finished.'

'And if there'd been an urgent call?'

'Then they'd have heaved the furniture out and got on

with it,' she told him. 'Honestly—do you think we're neg-
ligent or something?'

He thought no such thing. He didn't know what to think.
He walked over and sank down into one of the chairs—
and promptly stood up again.

One of the cushions had moved! Now it rose, shoving
itself to four feet, and it glared at him. What the...?

But Nell was smiling. 'Um...meet Ernest. Dr Sutherland,
Ernest. Ernest, meet Dr Sutherland.'

'Ernest.'

Who was Ernest? He'd just found out. Blake found himself looking at the most mournful, pathetic bag of bones
he'd ever come across in the doggy kingdom. The ancient
cocker spaniel, his black and white coat faded with age into
indiscriminate grey, was all jowls and floppy ears and huge
mournful eyes. He looked up at Blake as if he'd just
wounded him to the core.

'Hey, I didn't sit on you,' Blake said before he could
help himself. 'I nearly did but I didn't.'

The eyes still reproached him.

'Oh, for heaven's sake...'

'Take no notice of him,' Nell said blithely. 'Ernest's
greatest skill in life is making people feel guilty, whether
they deserve it or not.'

'He does a great job.'

'He does.' Nell grinned. 'I adopted him because he
looked so pathetic. It's his principal talent and he's really
very good.' She rose and crossed to give her dog a hug.
'I've had him for five months now. It's been a guilt trip all
the way, yet still I love him.'

Blake was still taking things on board. 'This is the Ernest
that's going to take up the third bedroom?'

'Well, I'm not going to sleep with him,' Nell said, horrified. 'He snores.'

Blake looked down at the ancient Ernest and he grinned.

'He looks like the sort of dog who'd snore.'

He got a really, really reproachful canine glare for his pains.

'Ernest's very sensitive,' Nell warned. 'You might find you have to pay for that remark.'

'He doesn't bite?'

'Bite?' Nell shook her head in disbelief. She crossed to the little kitchenette and opened the oven door. 'That requires energy. No, Ernest's principal way of punishing people is by ignoring them.'

'I can live with that.'

'You'll find you can't,' she warned him. 'It's very effective. He sort of embellishes his ignoring routine in all sorts of fancy ways. You'll see. Now... Dinner?'

Ernest was promptly forgotten. 'Dinner!'

'You haven't eaten?' She turned back to face him. 'I didn't see how you could have.'

'No, but—'

'Then there's dinner,' she told him as if he were stupid. 'I ate hours ago but I saved half the casserole for you. It's apricot chicken. Very basic but it is my first night. We stopped off at the all-nighter on our first furniture run so I could throw this together while the boys heaved sofas.' And then she grinned. 'I imagine it's set the town talking. An ambulance parked outside the minimart with a sofa sticking out the back.'

He imagined it might have. He should be angry. But there was apricot chicken casserole. His nose was giving him all sorts of messages, and every one of them was urgent.

And it was sort of funny...

'I don't approve,' he managed, and Nell nodded.

'Of course you don't. You're a very responsible doctor. I can see that. So you don't approve of ambulances filled with sofas, buying chicken drumsticks and cans of apricots. But you will still eat my casserole?'

He was trying hard not to laugh. For heaven's sake, she was ridiculous. 'I might.'

'Ernest will if you don't,' she said cheerfully, and Blake turned and glowered at the dog. Ernest glowered back.

But this was a dog after all. 'Don't even think about it,' Blake told him. 'Not even the scraps.'

'He's already eaten,' Nell said.

'Chicken casserole?'

'Dog food. The ambulance and sofa brought that, too. But he's not fussy and he's always up for second helpings.'

'I imagine he might be. That's quite some paunch.'

'Now you really are getting personal.' She scooped the casserole onto a plate and set it down on her gorgeous table. The whole room came together. The aroma of the delicious casserole. The furniture. The dog. The brilliantly dressed woman, heavily pregnant, ladling out food…

It was the sort of scenario that'd normally make him run a mile.

'Wrap yourself around that,' Nell told him, and she smiled.

Who could resist an invitation like that?

'Wash your dishes afterwards,' she said blithely. She hauled her dog up into her arms. 'We've done enough. Ernest and I are very, very tired and we're off to bed. We'll leave you to it.'

She left, and the room was desolate for her going.

CHAPTER THREE

SOMEONE was trying to smother him.

Blake woke to fur balls. Or fur mats. Something warm and heavy and limp was lying right across his face, threatening to choke him while he slept. He sat up like he'd been shot, and Ernest slid sideways onto the floor.

The stupid dog lay like he was paralysed, four legs in the air, eyes frantic, waiting for someone to set him to rights. Good grief!

'You dopey dog. Don't you have any respect?'

Ernest whimpered.

Was the creature injured? Blake flung back the covers, climbed out of bed and stooped to see.

Ernest promptly found his feet, took one agile leap and landed in the warm spot vacated by Blake.

'You damned dog... You're out of here.' Blake put a hand on his collar to haul him away, but it was easier said than done. Ernest lay like a dead dog. His eyes were closed and he snoozed as if he'd been asleep for hours, seemingly totally oblivious of anyone else's comfort but his own.

'It's either you or me, mate,' Blake muttered, and glanced at the clock. And then glanced again. Hell. That couldn't be right. The clock said eight-thirty. His alarm was set for six.

The alarm had been turned off.

She'd sneaked in while he'd been sleeping, he thought incredulously, and then wondered how on earth could she have done it. He would have woken. Surely?

The thought of Nell tiptoeing across his bedroom had him as unnerved as...as did her stupid dog sleeping in his bed!

39

'OK. I know. I have to get up,' he told Ernest. 'Sure, you can use my bed. Any time. Don't mind me.'

Ernest didn't.

He'd have to skip breakfast. There was a ward round to do before surgery at nine, and there wasn't time. At least no one had rung during the night, he thought as he showered and dressed, but that in itself was unusual. Worrying even.

He'd had the best sleep he'd had in months and he felt like a million dollars for it, but he'd have to pay by working doubly hard now. Harriet's heart problems needed urgent attention. He needed to persuade her to be transferred at least to Blairglen but preferably to one of the major coronary-care units at Sydney or Melbourne. That by itself would take hours.

Damn, damn, damn…

And on the other side of the wall, Nell must still be in bed.

'She's been a great help,' he told Ernest as he hauled a comb through his unruly thatch of hair. 'Some Christmas present she turns out to be. She turns off my alarm, she lands me with her dog and then she sleeps in…'

She was seven months pregnant. And she *had* made him apricot chicken the night before.

'But I don't need domesticity,' he told the somnolent Ernest. 'I'd rather eat baked beans on toast and be on time. How on earth can I fit everything in?' He slammed the bedroom door on the sleeping dog, walked out through the living room—trying to ignore just how good the newly furnished room looked in the early morning light—and stalked through to the hospital.

'Some Christmas present,' he muttered again, anger building at the thought of what lay ahead. 'Now I'll be late all day.'

Only he wasn't. Everything had been done.

Donald, the charge nurse, came to greet him, his face

wreathed in smiles. 'Well, well, if it's not Captain Snooze. Our Dr McKenzie told us you were having a wee sleep in and we could hardly believe it.'

'*Your* Dr McKenzie?'

'She's been here for two hours,' Donald told him. 'She had breakfast with the staff and we feel we've really got to know her. She's a great kid.' Donald was fifty. Anyone forty-nine or under was a kid to him—Blake included. Now he beamed like a Scottish patriarch, solving the problems of the world.

'And she's very, very competent,' Donald told him, ignoring the look on Blake's face and sounding as pleased as Punch. 'Louise couldn't get Elmer Jefferson's drip back in last night and she did it first go. Louise says she has fingers like you wouldn't believe.'

'You've let her near the patients?' Blake's voice rose to incredulous and Donald took a step back—but he wasn't a nurse to be intimidated by a mere doctor. They worked on equal footing, these two.

'Now, why wouldn't I have done that?' he demanded. 'Don't be a fool, man. She's a registered doctor, she's approved and paid by our hospital board, and Jonas and Emily from Bay Beach both rang me up personally to vouch for her training. I knew her when she was a kid, so I was tickled pink to hear she was coming back.'

Tickled pink hardly described how *he* was feeling. Blake stared at his charge nurse through narrowed eyes. 'You *knew* she was coming?'

'We all did,' Donald said smugly. 'Happy Christmas, Dr Sutherland.'

Great. The world had gone mad.

'Where is she now?'

'She's done a full ward round, sorted out any problems— not that there were any—only Elmer at five a.m.'

'Elmer's drip packed up at five and you didn't ring me? You know he—'

'Yeah, we know it's important. That septicaemia isn't

going to go away without a few more days of antibiotics. It was some spider bite he got.' He grinned, enjoying Blake's annoyance. 'So Louise rang Nell—just like she told us to.'

'When did she tell you to?'

'Last night, of course.' Donald grinned again. 'A couple of the nurses stopped by to lend her a hand with the furniture moving when they finished late shift. Me included. She got us hanging pictures and said you were taking turns with calls, starting last night, so when the drip packed up at five Louise rang her.'

'Rang my phone? I would have heard.'

'Louise rang Nell's cellphone,' Donald said patiently. 'She gave us the number. Easy.'

Easy...

His life had been turned upside down. By a nutcase.

'Is she wearing her purple patchwork pants?' he couldn't help asking, and this time it was Donald's turn to look astonished.

'Now, why should she wear purple patchwork to work? She's a professional. No. She's wearing a white coat over some sort of floral skirt. Very demure. See for yourself. She's in with Harriet.'

'Harriet?'

'Harriet's been busy planning how you could perform open-heart surgery here,' Donald told him, grinning. 'She wouldn't take no for an answer. I told Nell what the problem was and Nell left her until last. So she's still there. Want to see how she's doing?'

Blake did. He cast one more glare at his charge nurse—heck, Donald almost sounded as if he'd been bewitched—and then he stalked off down the corridor to Intensive Care. To see what damage had been done, and how best he could undo it.

Only, of course, no damage had been done at all. Harriet was lying back on her pillows, smiling up at the woman beside her bed, and Nell was holding her hand.

The night and the chest pain had taken their toll on Harriet. Her bravado of the night before had slipped, and fear was showing through. She was gripping Nell's hand like she was drawing strength from human contact.

She looked up as Blake entered—they both did—and he received two smiles of welcome. Nell's was warm and open. Harriet's was a bit wobbly.

'Dr Sutherland...'

He had the sense to focus on Harriet first. Nell and her damned managerial ways could wait.

'Hey there.' He walked across, took the old lady's hand away from Nell and held it himself. 'Well done,' he told her. 'You've had the night without any more trouble.' And then he frowned and looked sideways at Nell. 'At least, I assume there was no more trouble.'

'I would have woken you if there was,' Nell said blithely, and he almost choked.

Focus on Harriet...

'No more palpitations?'

'Nothing.'

'Great.' He hesitated. 'Harriet, we're going to have to get specialist opinion on this. I'm afraid that means a trip...'

'To Sydney.' Harriet managed a brave smile. 'I know. Nell...Dr McKenzie's just been explaining it to me.'

'Call me Nell,' Nell said promptly. 'Please. You used to call me Nell when I was a little girl. I don't see why you should change now.' She smiled fondly down at the old lady. 'Harriet used to run the general store and sometimes she gave me free sweets,' she explained to Blake, and Harriet's smile died.

'It was the least I could do. No one else ever did. Those dreadful—'

'That's enough,' Nell told her. 'The bad old days are over. Forgotten. And now aren't I lucky? Being a doctor, I can buy all the sweets I want.'

'Oh, my dear...'

But Nell was refusing sympathy. 'I've just been telling Harriet about my friend Matt who's the head of Coronary Care at Sydney Central.' She turned to Blake. 'Matt's a real sweetheart. He has a gorgeous wife and he has two sets of twins and a dog just like Ernest. In fact, he's Ernest's brother.'

Despite himself, Blake grinned at that one. 'Matt's Ernest's brother?' he asked incredulously. 'Don't go near him with a bargepole, Harriet. Ernest is the dopiest—'

'Matt's *dog* is Ernest's brother,' Nell said with dignity, but her green eyes twinkled. 'And haven't you made it up with my dog yet?'

'Two dogs like Ernest...' Blake said, raising his eyes to the ceiling, and Nell's twinkle deepened.

'Yep. Aren't they just wonderful?'

'Wonderful!'

Nell gazed at him thoughtfully for a long moment—and then shook her head. She put her mind back to business. 'Anyway, Harriet thinks she might just trust Matt to decide what's best to be done, so I've organised an air transfer to Sydney.'

'You've organised an air transfer?'

'With Donald's help, of course,' she told him. 'We decided Bob and Henry weren't really skilled enough for a coronary-care transfer.'

'And if Bob spends the day with the ambulance it'd mean the mail would be really late—if it arrived at all— and it's so near Christmas that it'd be a disaster,' Harriet chirped in, and Blake could only stare.

'But...'

'But what, Dr Sutherland?' Nell smiled. 'We haven't set in motion anything that you can't rescind. The air ambulance doesn't arrive until midday. But Harriet and I agree that you have quite enough on your plate without trying to implant a pacemaker before Christmas.'

'Harriet's agreed to this?'

'If Matt thinks it's necessary. Harriet wants to hang

around for the long term. She's agreed to help me set my house in order—oh, and knit me one of her famous capes. She knitted one for my grandmother once and I did so want one.'

'If I'd known,' Harriet said darkly, and Nell shook her head.

'No. How could you know? But now you do and you've agreed to make it for me so I'll have the wool ready as soon as you're transferred back. And I'll also ring Sonia, Matt's wife. She'll bring her latest set of twins in to see you and I'll bet she has you knitting for them before you can blink.'

Nell was fantastic, Blake thought reluctantly. Absolutely fantastic. In one fell swoop she'd persuaded Harriet to go to Sydney, she'd organised her company while she was there, she'd taken the depersonalisation out of Harriet's medical process—when Harriet met Matt she wouldn't think of him as a cardiologist but as the father of two sets of twins and one dopey dog—and Nell had given her something to look forward to on her return.

Whew!

'I probably need to go now,' Nell told Harriet, smiling down at her like a co-conspirator. 'I'm just about ready for a cup of coffee, and I'll bet Dr Sutherland wants to examine you.'

'There's probably no need,' Harriet said, but her eyes twinkled up at Nell. 'Oh, very well. We don't want to put his nose out of joint, I suppose.'

'Of course we don't.' Nell stooped and kissed her. '*That* would be perfectly appalling.'

He found Nell fifteen minutes later. She was sitting in the hospital kitchen, tucking into an enormous plate of eggs and bacon. As soon as he arrived she waved to the stove.

'Yours is there. Cook made it for you. I told her you were coming. If you're quick the eggs will still be runny.'

'I don't have time to eat.'

'Of course you have time to eat,' she said firmly. 'It's one of life's imperatives. Mrs Condie will be back in a few minutes and if she finds you haven't eaten it she'll be very hurt—especially when I told her how hungry you were.'

Was there no end to this woman's interference? 'How did you know I was hungry? I could have had breakfast at home.'

'I saw what was in your refrigerator,' she said darkly. 'Green bread, and bacon to match. Even Ernest would turn up his nose at that.'

The smell was delicious. She was infuriating—but she was also right. OK, he'd eat. To refuse would be petty. 'Ernest eats fillet steak, does he?' he muttered, scooping bacon and eggs onto a plate.

'If he can get it. Why wouldn't he?'

'Why indeed?'

Her green eyes widened. 'You don't like my dog?'

'Your dog,' he said with a glower, hunkering down in a chair on the other side of the table, 'is currently sleeping in my bed. *My bed!*'

'Whoops,' she said contritely. 'I couldn't have pulled the door fully shut when I switched off your alarm.'

'Now, about that—'

'Eat your breakfast before it gets cold,' she told him, popping another bacon rasher between her teeth. 'This is yummy.'

Blake ate a bacon rasher. And then another. And he glowered all the time.

'The wind'll change,' she said kindly.

'Excuse me?'

'If you keep that horrid expression on your face you could be in real trouble. I'm sure you don't mean to look bad-tempered, but if the wind changes while you look that way then you're stuck with it for life.'

'That's superstitious nonsense.'

'Oh, no. My best friend told me that when I was five so I'm sure it must be right.'

'Dr McKenzie—'

'Nell.'

'Dr McKenzie,' he repeated through clenched teeth.

'I suppose it's better than Miss McKenzie.' She sighed. 'What?'

'You had no business turning off my alarm clock.'

'But you were tired and I'm your Christmas present.' She said it as if it made everything fine.

'You still had no business interfering, and as for taking *my* calls in the night…'

'That's what I'm here for—and they're not *your* calls. They're *our* calls. The hospital board's employing me, so you have no right to act as if everything medical is yours. Now, this morning—'

'You've done enough already. This morning you can take yourself off.'

'Nope. I've organised it all with Marion.'

'You've what?'

'Organised with our receptionist,' she told him sweetly. 'She's pulled out all the patient files and I thought I'd run through them with you now. Before I see patients.'

'But *I'll* be seeing patients.'

'*You'll* see patients this afternoon.' She smiled again. 'I expect I'll be feeling a bit weary by this afternoon so I imagine I might take an afternoon nap, so you can take over all you want. Then.'

'Dr—'

'Won't you call me Nell?'

'It's impossible,' he burst out, and slammed his fist down on the table. Her coffee-cup jumped and coffee sloshed into the saucer. He glared across the table and found she was surveying him with care.

'You have a temper,' she said.

'*I* have a temper?' He thought back to the day before. 'How about you?'

She considered that, and found it reasonable. 'OK, we both have tempers, so let's moderate. Marion says you have any number of house calls banked up. The district nurse has a list and she says you've been going through them on a priority basis. But she says a morning off surgery would let you get the worst of them cleared. Is that right?'

Blake thought it through. 'Yes, I suppose so.'

'So there you go. I would appreciate it if you could run through the patient list with me first. Just so I know who's a hypochondriac and who's likely to be in trouble.' She smiled. 'I do miss the good old days before lawsuits where you could write "complete and utter nutcase" in the patient's history and get away with it.'

He struggled against a smile. 'But…'

'But what? Is that all you ever say?' Suddenly exasperated, Nell laid down her knife and fork and pushed back her plate. 'Are you still intent on arguing? Dr Sutherland, what have you got against me seeing our patients while you do our house calls?'

Our.

The word took Blake aback. It was a word that hadn't entered his vocabulary for two years. *Our…*

'I guess—'

'It's sensible,' she said firmly. 'Isn't it?'

It was. It was also…wonderful. To clean up his outstanding house calls… Whew!

'Now, you don't have to do them all today,' Nell urged, seeing where his thoughts were headed. 'I'll be here again tomorrow so you don't need to clear the decks completely. Marion thought you could spend a couple of hours doing home visits, then come back and take a run on the beach before lunch.'

'What business is it of—?'

But Nell was unstoppable. She had it all figured out. 'Marion says that's your very favourite thing and you haven't been able to go for a proper run for months. You've had to run near the hospital so you're available for emergencies. But today you can run where you want. Then you can come back about one o'clock, shower, lunch and be bright-eyed and bushy-tailed for afternoon surgery.'

'You have it all organised.'

'That's what I'm here for.' She rose and took her dishes to the sink. 'And you can't fight city hall. So you'd best just roll with the punches, Dr Sutherland. And who knows? You might even end up enjoying it.'

How could he enjoy it?

Blake spent the morning doing house calls but his thoughts flew back to the surgery at every available minute. What was Nell doing? Who was she seeing?

'I hear we've got a new lady doctor,' old Desmond Scott told him as he dressed his ulcerated legs, and Blake couldn't keep back the grimace.

'Is she that bad?' Des asked sympathetically.

Blake caught himself at that. What had Daniel at Sydney Central told him? *She's extremely competent...* Coming from Daniel, that was praise indeed.

So what on earth was he worrying about? he demanded of himself. Why couldn't he simply roll with the punches and enjoy it?

Because Nell was...bossy?

'Women make a real difference around the place,' Desmond ventured, seeing his thoughts stray sideways and trying to guess the reason. 'They stick their noses into everything. Can't help themselves. And they say she's moved into your house. You'll have a filing cabinet in the bathroom with a drawer marked "Razor" before you know it. And you'll be in trouble for leaving the toilet seat up! You mark my words.'

'There speaks a long-married man.' Blake relaxed a bit and allowed himself to grin. OK, maybe he was overreacting slightly.

'My Lorna would organise from dawn to dusk and never be happier,' Desmond told him proudly. 'She's gone across to her sister's now with a casserole because Madge is poorly, and she'll be so mad that you've come while she's away. She likes being here when you come, so she can give you a cup of tea and have a bit of gossip on the side. House calls in surgery hours is not what we're used to.' He chortled. 'I guess she'll have to get used to them now, though. This new doctor will free you up to do your house calls whenever. That'll mess with Lorna's routine no end.'

'Dr McKenzie's only here for four weeks.'

Des frowned at that. 'That's not what I hear. Grace Mayne popped in earlier this morning and she reckons she's home for good.'

'She's having a baby.'

'So Grace said, but should that stop her working? There's plenty of women these days work with a littly.'

Blake carefully re-dressed the worst of the ulcers, concentrating on the wounds rather than allowing himself to think about Nell being here permanently. Desmond's ulcers were deep and nasty. The old man's skin was like fine parchment stretched taut across the bone, and the least scratch turned into a mess. Usually dressing his ulcers upset him so it was good to see his attention diverted, even if it was toward the new lady doctor.

'We'll see,' Blake told him. 'There's time enough to worry about how much she works after she has the baby. And she can't stay in Sandy Ridge to have it.'

'You won't deliver her?'

'You know as well as I do that I need back-up if I'm to set myself up for deliveries.' Des was the retired town pharmacist and enjoyed talking medicine. In the interminable time it was taking to treat Desmond's succession of ulcers, they often talked about the problems of Blake's practice.

'I guess you have antenatal back-up now,' Des said thoughtfully. 'With Nell here you can deliver anyone but her.'

Blake applied the last of the adhesive and stood up, thinking it through. Des was right. Maybe he wouldn't make a habit of delivering babies—he'd still like a paediatrician on call before he did that—but he was better able to cope with emergencies now. Not just for antenatal work. For everything.

It was a really strange feeling. There was someone right at this minute doing the work he usually did, and the thought was taking some time to sink in.

He had back-up. Up until now he'd been too wearily confused and hostile to see it. Now he drove home and let himself think about what that back-up could mean.

The possibilities were endless.

He thought of Lyn Slater. Lyn was due to deliver in two weeks and the rule was to leave town and find somewhere to stay in Blairglen at least two weeks before the baby was due. But Lyn had been holding out until the last minute. She had two other children and hated the thought of up-rooting the family for Christmas.

The risks of delivering her had been a burden on his tired mind. Now at least they could cope with a Caesarean if they had to.

So Nell's Christmas present would be a gift not just to him. Nell could help him improve the standard of care to the whole district. If she was competent.

She's extremely competent, Daniel had said.

The thought was suddenly immeasurably exciting.

If only she wasn't so damned infuriating. So damned bossy. But what else had Daniel said?

She's such a mousy little thing.

If only she was, Blake thought grimly. Sure, it'd be great having a competent doctor around for Christmas, but she wouldn't be much help if she was strangled before Christmas Eve.

She'd told him to run. He did six house calls and was tempted to do more, but Nell's words rang in his ears. Go for a run on the beach... He hadn't run on the beach for months!

His running was his time-out. His only time-out. Ever since Sylvia... Well, ever since he'd needed to, he'd escaped into himself by running. He'd pound the pavements until his heart thumped inside his chest and the pain around his heart eased because there simply wasn't room for pain and exhaustion at the same time. Running had become almost a drug. He'd run or he'd go nuts, so every day, no matter how exhausted he was, he'd don running gear and do some miles.

And the beach here was lovely—long and golden and sun-drenched, it stretched for miles. The thought of it now was almost irresistible.

He shouldn't do it. He should go back to the surgery. But finally he couldn't withstand Nell's offer. He headed back to the house, disturbed Ernest's steady snooze, enquired politely if Ernest would like a run, too—well, you had to be courteous about these things, but Ernest looked at him like he'd lost his mind—and then headed to the beach.

He ran for an hour. Half an hour north. Half an hour south. Then, on impulse, because it was a gorgeous day and he may as well go for broke, he ran into the water and swam like a ten-year-old.

When he turned to the shore there was a woman and a dog sitting on the beach, watching. Nell and Ernest.

CHAPTER FOUR

HE WAS quite something, Nell thought dispassionately as she watched Blake come out of the water. If she was interested in men—which she wasn't—and if she was into bodies that looked like they'd come out of the centrefolds of *Women Only*, then maybe...

But she definitely wasn't. No.

'I've been stupid enough in that direction to last a lifetime,' she told Ernest, hugging him close. 'You're the only man in my life from now on.'

But there was no harm in watching.

Blake had hauled off his shirt and running shoes before he'd entered the water and he'd swum in his shorts. 'That's quite a six-pack,' Nell told Ernest knowledgeably, looking at the muscles rippling across Blake's chest and abdomen. 'Wow!' Then she looked down at Ernest's saggy midriff and grinned. 'Something you can only dream about.'

Ernest looked up and licked her.

'You don't want a body to die for?' Nell's grin widened and she hugged him again. 'I don't think Blake does either,' she told her dog. 'Em says he lost his wife three years ago and has been driven ever since. That's why he runs. It's also why he's not sure he wants me here.'

She thought back to the conversation she'd had with her friend when they'd been arranging this deal.

'He doesn't stop for a minute,' Em had told her. 'Maybe if he really tried he could get a partner at Sandy Ridge—or maybe Chris would have stayed on and worked part time in semi-retirement. But no. Blake has to take the weight of the world on his shoulders, and if he's not frantic with medicine he runs as if the world's chasing him. It's like if he stops the pain's going to catch up.'

'Was his wife really special?' Nell had enquired, and Em had shaken her head.

'I don't think she was, and I think that's the cause of the trouble.'

'I don't understand.'

'It's not my business to explain,' Em had said primly. Then she'd looked at Nell and her primness had faded to mischief. 'At least, that's what Jonas tells me, and I'm sure it means he doesn't know either. We're only going on hints of medical gossip and they lived in Western Australia before she died, which means the gossip's not very forthcoming. So you'll just have to find out for yourself!'

Drat! But there was enough to go on that was intriguing. Nell sighed. Then she went back to watching Blake walk out of the shallows, admiring the splendid muscles of the man—and waiting for him to register that she was sitting on the beach.

He couldn't get away from her. It was weird, coming out of the water and finding her there. It felt like a huge intrusion into his personal space.

People didn't wait for Blake Sutherland. Not like this.

But Nell was definitely waiting. She was wearing a maternity dress today. It wasn't as loud as her patchwork overalls. It was pretty and flowing—he'd glimpsed it under her white coat this morning—but now, on the beach, it was summery and nice and...

For heaven's sake, what was he doing, noticing what she was wearing? he demanded of himself. What did it matter? And she'd brought her blasted dog to the beach. Why? It wasn't as if Ernest was the slightest bit interested in exercise.

He glanced at his watch, suddenly hopeful. Afternoon surgery was due to start at two. Maybe he was rushed.

Damn. It wasn't yet one. He wasn't rushed at all and the novelty of being unrushed was almost indescribable.

But he still felt trapped. He saw her watching him—waiting—and there was nothing to do but to towel himself dry and stroll on up the beach, as if meeting pregnant women and crazy dogs on gorgeously sunlit beaches was something he did every day of his life.

'I've brought sandwiches.' She didn't greet him as such—just motioned to her picnic basket, and by the look of the crammed contents it didn't just hold sandwiches. It held a feast.

'You made this lot in between patients this morning?' he said in disbelief, and she chuckled.

'Yep. Superwoman. That's me.' Then she relented. 'Actually, Mrs Condie packed it up for me.'

The hospital cook. He frowned. At last—something he could object to. 'Mrs Condie has better things to be doing than making us picnics.'

'Hey, she offered,' Nell broke in before he could get any further. 'The staff were really pleased you'd found time for a run. I finished surgery, came out and discovered every nurse in the hospital knew you were down at the beach.' She grinned. 'Keeping secrets isn't this town's strong point. Anyway, I found this waiting for me on Marion's desk, with the suggestion that I might like lunch on the beach as well.' She beamed up at him. 'You know, you have very nice staff.'

He had very interfering staff.

'I need to go back.'

'To shower and change before afternoon surgery?' She nodded but she was flipping the cloth from the top of the basket. 'Sure, but you've got ages and there's chicken and avocado sandwiches. My favourite. And chocolate éclairs.'

He was backed up against a wall. 'I usually just have fruit for lunch.' It sounded pathetic, even to him.

'Then that's why you're skinny and I'm fat,' she said, and he grinned despite himself.

'No, Dr McKenzie. You're fat and I'm skinny because you're pregnant and I'm not pregnant. It has nothing to do with chocolate éclairs.'

Her twinkly eyes assessed him, running over the long lines of his body. She was assessing him the same way she'd have assessed a laboratory specimen, and he found the experience disconcerting to say the least. 'I guess you're not really skinny, but there's not an inch of spare fat on you,' she decided out loud. 'Whew. That's what the glossies call a body to die for.'

'What glossies?'

'Any glossies. Especially those ones that have six-pack men in the middle.'

'I'm amazed you read them.'

'They sure beat medical journals.' She grinned. 'Besides, I have high literary tastes,' she said with dignity. 'A girl has to keep informed of what's up to date. And in fashion.' Her eyes narrowed against the sun. 'I have to inform you— in case you don't already know—that your type of body is very much in fashion.'

'Gee, thanks.' He was so disconcerted he was almost at the blushing stage.

'Well, it's very nice,' she told him kindly. And then she sighed. 'I can tell you don't indulge in cream cakes too often. There's not a lot of chocolate éclairs in your biceps. I won't be as lean as you even after Brunhilda's born.'

That startled him out of his self-consciousness of stand-ing semi-naked and discussing his body build... He clutched this new straw and held on.

'Brunhilda?'

'This baby's been kicking me all morning,' Nell told him. 'So I said one more kick and she was being christened Brunhilda. Or Cornelius if he's a boy.'

He grinned at that. She really was the most extraordinary woman. 'And he—or she—stopped kicking immediately?'

'Nope,' she said sadly, handing him up a sandwich. 'I can see I'm about to have discipline problems. Cornelius or Brunhilda kept right on kicking. So that's it. They're doomed till they can come of age and change their names by deed poll. Never make a threat you don't intend to keep, that was my grandma's motto, and that's what I intend...'

And then her voice faded a bit, as if memory was intruding. 'Well, never mind. Maybe I don't intend all that much. Go on. Wrap yourself around your sandwich. There's heaps more where they came from.'

Why had she suddenly gone quiet?

She had him intrigued, he realised. He sat on his towel and ate his sandwich—and then another—and then another after that because really they were extraordinarily good, and he realised he knew not the first thing about Nell. And something about the way she was looking now said that it might well be hard to find out.

'You were raised by your grandparents?' he asked, and her face shuttered.

'Yes.'

It was about as communicative as a closed door. He tried again.

'But there wasn't a lot of love lost between you?'

'You might say that. Hey, there's lamingtons in here. Well done, Mrs Condie. Yum.'

He refused to be diverted. 'What happened to your parents?'

'I don't know. Or at least I don't know much.'

That raised his eyebrows. 'What do you mean?'

'I mean I don't know who my father was, and my mother dumped me here with her parents when I was three months old and was never seen again.' She bit into her lamington reflectively. 'Not that I blame her for never coming back, mind you. My grandparents told me she wasn't married—a whore was how they described her. Intolerance personified, that was Grandmother and Grandfather. So Sandy

Ridge was hardly a great place in which to be a single mum.'

Blake eyed her speculatively. 'And yet you've returned—presumably to bring up your baby alone.'

'My grandparents are dead,' she told him as if that explained all. 'There's the difference. I dare say if my grandparents were alive you'd have had second thoughts about living here, too.'

'As bad as that?'

'Worse.'

'Want to talk about it?'

'Nope.'

'Why not?

Attack was the best form of defence. 'Want to tell me about your marriage?'

'Um…no.'

'There you go, then.' Subject closed. 'Ernest, I believe this sandwich is spare. Can I interest you—?'

She got no further. She definitely could interest Ernest. He was very much a sandwich-eating dog. Or an éclair-eating dog. Or lamington. Or whatever…

Their picnic finished, the last scraps enjoyed to the full by garbage-bin Ernest, they were left with silence. Somewhat to Blake's surprise it wasn't an uncomfortable silence. They sat on and watched the sea, and their thoughts went in all sorts of directions, but it was an easy peace now that was settling between them.

Truce…

He had a partner, Blake thought, and the enormity of what was being offered slammed home once again. Someone to share his workload. Someone to give him time to run…

'You know, you don't always have to run,' she said into the silence, and it was as if she'd read his thoughts. His eyes widened but she ignored his surprise to continue. 'Beaches are good for lying on, too. Trust me. I know this. Sleeping in the sun is one of my splinter skills.'

He thought about it. Sleeping in the sun… Why would he do that? 'I enjoy running,' he said brusquely.

She nodded. 'I'm sure you do—like we both enjoy medicine. But there's more to life than medicine and running.'

'Such as?'

'Such as looking at glossy centrefolds. Or decorating a Christmas tree,' she told him, suddenly sounding annoyed. 'Which brings me to my next point. I can't believe you haven't done it. So tonight, after surgery, is decreed a Christmas-tree-decorating session. Write it in your diary in black ink. "Eight p.m. Help Nell with tree." Got it?'

'I'll be busy.'

'You'll be busy decorating the tree.'

'Nell…'

'Hey, you didn't call me Dr McKenzie.' She beamed. 'There's an improvement.'

He corrected himself. 'Dr—'

'You're slipping. It's Nell.'

'I might be very grateful for your offer to share my workload,' he said stiffly. 'But that doesn't mean I'm welcoming you to share my life.'

For heaven's sake—she was only asking him to decorate a tree. He was overreacting here, and the lurking twinkle behind her eyes told him she knew it.

'Now, whatever made you think I wanted to do that?' she asked, incredulous. 'I've done that once before, thank you very much. Shared my life with a man. And if you think I'm going down that road again, you're very much mistaken.'

'I didn't mean sharing in that way.'

'I know you didn't,' she approved. 'If you had, I'd be out of here. But decorating a Christmas tree's not sharing a life. It's just a part of sharing a house. Sharing a Christmas. They're very different things, Dr Sutherland.'

He could only agree. But he looked at the way she was looking at him, and he wasn't so sure.

She was a mind-reader, and the thought was very, very threatening.

Afternoon surgery was endless, if only because every single patient wanted to know about Nell. They remembered her from years back and were amazed.

'Is it true Nell McKenzie's back in town? And now she's a doctor like her grandpa was? Well, who'd have thought it? She was such a quiet little thing. And she's pregnant, they say? Poor lamb, just like her mother. Well, at least she doesn't have to face that harridan of a grandmother.'

Blake listened politely and fielded the questions as best he could, but over and over he found himself aching to ask questions himself. Somehow he forced himself not to, because if he asked questions about Nell, he decided, then it was possible she could ask questions of him, and he didn't want to think where that could lead.

They weren't sharing a life. They were sharing a house—and Christmas—and even that seemed threatening.

Finally he finished. He saw his last patient at about six, and then spent some time flicking through the histories of the patients Nell had seen that morning. He found her notes meticulous and she'd made no decision he wouldn't have made himself.

So, yes, she was competent, but somehow it didn't make him feel any better about what was happening. Sure, his workload had eased, but in its place was a problem. Invasion of personal space… He didn't like it. He didn't want it and he hadn't asked for it.

Eight o'clock came all too soon. Christmas-tree-decorating time. Write it in your diary in black ink, she'd ordered, but he hadn't needed to. It was indelibly planted in his mind. How could he avoid it?

But then… They couldn't get a tree, he thought with some relief. What had she been thinking of? It'd be too late now to take a trip out to the pine plantation, and the shops would be well and truly closed. Ha!

Nevertheless, he was taking no chances. He spent more time than necessary doing a ward round, he ate dinner in the hospital kitchen—suppressing just the faintest niggle that Nell might have cooked something—and it was almost nine before he finally made his way home.

There was a tree in his sitting room!

It wasn't just a tree, he thought, stunned. It was the mother of all Christmas trees. She'd arranged her grand-parents' furniture in a circle, there was a gorgeous Turkish rug in the centre of the room, and in a bucket in the centre of the rug was the pine plantation's biggest Christmas tree ever. It spread about eight feet in diameter, and its top just touched the cciling. It dominated the room, its sweet scent of pine making him think of...

Of Christmas.

He'd blotted it out, he thought blankly. He hadn't thought of Christmas for years. Not properly. Christmas was a family day other people celebrated, while he spent it fixing up broken legs from new roller skates or coping with perforated ulcers from too much pudding.

Now, in the time it had taken to haul one massive tree into his home, Nell had hauled up all these memories that he'd successfully buried for years.

'Do you like it?' she demanded the minute he walked in the door, and he could only stop and blink.

'Um...'

'Isn't it huge?' She was on her knees, threading popcorn. 'Help me do this before Ernest gets the lot. I've had to repop four lots already.'

There was popcorn everywhere. Strands and strands of multicoloured corn were roped around the tree, and more was scattered on the rug. Ernest was in his basket where he'd obviously been banished, looking at the popcorn with mournful eyes.

'Here you go.' She rose stiffly to her feet and before he knew what she was about there was a threaded needle and a bowl of yellow corn in his hands. 'I'm off to dye some blue. Finish that, will you?'

He didn't seem to have any choice. He sat—and threaded popcorn.

'Where did you get the tree?' She had him fascinated. She'd been in town barely more than a day and she was organising faster than he'd thought possible.

'Lorna and Des Scott sent their son around to see if I needed any help.' She beamed. 'Wasn't that nice of them? I remember Des as the chemist when I was a little girl, and Ron's just like him. I met Lorna when I popped around to Ethel's this afternoon to see how she was getting on, and they couldn't have been more helpful. The pair of them were like two old chooks, planning our Christmas.'

He was having trouble taking this in, but one thing stood out. 'You popped around to Ethel's?'

'I was worried about her,' Nell told him, shaking her corn in its blue dye. 'She was so upset yesterday about breaking her diet that I thought a follow-through this afternoon wouldn't hurt. But don't worry. She's stuck to her diet all day and I found her reading recipe books and planning Christmas to her heart's content.'

Damn, he should have visited Ethel himself—but those sorts of things hadn't been done in Sandy Ridge. Follow-throughs. Unless they were urgent there simply hadn't been time.

With a jolt he realised that now there was. Follow-throughs... They were a medical imperative and now he'd have time to do them.

If they weren't done first by Nell.

'She was really OK?' he asked grudgingly, and she smiled.

'She was great. She was up to her elbows in mince pies, but she hadn't eaten a single one. She's talked to Mrs Condie and she's cooking them for the hospital patients. Oh, and for us.' She held up a tray of mince pies. 'I arrived just as a batch were coming out of the oven and they're delicious. Like one?'

'No. Thank you.'

It wasn't that he didn't want one. It was that he hardly dared have it. Sitting on the floor, threading Christmas decorations and eating mince pies... Things were starting to look seriously out of hand. He glanced at Ernest and found he was being regarded with a look that was suspiciously like sympathy.

'Does she organise you, too, boy?' he asked, and Nell glowered from the kitchen.

'Hey, I heard that.'

'Ernest wants some popcorn.'

'Ernest will pop himself if he eats anything more. He ate all my yellow corn while my back was turned. And it causes flatulence. He's sleeping on *your* bed tonight.'

'Spare room again, Ernest,' Blake told him, and grinned at the dopey dog's expression. Honestly, you'd swear he understood. He was one crazy dog. 'Where did you get him?'

'Who, Ernest?'

'That's who I mean.'

'Why do you ask?' Nell had gone back to corn-popping. She was holding the lid of the pot tight and the sound of popping corn filled the room.

'It's just... He seems ancient.'

'He was born ancient.'

'How old is he?'

'The vet thinks about twelve.'

'So you've had him for twelve years?'

'Nope.' She set her pot aside and returned to kneel under the tree. Picking up the corn, she also started threading, so they were side by side, threading in unison. It was a strange feeling. Intimate... 'I said the vet *thinks*,' she told him. 'If I'd had him since a puppy surely I'd know the age of my very own dog.'

'OK.' Her voice was cross and Blake found himself apologising. 'I'm sorry. Tell me how he came into your life.'

'I've only had him for a few months.'

'Really?' Blake's mouth twisted into laughter. 'Don't tell me. You went to the lost dogs' home and picked out the most decrepit one you could see.'.

'There's no need to be rude about my dog.' She glowered. 'As a matter of fact, he chose me.'

'How?'

'It's a long story.'

'So I'm threading popcorn. I have all the time in the world.'

She hesitated and for a minute he thought she wouldn't go on. And then she shrugged. 'I was walking home from the hospital late at night and I was mugged. A group of four or five kids came from nowhere and grabbed me from behind. They hit me.' Her voice faded a bit. 'And…well, they took my bag and they hurt me. Not rape or anything, but they bashed… Anyway, when I finally figured out what was going on I was lying in the street, and Ernest was there. He was licking my face.'

Blake thought it through and watched her face. There was a heap going on here that he didn't understand and it behoved him to step carefully. 'Licking appears to be Ernest's specialty,' he said at last, and was rewarded with a smile.

'It is, isn't it?'

'I thought you were going to say he chased off the attackers.'

'Hey, there were five of them. Ernest had more sense. He knew the best course of action was to stay in the shadows and administer first aid.'

'And then what happened?' His eyes were still locked on Nell's. For some reason he found himself holding his breath. It was a sort of watershed, he realised. A chink in her armour. Maybe she'd finally tell him something.

'So I sat in the gutter and I howled and I howled, like a

great big sook. But I howled out a lot of stuff that had nothing to do with the mugging. I held onto Ernest and he licked me—and then I made a few resolutions.'

'I see.' The thought of her bashed filled his consciousness. Nell, sitting in the gutter, bleeding maybe, and sobbing... The image was light years away from the confident young woman he saw before him. It was jarring to say the least.

He didn't like the image at all. He found he was sitting by her Christmas tree with his hands clenching over fistfuls of popcorn—anger building at five unknown youths who'd dared to hurt her.

But she was no longer a victim. Not Nell. 'You don't see at all,' she said, a tiny smile flickering back. 'It was logical. I figured that was the end of me being a doormat. From that moment on, Ernest and I were going to take charge of our lives.'

He smiled up at her, and once again their eyes met. An unspoken message passed between them, and in that instant something changed. Something he couldn't define. But it was...nice. 'Well, bully for you and Ernest,' he told her gently, and she smiled.

'It is, isn't it?' Her beam returned in full. 'For one stray dog and one wimpish doctor we've done very well for ourselves. So maybe I should even be grateful to my muggers. Now...how's that popcorn going? Nearly threaded?'

'No. I—'

'Well, hurry up. There's more here.' And then she frowned. 'You did eat, by the way?'

'I ate over at the hospital.'

'Really?' She sounded as if she thought he was a dope for doing such a thing. 'Ernest and I made chicken pie. And chocolate pudding.'

He'd had cold mutton and salad. Damn.

Maybe he *was* a dope.

Maybe he didn't know what the hell he was any more.

So he sat and threaded popcorn, because that was all he could think of to do.

The nights were the longest. Would he ever be able to close his eyes at eleven and wake at seven with eight hours' uninterrupted sleep? Blake lay in the darkness, listening to a rising wind. His hands were linked behind his head and he stared up into the night with all the old familiar demons doing their haunting.

Curiously, though, tonight they were changed. Different.

He could still see Sylvia's face. That'd stay with him for ever. But tonight he wasn't seeing her as he'd seen her at the end. He was watching her as he'd first noticed her. At Christmas...

'Not the orange ones. You dingbat, can't you see I have a pink and white theme?' Her gorgeous face had laughed down at him from the ladder as she'd attached baubles to the ward Christmas tree. 'Yes, that's lovely,' she'd approved. 'Now, just stand there and hand them up, there's a lamb. But nothing that clashes.'

Sylvia would have hated Nell's tree, Blake thought. There wasn't a thing on the branches that went with anything else. It was a garish, outlandish jumble of everything she'd been able to scramble together.

'Well, you don't seem to have boxes of Christmas decorations lying around and I don't have cash to splash,' Nell had told him when he'd fingered the decorations in amazement. 'So a girl's got to do what a girl's got to do.'

What a girl had to do had stunned him. She'd fetched his waiting room's collection of magazines to the apartment and she'd ripped them into pieces. Now they were reassembled as masses of paper chains, looping through her threaded popcorn, and she'd made scores and scores of tiny paper lanterns to hang all over.

'Look,' she'd said, laughing and motioning to the highest

lantern. 'This one's a lantern made with Brad Pitt's six-pack. What a way to make a Christmas lamp.'

He grinned into the night at the thought of it.

But Sylvia would have had a fit.

Damn Sylvia.

The thought came from nowhere, astounding him. It was the first time he'd thought it. Up until now the guilt had been all-consuming. But now…

It was a great Christmas tree, he decided, and then he gave the image of his dead wife a grimace. 'Don't you spoil it for me.' As she'd spoiled everything else…

He sat up and flicked on the light, as he'd done every night now for over three years. But now it wasn't Sylvia he was thinking of.

The top of the tree was bare.

'We need an angel,' Nell had said sadly just before they'd retired for the night. She'd stood back and stared at the tree's tip with regret. 'We'll never find one now. I'd splash out and buy something as important as an angel, but the shops will have sold out long ago.'

And now, in the dark, a memory crept back—a long-ago memory from when he'd been about five years old. Back to kindergarten days.

'Fold here. Now cut. See, if you leave just a little bit on either wing, they'll join.' He'd made paper angels. Chains of paper angels.

They'd run out of paper.

He stared down at his bedside and his medical journals mocked him. Hmm. He could but try.

It was four in the morning. Nell had slept for five hours, but then she woke. The surf was starting to crash in the rising wind, and junior was kicking in no uncertain terms.

'Cornelius,' she threatened, but it was no good. Cornelius or Brunhilda kicked on. Finally she sighed, threw back the covers and emerged to the living room.

There were angels circling the top of her tree.

For a moment she thought she was dreaming, but then she looked again.

Blake had cut them with care. These were kindergarten angels cut by a man who'd trained as a surgeon. You could see the skill of surgeon's fingers in the way he'd cut the gorgeously intricate wings.

They were identical—well, they would be as he'd folded the pages into three and cut them as a chain. Then he'd joined the wing of the first and the third to form a ring. Now the ring of winged angels circled the tip of pine, and they beamed down…

How had he done the faces? How had he made them smile?

He'd cut them! The deep green of the tree made the intricate cuts in the glossy paper stand out as beaming smiles. Wondrous smiles. Smiles of blessing…

Nell stood back, stunned. They really were very, very good, and they completed her Christmas tree magnificently.

But he'd cut them from his medical journals.

There was an advertisement for haemorrhoid cream running around the base of the first angel!

Haemorrhoid cream advertisements on Christmas angels?

He was a nut, she thought, and found herself giggling. A nice nut. Underneath that grumpy, repellent shell she was starting to discover a very nice person.

She'd just have to struggle to expose it.

Which posed a dilemma. Why would you bother exposing anything? she asked herself. You're not interested in men.

It's just I'm interested in him as a person, she said to herself defensively. Not as a male.

Yeah, right. You dope, Nell.

I'm not a dope. I know what I'm doing. I can take care of myself.

Maybe she needed to go back to bed and stop thinking about it. Hmm.

The phone went at six, blasting through the sounds of wind and surf and waking both doctors. The hospital staff had been told to ring Blake again during the night, and the phone was by his bed, but Nell heard it. She'd left her door wide open and she saw him as he walked out of the bedroom, still talking on the mobile handset.

Well, why wouldn't she look? He was only wearing pyjama pants, and there was that chest again…

For heaven's sake, Nell McKenzie, she told herself as he flicked on the living room light and his body was clearly delineated in the frame of her bedroom door. Get a grip! And listening to him, her concentration on his chest faded immediately. She did indeed get a grip.

'How many? Right. You've contacted the ambulance? What about the coastguard?'

That was enough. Nell's covers were thrust aside and she padded out fast to see what was going on.

Ernest was there, too, awake and alert and looking only slightly hungry. Woman and dog stood beside the Christmas tree, and waited for Blake to finish. Blake's voice was curt and incisive, but mostly he listened.

'Yeah. Right. OK. Tell the ambulance to pick me up in two minutes. You might be able to winch me down from the top.'

And then he clicked off the receiver and headed back to his bedroom. Leaving the door open, he was throwing on his clothes regardless of the fact that Nell was standing by his bedroom door. He simply didn't notice.

This, then, was real trouble.

'Is there anything I can do?' Nell asked.

'No.' That was to the point. He was zipping his trousers and hauling on his shirt almost in one motion.

'What's happened?'

'A group of locals fishing from the clifftop.' He shoved his shirt into his trousers and reached for a sweater. 'Damn fools. They know these cliffs are unstable.'

'There's been a slide?'

That made him frown. He'd forgotten she was a local. She'd know what the problem was. The sandstone cliffs were notoriously unstable here, yet time and time again he'd seen fishermen edge closer to get their cast to land inches further out into the surf.

'Yes.'

'To be out in this wind...' She thought fast and knew they'd have selected this morning especially. With the wind behind them they could cast their lines further out to where the fish ran. 'How many fell?'

'Three. One's in the water. The coastguard's on the way, but God help him. Two are stuck on a ledge halfway down and one seems badly hurt.'

'I'll come.'

'You're seven months pregnant,' he said explosively. 'You'll only be in the way.'

And that was that. He hauled his sweater over his head, grabbed his boots and headed for the door.

CHAPTER FIVE

'YOU'LL only be in the way.' How often had she heard that? All her life, Nell thought bitterly, and it made no more sense now than it had all those years ago. 'Get out of my kitchen. Leave your grandfather alone. Go to your bedroom, Eleanor.'

'Why?'

'You're in the way.'

That statement was now a red rag to a bull, Nell decided as she hauled on her clothes. Damn the man! Who did he think he was?

'These are my people,' she told Ernest fiercely. 'I was brought up here. If there's fishermen stuck on the cliffs or in the water then I'll have known them for ever, and I'm trained in emergency medicine.'

Ernest looked at her with understanding, and as she raced to the door he sniffed after her.

'Sorry, boy,' she told him, not without irony. 'Not today. Believe it or not, you'd only be in the way.'

Someone—whoever had phoned—had obviously collected Blake. Nell had heard their vehicle accelerate away while she'd been throwing on her clothes—the same purple overalls Blake had first seen her in. They might be flamboyant but they were practical. Now she emerged to the windswept dawn to find no one.

The hospital residence was on a bluff overlooking the town and the wind across the bluff almost blasted her sideways.

The fishermen must be on the north cliffs, she decided as she headed for her car. They must be. At this time of year

71

the tailor—a popular eating fish—would be running and the fishermen would be casting off the cliffs north of the river mouth. The cliffs were forty feet high, they were known to be dangerous and she knew about twenty men in the town who'd be stupid enough to fish there.

So she knew where to go. No thanks to Blake.

'Damn the man,' she muttered under her breath as she steered her Volkswagen northwards. 'Who does he think he is?'

He thought he was a hero!

Nell pulled up on the clifftop, parking well back from the ambulance and other vehicles. There was a cluster of men gathered where the cliff dropped to the sea, and as she climbed from her car she caught sight of Blake's dark sweater and gold-brown hair. He appeared to be sitting on the cliff edge.

He wasn't just sitting. As she ran closer she saw that he was in a harness, and as she watched in horror, he was lowered over the face of the cliff. Her breath caught in fear but she was too late. He was gone.

'What the hell do you think you're doing?'

Nell's barked command had men turning toward her. She was striding toward the cliff with a fierceness born of fear, and the wind was tearing at her back, almost pushing her out to sea. She had to raise her voice to be heard above wind and surf.

'Of all the stupid... Look how close you are! Will you get back?' There were six of them standing right on the edge. 'If the edge has crumbled already, don't you realise it can go again? Bring Dr Sutherland back up. Now!'

'We can't do it, Nell,' one of the fishermen said dully, turning back to stare down the cliff with eyes that had room for only one thing. 'The only other way to reach them is with a helicopter and we can't wait. Tom's down there, and Dan, and Dan can't breathe. Tom yelled up that he was turning blue. He's unconscious and there's blood coming out of his mouth, so it was send the doc over or have him die before we could reach him.'

Nell was forced to leave Blake on the ledge. A man could be dying of airway obstruction. Blake had gone down because he could focus on only one thing, so it was up to her to focus on others—like getting these fools back from the cliff edge before Blake ended up with more patients down there.

'Where's the fire chief?' she snapped. When she'd left town twelve years ago the fire chief had been the man to turn to in emergencies. Allan had a fierce intellect, enough courage for a small army and, in times of drama, there was no one she'd rather rely on.

'He's in Brisbane for his daughter's wedding,' one of the men said helplessly, and Nell realised with a sinking heart that the trouble with having someone so competent in charge was the void it left with him gone.

And all the men were looking at her. Good grief! Ten years ago the townsfolk had looked at her like she was a scrap of an unwanted kid. Now, because she'd raised her voice in anger and because she was deemed a doctor, she was looked to for answers.

And of all the fishermen in the town, these were the stupidest. So the void had to be filled by her.

'OK, move back,' she told them. 'Now!' The rope they were holding had gone slack. Blake had presumably reached his ledge. Then, once the rest of the men were back from the edge, she ventured forward herself, crawling on all fours to see.

Yes, Blake had reached the ledge. A rocky outcrop fifteen feet down had caught the two men. Blake was there now, crouched over a prone figure while another watched with helpless dismay.

It was better than she'd dared hope. The ledge seemed solid. A mass of loose dirt seemed to have come from the top when it had crumbled, but the ledge itself looked as if it might hold.

She stayed where she was, lying on her stomach—with difficulty because of her pregnancy—and watched what Blake was doing. The way Blake was moving, she could tell that every ounce of his concentration was on the injured man. If Dan was dying of airway obstruction, it'd take every bit of Blake's skill to keep him alive in such a situation.

'Is Blake carrying his phone?'

'There's no reception out here,' someone told her, and she bit her lip. Damn.

OK, she had to think for herself—and for Blake. She couldn't yell down to him. From where she was he probably wouldn't hear and it was too dangerous to lean right over.

'Right.' She inched back and stood up, walking away from the edge and pushing into the wind as she gazed swiftly around the remaining men. Three fishermen, two fire officers and one ambulance officer. She knew them all.

'Bill, you inch forward and take my place,' she ordered. 'Stay on your stomach and put your weight as far back as you can.' Then she explained her reasons to the others. 'We need someone to direct the winch, and Bill's the only one whose family are grown.'

They saw the sense in that. If anyone had to risk their life, it should be someone without dependants. 'OK by me,' Bill said grimly.

'Blake'll need oxygen,' Nell told them. She'd seen that he'd carried his doctor's bag down with him—he therefore had the means to do an emergency tracheotomy if he must— but he'd had no time to organise more. She didn't want Blake wasting time now, calling up directions and waiting for equipment. She turned to the ambulance officer. 'Henry, do you have a portable oxygen cylinder in the ambulance?'

'Sure thing, Nell. I mean Doc…'

'Give it to Bill before he goes close to the edge. And give him another rope. The fewer trips he has to make back and forth to the edge, the safer it'll be. Send saline solution down, too, and the things Blake needs to set up a drip.' She hesitated. 'Bill, are you sure you're OK with this? I can do it if you can't.'

'You can't,' Bill said heavily. 'You've got a littly on board. Have a bit of sense, Doc.'

She nodded, but in her mind she'd already moved on. Apart from supplying Blake with equipment, if Bill was willing to stay by the edge there was little more she could do here. So triage... Move to the next priority. They'd said there were three men.

'The man who fell into the water...'

'The coastguard's reached him.' One of the men gave a rueful grimace. 'Their boat was out already—well, it would be if the fish are running, 'cause they always do a bit of fishing on the side—and they saw what happened. They damn near splintered their boat on the cliffs, getting him aboard, but they did it. But he looked unconscious when they hauled him in.'

'And now?' Nell looked out over the white-capped sea but she couldn't see the brilliant orange of the coastguard vessel. 'Where's the boat now?'

'It's taking him back to harbour.' The fisherman hesitated. 'Dunno if they'll get in until the tide turns, though, but they're going to try.'

'I'll go down to meet them,' Nell told them. She didn't want to. She felt sick to the stomach at the idea of leaving Blake in these incapable hands—of leaving three men stuck on the crumbling cliff face—but there was an injured man being brought back into harbour who could well need her services more.

What else was needed here? The men were looking at her in helpless dismay and she wanted to knock a few heads together.

'Get more men out here,' she ordered. 'I want the fire crew.' Surely if the whole fire crew arrived there'd be someone with more intelligence than this lot. 'But don't let anyone but Bill go near the edge. Get long planking laid between here and the edge so when you're winching equipment, the pressure's not on the absolute edge. And, for heaven's sake, wait for the helicopter to bring the men up. If you try and take their weight from here…'

She didn't need to say more. The fear was in her voice and it was reflected in all their faces.

Oh, Blake, she thought as she ran back toward her car. She stopped at the ambulance and grabbed a few things she thought she might need herself.

She should be praying for all of them, she thought. She was. But mostly she was praying for Blake. She'd only known him for two days. The way she was feeling didn't make sense but, sense or not, that was the way it was.

A sudden image of Blake's paper angels sprang to mind. As she turned her car down toward the harbour she felt tears stinging at the back of her eyes. 'You look after him,' she commanded, and it was a direct order to his three paper angels, their crazy haemorrhoid cream included.

'Dear God…' Things weren't destined to get any easier. Nell pulled up at the jetty and what she saw made her feel sick all over again.

'The tide… Oh, no…'

Sandy Ridge harbour was formed by a river mouth, and behind the town the river broadened into a massive tidal lake. Tides were, to say the least, impressive. The water movement was massive.

Local fishing boats would normally wait until ebb tide before attempting to come back into harbour. To attempt anything else in weather like this was almost suicidal. As she pulled up, she could see waves breaking over the rocky entrance. Help!

And then she saw a face she knew. 'Grace!' Here, at last, was someone who was capable of sharing responsibilities.

Grace Mayne had fished with her father and then her husband since she was ten years old. She was now well into her eighties, she was fiercely intelligent and if anyone could help Nell it was Grace.

The old woman had been standing on the jetty, eyeing the harbour mouth with disfavour. She turned to Nell as she approached, gave her a flicker of a welcoming—and assessing—look and then went back to staring at the sea.

'The coastguard boat…' Nell managed.

'We've heard.' Grace didn't turn back as Nell reached her. She was staring out to sea with eyes that had seen it all. In her dingy overalls, with her weathered skin and her washed-out green eyes and faded copper hair, the old lady seemed almost a part of the sea itself. 'The coastguard radioed in to say they picked up Aaron Gunner. He's in a pretty bad way, but they can't get in. Not yet. They'd be pushing against the tide with the water breaking forward. I wouldn't try right now. No one would.'

'How long?'

'It'll be a good two hours before the ebb.'

'Do they say what's wrong with Aaron?'

Grace nodded. 'Leg's a mess. Bone sticking through the skin. Bleeding like a stuck pig. He was unconscious when they hauled him out of the water but he's coming round now. Screaming, they say.'

Dear God…

'The chopper's coming from Sydney,' Grace told her. 'Marion's been on the radio to the ambulance, trying to find out what's going on, because Doc Sutherland's phone's out of range. The ambulance boys told her you were coming here. She said to tell you the chopper'll be an hour or maybe a bit longer, but they'll need it for the men on the cliff first.'

Grace paused and surveyed Nell's face with care. 'Looks like Aaron mightn't make it?' And it wasn't a statement. It was a question.

'Mmm.'

Silence. Nell shaded her eyes and both women stared out to the river mouth. There was a wash of white water, almost like rapids, bursting out toward the open sea. To try and fight that current to bring a boat in... Impossible!

But maybe there was another way. The tidal flow seemed at maximum so the surge of water outward was massive, stronger than the incoming rush of breakers. Nell turned to Grace, a sudden flare of hope in her eyes.

'Grace, I know getting into harbour's impossible, but could you get me out?'

Grace stared. 'What, through that?'

'I remember you fought a tide like this a few years back,' Nell told her, and managed a smile. 'Mind, that was a real emergency. There was a bushfire, the road was cut off and the town was out of beer. Half the fleet took off for Bay Beach.'

'Wasn't like this, though.' Grace went back to assessing the river mouth. 'It was later. The flow wasn't as strong and there wasn't as much wind.' She wrinkled her already massively wrinkled face. 'Going out now'd be like riding the rapids.'

'But we'd be going with the flow of the water.'

'We?'

'I want you to take me out there,' Nell said urgently. 'Can you do it?'

'But—'

'You know I'm a doctor.'

'Yeah. Just like your grandpa.' But Grace's eyes narrowed. 'Though maybe not like your grandpa if you want to take these sort of crazy risks for Aaron.' She took a deep breath. 'I'm eighty-three,' she said at last. 'Everybody I care for's dead. It doesn't matter if I go down with the boat. But you've got a baby aboard.'

'And I'll bet Aaron has a family.'

'He has,' Grace said grudgingly. 'Three littlies. Nice wife. Stupid, but nice.'

'There you go, then.' Nell swung back to her car. 'I'll grab some equipment and then let's go.'

'You're mad,' Grace told her, but she was speaking to no

one. Nell was heading for her car, and for a long moment Grace stared after her.

There were more fishing boats lined up on the wharf. If she didn't take Nell, Nell would persuade someone else to take her, she thought.

What had she told the girl? *Everybody I care for's dead.* It wasn't quite true. Not now.

With a sigh Grace climbed aboard her boat—and then she grinned, the dreary blanket of depression that had been hovering over her since the death of her husband lifting like magic. 'We're both mad,' she muttered. 'But who dares wins. Right?' She chuckled as Nell came running back with her equipment. 'Welcome to town, Dr McKenzie. We're very pleased to see you home.'

In the end they didn't do it alone. As soon as Grace gunned her motor they had every fisherman not already at sea rushing to their boatside.

'What the hell do you think you're doing?'

'You know Aaron's dying and they can't get him into the harbour,' Grace said curtly, motioning to Nell who was storing equipment in the cabin. 'So we're going out. I'm taking Dr McKenzie out to see if there's something she can do.'

'Not alone, you're not' was the consensus, and when they finally slipped their moorings they had a crew of four. All of them were as old as Grace or older, but they had no intention of taking unnecessary risks. Each of them was weighed down with safety gear.

'Because we might be old but we're still good for a few years yet,' the ancient fishermen told Nell, grinning at her as they slipped through the last patch of calm water. 'Between us we must have more than three hundred years of seagoing experience. Let's hope some of it pays off.'

They told Blake what was happening and he nearly had them winch him up straight away.

'They radioed from the harbour,' Bill told him from the clifftop. The wind had eased just a bit—enough for them to hear themselves speak. 'Grace Mayne has taken her boat out to meet the coastguard, and she's taken Nell with her.'

'Through the outgoing tide?' Blake's voice was incredulous. 'In these conditions?' They had to be mad.

'Yeah.' Bill sounded as sick as Blake felt. 'Can't say I like it.'

Like it? The man was a moron. Blake turned back to his patient and it was just as well the fisherman took most of his attention or he would have gone crazy. Once more he checked on Dan's airway, clearing the blood that filled his mouth almost as soon as he swabbed it away. He had Dan lying on his side. The blood came from fractured teeth that had torn his gums. It wasn't life-threatening—as long as Blake concentrated—but Bill's news made that almost impossible.

Damn the woman. She was pregnant, for heaven's sake!

She'd gone out with Grace... And Grace was suicidal. He knew it. The elderly woman had told him so herself. She was refusing to take antidepressants, and here she was, pushing her boat at something that was likely to kill her. And she wouldn't care.

She'd take Nell with her.

The thought was savagely, piercingly dreadful. He felt sick, so much so that the other fisherman on the ledge leaned toward him with concern. 'You all right, Doc?'

He caught himself. 'Yeah. Never better,' he muttered, and reached for another swab.

Dear God. Nell...

Which was pretty much exactly what Nell was thinking. Crossing the harbour entrance was the most hair-raising thing she'd done in her life. It was white-water rafting at its most dangerous—not on a raft, but on a bathtub of an ancient fishing boat. All the decent boats with more powerful motors were already at sea, so it was Grace's ancient tub or nothing.

Nell was strapped into a lifejacket, clipped to a lifeline and told to stay put.

'You're under orders,' Grace yelled at her as one of the fishermen helped her fasten herself her onto the sheets. 'If the boat rolls, then you undo that clip. Fast. The line'll keep you safe while we're upright, but if the boat goes under then it'll tie you there. You'll drown.'

'Gee, thanks…'

They all had clips. They might be ancient and they might also be desperate to help, but they were taking minimal chances. Grace was taking minimal chances. She was using every ounce of skill she possessed to keep the boat safe.

She was wonderful, Nell thought. Her geriatric saviour!

And then they hit white water, and Nell thought of nothing but keeping alive.

There was water all around her. The mass of water rushing out of the harbour was so great that it was seething into the stern of the boat. There were waves breaking in front of them, creating eddies and whirlpools like something out of a nightmare.

It was a pretty wet nightmare! Maybe there was a better metaphor but she couldn't see it. In fact, after the first rush of white water she couldn't see anything at all. She was soaked and she was blinded and she was concentrating only on each sodden breath.

'Go to it, Grace,' she prayed over and over. But it wasn't just Grace. There were three of them on the wheel, using their combined strength to hold the boat on course and stopping it slamming into the harbour wall. The other fisherman was monitoring the pumps, and it was only Nell who stood uselessly where she'd been clipped.

'You'd only get in the way,' Grace told her when she'd wanted to help, and she'd grimaced.

That's what Blake had said to her, and they were her grandmother's words, echoing down through the years.

But this time it was different. This time she knew it was true. Grace knew her boat and she didn't, and it'd be little use to anyone if they managed to get through the harbour mouth only to have the doctor they were carrying washed overboard. So Nell accepted her role of idleness, but she felt very small and very vulnerable and, to be honest, she also felt very, very afraid.

For the first time she wondered whether this was fair on her unborn baby, and she knew it wasn't. She'd raced into it without thinking. They advised pregnant women to give up smoking because of the threat to the unborn child, but this... How much greater threat was this?

She put her hand protectively on her stomach.

'If I get through this I'll never threaten you with Cornelius or Brunhilda again,' she whispered to her little one. 'I promise.'

She hoped to God it was enough.

And then they were through. The last rush of water shoved them forward like a cork from a bottle, and they emerged to sunshine and water that was rough but, compared to what they'd just been through, it was like a mill pond. Nell gasped and wiped water from her eyes and then proceeded to count heads. Her four wonderful geriatrics were all beaming at her like they'd won the pools.

'Who said only the youngies know how to handle a boat?' Grace chortled. 'Well done, us.' Her eyes rested on Nell for a moment, her old eyes meeting Nell's young ones in a flash of triumphant recognition. Then it was back to business. 'Adam, how much water do we have on board?'

'Don't take on any more,' Adam advised. 'A sparrow lands on this deck and we're under.' But the pumps were going full throttle, spurting the water out behind them, and for now things could only get better.

They had to find the coastguard boat with the crew and Aaron.

'They tried to come into harbour but when they couldn't they went back to the shelter of the north cliffs,' Grace told her. She'd left the wheel to one of the others and had checked the radio. 'It's calmer there and they're standing off far enough to keep from getting pounded on the rocks. But Aaron sounds...' She faltered, and this time her eyes didn't meet Nell's. 'Well, he's lost consciousness again and they can't stop the bleeding. I hope to hell we haven't come this far for nothing.'

She was there. Grace's old tub of a boat rounded the headland and Blake nearly stood up and cheered. He counted heads. There were five on board and he could see Nell's crazy patchwork overalls from here. Bless the overalls. He hadn't realised how much he loved them.

Loved them? Liked, he corrected himself, and suddenly it mattered to him that he did. Liked. That's what he did. He didn't do love. Nell was a competent doctor; she was working alongside him and he owed her a responsibility. That's why he'd felt sick—nothing more.

Under his hands Dan stirred and moaned and Blake adjusted his air-flow. 'Take it easy, mate,' he murmured, but it wasn't quite a murmur. There was jubilation in his voice, and he felt like a kid who'd been handed a Santa sack all for himself.

The men on the coastguard boat watched the geriatric crew approach with amazement, and when they saw Nell there was even more amazement.

She must look a real sight, Nell thought ruefully—a half-drowned doctor, very pregnant, wearing soaking purple patchwork. But she had work to do. There was no time to think about her appearance.

She sorted equipment to be taken on board and then, finally, she allowed herself one uneasy glance up the cliff face. Only one. She shouldn't even take that. There was nothing for her to do even if Blake had fallen. It was the first rule of medicine in an emergency to not allow oneself to be distracted by things you could do nothing about, but...

Please, God. Protect Blake…

And blessedly, joyously, he was still there. He was still crouched over the injured fisherman, and that had to be a good sign. It meant his patient was alive, and there hadn't been a further fall.

But from underneath, the ledge didn't look nearly as solid as it had from up top. In fact, from here the ledge looked as if it could give way at any minute.

'Don't think about it,' she told herself fiercely. 'Triage, Dr McKenzie. Concentrate on what's important.'

Which was Aaron, not Blake! Thinking of Blake only led to trouble—in more ways than one.

And Aaron certainly needed her.

Her transfer from boat to boat, tricky at the best of times, was achieved with Nell hardly thinking about it. She couldn't. Her mind was already assessing what needed to be done. She took one look at the man lying on the deck and her heart sank. Back at Sydney Central she'd have had him in Theatre in minutes. She'd have had blood banks on the line, she'd have been cross-matching, she'd have had surgeons and…

Well, here she had herself and only herself, and she was already kneeling beside him as her equipment was transferred after her.

'Good luck,' Grace called as the boats pulled apart, and Nell knew that she was going to need it.

What she needed, in fact, was Blake—or at least another doctor—but she was all she had.

Nell did a fast assessment which was harder than she'd thought on the rolling boat. There was no head wound. The lack of consciousness must be due to shock and loss of blood, she thought. The fracture was compound, and it bled sluggishly even though the coastguard crew had tied the upper leg with a tourniquet. And that couldn't stay there. Nell felt his foot and flinched at the coldness of it. Soon he'd have tissue death.

Or complete death. How much blood had he lost? The deck was awash with it.

The first thing to do was to stop the bleeding. There must be a severed artery. 'There's antiseptic in my bag. Do you have any more?' Heck, she needed antiseptic by the bucket load. To tie off an artery in these conditions... She had no choice.

'There's a light in the bag. I want it held straight down at his leg,' she ordered, shoving her bag into someone's hands as she applied a fist to the pressure point above the wound. 'And I want fishing line.'

She was thinking fast as she ripped Aaron's already shredded trouser leg. 'You.' She picked a random man of the half-dozen clustered around. 'Hold yourself steady against the rail and hold the plasma. Don't move. And, you... Kneel here and take over. See where I'm pressing? I want you to do the same.'

She worked swiftly and incisively, her training allowing her to almost forget her surroundings. She'd used human dripstands before. This was the stuff Nell was trained to do. As doctor in charge of a busy city casualty ward—and at the scene of accidents when needed—she'd been at the coal face time and time again. When patients had been stuck in damaged cars and couldn't be shifted, she'd been able to cope.

She'd had back-up there, though, she thought. Trained ambulance crew. Paramedics. But here... Here there was no one. And Blake was still on that dreadful ledge.

Don't think of Blake! Think of what she needed to do.

She'd only brought four units of plasma, she thought grimly as she searched through the damaged flesh, trying to locate the artery. Four units didn't look nearly enough. And where was the artery?

Ah, there it was, under her fingers, still spurting blood despite the tourniquet. She had no choice but to tie it off, even though it might mean losing the foot.

The foot might be the least of Aaron's troubles. She used

fishing line to tie off the artery and allowed herself a few deep breaths. Then…

'When did you say the helicopter'll be here?'

'Maybe an hour.'

An hour! Help.

'Does anyone here know their blood group?' she demanded. It was a forlorn hope, but she had to ask. 'There isn't anyone with O-negative blood, is there?' O-negative was the universal donor. Without the facilities to cross-match, that was her only hope. Or Aaron's only hope.

And amazingly there was. Two men—brothers by the look of them.

'We're blood donors,' they told her. 'Doc Sutherland uses us a lot. Because, yep, we're O-negative.'

Miracle of miracles. O-negative and blood donors… If Blake used them regularly she could assume their blood was safe. Another glance at Aaron's deathly white face confirmed what she believed. He was unconscious and he'd lost so much blood there was a risk of brain damage. The extra risks from not cross-checking would be more than outweighed by Aaron's increased chances of survival.

But could she do a blood transfusion on this heaving boat? She did a frantic visual check of equipment, thought it through and then nodded. She could but try. She had no choice.

'OK. Lie down and swab your arms with antiseptic,' she told them. 'As soon as I have this bleeding stopped, I'll be using you. I need all the blood I can get.'

Her confidence silenced them all. The men were staring at her in amazement. These were local men and they knew her—or they'd thought they knew her. This was Nell McKenzie. Nell! The sad little town girl who'd been more trouble than she'd been worth.

'Just do it,' she said, sensing their uncertainty. 'You need to trust me.'

They looked again—and then both her potential blood donors nodded. Trust her? They did.

* * *

The helicopter finally came from the north, and Nell was never more pleased to see anything in her life. By that time her major anxiety was for Blake and the other two men trapped on the ledge.

She'd done all she could for Aaron. He desperately needed surgery if they were to save his leg, but she'd stopped the bleeding and given him enough blood to avoid brain damage. Or more brain damage. She'd feel a whole lot better if he gained consciousness. But now there was nothing else for her to do but to gaze up to where the ledge looked more and more fragile every time she looked. To Blake.

But then the helicopter appeared. The men and women on board were competent and professional. They swung in over the cliff, a stretcher was lowered and within ten minutes everyone on the ledge had been winched to the top. Blake was winched up last, and as Nell saw him being hauled upward she felt almost sick with relief.

Then there was a brief pause when they landed on the clifftop, followed by the wail of the ambulance siren receding into the distance. Presumably Blake and the injured fisherman were on their way to hospital. Nell could finally let out her breath on Blake's behalf. Dear God, thank you.

Why had she felt sick? She hardly knew the man. She'd met him two days ago. It didn't make sense. She was accustomed to trauma—why should Blake's fate worry her more than others?

She only knew that it did. It wasn't sensible in the least—but still it did.

Then it was their turn. The chopper was back, lowering a stretcher for Aaron. It was a tricky operation on the choppy sea but this crew was good! Two paramedics were lowered as well. It hadn't been safe to lower anyone not absolutely essential onto the ledge, but onto the boat it was different. Nell was suddenly redundant in the face of these people's far superior training in moving the injured.

'We'll take him straight to the hospital,' the paramedics

told her, strapping Aaron onto the stretcher with skill and speed. 'The chopper should reach the hospital almost as soon as the ambulance, and your Dr Sutherland will be there to meet him.'

Her Dr Sutherland... The thought brought an unexpected jolt of comfort. She didn't understand why, but it did.

Finally, the winch was lowered once more. 'This time it's you, Doc,' the paramedics told her. 'It'll be more than an hour before the boat can get you into harbour. There'll be two patients back at the hospital now and Doc Sutherland needs help. He doesn't want to send either man to Blairglen—at least until they're stable—so he's asked us to bring you in.'

It made sense, Nell thought, but the idea of stepping into the harness and being winched upward made her feel ill. She had a baby on board.

She looked at the harness, saw that her weight wouldn't hang too heavily against her abdomen and shrugged.

'I'm really sorry, baby,' she whispered as she was roped into the harness. 'If we get through this I'll buy you the safest, snuggliest bassinet known to man, and I'll never put you at risk again. Promise.'

And then she was whisked up into the sky, to the chopper waiting overhead. To the hospital.

To Blake.

And it was a Blake who was seething.

'What the hell do you think you've been playing at?' Nell was no sooner through the door of Casualty than Blake's pent-up anxiety exploded into unreasonable fury. 'To go through the harbour mouth at that time. It was madness!'

But Nell wasn't in the mood for apologies. She was feeling sick with relief at being on firm ground, and she wanted to yell herself.

'You know I had no choice.' She took a deep breath and steadied. 'How's Dan?'

Her carefully produced matter-of-fact tone had its effect,

and only Nell herself knew how hard it had been to produce it. 'Stable.' Blake caught himself and grimaced. If she could act professionally then he'd better match it.

'He's broken his nose, smashed some teeth and knocked himself out. The combination almost killed him—he was breathing blood—but once I had an airway established he was fine. He's conscious now, his breathing's regular and I'm happy with him.'

'Right.' Nell was now purely in professional mode. In truth, the events of the morning had left her feeling dizzy, but there was work to do before she could indulge her own emotions. She couldn't afford to let herself be anything other than a doctor.

And she certainly couldn't afford to do what she wanted— which was to put her arms around this damned man and hug him senseless. She hadn't realised how frightened she'd been until then. Frightened for herself, frightened for her baby— frightened for Blake!

Frightened for Blake? Why should she have been more frightened for him than for anyone else on the ledge? Why was he making her think like that?

Medicine! Concentrate on medicine. And somehow she did. 'Then Aaron needs our attention first.' She motioned down to Aaron's gory leg. 'The leg fracture needs reducing.' She didn't explain further. Blake could see for himself what the problem was. The blood supply to the foot was almost completely blocked and the leg was flaccid and white.

'I've tied off an artery, and the compound fracture is obstructing what remains of his blood supply,' she told him. 'We need to straighten it enough to get blood through until he gets to a vascular surgeon.' She took a deep breath. 'He'll need to be taken to Blairglen for that, though.'

'I can do that—if you'll back me up with anaesthetic.'

She stared. Vascular surgery… 'You're kidding!'

He shrugged. 'Vascular surgery was my specialty. I've done very little since I moved here but I can do what's necessary.'

'Right.' She believed him. There was something about Blake Sutherland that said he wasn't a man to blow his own trumpet lightly. If he said he could do it, she wouldn't argue, and the time difference between operating now or waiting to operate until after transfer to the city might very well be the deciding factor in saving the foot.

She cast one long assessing look at Blake, and she made up her mind. Aaron was loaded with morphine and drifting in and out of consciousness, and she squeezed his hand. 'Aaron, can you hear us?'

There was a faint return of pressure on her fingers. Which was wonderful. If he was responding now, it meant that the possibility of brain damage through blood loss was minimal.

'That's terrific,' she said. Blake was watching her, the last traces of his anger fading in the face of her professionalism. 'Your leg's at an odd angle and it's blocking the blood supply to your foot,' she told him. 'Dr Sutherland and I are going to put you to sleep and straighten it out. Is that OK with you?'

Another squeeze.

'Well done,' she said gently. Then she looked through to the waiting area. 'I'm guessing that's your wife outside, waiting. Wendy, isn't it? I recognise her from school. We'll bring her in before we pop you to sleep.'

Then she moved back to Blake's side, out of Aaron's hearing, and she focussed on what lay ahead and only that. If she let herself feel exhaustion or let the terror of the morning take hold, she'd never get through this. 'You're sure you can do this?'

He was watching her face and he was concerned. 'If you're sure you can do the anaesthetic.'

'I don't see we have a choice. If this fracture's not reduced soon, he'll lose his foot. And I've done my first part anaesthetics. It's the major reason I had the job as senior casualty officer. I could put drips in better than anyone else in the hospital.'

And she, too, wasn't boasting. It was the simple truth, and Blake had the sense to recognise it.

He cast her one last long look, though, and she knew he was seeing past the professionalism to the tumult of emotions that lay beyond. Sensibly, however, he accepted that they had to be ignored.

'Then let's go,' he said. 'Together we can do this.' And he touched her lightly on the arm. 'Together...'

Finally they were finished. With Aaron in Recovery, Donald hovering by his side as the most competent attendant nurse they could wish for and Dan settled into the ward, there was time to stand back and take stock.

Not bad. Not bad at all, Nell decided. All that drama and no deaths.

But now that the need for action had passed, exhaustion washed over her like a heavy blanket. She ripped off her surgical gown and let it drop beside her. Suddenly she didn't have the energy to move it an inch further.

Blake was watching her. They'd been operating for over two hours, and he was almost as exhausted as Nell, but his eyes were only for her.

'Sit down,' he told her.

'I don't—'

'Sit down.' Before she knew what he was about he'd placed his hands on her shoulders and propelled her into a chair. 'You look like you're about to fall over.'

'I'm not—'

'Don't argue. You have every right to fall wherever you want.'

She looked up at him, stunned. Good grief! There was something in his voice that she hardly recognised. Tenderness? Surely not!

'That was a magnificent effort,' Blake told her, and this time there was no mistaking the emotion behind his voice. 'From start to finish it's been little short of miraculous. To tie off the artery… To do blood transfusions on board a boat in filthy weather. And that anaesthetic…'

After that amount of blood loss they really should have stabilised Aaron first, but it was operate immediately or have him lose his leg. And Nell pulled him through. 'Daniel told me you were good,' he said. 'But until now I hadn't realised just how good.'

She managed a smile. 'I try to please—and you're not bad yourself.' That was an understatement. His skill as a vascular surgeon had left her stunned.

But he wasn't listening. He was focussed on her. 'Hell, you're past exhaustion.'

'Maybe.' She wasn't about to commit herself any further.

'And I'll bet you're still wet from that damned boat.'

'I am not.' Somehow Nell raised a hint of indignation and a smile. 'Even my knickers are dry by now.' She lifted her legs out and her crazy overalls were as stiff as board before her. 'See? Dry as a bone, though I've got so much salt stuck to me…'

'And blood.' Blake was gazing down at her patchwork legs in disgust. 'And I can see—and smell—the odd fish scale or two. Plus, there's grease and antiseptic and heaven knows what else. I'm putting up Aaron's antibiotic level to maximum and then some.'

She could only agree, but she was too tired to care. Blake was in charge now. 'Mmm.'

He smiled. 'How about taking your wonderful overalls off and I'll get someone to take to the cleaners? It'd be a shame to lose them.'

She blinked. 'My wonderful overalls?' Was she hearing right? 'Excuse me,' she said cautiously, 'but you don't like my overalls.'

'Who said I didn't?'

'I'm sure you didn't. Your face said you didn't.'

'Then my face said wrong,' he growled. 'There's nothing wrong with your overalls. In fact, there's nothing wrong with you.' He hesitated. 'Nell, if it wasn't for you, Aaron would

be dead now. And those no-hopers at the top of the cliff...
I told them to move back but they have the brains of sheep.
I was never more grateful for anything than when I heard
your voice.'

'Being bossy.'

'Bossy's great, especially when it means I don't have another couple of fool fishermen landing on my head.' He
smiled down at her—and such a smile! It made her catch
her breath in something akin to panic.

'I'll hold you to that,' she said, and if her voice was a
trifle unsteady, who could blame her? 'I... Maybe I'd best
see to Aaron and talk to his wife. He should be almost
awake.'

'I'll see to Aaron,' Blake told her. He smiled again, deepening her sense of unreality. 'And then I'll do afternoon
surgery while you, Dr McKenzie, take off those disgusting
overalls, shower, get into bed and sleep. For the rest of the
day.'

'But—'

'No argument,' he told her firmly. 'Do you want to risk
losing your baby?'

That stopped Nell. Maybe she had done a bit much today,
she acknowledged. If anything happened to this pregnancy...
'No! I mean...of course I don't!'

'There you go, then,' he told her. 'Bed. Now! And you're
not to stir until I come and wake you.'

There was nothing more to be said. Except...

'Yes, sir,' she said meekly—and took herself off to bed.
And the caring in his voice stayed with her until she went
to sleep, and longer.

CHAPTER SIX

IT WAS nearly seven p.m. when Blake woke Nell. He was reluctant to wake her even then, but she hadn't eaten lunch. They'd operated straight through. Now there was no evidence to show him that she'd eaten anything before she'd fallen into bed.

Dinner was ready. Damn, he *was* a doctor, she *was* pregnant and she had to take care of herself, but when he opened her door a crack to discover she was still fast asleep, his reluctance deepened. Her hand was curled under her cheek and her bright splash of copper curls looked vivid against the stark white of the pillow. She looked like a child.

She was anything but a child, he thought, letting his mind drift through the morning's events. Her skills had stunned him. She was an amazing doctor.

She was an amazing woman.

She was his Christmas gift, he thought suddenly, and he was incredibly lucky to have her.

As was Aaron. Blake was under no illusions. If Nell hadn't been here this morning—if she hadn't taken the risks she had—Aaron would be dead and there'd be a wife and three children facing a dreadful Christmas. Instead, they'd have a Christmas with a grumpy fisherman with his leg in a cast, but it definitely beat the alternative.

Ernest was shifting on the foot of Nell's bed. He saw Blake and wriggled his rump, thumping his disreputable tail against Nell's legs so that Nell stirred and opened her eyes.

And she smiled. Dear heaven… That was some smile!

He was standing there like an inane fool. Somehow he

managed to give himself a mental shake and haul his thoughts back on track.

'Hi, sleepyhead. Are you hungry?'

'Oh…' It was a lovely, drawn-out sigh. She stretched out in her bed like a cat. 'Oh, I guess I am.' She glanced at her bedside clock and her eyes flew wide. 'Seven!'

'You've slept most of the afternoon. If you'd slept any longer it would have turned into morning, and I thought you should eat before settling for the night. For the sake of junior.'

'Junior hasn't been getting such a good deal lately,' she admitted ruefully, and sat up. And then, as the sheet fell away, she gasped and hauled her bedclothes hastily back against her. She'd fallen asleep stark naked. Blake had a glimpse of full and gorgeous breasts, and then she was covered again.

She didn't blush. Instead…she giggled!

'Whoops,' she said, and hauled her sheets tighter against her. 'Sorry. I couldn't find my nightie. I looked for a whole two seconds and then bed called so urgently I couldn't resist.'

'Don't mind me,' Blake managed, though only just, and her smile widened at his discomfort.

'I don't. Ernest thought it didn't matter, and seeing as he's the only man in my life…'

'Lucky Ernest.'

'He is, isn't he?' She gave her dog an enormous hug— and Blake had another glimpse of those breasts!

For heaven's sake! He was a doctor and she was a pregnant woman. The glimpse of a bit of breast shouldn't have the capacity to knock him sideways.

But it did.

He was tired, he told himself. That was all it was, nothing more. Make yourself talk sensibly, Sutherland. Now!

'Dinner's ready when you are.'

'Great.' She made to throw her covers off and then thought better of it. 'Whoops,' she said again. And grinned.

'I'm determined to be unrespectable. Sorry. Could you and Ernest please leave?'

'We know when we're not wanted.' Blake struggled to find a smile himself. Keep it light... He clicked his fingers. 'Come on, Ernest. The lady wants some privacy.'

She wasn't fooled for an instant. 'It's not me who's embarrassed,' Nell called as he beat a hasty retreat. 'Where's your professional detachment, Dr Sutherland?'

He didn't have any and he knew it. He and Ernest headed for the kitchen and closed the door, and it was all he could do not to lock it after him.

Dinner was steak, chips and salad—Blake's staple diet. Every evening he followed almost the same routine. He threw frozen chips in the oven, had a quick shower and then emerged to fry steak and toss a bit of salad. It was an unexciting diet but it kept him alive.

Nell wasn't complaining. Wrapped in her voluminous crimson bathrobe, she walked into the kitchen and wrinkled her nose in appreciation.

'Yum. No one told me you could cook.'

'It's hardly gourmet cooking.' He looked up from his frying-pan and found her eyes doing a careful assessment of him—from the toes up. The sensation was unnerving, to say the least. 'How...how do you like your steak?'

'Medium. So I'm sure it's dead.' She sniffed her appreciation. 'And chips, too. Wow! What a man!'

'You'll make me go all bashful,' he told her, grinning and trying desperately not to do just that. He was practically acting like a schoolboy! 'Sit down.' He went back to concentrating on his steak, but he was searingly aware of Nell's eyes following his every move.

'You can have some wine if you like,' she told him. 'I've slept all afternoon, and it's my turn to be on call, so you can eat and drink all you like and then fall into bed.'

Wonderful thought. Ridiculous thought!

'I need to go back to the hospital. I haven't done my rounds yet.'

'I can do those for you.'

'They're my responsibility.'

'You're sharing responsibility, remember?' She smiled up at him as he placed a loaded plate in front of her, and her smile made his guts move sideways. 'With me. And you've worked all afternoon while I've slept.'

'You're not doing my ward rounds.'

She glared. 'I'll sulk.'

'Sulk away.'

'I'll ring up Jonas and tell him you're not co-operating.'

'Fate worse than death. I can cope.'

'I'll strip naked!'

Blake's eyes flew wide at that, and she chortled. 'Got you there. That is a fate worse than death.' She looked down at her very pregnant bulge. 'And maybe you're right to back away in horror. Sexy I ain't.'

Sexy she most certainly was, with her gorgeous crimson robe and her tousled curls and her wide green eyes, but he wasn't saying that for the world.

'So tell me about your wife,' she said conversationally, ignoring his astonishment and popping a chip into her mouth. 'What was she like?'

That was enough to kill any vestige of amusement. 'You don't want to know about my wife.'

'Of course I want to know about your wife.' Another chip went the way of its predecessor and she twinkled. 'I'm the world's biggest sticky beak—that's me—and Jonas and Em told me just enough to be tantalising.'

'Well, get untantalised. I'm not talking.'

'Why not?'

He ate half his steak before answering, but his silence didn't work. Instead of being abashed, she was eyeing him like an inquisitive sparrow, and her probing laughter was almost impossible to resist. She ate and watched him, and he had the feeling she was laughing inside at his reticence. Finally he laid down his knife and fork and glared.

'You tell me first.'

'Tell you what?'

'I assume there's been a man in your life.' He was goaded into asking this. He didn't want to know, he told himself, but it might shut her up. And...he wouldn't mind knowing.

'You mean the father of my baby?'

'That'd be the one.' He lifted his fork again and pierced another slice of steak. Trying to pretend it didn't matter.

'You don't want to know about him. It's boring.'

'Then you don't want to know about my wife.'

She tilted her chin and regarded him across the table—considering. 'If I tell you mine, will you tell me yours?'

'We'd bore each other stupid.'

'But Emily says you've locked away what's happened and won't talk about it and it's driving you crazy.'

He grimaced at that. 'Em should mind her own business.'

'Em's a wonderful doctor. She cares.'

'She sticks her nose in—'

'Where it's not wanted. That's what good doctors do. You know as well as I do that the worst problems present as a grazed knee or a request for hayfever tablets, and then, if you leave a chink of silence at the end there's an "Oh, by the way, Doctor..." and out it all comes. Something really major, like they're feeling suicidal or they have a lump in their groin. And if you don't leave that chink, there's trouble.'

'But I don't need—'

'You do need.' Nell's smile faded and the look she directed at Blake was searching and concerned. 'Em's right. You've locked everything up and it's doing damage.'

'Don't be ridiculous.'

'So just tell me.'

'You tell me,' he said, goaded. 'If you have your life so under control...'

'I don't have my life under control.'

'Tell me about your baby's father.'

She took a deep breath. 'And you agree to tell me about your wife?'

He sighed, pushed to the limit. 'If I tell you, will you get off my back?'

'Never another word,' she said virtuously. 'Cross my heart and hope to break a leg.'

'Then tell me about yourself first,' he muttered, and tried to think back to how this conversation had ever got started. He should draw back right now. But she was sitting across the table from him, eating chip after chip, and her eyes were smiling and kind.

Damn it, he did want to know about her, and if the price was simply telling her about Sylvia...

He could wear it, he thought. Maybe.

'Who's the baby's father?' he growled. And waited.

To his surprise, her response took a long time coming. Nell finished her meal, pushed her plate away and sat looking down at the table for a long, long time.

She was as reluctant as he was, Blake thought, and the knowledge surprised him. Sylvia...well, Sylvia was a tragedy, but surely there was no tragedy with Nell. An indiscretion, maybe, but...

'I thought my baby's father was my husband.' Her soft voice cut across his thoughts and his eyes flew to hers.

'What?'

'Silly, wasn't I?' She gave a self-deprecating grin, but her laughter was completely gone. It was a forced grin. A smile of humiliation.

'Will you explain?'

'Maybe I need to go back...to go back further.'

'I have time.' He glanced at his watch. There was half an hour before he'd told the nursing staff he'd be back, and if she took all that time then maybe he wouldn't have to talk about Sylvia.

'Richard was the son of my grandfather's accountant.'

'I see.' But Blake didn't. 'Your grandfather was the local doctor here.'

'That's right.' She took a deep breath. 'He certainly was. But he hated me. As did my grandmother.'

'Surely not.'

'Of course they did. Ask anyone. My mother was their only child. She was brought up in a house of repression and dislike, and she got herself into trouble. With me. Then she disappeared, leaving my grandparents with what they termed the consequence of sin. It was their Christian duty to rear me but no one ever said they had to like it. They couldn't look their neighbours in the eye while I was around, and I couldn't leave.'

'Hell,' Blake said faintly, and Nell nodded.

'It was hell. My mother left when she was fifteen, and I should have left then, too. But somehow...' She sighed and looked up, meeting Blake's eyes over the table. 'I was good at school,' she told him. 'The teachers were kind, and I guess in some strange way I thought that maybe if I became a doctor—someone of worth like my grandfather—then I'd gain my grandparents' approval. I might have known it could never happen.'

He nodded. 'And so?'

Nell shrugged. 'So I worked my butt off, I won a scholarship to university, became a doctor and once I'd left, I never came home. Until my grandmother died.'

'Which was?'

'Two years back.'

'That's right.' His brow cleared. 'I'd just arrived in town. She was the old lady out on Beacon Point.'

'That's the one. My grandfather had died some years before and I contacted her then—while I was still at university. But she told me not to come home for the funeral because my grandfather wouldn't have wanted me there. So I didn't. But I came home to bury my grandmother. She had no one else.'

'And...'

'And I met Richard.' She sighed. 'He was with his father when they told me I'd inherited everything from my grandparents' estate.'

'So your grandparents were fond of you after all.'

'No way.' She shook her head. 'To leave me money would have been unthinkable. Heavens, I might have spent it! But they were so old-fashioned that Gran never thought about making a will in her own right. Grandpa left everything to her, and if she predeceased him then he left it all to charity. I guess he figured that'd cut me right out. But he was too private and too proud to use a lawyer, so he omitted planning for what eventually happened. Gran outlived him. She therefore inherited the lot and failed to make a will in her own right. Which left me with everything. By default.'

'Lucky you.'

'Maybe I was.' She gave a rueful smile. 'I didn't know how lucky. But Richard did. His father told him. They were misers, my grandparents, and I was suddenly worth a fortune. Do you see the irony in that? Poor, downtrodden Nell who everyone was told was worthless was suddenly almost a millionaire. Until then all I'd known was hard work. And then—my grandparents were gone and there was Richard.'

Richard... Blake thought back to vague gossip he'd heard just after he'd arrived in Sandy Ridge. And then more recently. The gossip hadn't been pleasant. 'Richard Lyons?'

'That's the one.'

'I see.' He did, too. Hell! 'And you fell for him?'

'Richard would have charmed blood from a stone,' she said bitterly. 'And I was so stupid I married him.' She shrugged. 'You have no idea what it was like... I'd been so damned alone, and my grandparents' deaths made me feel appalling. Richard was the wrong man at the wrong time. So I was a fool. He'd come here to spend time with his father—in fact, he'd come to ask for money but I didn't know that. He was desperate and I was the answer to his prayers.'

'And you married?'

'We married. Fast. Why wait? he said, and it made sense. I'd been alone too long, and he was so…loving.' She hugged herself and a shiver ran right through her. Suddenly Blake felt an almost overwhelming need to reach out and touch her—comfort her—but she kept speaking, and somehow he held back.

'Richard had a dubious accountancy practice back in Sydney,' she told him. 'It was near Sydney Central, so he moved into my flat and I kept on with my medicine. But the marriage wasn't happy. It didn't take me long to realise what an idiot I'd been. And then, just as I was thinking I should walk away, I became pregnant.'

'And…'

'And Richard demanded I have a termination. I wouldn't—I was so upset—and I caught the flu and I was morning sick and miserable. I was on night duty and my boss sent me home.' She shrugged. 'So I came home unexpectedly and it was the old story. I found Richard in bed with someone else.'

'I…see.' It was an inane comment but the best he could come up with.

'You don't see at all,' she said bitterly. 'You don't know how close I came to throwing it all in. And I mean everything. Suicide had never looked so good. But then I started walking—and walking the streets of Sydney at night when you're alone is not a good idea. It ended with me being mugged. And finding Ernest. Somehow we pulled ourselves together, we drove back here out to my grandparents' house and sat on the bluff and looked out to sea—for hours. And then I made a few decisions.'

'Which were?'

'To take control,' she said, and her chin jutted in a way he was coming to know. And like. 'To stop trying to please everyone and subjugating myself for scraps of affection.' She took a deep breath and she met Blake's gaze head on. 'I had a new little life aboard and I don't want my baby to have a doormat for a mother. And I had the world's best dog to take care of. So I headed to the best lawyer I could find. Nick Daniels at Bay Beach. He's a county court judge now but as a lawyer he's the best.'

'He helped you?'

'He certainly did.' Nell smiled. 'I had one piece of luck. I'd walked into the flat and heard Richard and his woman in bed, and I'd walked straight out again without them knowing I'd seen, so Richard still thought I was the adoring stupid little woman. He didn't have a clue I was onto him. And I was just in time. I rang Richard and told him I'd been called urgently to Bay Beach because a friend was ill. Then Nick and I started asking questions. I discovered so much of mine had been shifted to both our names—ready for Richard to remove everything. Nick was appalled. Apparently Richard had had it organised for months. But I forestalled him, and I won. For the first time in my life I won.'

'Good for you.'

'It was, wasn't it?' Laughter sprang back. 'Then I went back to Sydney, kicked Richard out of my flat and I got the king-sized quilt I'd been making. You have no idea how stupid I felt. I'd spent hours and hours making a stupid quilt for a marriage that was nothing but a fraud—and I chopped it up and made it into maternity overalls. And then I made a few more decisions. One of them was that I wanted to work here.'

Blake thought that through. 'Richard disappeared?'

'He and his lady had been planning to leave for a while,' Nell said bitterly. 'So, yes, they scampered—with lots of clients' money but, thanks to Nick, not mine.' She shrugged. 'He hurt a lot of people.'

'Including you.'

'No.' She shook her head. 'He didn't hurt me. He woke me up out of my stupor. He made me realise just how damned stupid I'd been and for how long. So I'm almost grateful.'

'Yeah?'

'Yeah.' She chuckled. 'Except if I saw him again I'd personally castrate the toerag. In the nicest possible way, of course.'

He raised his eyebrows at that. 'Oh, of course.'

'And the best thing was, when the police dug really deeply into his background they discovered he'd married before. About ten years ago. Even though it only lasted a few months he'd never bothered to get a divorce, so I wasn't married after all and I wasn't in any way responsible for all the debts he'd run up.' She took a deep breath. 'So now you know,' she told him. 'That's all. Now, are you going to tell me about you?'

'Me?'

'Yep, you, stupid. And your wife. Sylvia.'

'I...'

'Fair's fair and a bargain's a bargain.'

But then the phone rang. Saved by the bell, Blake thought thankfully, but Nell beat him to the receiver.

'Dr McKenzie here.' Then she listened. 'Right,' she said at last, her eyes on Blake's face. 'We'll be there in three minutes.'

She replaced the receiver. 'This doesn't let you off the hook,' she told him.

'No. But what is it?'

She was already moving toward the door. 'Grace Mayne's on her way in. Her neighbour found her. She's unconscious and the ambulance boys thinks she's dying.'

Hell! Grace...

'I'll go,' Blake snapped, reaching the door at the same time she did.

'Grace saved my life this morning,' Nell told him, her voice shaken yet determined. 'And Aaron's. We'll *both* go.' She hesitated. 'And then we'll come straight back here and take up where we left off.'

The ambulance boys had had a long day today. For minimally trained volunteers it was almost too much. Professional detachment wasn't in their job description. Bob and Henry stood by the stretcher and almost wrung their hands. They might enjoy a bit of drama, but not when it was as serious as it had been today.

'What happened?' Blake demanded answers before he reached Grace's side. He was moving so fast Nell almost had to trot to keep up with him. The fact that she was wearing her grandpa's overlong bathrobe didn't help at all.

But she was determined to keep up. Blake was determined to practise alone, and the only way to break him of the habit was to stick by him. Like glue.

And this was Grace... Oh, no. Grace! No wonder Bob and Henry looked sick. The old lady had held a place in the town's collective hearts since Nell had first met her. Whenever there'd been trouble, there'd been Grace. Whenever anyone had needed help, she'd been there. She had a heart so big...

Her heart. Please, let it not be her heart, Nell thought. If this morning's exertions were to kill her... Dear God, no!

But Grace looked dreadful. Blake already had his stethoscope out and his fingers were on the old lady's wrist, feeling her pulse as soon as he reached her. 'Does anyone know what happened?' he demanded again, and the ambulancemen nodded.

'Her neighbour, Adam Roberts,' Henry whispered, dragging his eyes from Grace's chest. It was hardly moving. She was hardly breathing. 'Adam was on the boat this morning, too.'

'And?' Blake's voice was clipped and decisive, dragging professionalism from him, and with an effort Henry made himself concentrate.

'Adam said they drove home together as soon as the boat moored,' he told them. Both ambulancemen were totally focussed on Grace. They hadn't spared Nell's startling outfit a glance. In fact, Nell had now shifted from being just another local. They no longer saw her as Nell. They saw her now as another doctor—more help—and the bathrobe didn't register at all.

'She was fine,' Bob continued. 'Adam said she ate a huge lunch—latish like. They cracked a bottle of champagne and Grace had three glasses. And then she felt a bit wobbly so she went for a lie-down. Adam was a bit concerned, so he popped in after dinner. He found her...' His voice broke off in distress.

Blake lifted the wrinkled eyelids. Grace's pupils were dilated and unresponsive. Nothing.

'Is it her heart?' Bob whispered, his face almost as ashen as Grace's. 'Hell...Grace... We thought Grace'd live for ever.'

So had everyone, Nell thought, feeling sick. She'd asked the old lady to take her out to sea. She'd done this to her!

'Had she taken her diabetic tablets?' Blake demanded across their grim thoughts, and Bob frowned.

'Diabetic tablets?'

But Henry knew. 'Yeah, she did,' he volunteered. 'Adam said to tell you that. He said they were late having lunch and with the champagne and everything she thought she should take two.'

'Two,' Blake said, his face clearing like magic. 'Nell, would you—?'

But Nell was already scrambling for the blood-sugar monitor. She handed it to Blake, and her heart was lifting. Two... Thank you, God. Oh, thank you. Wordlessly Blake took a pin-prick of blood. Seconds later he had the answer—and it was great!

'She's having a hypo,' he told them, unable to conceal his delight, already finding a vein. 'Her blood sugar's way down. It's almost zero.'

'You're kidding.' Bob and Henry had enough medical training to realise what that meant. 'Hell,' Henry said, staring down at Grace's limp form. 'You mean if we'd just given her juice... But...' His face clouded again. 'We couldn't. She was unconscious. Doc, she looks…she looks almost dead. Is it too late?'

'She's not and it certainly isn't,' Blake said firmly. 'Though she's obviously past a cure by a glass of juice. But I'm betting if we give her an injection of glucose she'll be back to normal in no time. Watch.'

And that was the way it was. Almost at the prick of the needle, Grace stirred and woke. It was one of medicine's nicest miracle cures, Nell thought, almost delirious with relief. Not a heart attack. Only a hypo. She closed her eyes and sat down in a nearby chair, her professional detachment flying straight out the window. Oh, Grace…

'I… Where…?' It was a faint whisper, echoing gloriously through the examination cubicle. The old lady was confused and upset, but she was already coherent, and Blake took her hand and held it. Hard.

'You've had a diabetic hypo,' he told her, his voice gentle but steady. 'You remember? It's the thing I'm always warning you against. Taking two tablets indeed…'

Grace's eyes creased in confusion, but Blake's eyes were sure and reassuring. Finally she searched the room and her eyes found Nell. 'It's Nell,' she said, her voice wondering.

Nell thought, She recognises me. All this and she still recognises me. But she hardly knows me. 'You scared the life out of us,' she managed. 'Oh, Grace…'

'I never meant to. Oh, girl, I'm so sorry.'

'Don't you be sorry.' Nell found her feet and found her smile and stooped to hug Grace. 'Don't you dare be sorry. After all you've done today… You deserve to do whatever you want.'

'Except kill yourself with neglect,' Blake growled, trying to keep his own emotions under control. 'OK, Grace. We'll organise you a meal. We'll keep your blood sugar monitored all night and you're not going home until it's steady.' He shook his head. 'I've had enough trouble with the fishing community for one day.'

Grace was recovered enough to grin. 'No. How can you

say that? You just got to sit on a ledge while we risked life and limb.'

'Yeah? A ledge made of crumbling sandstone...'

'It's the women who're the toughest,' Grace said serenely, and for some reason her old eyes rested on Nell's with something that looked astonishingly like affection. And caring.

'Says who?' Blake's relief at the outcome was making him feel fantastic. With Nell safe by his side...

Now why had he thought that?

'Let's get you into the ward,' he growled, and he found all of them were looking at him in astonishment.

'Do you need to sound grumpy?' Grace shook her head. 'And I'm not staying here. Bob, take me home.'

'Bob, wheel her into the ward.' Blake had himself together again—almost. He lifted his syringe. 'You need a meal and then a sleep, with us monitoring your blood sugar at regular intervals, and you're not going home until I'm convinced you're settled.' He held the sharp needle against the light, and then looked at Grace, considering. 'So...do you want to go quietly, or do you want to suffer the consequences?'

And Grace laughed and held up her hands in mock surrender. 'OK, Dr Sutherland,' she conceded. 'You're the boss.'

'That's just the way I like it,' Blake said, and Nell grinned. She did like a happy ending. Especially this one.

'It's time you went home to bed, too,' Blake told her. 'I'll stay and do my ward rounds.'

'I'll do them with you.'

'There's no need.'

'You know damned well there's a need,' she said severely. 'Grace, this man's avoiding me. What do you make of that?'

'I think any man who avoids a girl in nightwear as gorgeous as yours needs his head read,' Grace said stoutly, recovering by the minute.

Her nightwear... 'Oh, help.' Then Nell grinned and did a pirouette right there and then. God was in his heaven, and all was right with Nell's world.

Grace smiled, and this time there was no mistaking her affection. 'It makes a change from a white coat,' she told her.

There was that. 'It does indeed,' Nell agreed. And then, before he could guess what she intended, Nell tucked her hand in Blake's. 'Come on, Dr, Sutherland. Let's get on with it.' She smiled at Bob and Henry, and then at Grace, encompassing them all in her happiness. 'Dr Sutherland and I are going to do his ward rounds and then he's going to tell me his life story. What do you think of that?'

Grace smiled. 'I think Dr Sutherland had better be careful.' She hesitated. 'Looks like the days of a lone medico are over. By the look of the pair of you, in thirty years Nell could be as entangled in the concerns of this town as I am.' And her smile said she thought that was no bad fate at all.

Not like Blake. His hand in Nell's was suddenly rigid. 'I don't think so.'

'Don't fight against the tide,' Grace told him, still smiling. 'There's nought you can do about it—and would you really want to try?'

Yes!

But for now he had no choice. Nell's hand lay in his, she was waiting and he had no choice but to get on with it. It was either that or pick her up bodily and put her out of the door. That was maybe an appealing option, he thought grimly, but she was smiling at him, too.

Fight against the tide? Some things were just impossible.

CHAPTER SEVEN

IT WAS over an hour later before Nell had Blake where she wanted him—back in the kitchen with a pot of coffee between them. 'Now,' she said severely, and he shook his head.

'Now I need to finish my coffee and go to bed. I'd imagine you do, too.'

'I'm not going anywhere. I slept all afternoon and I'm not tired, so stop prevaricating. It's your turn to talk, Dr Sutherland. I told you the "How Nell Was a Dope" story with all the gory details. Now you tell me "Why Blake Swore Off Relationships For Ever". I'm listening.'

He didn't want to. He drank his coffee too fast and then rose from the table. Nell's hand reached out and caught his, pulling him back.

'No,' she said severely. 'Sit.'

He managed a smile at that. 'Hey, I'm not Ernest.'

'No. But sit, all the same.' She didn't release his hand, and he stared down at their intertwined fingers. Her hand felt warm and strong. Despite his wish to stay uninvolved with this amazing woman, the story she'd told him flooded back.

What sort of people had her grandparents been? he wondered. He remembered the old lady—fiercely independent and almost paranoid with pride. It had taken every inch of his skill to persuade her to allow nurses into her home for those last few months. He hadn't warmed to her at all.

And now... Letting his hand rest in Nell's, he felt an almost overwhelming longing for the old lady to still be alive. So he could go and shout at her—ask her what the hell she thought she'd been doing to allow Nell to have that sort of dreadful, barren childhood.

If she'd been adopted she'd have been loved to bits, he thought. Anyone would love her. She deserved to be loved.

If she'd been loved in childhood she wouldn't be in this mess, he thought bitterly, and then the thought came out of left field.

He wouldn't be in this mess!

'Hey, it's not that bad,' she murmured, and his eyes flew to hers.

'What?'

'You look angry. Does sharing your past make you cross?'

'No, I…'

'You are going to tell me—aren't you?'

Blake took a deep breath. 'There's nothing to tell. I was married and now I'm not. Sylvia's dead.'

'I know that. Em said your wife was killed in a car crash.'

'That's right. End of story. So what else do you want to know?'

'Why Em says the mention of her name makes you clam up. Why you can't talk about her. Why it still hurts so damned much.'

'She was killed.'

'Yes, but that doesn't explain it,' she said as if he was being deliberately obtuse. 'After three years she should be fading to a beloved memory. She shouldn't be stabbing you with pain. Stopping you living to the full.'

'You don't understand.'

'So explain. Make me understand.'

He glared. 'You need to be in bed.'

And she glared back. Desperate measures were called for. How had she made him do what she wanted in the past? Yeah, right.

Nell grinned and felt for the top button of her bathrobe. 'Blake Sutherland, you have two minutes,' she said, exasperated. 'And then I'm starting to strip.' She undid her top button, her eyes daring him. 'One button at a time. All the way.'

Good grief! He eyed her uneasily. Make a joke, he told himself desperately. Hell, how else could he cope? 'Is this the line you try on patients who are reluctant to tell you their problems?'

'All the time,' she said serenely, and he almost choked. 'I don't believe you.'

Her fingers moved to the next button. 'Try me.'

'I'll head back to the hospital.'

'I'll follow you to the hospital,' she said. 'Stark naked.'

'You wouldn't dare.'

'No?' Her green eyes sparked with mischief, and she undid the next button. 'Are you sure?'

And then she undid the next...

Blake didn't depend in the least on her good sense—or her sense of decency, he decided. Her good sense should have prevented her trying to go out through the harbour mouth this morning, and she'd risked drowning instead. Compared to that, a naked display in the grounds of the hospital would be nothing.

Despite himself, his lips twitched. She saw, and she smiled encouragingly.

'You should know I don't threaten what I can't deliver. So tell me.'

'You're incorrigible.'

She chuckled. 'That's the nicest thing anyone's ever said about me. Incorrigible. I like it.'

'Nell...'

'Just tell me.'

He sighed. He sighed again but her look was stern.

'Come on.'

And there was no choice. Tentatively he tried, but it hurt. It hurt even to say the name. 'Sylvia...'

Nell sighed, exasperated. 'Your wife's name was Sylvia. I know that. What else?'

'She was a mistake.'

'Well, join the club,' Nell said without rancour. 'You and Sylvia. Me and Richard. I bet Richard was the biggest disaster, though.'

'Not necessarily. In fact, not even remotely.'

He still seemed reluctant to continue so Nell prodded some more. 'So let me guess. She was a nymphomaniac who insisted on sleeping naked?'

He couldn't help it. His mouth twisted into a smile, and Nell smiled with him. 'That's better,' she approved. 'Tell me more.'

'I...'

'Oh, for heaven's sake, just do it,' she snapped, losing patience. 'Now.'

And he cast her one last long look—and started to talk.

'Sylvia was another doctor,' he said, and his tone was different now. Dispassionate. It was as if what he was talking about concerned someone else—not him. 'We met in final year—at a hospital Christmas celebration. She was gorgeous, intelligent, funny... In fact, she was everything I thought I wanted in a wife.'

'I see.' There was a tiny bit of Nell that didn't like this, but surely it was illogical. What he thought of his dead wife had nothing to do with her—did it?

'I'd been a swot,' he told her, his voice still expressionless. 'Like you, I was a scholarship kid. If I didn't do well, I lost my funding, so I'd been head down, butt up in my books for years. It was Christmas. I'd just passed my final exams, I raised my head from my books and almost had it knocked off by Sylvia.'

'You fell for her?'

'Hook, line and sinker.' He shrugged, and smiled a smile that didn't reach his eyes. 'So much so that I asked her to marry me.'

'And she did?'

'No.' He shook his head, and his gaze fell to the wedding ring on his finger. 'Not then.'

'Why not?'

'Sylvia was having too much fun. She was so smart…' He shook his head again. 'She'd hardly had to study. Exams were something the rest of us fretted about, but not Sylvia. If she couldn't get away with her extraordinary intelligence she charmed her way through them. And she seemed to hardly need sleep.'

He shrugged. 'Anyway, as soon as the Christmas break was over and we settled back to work I could see the whole affair was stupid. Doomed. I wanted to do my surgical training so I needed to sleep and to study, and she didn't. She thought I was boring. So… We graduated, I took up surgery and she took off for Europe. I expected never to see her again.'

'Poor dear.' Nell smiled with mock sympathy. She could imagine Blake as a recently graduated doctor, and she could also envisage what life must have been like for him then. Medical students might be too busy for a love life, but absurdly good-looking fully qualified young doctors as Blake must have been most definitely were not. 'I can't actually see you broken-hearted and bereft.'

He glanced up at that and met her dancing eyes, and he managed a grin himself.

'Well, no. Not really.'

She chuckled. 'You hardly have the look of a man who'd go unnoticed by the female population in general. After leaving the rigours of medical school behind you, I bet you went from girl to girl.'

'Hardly that. But…' His grin faded. 'OK, I had a good time, but I never felt settled. Even when I finished my surgical training, it was like Sylvia had left a shadow—a ghost I couldn't exorcise. After a while I left Sydney and took up a consultant's post at Niribil in Western Australia. Niribil's about the size of Blairglen. I did general surgery rather than vascular surgery but I enjoyed the country. I enjoyed a smaller, familiar practice where everyone knew everyone.' He took a deep breath. 'And then Sylvia came home.'

'I see.'

'I bet you don't.' His voice was suddenly savage. 'She was different. More fragile somehow. Brittle. But still breathtakingly lovely. She was on my doorstep when I got home from hospital one night, and she said simply that she'd missed me dreadfully and if I still wanted to, we'd be married. Straight away.'

'So you were?'

'Well, what would you have done?' Blake closed his eyes in remembered pain. 'Hell, I'd asked her more than once. I'd said if ever she changed her mind I was still there for her. And she was still lovely.'

'But?'

'Yeah, there's a but,' he said grimly. 'Of course. I should have waited. It had been years since we'd been together, and we needed time. She didn't give us time, and when I discovered what was wrong we were well and truly married. She was up to her neck in substance abuse.'

'Oh, no...'

'She'd thought she was so clever,' he said grimly. 'Apparently it had started before she finished medical school. Uppers to get her through the exams, tranquillisers to get her to sleep and then a frightening progression to the heavy stuff. When we'd thought she was just naturally bouncy she was really as high as a kite. Much of this, though, I didn't find out until later.'

'How much later?'

'After she was dead.'

Nell drew in her breath. 'Oh, Blake...' Then she went on gently, 'Do you want to tell me? I won't insist.'

There was a moment's pause. And then he shrugged. 'Why not? Why not tell you everything? I've come this far.' He took a deep breath. 'As soon as she arrived, Sylvia applied for a registrar's job at Niribil. There was no hesitation in employing her. After all, I knew her qualifications were sound. In view of the fact that I vouched for her—and that I was marrying her—the hospital board didn't even bother to check her employment record in Europe. If they had...'

'If they had?'

'Then they'd have found out she had two malpractice suits coming up against her. Major ones. For gross negligence. Which was why she'd fled back to Australia.' He chewed his bottom lip. 'Anyway...'

'Anyway?'

'Anyway, we married,' he said grimly. 'And I started worrying almost straight away. You can't live with someone for long without suspecting things aren't OK. But I didn't know for sure, and I didn't say anything. After all, how could I be so crass as to suggest my wife was a drug addict?'

'It wasn't obvious?'

'It was obvious that she was either high or low. Almost as soon as we were married I saw the mood swings that she'd been careful to keep from me, and I suspected psychological problems. But before I could do anything about it a little boy came into Casualty with meningitis. Sylvia had been employed as the emergency registrar, but she'd gone home early, leaving no doctor on duty. The nursing staff saw him and were worried, suspecting meningitis. So they rang Sylvia. But Sylvia couldn't be bothered to get out of bed. She gave phone orders for a dose of antibiotics that was a tenth of what was needed, and said she'd see him in the morning.'

'Oh, no... Oh, Blake...'

'When the child's condition worsened they tried again,' he went on inexorably. 'But they couldn't raise Sylvia any more. And no wonder. She was zonked out of her brain—almost unconscious.'

'Where were you?'

'I was up to my neck in Theatre, dealing with a car-accident emergency. When the little boy started deteriorating the charge nurse came to find me to ask how they could raise Sylvia, but by that time the kid had been in trouble for six hours. And he'd lapsed into a coma. I changed the antibiotic orders—any fool would have and the charge nurse should have seen it himself. When I finished operating I took over Sylvia's role, but it was far, far too late. And when the little boy died, I went to find her.'

It made everything so clear. Dreadful but clear. 'And...'

'And I couldn't wake her. So I went through her bedside cabinet. Six weeks married.' He gave a harsh laugh. 'I couldn't believe what I found. I couldn't believe I'd been so stupid. She'd taken so much...'

He closed his eyes on remembered pain. 'I was so furious. Unbelievably—explosively angry. And then, when she finally woke and I told her what had happened, she turned into the Sylvia who'd laughed when I'd first proposed marriage. Supercilious. She said I was being ridiculous, and she didn't have to put up with this. Before I could stop her she'd headed out to the car and driven off. Fast. Too damned fast. I sent the police after her and went searching myself, but she went over the cliff a couple of miles out of town.'

'Oh, Blake...'

'Pathetic, wasn't it?' He gave a ghost of a dreadful smile. 'The town had employed her because of me, and I was too stupid to see what was happening. I failed them.' He looked down at his hand, and he twisted the ring. 'And I failed Sylvia.'

'How do you figure that?'

'I should have seen. Maybe I did, but I didn't want to know. I was so damned busy. I was too damned smitten.' He took the ring from his finger and then replaced it, like it was a chain that held him a prisoner. 'Anyway, I moved. I came here. I decided I'd practise alone. I wouldn't depend on anyone.' He raised his head and met Nell's look head on. 'And I don't.'

She hesitated. 'But you need me.'

'I don't need you,' he said flatly. 'I don't need anyone.'

'You're running yourself into the ground.'

'No.'

Her hand came across the table again and took his. She held it firmly, using both of her hands to hold his one, and her eyes were direct and deadly serious.

'Blake, you can't stay alone for ever because of one stupid mistake.'

'Tommy Vanderboort will be dead for ever because of my mistake. He was six years old and he's dead. And so is Sylvia.'

'So one day we'll all be dead,' she said, exasperated. 'But, meanwhile, you need to get a life.'

'I have a life.'

'Yeah, medicine, which can very easily be shared. That's why I'm here.'

'For four weeks.'

'I'm here for ever,' she said bluntly. 'And I want to work. You may as well use me.'

But Blake's mind had closed against her. The remembered pain was still reflected in his eyes. 'I'll use you over the Christmas rush,' he told her. 'Until you need to go to Blairglen to have your baby. But that's all. I won't depend on anyone else.'

'So you'll take the medical needs of the whole community on your shoulders alone—for how long? Until you collapse of a nervous breakdown?'

'Don't be ridiculous.'

'It's you who's ridiculous,' she snapped.

'Look, let's leave it.'

'No.'

His face shuttered in anger. 'Leave it, Dr McKenzie. You're employed for four weeks. No longer. The board won't put you on permanently without my approval.'

'And you won't give it?'

'That's right.'

'Then you're a fool.'

'Thanks very much.'

'Think nothing of it.' And then her mood suddenly seemed to lighten and she smiled. It was an extraordinary smile, given the circumstances. 'Hmm.' She pushed herself back in the chair and surveyed him thoughtfully. 'Look, this is crazy. You and me…we're a right pair. We've both had marital disasters. The only difference is that I refuse to let it wreck my life—in fact, I figure it might well have been the catalyst for me to start living. You've decided otherwise. So I only have three weeks left to change your mind.'

'I won't change my mind.'

'I'm not a drug addict.'

'No, but you're a…'

'A woman?'

'Yes!'

'Well, how about that?' she said slowly, and her smile widened. 'Well, well. So, if I had a sex-change operation, it'd be OK to employ me?'

'No, but…'

'But what?'

'Nothing.' Blake shoved himself back from the table so hard the chair fell over. 'Nothing at all. I'm going back to the hospital.' He hesitated. 'There's some orders for Aaron I forgot to write up.'

She didn't believe him, and it showed, but she was being polite. 'You do that, Dr Sutherland,' she told him cordially, and her smile didn't slip. 'Off you go. Minister to the sick and needy all by yourself.'

'I—'

'Don't let me stop you.' What the hell was she playing at? She was still laughing. 'What a hero. But if you're setting yourself up as a hero, then I'll be a heroine.'

'What do you mean by that?'

'Meaning that if you can be a drama king then I can be a queen to match,' she said kindly. 'I made a fool of myself over a man, and you did the same over a woman. But I took off my wedding ring and threw it into the middle of next week. You should do the same.'

'No.'

'You will.'

'Nell…'

But she appeared to be thinking and her attention didn't seem to be on him. 'Three weeks. It's not very long.'

'I can't—'

'But Christmas is in between.' She wrinkled her forehead, deep in thought. 'All that brandy sauce. It might do the trick.'

'Nell!'

'Now, don't you worry about a thing.' Her smile deepened. 'Leave it to me.'

'Leave what to you?'

'Curing your broken heart, of course,' she said. 'After all, I'm an expert. I chopped up my king-sized quilt and it fixed me. What can we chop up of yours?'

'Nothing.'

'I'll think of something.' Her brow creased even more. Then she looked up at him and smiled. 'What are you waiting for? You have work to do and I have thinking to do. So let's start now.' She waved him away and she smiled. 'Go on, then. Shoo!'

'But—'

'But nothing,' she told him. 'Just go! Leave Ernest and me to our thinking.'

He'd never been told to shoo in his life before. But he had no choice. Blake Sutherland…shooed.

It was a tricky problem.

Nell sat underneath the Christmas tree and threaded a bit more popcorn and ate a lot more, and then she hugged Ernest and fed him the rest. 'Because I'm getting as fat as a whale,' she told him. 'If this bulge is all baby then I'm having a twenty-pound whopper.'

Ernest looked at her with sympathy—and obligingly scoffed her popcorn.

'But what will we do with Blake?'

Ernest patently didn't know.

'So it's over to me.'

Ernest scoffed the last of the popcorn and looked hopefully toward the kitchen—just in case she was thinking of popping more. Which she wasn't.

'You're thinking it's none of my business?'

It was certainly none of Ernest's business. All he could focus on was popcorn.

'I certainly don't need the complications of hauling Blake Sutherland back to the real world.' Nell nodded and considered. 'But I do need a part-time job in medicine. I don't want to give up my medicine for ever, and I want to stay here.'

Hmm.

'You think I should leave all this until after this baby's born?' she demanded of Ernest. 'Let Blake stew in his own juice for a bit? Maybe that'd work. But Emily says he's headed for a breakdown and she's right.'

Ernest licked her hand, but Nell was oblivious. She scratched Ernest's ear, deep in thought. 'So should we let him break down, then leap into the breach and fix it? Like a true heroine? And a true heroine's dog?'

She gave a rueful grin to herself and ran a finger down the small of Ernest's back. Ernest almost turned inside out with pleasure.

But Nell was still thinking. 'That way I might lose him completely,' she said out loud. 'We all might. And the town doesn't want that.'

'Why not?' she demanded of herself.

'Because he's a wonderful doctor,' she retorted—but there was a part of her that knew she was lying. This wasn't anything to do with the fact that Blake was a wonderful doctor. And it had nothing to do with the medical needs of the town.

He was a very intriguing man. And maybe he was something more that she was hardly admitting to herself.

Yet...

CHAPTER EIGHT

FIVE a.m. Blake stirred from sleep and peered at his bedside clock. Something had woken him. Not the phone. What?

He threw back his covers and made his way out to the living room—and stopped short.

Nell was sitting beneath the Christmas tree. Ernest was snuggled in by her side and she was balancing a cup of tea on her very pregnant tummy.

She was wearing pyjamas covered with pink elephants. She looked cute and desirable and very, very alone. She looked like someone who he should just walk across to and gather into his arms and...

Hell! What on earth was he thinking of? He gave himself a mental shake and pushed the door wider. 'What are you doing?' he said carefully, and her cup of tea jumped on her bulge, splashing her pyjamas.

'Damn,' she said crossly. 'That's the third time I've sploshed.'

'The third time?'

'My bump actually doesn't make a very good table,' she admitted. 'Not when junior kicks. He's bumped it twice and now you've scared me into bumping it again.'

'I'm sorry.' He paused. 'What did you say you were doing?'

She smiled up at him, and his impression of cuteness and desirability and...and, despite the smile, forlornness deepened even further. 'I didn't,' she told him.

'Oh.' He paused. The situation was weirdly intimate. He was suddenly conscious of his own pyjamas—and the fact that he was wearing only the trousers. His chest felt very bare—and Nell was so damned close that...

123

Stop it!

What on earth was she doing? 'Are you going to tell me?' he demanded.

She considered. 'Would you believe I'm waiting for Santa Claus?'

He grinned. 'You'll have a long wait. There's still a week to go.'

'I'm a very patient woman.'

'You're a very pregnant woman,' he said gently. 'You should be in bed.'

She looked up at him then, surprised by the gentleness of his tone. Touched, even.

'Thanks, but you try telling that to Cornelius.'

'He's giving you trouble?'

'He's kicking his mother,' she said with dignity. 'You'd think he'd know better. Boy, will I have some words to say to him when he comes out.'

Blake hesitated. He should go back to bed. He should leave her there. But the temptation to do the opposite was suddenly impossible to resist.

He resisted no longer. He crossed the room and sat down beside her, and her look of surprise deepened.

'So what's your excuse?' she asked. 'Who's kicking you?'

'No one,' he admitted. 'But Ernest's thumping woke me up.' That's what it must have been, he decided. The goofy dog was in seventh heaven. His head was on Nell's knee and his tail was banging against the floor like a drumstick going flat out.

'Oh, heck.' Nell shoved a hand down and tried to still the offending thumping appendage. 'I'm sorry. I'll make him stop.'

Which was easier said than done. Her hand moved up and down with the tail. Ernest was as strong as a horse and his tail was determinedly cheerful.

Blake grinned. 'Right, then, Dr McKenzie. You'll make him stop. So how are you going to do that?'

'Most cocker spaniels have their tails chopped off at birth,' she said. And then she looked at the tail. Its thumping was an expression of pure bliss. 'Though how anyone could...' She sighed. 'I guess that's another way of saying I haven't a clue. I think as a disciplinarian I'm a failure.'

'You're not a failure.' Blake was sitting on the plush Turkish rug beside her. Above their heads were his three Christmas angels. They should have twinkly lights, he thought inconsequentially, and made a mental note to buy some, because suddenly it seemed important. Meanwhile, somehow he forced himself back to what Nell was saying.

'It's nice of you to say I'm not a failure, but so far I don't seem to have managed very well,' she told him. She took a deep breath. 'And how I'm going to manage being a mother...'

'You'll be a wonderful mother.'

She cast him an unsure glance. 'Do you think so? It scares me stupid.'

'Why wouldn't you be a good mother?' he demanded, and her look of uncertainty deepened.

'I have no role model. Except my grandparents. And they were great teachers—I don't think! If I follow their example, the very first time my baby annoys me I'll order her to leave home. I'll tell her she's useless and that she's only in the way.'

He grimaced. 'That's what you were told?'

'All the time.'

'Do you know what happened to your own mother?' he asked carefully. This wasn't a scene he would have chosen to share—it was too damned intimate for his liking—but leaving her alone now would have been selfish.

Selfish on whose part? Not his, he had to admit, because he wanted to stay.

'She's dead.'

'You're sure?'

'Mmm.' Nell nodded. 'I made enquiries almost as soon as I graduated and earned enough to pay an investigator.'

She shrugged. 'So I found out, but it doesn't make pretty telling. Fifteen-year-olds who are kicked out of home because they're pregnant rarely end up living happily ever after.'

He nodded wordlessly. As a doctor, he'd seen enough of the lives street kids led to know she was speaking the truth. 'Your grandparents have a lot to answer for.'

'They do at that.'

'But you're not in the least like them,' he told her, sure of that at least. 'And your mother and father must have been really special people to have produced you.'

'I don't even know who my father was.'

He looked at her sideways and thought this through. And smiled. 'I bet he had freckles.'

'Probably. And red hair because my mother was a blonde.' But she didn't smile. Her eyes had lost their customary laughter and the echoes of sadness were there in its place.

'You'd like to know your father?'

'I'd like to know anybody,' she said simply. 'My grandparents didn't want me. My mother's dead. I have no one.' She took a deep breath. 'Normally I don't mind but sometimes it's so damned lonely. I guess that's why I was stupid enough to fall for Richard.'

'You won't be alone for ever. There'll be someone else.'

'Oh, sure. I'm *so* desirable.' She managed a smile then, but it was a feeble one. 'Me and my baby and my best dog, Ernest.'

Blake wasn't to be deflected. 'Lots of men would think you were desirable.'

She fixed him with a look. 'Ha! You don't.'

'But I'm…'

'Different?' She tried to smile again but it didn't quite come off. 'I know. You've told me. Alone for life. Just like me. Only my aloneness isn't by choice.'

'It really worries you?'

'It's so damned hard,' she blurted out. 'Not the loneliness

bit. At least not for me. I can cope with that. But my baby…
Hell, my baby's father doesn't want her. He wanted me to
have a termination, and I'm betting he never comes near
me. In fact, even if he does surface he'll end up in jail, and
how useful's a jailbird as a father? If anything happened to
me, what would happen to my baby?'

He met her fear head on. 'Then it's lucky you're as
strong as a horse.'

'That sounds defensive.'

'It wasn't meant to sound defensive. It was meant to
sound reassuring. Pregnant women get odd fancies…'

'That they might die in childbirth.' She was glaring at
full strength now. 'Yeah. Really unrealistic. But you're a
doctor. You know it happens.'

'What happens?'

'Mothers die. If I got eclampsia…'

He was startled at that. Eclampsia… 'You're being
checked?'

'I'm checking myself.'

'You shouldn't be checking yourself.' He felt a surge of
real concern. Hell, if she did have eclampsia… 'Nell, for
heaven's sake. Are you OK?'

'Well, yes.' she admitted. 'I guess I am. Emily checked
me over last week and before that I saw the best obstetrician Sydney Central has. But…'

Blake's breath was let out in a whoosh of relief. 'There
you go, then. What's your resting blood pressure?'

'Ninety over seventy.'

'That's great. Perfectly normal.'

'I know that.' She glared on, refusing to let go of her
terrors. 'But I still might get eclampsia. And I might die.'

'Is that why you're sitting out here, then?' he demanded,
things becoming clear. 'Worrying about dying?'

She hesitated. And, finally, she let go. 'A bit,' she admitted. 'I guess I've been worrying about who'll fill my
daughter's Christmas stocking next year if I do.'

'Or your son's?'

'As you say. Or my son's.'

He thought about this, trying to be professional—as he'd be if he were sitting on one side of his desk while his patient voiced her fears from the other. 'You really do have no one?'

'I really do have no one.' She took a deep breath, fighting to regain her normal cheerfulness. 'There's only Ernest and I can't see him changing nappies. Bay Beach has great children's homes, though.'

'You're so worried you checked out the orphanage?' he demanded, startled, and she gave a shamefaced nod.

'Just a bit.'

'Just a lot!' He could see it all now. Rationality had gone out the window. She'd been alone throughout this pregnancy and she'd lost perspective.

So she needed reassurance. Tell her she'll be fine, he told himself. Tell her there was less than a chance in a thousand that things would go wrong. Tell her...

But suddenly he knew what he'd tell her, and it was none of the above.

'I'll look after your baby if anything happens to you.'

He'd said it—and neither of them could believe he had. They sat on the floor and stared at each other and he thought, What on earth have I done?

And she thought, What on earth is he saying?

'Blake...'

'Nell?'

'You don't...you don't mean it?' she whispered, and the look on her face was one he was starting to know. And he didn't like it. It was her Nell-against-the-world look. Nell declaring she didn't need anyone.

It was Nell kick-starting her new life in her wonderful patchwork overalls and with a heartful of courage that was so much greater than any he had.

What he was offering was a tiny thing, he thought—a promise for an outcome he knew would never happen. But it meant the world to her. Her eyes were shining, shimmering with unshed tears, and her hand caught his and held.

'Blake, how could you? You don't have the least idea of what you're saying. You're a dyed-in-the-wool bachelor and the last thing you need is a baby.'

Yeah, but it'd be Nell's baby.

The thought hit home with quite amazing clarity that he wouldn't mind so much. If this baby was like Nell. A child... He could get a housekeeper, he thought. Bring it up here. Keep Ernest...

Hell, Nell wasn't going to die! But if she did...

It was a dreadful thought. Appalling. And he'd have a baby.

'Where would you squeeze a baby into your schedule?' she demanded, and he chuckled at the horror in her voice.

'So I guess you'd better live, then.'

'But...you are serious?'

Blake's laughter died. 'Yes, Nell. God knows why, but I am serious.'

'Even though you never want to marry again? You never want a woman? But you'd still take on a child.'

'If he or she needed me. Yes, I would.' And he knew, suddenly, that he spoke the truth.

'Oh, Blake...'

He gazed down at her upturned face, still trying to come to terms with what he'd offered. He must be mad. But he didn't feel in the least mad. He felt sure and strong, and warm and tender and...

And then, before he knew what she intended—before he could even guess—she'd twisted and taken his face between her two hands. And she'd kissed him full on the mouth.

The kiss was supposed to be one of gratitude—of surprise and pleasure and overwhelming thankfulness that he'd made such an offer—that he'd eased such an aching fear within.

But it never could be simple gratitude. Never. Because

the two of them had been apart for too long—partnerless—each of them aching with loneliness and with need. So there was that between them which neither understood but which became apparent at the first touch of lips to lips.

And it was something that was mind-shattering. It was like their world was blown apart at first touch.

Fire to fire...

That was what it was like, Nell thought dazedly. Wildfire! She'd made the first move—she'd reached up to kiss Blake—but the moment they touched she was no longer in control. Her body had a life all of its own, and it was an all-engulfing blaze of white-hot heat.

Her mouth met his, and was it hers who claimed his or the other way around? Who knew? Nell didn't. All she knew was that there was warmth where there had only been ice before, and there was comfort and longing and aching, aching need...

He felt so good. He felt so right! From the first time she'd seen him she'd felt this magnetic pull between them, and it had grown stronger with every piece of evidence that here before her was a wonderful human being.

No. Not just a wonderful human being, she thought dazedly. A wonderful man.

He was big and tender and caring, and aching with the desolation of loss himself. He was as different to Richard as he could be.

He was...

He was Blake. Just Blake. And that was enough and more for her body to respond. She melted into him, aching to have his arms come around her and hold her. And when they did she could hardly believe it. Miracles did happen. Love could flower where there'd only been barren waste...

Love.

She was falling in love, she thought, bewildered beyond belief, and then she thought, No.

She wasn't falling. She'd fallen.

She was head over heels in love with Blake Sutherland,

she decided right there and then, and there wasn't a darn thing she could do to stop herself being just that.

And she wasn't going to begin to try.

And Blake… He had no idea what was going on. No idea at all. One minute he was sitting on the living-room floor under the ridiculously decorated Christmas tree, trying hard to be professional, trying hard to be concerned, and suddenly the axis of his world had tilted.

He hadn't meant to make such an offer. He hadn't meant to get involved at all. Hell, he never got involved. He was a doctor, for heaven's sake, and he heard hard-luck stories every day of the week. What if he offered every single mother the reassurance he'd just offered Nell?

But this wasn't any single mum. This was Nell.

It didn't make any sense at all, he told himself desperately, but the way his body was responding to hers, the way his head was threatening to explode and his thighs were on fire and his body was screaming his need and…

And hell!

If only he was wearing something on his upper body! But he was naked to the waist and her crazy pyjamas were brushing his bare skin, and her breasts were against his chest and…

And his arms came around and held her to him. It was a measure of reassurance, he told himself desperately. Not so he could deepen the kiss. Not so he could feel her gorgeous body against his. Both those things were side issues and they didn't matter.

Like hell they didn't matter! They were *all* that mattered. His mouth was plundering hers, starving for something he hardly knew he'd been missing. Or something that he'd never had.

Had he ever felt this way with Sylvia?

No. No and no and no.

Sylvia…

But suddenly she was there. His dead wife. She was in

his brain, screaming at him that letting his emotions rule
his head led to disaster. Not just for him. For everybody.

A tiny six-year-old was dead because of his stupid emotions…

Once before he'd let his emotions hold sway and two
people had died because of it. It was a desperate lesson,
but it had been drilled in so far that even now it surfaced.

The way he was feeling was crazy. Terrible! The way
Nell made him feel… Like it or not, he was emotionally
involved, and this was the way of madness.

What was he doing? he thought dazedly. It was one thing
to offer to care for a child when he knew that offer need
never be taken up. It was another to kiss the child's mother
as if he meant it.

He was falling toward… Falling toward he didn't know
what, and it scared the life out of him. He didn't want this
sort of involvement. *He didn't.*

And so, finally and with a shuddering gasp that left him
feeling desolate with loss, he managed to pull away.
Confused, Nell fell back, and she looked up at him in the
dim light with eyes that were enormous. Her eyes reflected
his confusion and his…his fear?

And that's what it was all about, he thought bitterly.
Fear. Somehow he dragged himself to his feet, though afterwards he could never figure out how he'd done it. How
he'd managed to break the link.

He was afraid, but at least he had the sense to admit it.
To run before it could get any worse. 'I'm sorry. Nell, I'm
sorry.' His voice was a husky whisper.

'Hey, I'm the one who kissed you.' She was striving for
lightness but it didn't come off. How could it? 'I guess
we've both been alone for two long. Sex-starved medicos,
that's us.' And if her voice hadn't trembled he'd have
thought she was joking.

'I—'

'It's just as well I'm pregnant already,' she continued,
her voice growing firmer in the face of his uncertainty.

'And I deserve to be. Wandering round strange men's houses in the middle of the night, wearing nothing but elephant pyjamas.'

He stared down at her, and somehow she managed to get her face in order to smile back at him. Keep it light, her brain was screaming, while all her body wanted to do was rise and...

Nope. Listen to your mind, Dr McKenzie, she ordered herself. It's the only safe course.

She didn't want to be safe. She wanted more! More of Blake Sutherland. More of Blake Sutherland right now!

But he was managing a smile as well, albeit a pretty strained one. His eyes were as wary as hell, and he backed a couple of feet like she wasn't safe.

'I'm sorry.'

'For a kiss?' Her eyes mocked. It wasn't too bad that he was disconcerted, she decided. Normally he was too damned...*concerted* for his own good! 'I refuse to accept your apology. No one apologises for a kiss as good as that one.' She twinkled. 'Together we pack a powerful punch, Dr Sutherland.'

'We do indeed.'

'So you'd best be safely off to bed before we do something we might regret?' She ended on a note of interrogation, and he nodded.

'Yes.'

'Me, too.' She struggled to her feet. He couldn't help himself—his hand came out automatically to help, but after she was steadied he withdrew again. His eyes were like those of a watchful jaguar, a big cat not sure whether what he was watching was hunter or prey.

Nell hesitated. She should bolt for cover, she thought. She should. But...

'You did mean it?' she whispered. 'About caring for the baby if anything happens?'

'I dare say I'd be in a queue. After Emily and Jonas and—'

She didn't let him finish. 'But you did mean it?'

There was a long silence. 'Yes, I did mean it,' Blake said heavily, committed despite himself. 'I did.'

'Thank you,' she whispered, and then, because there was nothing else to say—nothing else to do—she clicked her fingers for Ernest to follow her and she headed for bed.

She stopped at the door and looked back. He looked desperate, she thought. Gorgeous and manly and very, very sexy, but desperate for all that. She so wanted to go to him. To hold him.

But all they had in common was medicine and it was a pretty tenuous link.

'You sleep in tomorrow,' she told him. 'To make up for tonight. I'll do ward rounds and morning surgery.'

'Just morning surgery.'

'Blake...'

'That's all I want,' Blake said heavily. 'Nothing more.' And both of them knew he was talking about something other than medicine.

'Fine.' She was suddenly angry. 'Fine by me, Dr Sutherland.' She clicked her fingers again. Ernest had been dozing underneath the Christmas-tree popcorn, waiting for some to fall on his nose. It was like wishing for the moon, Nell thought bitterly. Or like wanting emotional response from Blake Sutherland. 'Come on, Ernest. We know when we're not wanted.'

Ernest made to follow her, but when he reached her side, he too looked back, as if he would really, really like to stay.

And, amazingly, he was looking at Blake and not at the popcorn. 'Come on, Ernest,' Nell growled again, and cast a last hostile look at the man who was messing with her equanimity. And her dog's equanimity. 'Let's go! We ought to learn when we're not wanted. Heaven knows, we should be good at it by now.'

*   *   *

And after that she couldn't get near him. Even with medicine Nell had to fight him every inch of the way, and after a couple of days she was ready to scream.

Blake—graciously—allowed her to conduct morning surgery, which went on for three hours, but that was it. Everything else she tried to do she was politely told to butt out. And sometimes he wasn't even polite. He just ordered.

'Who do you think you are?' she demanded five days before Christmas. They'd just eaten dinner and Blake was about to head out yet again, for the fifth house call for the day. 'I'm being paid as much as you are. What gives you the right to do all the work?'

'You're pregnant.' He was holding himself stiffly away from her, as if she had body odour, and she felt like slapping him. Or throwing the dish she was holding at him. Of all the stupid, pig-headed, obstinate...

'And you're exhausted,' she snapped.

'I'm not exhausted.' He was so matter-of-fact that it was almost impossible to argue with him. 'You're giving me time off.'

'Ha! You do house calls when I'm doing surgery. Time off indeed.'

'It gives me time to run.'

'And that's another thing,' she said darkly. 'You don't need to run for miles every day. It's not normal. It's not even natural.'

'It's healthy.'

'Is it? I believe I was given a certain number of preordained breaths and I'm not going to waste a single one of them jogging.'

'That's the difference between you and me,' he said virtuously, striving for lightness. 'You're indolent.'

'I'm only indolent because you won't let me be anything else.'

'You could spend more time out at your grandparents' house. That way you could move out there earlier.'

'Meaning you could get rid of me earlier?'

'Yes,' he said promptly, and she glowered.

'I can't go out there. They're restumping, and if you think I can live in a house while it's stumpless... Of all the mean things. And it's Christmas, too. Blake Sutherland, you are less than polite.'

'I need to be. It's my only defence.'

'You sound like you're afraid of me.'

'I'm not.'

'And you're looking forward to having Christmas with me?'

'I'm not looking forward to having Christmas with anyone.'

'You, Blake Sutherland, are being too stupid for words.' She rose and slammed her dishes in the sink. One cracked. She stared at it, and then the corners of her mouth creased upward. 'Whoops...'

It was her favourite word, he thought, and why it had the power to twist his thoughts so he hardly knew what he was thinking...

Nell was right. He was being too stupid for words. But something was being threatened here and he didn't know what.

Hell, he was running and he didn't know why.

But Nell suspected. Blake was scared stiff of commitment, she thought. Well, so was she, but it didn't make her mutton-headed.

Blake was a wonderful doctor, she thought time and time again as she watched him at work. Wherever she went there were instances of his skill—and his compassion.

Grace Mayne was a prime example. The old lady came into the surgery the next morning with her hand wrapped in a bloodstained bandage. She'd been filleting fish and had almost filleted herself in the process. The jagged cut needed cleaning and stitching, which took quite a while.

'What on earth are you doing to yourself?' Nell demanded. 'For heaven's sake, after all our trouble with your diabetes... Are you determined to keep us busy?'

'Just stick a stitch in it and don't fuss, girl,' Grace told her. Then she hesitated. 'Actually, I was coming in anyway so Dr Sutherland wouldn't have to come all the way out to my place.'

Nell frowned. 'Why would he come out to your place?' She carefully cleaned the jagged cut, stitched the edges neatly together and tied off her thread. Then, with the task done, she probed some more. 'Your diabetes is stable again, isn't it?'

'Yes, but...' Grace hesitated again and then decided to continue. 'You know my Jack died a couple of months back?'

'Blake told me that.' Her voice gentled. 'I'm sorry.'

'Yeah, well, I didn't take it very well. It seems sometimes that I've lost everyone. Our daughter died of whooping cough when she was just a baby. Mike, our son, was drowned surfing when he was nineteen. And now Jack...' She took a deep breath. 'Anyway, Dr Sutherland comes a couple of times a week—just to make sure I'm OK.'

'And are you OK?' Nell probed gently, and Grace shrugged. Then she smiled. 'Actually, I am,' she said. 'At least, I'm better. The rescue in the boat—it made me feel like I was still useful. And with you in town...' She broke off, as if she feared saying too much, and Nell was left confused. But Grace was moving on.

'It was Dr Sutherland who got me fishing again,' she said, and Nell knew she was changing the subject but didn't know why. 'I've been fishing for garfish for the nursing-home patients—there's a couple of oldies who love them and he knows I'm good at catching them. That's what I was doing when I sliced myself.'

'You were filleting garfish?' Nell was successfully diverted. 'Grace, they're tiny. I've never filleted gars.'

'Yeah, but the old folk don't want bones. I've got time enough to do it and the nurses were good enough to my Jack. It doesn't hurt me to give something in return.' She looked down at the crisp white dressing Nell was placing on her hand and sighed. 'I guess I'll have to wear a glove now.'

'You mean you're going back fishing?'

'It's Christmas in a few days, so fish are in demand, and I might even catch something for myself. It's not worth having turkey on my own. My next-door neighbour goes to his daughter in Sydney and there's no one else.' Her smile slipped, replaced by a pain that was firmly put away. 'Anyway, I reckon I know where I can catch some Moreton Bay bugs. Bugs would be great at Christmas as a meal for one.'

Grace was such a brave old lady, Nell thought. Damn, why was she so alone? She forced herself to smile, following Grace's lead. 'You can really catch Moreton Bay bugs?' She'd had the tiny, lobster-like crustaceans before and they were delicious.

'Cross my heart.'

'You wouldn't like to catch a few for me and Blake?'

'Don't tell me you and Blake are sharing Christmas?'

'Yes. Yes, we are.' At Grace's look of amazement Nell gave her a rueful smile. 'Whether he likes it or not.'

'Then it'd be my pleasure.'

Nell's smile broadened. Grace's pleasure was obvious, but Grace had said she was having Christmas alone. And Nell and Blake…

Nell knew instinctively that Blake would make some excuse to head off for house calls. She'd never see him, and the thought of pulling a solitary Christmas cracker was suddenly less than appealing. 'Grace…'

'Mmm?' Grace was admiring her dressing.

'You wouldn't like to join us for Christmas dinner?'

Her head came up. She was a weathered old fisherwoman, not given to displaying emotion, and she didn't show any now. Instead, her eyes narrowed into a question. 'Why?'

Nell laughed. 'That's a bit rough. It's a very nice invitation.'

'It is, indeed.' She continued to eye Nell and ran a hand through the fading copper of her hair. 'But if you and Blake are having it together…'

'You needn't think you'll be interrupting any tête-à-tête,' Nell said bluntly. 'Blake will find something to keep him busy and I need someone to help me carve the turkey.' She smiled. 'Someone with garfish filleting skills might just know how to do the job.'

Grace gazed down at her hand, and she relaxed. 'You'd let me carve the turkey? That'll keep you busy for the rest of Christmas—bandaging what's left of me.'

'But you'll come?' Nell was pressing, but all of a sudden it seemed important.

'You really are making an effort to be part of this town,' Grace said slowly, and Nell nodded.

'Whether Blake likes it or not. It's home.'

'It never was when you were a child.'

'No, but it should be now. Inviting everyone who needs a Christmas will make me feel more at home.'

'Does Blake know you're doing this?'

'No, but—'

'You don't think you ought to ask him first?'

'No way.' She shook her head. 'He'll find an even bigger reason not to be there. But will you come?'

Grace looked at her for a long, long minute, a strange questioning expression on her face. Finally she nodded, and for some reason it seemed the decision had been momentous. 'Yes, girl, I'll come,' she told her. 'I always was a damned fool for Christmas.'

'Me, too.' Nell fastened the last of the tape and their smiles met. 'Not that I've ever had one.'

'What do you mean?' But then Grace paused, thinking back. 'Your grandparents didn't celebrate Christmas, if I remember.'

'No. And my husband wasn't very much into the Christmas spirit either.'

Grace sighed. 'Oh, girl…' But then she brightened.

'Then it's up to us to make your first proper Christmas great. Who else are you inviting?'

Nell took a deep breath. 'Who do you suggest? Let's make it big. Anyone without someone to share it with them.'

Grace gazed at her, still with that strange half-smile. 'You're giving us a Christmas? After all this town's done to you?'

'What do you mean?'

'I mean you had the pits of a childhood,' Grace said, her voice suddenly harsh. 'No one stood up to your grandparents. Your grandpa was the town doctor. We needed him and you and your mother were treated like dirt. What they did was almost child abuse. We stood by and watched, and now you're organising a Christmas for everyone who needs it.'

'It'll be fun.'

'We don't deserve it.'

'Grace, you've always been kind.'

'No.' She seemed seriously troubled, and Nell laid a hand on her arm.

'Please, Grace. Can we forget my childhood? It's Christmas. I just want to enjoy it. My last Christmas without responsibilities.'

'You're taking on a load of responsibility, even without the baby. You're taking on half of Doc Sutherland's work, and you're taking trouble over us.'

'Grace, please…'

Grace took a deep breath. She met Nell's look head on, and she sighed. 'You really want to do this?'

'I do. It'll be fun.'

'And you don't expect anything in return?'

'What on earth could I want?'

Hmm. Grace was silent for a long time, and then she hauled a blank piece of paper toward her and lifted a pen.

'Christmas,' she said, and her thoughts seemed far away. 'A proper Christmas. How wonderful. Let's make a list.'

But she hadn't answered Nell's question.

CHAPTER NINE

'MRS CONDIE wants to know whether you want Christmas dinner in the hospital.' There were three days to go.

Nell had spent all her spare time organising her Christmas dinner, and now Blake's question caught her unawares. She looked up from wrapping candy canes in red Cellophane, and forced herself to focus.

'You know I've asked a few people. I thought we'd eat here. I'm organising food.'

'Mrs Condie will organise it for you. I don't know how many you have coming but—'

'Grace says maybe twelve.'

'Twelve!'

'There's a lot of lonely people in this town. But I don't want Mrs Condie cooking. The hospital kitchen's cold and sterile and about as unChristmassy as can be. I can do it here. If you help.'

If he helped… He might have known. 'I'm normally busy on Christmas Day.'

She sighed, exasperated. 'Dr Sutherland, that's hogwash, and you know it. In every hospital I've ever been in at Christmas—and, believe me, I've been in a few—there's always a lull at midday. Morning's present-giving and church. Then dinner, which lasts for hours. Then it's time to try out the new skateboard and test the limits of Great-Uncle Donald's peptic ulcer, so our work begins. But that's not until about four. What's your problem?'

His face was shuttered. 'Nell, I didn't ask you to organise this Christmas dinner. It's all very noble of you…'

'Noble. Is that why you think I'm doing it?' She was astounded. 'So I can feel virtuous?'

141

'I didn't say that.'

'You implied it.' She met his gaze, her green eyes flashing anger. 'You don't think I'll get as much from this as I put in?'

'I don't understand.'

'I mean I want to get involved with this community,' she told him. 'I want people to like me and I want to like them. In short, I want emotional attachment—something you're running scared of.'

'I'm not.'

'Don't kid yourself. You are. And for heaven's sake, what harm can it do? There's twelve of the town's old folk coming to Christmas dinner. They want a good time and so do you. And it could happen. If you let it.'

But his face was closed. As far as Blake was concerned, the conversation was ended. 'I'll eat with you if I can.'

'Gee, thanks.'

'I'm sorry.' And suddenly he was. He looked at her face and thought he'd hurt her. She was trying to hide it, but there it was. Hell, he'd hurt her and she'd had enough kicks already. But she wanted something he wasn't able to give.

She wanted commitment—not just to the town's elderly, but to her.

And he couldn't give it.

'I'll try and share my meal with you,' he said gently, and her eyes flew to his, her temper flaring.

'There's no need to patronise me.'

'I didn't mean—'

'Mean it or not, it reeked of patronising. Blake Sutherland, we're stuck together for Christmas so you may as well be civil about it.'

We're stuck together… He stared at her for a long moment, and then he spun on his heel and stalked away—because he didn't have the faintest clue how to deal with what was happening. Because he didn't even know what was happening! And he didn't want to know.

*   *   *

For how long were they stuck together? he wondered desperately as he tried to sleep that night. It was getting harder and harder to sleep. Nell was just through the wall, and the memories of that kiss were enough to keep him staring at the ceiling for so long he thought he'd go nuts.

She could well be here for the whole month. Over two more weeks and maybe longer. He'd driven past her house a few days back and seen it in its unstumped glory. It had broken windows, there were boards missing from the verandah and the whole house was layered with dust. In this town things moved slowly. She'd be lucky if it was finished by the time her baby was born!

How would he cope with that?

He wouldn't have to, he told himself hastily. She'd go to Blairglen for her baby's birth. She needed to go there at least two weeks before the baby was due, so that gave him an end point of five weeks at the latest. In five weeks he could be rid of her.

But how would he cope for that long?

'Please, let it be shorter,' he pleaded to the silence as he waited for elusive sleep. He didn't want her near. He didn't want her in this house—he didn't want her dog, her furniture, her silly damned Christmas tree. He wanted to be alone!

He slept at last, but if he could have known it his prayers were being answered right now. Because out on the bluff, the town was very much still awake.

The population of Sandy Ridge was working on making Dr Sutherland alone again.

'Dr Sutherland...'

It was late afternoon on Christmas Eve and they were nearing the end of Theatre. Scott Henderson had presented that morning complaining of abdominal tenderness. He'd seen Nell, Nell had admitted him and they'd watched for a couple of hours, hoping it might settle. Then suddenly there'd been rebound. A grumbling appendix had burst and a procedure they'd hoped he could have been spared until after Christmas was suddenly urgent.

At least such an operation was possible now in Sandy Ridge. With Nell there, they'd been able to operate fast and effectively. The appendix had been removed, the peritoneal cavity had been cleaned, a heavy dosage of antibiotics was already being fed in through the intravenous drip and Scott had every chance of being able to eat a Christmas dinner. He'd be stiff and sore, but he should be fine.

Now there was only the wound to finish suturing. Blake was concentrating totally—that way he didn't have to chat. If he chatted with anyone it had to be with Nell, and that seemed impossible. So Nell chatted with the theatre staff as she started to reverse the anaesthetic, and Blake was left to indulge in what was starting to seem like sullen silence.

For heaven's sake, he was behaving like a spoiled schoolkid, he thought as he sutured. He was being unreasonable. Stupid. And why?

He didn't know why. He only knew that to hold himself apart was the only way he knew of protecting himself—so when Marion put her head around the door to call him, he was almost relieved to be called. If he was needed, then Nell could take over and he could get out of there.

'Yes?'

'There's been an accident,' Marion told him. 'One of the builders. Out at Nell's place.'

'What sort of accident?'

'Collapse of a part of a wall. There's a couple of men trapped.'

Hell!

Nell was staring. 'How can a wall have collapsed?' she asked, puzzled. 'They weren't doing any major structural work.'

'They're reblocking.'

'That shouldn't make a wall collapse.'

'You don't know the tradesmen in this town,' Blake said grimly. He tied off the last stitch and motioned to Donald to apply the dressing. 'These guys have been inbreeding for generations and sometimes I think if they had one neuron collectively it'd be lonely.' He motioned toward Scott, and he was already stripping off his theatre gown. 'Can you take over here?'

'Of course.' But Nell bit her lip. 'Blake, it's my house. I'm coming, too.'

'I need to go straight away.' It was as if he was desperate to get away from her, Nell thought grimly, but he was right. He had to leave and she couldn't go yet.

'I'll follow. As soon as I've reversed the anaesthetic and Scott's stable…'

'I'll contact you if I need you.' Blake let his eyes rest on the bump of her pregnancy. 'You've had a big day, and it'll be dirty and dangerous out there.'

'It's my house,' she said belligerently, and his eyes softened.

'Yeah, I know, but you're tired. I'll let you know the damage as soon as I can.'

'I'm coming. As soon as Scott—'

'OK.' He held up his hands in surrender. There wasn't time for arguing. 'I'll see you soon.'

She *was* tired. Half an hour later Nell was in her little car, travelling out toward her house and hoping desperately that there was nothing major wrong, but overriding her problem was the wave of fatigue that was threatening to overwhelm her.

The last few days had been busier than she'd ever expected them to be, she thought as she drove. There'd been all the organisation for Christmas, and, as well as that, she seemed to have been needed medically.

She grimaced as she rounded the headland and steered the car up the long driveway to the house. Blake had insisted that she still only do morning surgery, so she should have had heaps of time. She should have been out at her house every day, seeing what the builders were doing.

But it seemed like every time she went toward her car there'd been someone hurrying toward her, or the phone would ring and it would be…something. Marg Connors wanting a woman-to-woman chat about how to tell the facts of life to her daughter. Grace wanting to talk about the merits of installing a security system so if she fell at night she could get help. Bob wanting to know whether his mother should move into a nursing home. It was always things that might normally merit a trip to the doctor, if the doctor had been less pressed than Blake.

The town had elected her their alternative doctor, Nell thought as she drove, and she should be grateful. She was sparing Blake work. But now she didn't have a clue what was happening to her house and her back ached with a dull, sickening throb.

She'd been standing too long over surgery, she thought. She should have sat to give the anaesthetic, and now she had to cope with a collapsed house and injured men—and a turkey that needed stuffing before she went to bed that night!

'Merry Christmas, Dr McKenzie,' she told herself wryly as she drew to a halt. 'After all, you asked for this…' And then she stopped, and stared up at the house.

It wasn't the same house.

She must be dreaming. But she wasn't. The house was standing where it had stood for a hundred years—her grandparents' house—but what a difference!

Gone were the broken windows, the peeling paintwork, the tilting verandah. This was a house that hadn't been seen for years—in fact, Nell didn't remember her house ever looking like this.

From her grandparents' time the house had been painted a dull mission brown. Now the house was the palest of soft yellows, almost cream but not quite, and it was trimmed with a grey-blue that took its inspiration from the sea. The windows were spotlessly clean and there wasn't a broken pane. They swung wide to the sea and they were laced with curtains that Nell had never seen, each of the same blue with the softest cream on their inmost border.

What else? The wide verandah had a new railing. The floorboards were polished redwood, smooth and gorgeous. Nell climbed out of the car and crossed the verandah, still feeling as if she were dreaming.

She hadn't been near the place for a week, she thought dazedly. When she'd rung the builder she'd been told he was struggling to get things done. He'd sounded totally unorganised and Nell had despaired of moving out of Blake's before the baby was born.

And now she could.

But…the wall? The collapsed wall? Where on earth…?

It didn't exist. Of course it didn't exist. It had simply been a ruse to get both doctors here. Instead of casualties, as Nell opened the wide front door there were a hundred people—maybe more. Balloons. Banners. Huge signs. 'Welcome home, Nell. Welcome home!'

She couldn't believe it—but they were all watching her, waiting for her reaction. Blake was there, too, with a very strange expression on his face. He must have been surprised as well, she thought. They'd kept this a secret from both of them. People were smiling at her. Laughing.

Blake wasn't smiling.

He should be. This meant she could get out of his life earlier than either had dreamed possible.

She could go now.

'What do you think?' It was Grace, the lovely wrinkled old fisherwoman, still in paint-spattered overalls as if she'd just this minute put the finishing touches to the walls. Which indeed she had.

Nell turned to her, and hugged her hard. There were tears glistening in the old lady's eyes, and they were mirrored in Nell's.

'Was this your idea?'

'It might have been,' Grace said noncommittally, and Nell knew it had.

'It's beautiful.'

It was all beautiful. The inside had been worked on as well as the outside. From the doors leading from the sitting room, Nell could see that every room had been painted and the floors and furniture washed and polished till they shone. All her grandparents' furniture looked wonderful...

Including...

'You've brought back the stuff I took to Blake's.'

'It's yours.' The ambulancemen were there, too. Bob and Henry were laughing at her shock and enjoying themselves hugely. 'You can't believe the trouble the townsfolk have had keeping you away from this place for the past few days—the complaints they've had to make up to distract you. We've worked in shifts to keep you away from here. Scott's appendix was a blessing. And we thought Blake'd hardly mind if we shifted your furniture back home. After all, he's got his house to himself again. Losing the odd sofa'd hardly matter.'

'You left him the tree?' Suddenly it seemed absurdly important that they had. He had to have something. He needed his Christmas angels!

But they had left them so she could stop worrying. 'We made you your own,' Grace told her, motioning to the corner where Christmas lights twinkled. Her arm was still around Nell's in an out-of-character display of affection. 'The town thought...well, you've been home for less than two weeks and already you've risked your skin saving one of us, and now you're putting on a fantastic Christmas for us oldies. Nell, we never stood up for you against your grandparents. We figured the least we could do was to see you had Christmas in your own home.'

'Oh, Grace...' She gazed around at them. At her people. *Her* people. And they beamed back, hugely satisfied with her pleasure.

Except Blake. He was standing on the sidelines, watching but not saying a word. Her gaze swung to his face and found his eyes creased, as if they were puzzled.

He was puzzled. Not pleased. Not displeased. Just... puzzled. Why?

He'd have his home to himself for Christmas, she thought. That should please him.

'I'm sorry about your furniture,' she said softly, and he managed a smile. His gaze moved from Nell's face to Grace's, and then back again, and the trace of puzzlement remained. She didn't understand it, but finally he dragged himself back to what she'd said. The furniture. Right.

'I can live without your furniture,' he told her. 'I have for the past two years.'

There was a pause—a moment when silence fell over the whole room. It was as if the room were witnessing a declaration.

He could live without her furniture. He could live without her. Of course he could. Why had she ever imagined differently?

After all, she was plain Nell McKenzie, a woman who was pregnant with another man's baby, a woman who was so different from his beautiful Sylvia that...

She blinked. What was she thinking of? The town's people had just given her this house and here she was fantasising about things that were totally ridiculous. Like a relationship with Blake.

He didn't need her, she told herself. He didn't want her, and if she gave any hint to the contrary then she'd make their working relationship untenable. When her baby was born she wanted part-time work here. She wanted to be his part-time partner.

Not his full-time love.

Or rather she did want that—very, very much—but she knew very well that trying for the second would destroy completely her chances of the first. So she just had to get on with it. With a wrench she forced her gaze away from Blake, back to the townspeople surrounding her.

'I suppose you haven't all gathered here to haul some injured builder from under a collapsed wall?'

There was general laughter and then someone handed her a glass of champagne, someone else started to play on her grandmother's piano, a fiddler tuned his instrument to the piano—and the party to end all parties began. A party to welcome Dr Nell McKenzie back amongst her own.

Blake left. Pleading the excuse that he needed to check Scott, he gave it an hour and then headed back to town. He did it via a detour. The beach was calling. The sea...

He desperately wanted to run. Desperately! He parked on the headland and stared down at the moonlit ribbon of sand stretching away to the horizon. He wanted to run and run, and never stop running. Away from here. He wanted to leave! He didn't want Nell staying in this town, disturbing his precious solitude.

She wouldn't be disturbing it now, he told himself. She'd no longer be sleeping just through the wall from him. She'd be in *her* house. He wouldn't have to see her. She'd be gone.

But she'd still be...there.

Damn. Damn, damn and damn. His hand thumped down onto the steering-wheel and he hit the hooter without meaning to. A bunch of dopey seagulls squawked their indignation at being rudely wakened and then settled again to their nightly roost.

He should go. Scott was waiting.

The beeper was on his belt. The nurses would beep him if he was needed.

Hell, why didn't they beep him? He was going nuts.

Finally he turned on the engine and forced himself to steer homewards. Ernest would still be at the apartment, he thought suddenly. Everything else of Nell's had been moved. He'd seen that she had it all—the energetic townsfolk had shifted everything, even the food for tomorrow's Christmas dinner. But her dog hadn't been at the party. They must have thought so many people in a strange place might upset him so they'd leave Ernest for Nell to collect later.

The thought was good. Ernest would still be still there, so she'd have to come to...

'Oh, for heaven's sake, Sutherland!' He didn't want Nell to come. He didn't want anyone! He was sure of it. But it was with a heavy heart that he headed back toward the town.

Toward the flat. Toward Ernest. Toward all that was left of Nell McKenzie.

When Blake woke it was Christmas, and Nell wasn't there. He lay and stared at the ceiling for a long time and tried not to think just how 'not there' it felt. Which was pretty much overwhelming.

Six a.m. There was plenty of time before he had to get up. He'd scheduled surgery from ten to eleven for urgent cases—the earaches and fevers that couldn't wait. He needed to do a ward round before then, but they'd look askance if he came in now, so the next couple of hours were his to do with as he wished. But he didn't wish to do anything.

He'd run, he thought. That'd be a good start to the day. Having made his decision, he threw off the bedcovers and headed for the living room, to discover Ernest fast asleep under the Christmas tree.

'What on earth are you doing?' he demanded. The dog was lying on his back, staring up at the tree like it personally had robbed him. 'You weren't hoping Father Christmas would drop in, were you?'

Maybe the dog had been hoping just that. The gaze that Ernest turned on him—reproachfulness personified—said he certainly wasn't happy. Blake sighed and crossed to the fridge.

'OK, I don't see why Santa should desert both of us.' There was a portion of leg ham in the fridge—small enough for one person to demolish over Christmas. All the wonderful food that had been there the day before had been taken out to Nell's but they'd left him enough to get by. Just.

'You'll be eating your main meal with us so there's no need to leave you all the trimmings,' he'd been told by Grace, and he could only agree, even if he didn't intend to eat anywhere near Nell.

So there was ham, eggs, a bowl of strawberries and not a lot else. Blake sliced the ham from the bone, ate a slice himself—well, he should do something to celebrate Christmas—and then he offered the bone to Ernest. 'Merry Christmas,' he told him.

But Ernest wasn't in a Christmas mood. He sniffed the bone and sighed heavily. Slowly, deliberately, he carried it to where the plain rug had replaced Nell's Turkish ones on the living-room floor. Without looking at Blake again, the dog scraped the rug back, deposited the bone underneath and proceeded to lie on top of it.

His body language was unmistakable. I'm miserable now. I appreciate the gesture and maybe I'll eat it later, but I'm too sad to eat just yet.

'You're supposed to eat it now,' Blake told him, lifting a piece of ham and biting. 'Like this. It's Christmas now.'

But Ernest wasn't happy and Blake knew exactly how he felt.

'You're missing Nell?' Blake stooped to pat the velvety head. 'I thought she'd come and get you.' He had, too. Blake had lain awake until the small hours, thinking that Nell might sleep here. Her bed was still made up and her dog was here and... And he was here!

Damn, that'd make no difference at all. He was being ridiculous.

'How about you come down to the beach and run with me?' Blake enquired, and Ernest looked so unenthusiastic that he almost laughed. Almost.

'OK.' Blake knew when he was beaten. 'Give me five minutes and we'll take your damned bone and we'll give the pair of you back to your mistress.' And then he'd really be alone for Christmas—which was the way he wanted it. Wasn't it?

Maybe.

In the end it was eight before he reached Nell's, which was maybe just as well as Nell would hardly have appreciated a six a.m. wake-up call. But he'd been delayed. Jodie Farmer had sat all night in a steam tent with her croupy baby and had waited until dawn to bring her baby in.

'Because I know last night was a big night and I didn't want to bother you. Did you enjoy the party?'

'Very much, thank you.'

Jodie had surveyed him with care. She was almost as wide as she was high, big-hearted with it and as sharp as a tack. 'You and Doc McKenzie had a fight, then?'

'No. Why would we fight?'

'You didn't stay out there?'

'Of course I didn't. It's Nell's house, not mine.'

She wasn't satisfied. 'But you still fancy her?'

'Of course I don't.'

'No "of course" about it,' she said bluntly. 'My old man put ten quid on the pair of you being married by the time her baby's born.' She grinned. 'Got long odds, too, so we'd appreciate it if you'd oblige.'

'Not even for you, Jodie,' he said, goaded. Good grief!

'So what's wrong with being married?' Jodie looked down at the baby in her arms and she grinned. 'Last night was the pits but we wouldn't give her back, and me and Daryl think marriage is great! And now you'll even stick Lily in hospital so we can have Christmas dinner in peace. Bliss.'

'You'd be well served if I didn't admit her.'

'Then I'd fall asleep on top of her and you know it. Daryl was out all night, fishing, so he's no help. I'll see her settled, crawl into bed with my hubby and wake in time to have Christmas dinner with my in-laws. Marriage is great, Doc Sutherland. You ought to try it.'

'No, thanks.'

'You couldn't be talked into it?'

The woman was impossible. 'I've been married already,' he said curtly, but even that wasn't enough to shut her up.

'Doc McKenzie's different,' she told him, refusing to be silent. 'She's special.'

'So was my wife.'

'Yeah, well.' She shrugged, but she still grinned. 'Not from what I've heard, but have it your own way. I'm still backing Daryl's bet. I might even have a flutter myself.'

'You'll lose your money,' Blake told her, striving desperately to bring this crazy conversation to an end. It was at times like this that he wanted to be something other than a doctor. Like a hermit! But he lifted Jodie's baby into his arms and felt a jabbing ache of uncertainty. Lily's tiny face was so innocent. So trusting.

'Hey, you're ripe for marriage,' Jodie said, watching him and smiling.

'I've got all I can cope with, looking after everyone else's kids,' he retorted. He forced himself back to the business at hand. 'Her breathing's still a bit blocked, Jodie, so we will admit her.'

'I knew you would.' Then, before he knew what she intended, she grabbed him—and her baby—in an all-enveloping hug. 'I think you're the greatest,' she told him. 'And so's Dr McKenzie. So off you go and win Daryl's bet for me. Right now.'

CHAPTER TEN

THOROUGHLY disgruntled, Blake walked up the front steps of Nell's house and hoped she was awake. He'd offload the dog and be out of here, he told himself. Fast.

He knocked on the back screen, Ernest by his side, but they were met by silence. He knocked again and the door swung inwards. Instead of Nell, though, he was confronted with Wendy Gunner.

Wendy was Aaron's wife. He'd seen her the day before at her husband's hospital bedside, with her three children in tow. Things had been looking good for her—her husband was recovering fast—and she'd been bright, cheerful and bubbly.

She was none of that now. She looked pale and drawn. She was still dressed in her nightwear and her two littlest children were clinging to her side.

'Wendy!'

'Dr Sutherland!'

His stomach lurched somewhere toward his feet as he heard her fear. His hands came out and gripped hers, holding hard. 'Wendy, what's wrong? Where's Nell?'

'She's…she's in the bathroom.'

'The baby…' Hell, the baby!

But it wasn't the baby. Wendy gave a choking sob and shook her head. 'No. It's not the baby. It's Jason.'

'Your Jason?' He didn't understand. Jason was her eight-year-old. 'What's going on?'

'He got a bike for Christmas.' Another sob. 'The kids have been up for hours. Jason took the bike straight out onto the gravel drive and while I wasn't looking he stuck a plank on some bricks to make a jump. Of all the stupid things…

155

And now his leg… You should see it. There's blood and gravel and he's ripped his pyjamas and I know I should be in there helping, but all of a sudden I felt sick and I couldn't…' She buried her face in her hands.

'Hey, Wendy.' Blake's arms came around and held her. He could guess what was happening. While her husband's life had been in danger and afterwards, Wendy had been fantastic. She'd held herself composed and cheerful and optimistic throughout.

But now the accumulated strain of keeping cheerful for Aaron's sake and the after-effects of the terror had proved too much. One damaged knee was all it had taken to push her over the edge.

Blake needed to find out how badly the child was hurt. There were murmurs coming from the bathroom, but Wendy needed help first.

'Kyle.' Blake looked down at the second of the children. Kyle was six years old and was lost in the face of his mother's distress. Blake knelt and met him at eye level. 'Kyle, your mother's upset. Jason's sore knee has made her sad. But there's nothing to worry about. I bet Dr McKenzie is bandaging it really well, and I want to help her, so do you think that if your mum sits on the sofa right here, you and Christy could give her a cuddle?'

Kyle considered the matter gravely. His thumb was permanently stuck in his mouth and his eyes were huge. He stared up at his mother in bewilderment.

'Mummy's crying.'

'That's why she needs a cuddle.' Blake turned to the four-year-old. 'Christy, can you help?'

Wendy's daughter was made of sterner stuff than her brother. She nodded at once.

'Sit down, Mummy,' she ordered, and Blake grinned and put his hands on Wendy's shoulders and propelled her to sit.

'Now cuddle,' he ordered, and Christy did just that. After a moment's doubt, Kyle followed.

'Don't you let your mother up,' Blake ordered as Wendy's

arms came out in an instinctive reaction to hold them both close. 'She's not to move.' He motioned to the dog who'd followed him hopefully into the house. There were good smells coming from here. Christmas smells. Food smells. It was enough to make a dog really optimistic. 'If she stands up, you tell Ernest to lick her,' Blake told the children. 'That'll fix her.'

'Does he bite?' Kyle asked, diverted from his mother for a moment.

'No. His specialty is licking. Very, very wetly.'

'He'll lick our mummy?'

'Only if you let her up.'

It appealed enormously to the two children. They stared at Ernest for a long moment, Ernest stared back, and they got the message. They got on with the important task of mother-cuddling.

Blake found Nell, with the little boy sitting on towels on the bathroom floor. She'd ripped the pyjama leg aside to reveal a nasty gravel rash. By the look of Jason's face— stoic rather than in pain—she must have given him a local anaesthetic, but it was a big job. He'd scraped not only his knee but his leg almost down to his ankle.

'Well, Jason Gunner. You've made a right proper mess,' Blake growled as he entered the room, and Nell looked up with relief. She'd been kneeling on the floor as she worked, and by the look of it, the floor wasn't at all comfortable.

'Blake...' There was no hiding her relief, and Blake felt a small surge of satisfaction. Actually, quite a large surge.

'Can I help?'

'If you would.' She winced, grabbed the towel rail and hauled herself to her feet before he could help. Her hand moved to the small of her back and she grimaced again. 'Operating on the floor when you're this far pregnant is hardly fun. I should have used the kitchen table—except that the turkey's using it.' She managed a smile, but it was a wan one. 'I've given Jason a local anaesthetic so we can get all the gravel out without hurting him, but I'd be very grateful if you could take over.'

Blake didn't hesitate. He crossed to the basin and started washing. 'Of course. What on earth was Wendy thinking of, coming to you?'

'It's Christmas,' Nell said simply. 'They're my next-door neighbours and they didn't want to disturb you.'

Right. It was a major hazard of being a country GP. Patients thought it was somehow easier for all concerned to land on the doctor's front doorstep rather than come to the surgery. It wasn't and, by the look of Nell's face, she'd been feeling the strain.

'Not up to taking on my full workload?' he asked, and she flushed. Damn. Why had he said that? She was distressed, he thought, and it was he who'd distressed her.

'I'm sorry. That was uncalled for.'

'It's true. I'm useless. I'm not usually—'

'Usually you're a really fine doctor,' he told her, meeting her eyes and smiling—trying to make her smile back. 'But kneeling on the floor when you have ten-ton Tess aboard is hardly sensible.'

That made her indignant—which was just the reaction he'd been angling for. 'Hey, my baby's hardly ten-ton Tess.'

'He looks like it—doesn't he, Jason?' Blake had swiftly washed his hands and was already stooping over the injured knee. 'Holy cow, how much gravel did you get in here, Jason Gunner? You must have been travelling at a hundred miles an hour. It must be some bike that Santa left.'

'It's red,' Jason told him proudly. 'And it's got little wheels so I can do heaps of tricks.'

'Well, you write a letter to Santa and tell him he forgot knee and elbow pads,' Blake said sternly. 'What was Santa thinking of?' Then he relented. 'You didn't hurt your bike?'

'No.' Jason managed a gap-toothed grin. 'I checked it before I had a look at my knee.'

'You're born to be a Formula One driver.' Then Blake glanced up at Nell and his smile faded. She was almost as white-faced as Jason. 'Go and make yourself a cup of tea, Dr McKenzie,' he suggested. 'I can finish here.'

'I don't need a cup of tea.'

'Well, ten-ton Tess might.'

'Is your baby really ten tons?' Jason asked, interested, and Nell managed a smile.

'I hope not, but he sure feels that way at the moment.'

'When exactly is your due date?' Blake asked, focussing in sudden concern. The baby had dropped, he thought. Nell looked different. The baby was no longer a neat bundle around her midriff. Had it dropped in preparation for delivery? Surely not.

'February eight. There's a good six weeks to go.'

'You're sure of your dates?'

'Of course I'm sure. I'm a doctor, aren't I?'

'You've had an ultrasound?'

'No, but—'

'But nothing. Hell, Nell...'

'Do you mind?' she snapped, motioning to the boy. 'Concentrate on Jason.'

'Sorry, Jase.' Blake turned back to what he was doing. 'You didn't hear what I just said.'

'Hell?' Jason enquired, and Blake smiled.

'It's not a word to say in front of ladies. I only said it because I was provoked.'

'What's provoked?'

'Something Dr McKenzie is very good at. She's a very provoking lady.'

Jason thought that through. 'Does provoking mean pretty?'

'That's part of it.' He'd determined to keep his mind on the job. There was only a tiny area of the wound left uncleaned. He scrubbed the top layer, scrubbed harder and then used tweezers to remove the last of it. Finally he looked around to find a dressing and Nell placed it into his hand, unasked.

Her presence was strangely disconcerting. 'I thought I told you to go and have a cup of tea,' he growled.

'I told you I didn't want one.'

'See?' Blake demanded of his patient. 'Provoking. Provoking, provoking and even more provoking.'

'She is pretty,' Jason agreed, and Blake grinned.

'She's pretty fat.' Ignoring Nell's indignant gasp, he came to the point he needed to focus on next. 'You saw Emily last week?' he demanded of Nell.

'Yes. Why do you ask? You know I drove across to visit her.'

'And she examined you?'

'She says everything's fine.'

'But she examined you?'

'Yes!'

'And she agrees with your dates?'

'Why wouldn't she? I know I'm right.'

'Have you got a bassinet yet?' Jason asked, interested. 'Cos there's one at my place.'

'I won't need a bassinet for ages,' Nell said, a trace of desperation in her tone. 'I'll worry about that when I stop working—in two weeks!'

'You're exhausted now,' Blake told her.

'No. Yes! Maybe I am, but only because I danced until the small hours last night, and then I had to stuff the turkey and lay the table.'

And Jason was on her doorstep to stop her sleeping in, Blake thought—but she must already have been up and dressed. She was looking great, in a gorgeous crimson maternity dress. It was a simple sundress with shoestring shoulder straps, cut low across her breast and then flaring in soft folds to mid-calf.

She was pretty, Jason had decreed, and Blake agreed entirely.

'What else have you got left to do?' he asked, fitting white gauze across Jason's knee and lower leg.

'Not much.'

'You have a dozen people coming for Christmas dinner. That's hardly not much.'

'They're all bringing something. My job's the turkey and the roast potatoes. Everything else is done—oh, except the brandy sauce.'

'So after the brandy sauce you can have a rest before everyone gets here.'

'I guess.' She sounded doubtful as she glanced at her watch.

'Right.' Blake lifted Jason and set him on his feet. 'That's you fixed—which gives me time to help Dr McKenzie with the brandy sauce before morning surgery.'

'Are you having Christmas dinner with Dr McKenzie?' Jason asked, and Nell butted in before he could answer.

'Of course he is.'

'Maybe...'

'We're having Christmas dinner in Dad's room at the hospital,' Jason said proudly, oblivious to the tension that was suddenly filling the bathroom. 'But afterwards... If I promise not to fall off, can I ride my bike over to show it to you?'

'We'd love to see it.' Nell smiled at Blake. 'Wouldn't we?'

Blake glowered. 'I don't know whether I'll be here. I don't know how busy I'll be.'

'You can't be too busy for Christmas dinner,' Jason said, shocked.

'We'll see.'

They took Jason out to the hall to discover Wendy had pulled herself together and was in control again. Just. 'I'm really grateful,' she told them. 'And, Nell, I'm so sorry for disturbing you on Christmas morning.'

'Think nothing of it.' Nell was watching Wendy's face, taking in the strain around her eyes. 'It's been a crazy Christmas for you.'

'Yes.' Wendy faltered, but tried to keep her voice bright. 'It's an odd one. Just me and the kids. We were supposed to go to my sister's in Blairglen. All the family are going.'

'Instead of which, you're pandering to the invalid.'

'It feels funny.' Wendy blinked, determined to hold back the tears which were just behind her eyes. 'When Aaron was hurt, the family offered to come here, but my sister's eight months pregnant and I thought it wasn't fair. I mean...' Her eyes flew to Nell's tummy. 'Well, eight months or not, she could have it any minute.'

'Hey, I'm not due for six weeks,' Nell said decisively. 'And first babies are always late.'

'Yeah.' But both Blake and Wendy were looking at Nell's tummy like a coiled snake.

'Oh, cut it out, the pair of you.' Nell managed a laugh. 'Wendy, are you saying that after you leave hospital you're going home alone?'

'With the kids. Yes.'

'You'd better come here, then,' Nell told her. 'It's open house for anyone who can sing Christmas carols. We don't mind if you come late and have eaten heaps already. You can help finish the brandy sauce.'

'I couldn't.' But it was obviously enticing. 'Oh, Nell...'

'I'd love you to. We both would. Wouldn't we, Blake?' Nell grinned and tucked her arm into Blake's, whether he liked it or not, making them an instant couple. 'The average age of my guests is about a hundred and six. I suspect one tablespoon of my brandy sauce and they'll be out for the count, so I depend on you and Blake to keep me company.' She twinkled at Wendy and then she turned her smile on Blake. 'And to help me wash up.'

Wendy smiled back. 'If you put it like that.' She looked a question at Blake. 'And if you're coming, too...'

He was stuck. They were all watching him, two women and three children, their faces bright with expectation. And Nell was by his side, holding his arm in hers and smiling up at him. Her body was warm and close and... And it was suddenly all too much.

'I'll come if I can,' he said, goaded, and Nell grinned.

'What a very polite way of accepting.'

'It's the best I can do.'

It was only a meal, for heaven's sake. Why did it feel like he was signing his life away? *I'll come if I can*... Heaven knew that he couldn't.

Wendy took her children home, the four of them skipping down the track with Jason barely limping.

'Kids are amazing,' Blake said, watching them go. 'You and me'd be in bed after falling like that.'

'You think Jason would go to bed when there's a new bike to be ridden?' Nell laughed. 'I wouldn't be surprised if he's back, having the other knee bandaged, before nightfall.'

'He'll be back anyway—for your party.'

'He will, too.'

'It's too much for you,' Blake said savagely, watching her face. Despite the gorgeousness of her crimson dress, she still looked pale. 'Hell, Nell, why do you—?'

'Do you mind not swearing at Christmas?'

'I'll swear if I want to.'

'Ernest is shocked.'

'Ernest is concentrating entirely on turkey, and stop changing the subject. Nell...'

'Are you going to help me with the brandy sauce?' she demanded. 'Or are you just planning to stand around, getting in the way? Because if you are, I promise I'll hang mistletoe on your nose. And there's six widows coming to my dinner, and they all know what mistletoe's for.'

Blake smiled but he was still worried. 'Nell...'

'Just shut up and work,' she told him, pushing him into the kitchen. 'Do you know how to separate eggs?'

'Separate eggs. You mean one from the other?'

'And you a surgeon,' she told him, exasperated. She plonked a carton of eggs in front of him. 'I'll show you one, and you do the other eleven.'

'A full dozen! How much brandy sauce do we need?' he demanded, startled, and she chuckled.

'How long's a piece of string? Goodness knows.'

'So what's it got in it?' He picked up the recipe book,

and saw it written in a child's handwriting. 'Where did you get this?'

And for a moment she hesitated. 'Um…'

His attention was caught. 'Don't tell me it's a secret.'

'No.'

'Then what?'

'It was written on a slip of paper tucked into one of my mother's books. I found it stowed in the garage with everything else of my mother's. Heaven knows where she got it, because my grandmother certainly never made it, but now it's one of the few things left to me.' She put a cream container on the table and reached for an apron. 'So I guess you could say it's a family recipe. *My* family.'

Blake felt his gut wrench at that, a feeling he was starting to recognise. She'd had so little, and she could have so much more—but, then, for Nell to have more, he'd have to give. So what was he thinking of?

He knew what he was thinking of. He knew what he wanted. He wanted Nell to have a family, and he wanted that family to be him! But for him to be Nell's family he'd have to break down barriers that had taken him years to build, and he didn't want that. Did he?

No. No and no and no. Definitely not.

'If you don't hurry and break those eggs, you'll miss morning surgery,' she was saying. 'Mind, I've done half your work for you.'

With a start he jerked himself back to the job at hand. Brandy sauce. The important things in life. Right.

She was supposed to be sleeping. After Blake left, Nell tried to settle. Instead, she wandered around the house like someone lost, Ernest trailing behind her. Her back still ached, she was weary and she was downright miserable.

Would he come back? Even though he'd promised, she didn't think so. He'd find some urgent medical need and he'd phone with an excuse that she couldn't fault.

'You're a fool, Nell McKenzie,' she told herself for the

fortieth time. 'You have a house. A dog. Friends. People coming to Christmas dinner who you care about. What else do you want?'

Blake.

The answer was written across her heart as if it had been branded by fire. She wanted him so much, and she was stupid, stupid, stupid. Because Blake didn't want her. He didn't want anyone, and she simply had to accept that and get on with her life—as best she could.

But she certainly couldn't sleep.

'Merry Christmas!'

Ethel Norris was the first to arrive, carrying a boiler almost wider than she was. The pudding lay on the back seat of her car as Nell came out to greet her, and it was bigger than a basketball. 'I know I'm early but if the pudding doesn't go on soon it won't be ready.'

'What a pudding!' Nell lifted it and groaned with the weight. Her back stabbed again with the pain she was starting to expect. She hid her grimace as best she could. 'Heck, Ethel, what did you put in this?' Drat, what was wrong with her? Her legs felt like jelly.

But Ethel was too busy to notice. 'Everything but the kitchen sink.' The big woman beamed. 'I've never made such a pudding. It should have been made a couple of months ago, but with this party planned just this week I had to put more brandy in to compensate.' Her beam widened, and Nell thought back to the miserable Ethel she'd met when she'd first come back to town, and she could only wonder.

'Hey, and I've lost two more pounds,' Ethel told her, guessing where Nell's thoughts were headed. 'How good's that?'

'You're not dieting today!'

'No fear. No, Dr McKenzie, I'm following your advice and very good advice it is, too. Now, let's get this pudding on the stove and see what else needs to be done.'

Soon after Ethel came Grace, bearing trays of Moreton

Bay bugs, gleaming in their crimson glory, with bowls of home-made tartare sauce and slices of fresh lime.

Then old Norman Harper arrived with oysters, Harriet Walsingham with salads made from her own garden—a Harriet complete with pacemaker on board and details of her Very Interesting Heart Surgery—Bert with baby potatoes dug that morning, Marg with fresh peas, the ancient Toby with a whole bucket of fresh cream he'd scooped off his magnificent Jerseys' milk, Elsie with strawberries, Clare with home-made chocolates...

By the time they sat down to dinner the table was groaning, and Nell looked around at the sea of smiling faces and thought, Why wouldn't you do something like this? If not for this, all these people would have sat down to Christmas dinner alone, and they'd have been collectively miserable.

The only dampener to her spirits was that Blake still wasn't here, and she couldn't stop thinking of him. Drat the man. He hadn't even phoned. Somewhere he was eating his Christmas dinner alone. He'd be in the hospital kitchen, she thought, or in his apartment with his boneless ham and his one punnet of strawberries. She wished suddenly that she'd sent some of this food over to him. She couldn't bear that here there was so much and he had so little.

But he had to make the first move himself, she told herself fiercely, and he wouldn't. He wanted to be solitary!

'Pull my cracker,' Tom told her, and then Grace and Ethel carried in the turkey between them. The bird was golden brown and so succulent Nell could almost taste it before she raised it to her mouth.

'Happy Christmas,' Grace said, and raised her champagne flute across the table to Nell. 'Welcome home, Dr McKenzie. Welcome to your first proper Christmas at Sandy Ridge, and may there be many more.'

There were cheers all around, and Grace was watching her with a look that was almost tender. Nell found her eyes filling with tears. This was what she'd wanted so desperately, for herself and her baby. She had a home.

But where was Blake?

Blake was trying hard not to be there. Really hard. But there wasn't enough work.

Jason Gunner must be the only casualty in the whole of Sandy Ridge, he thought desperately as he stood at the nurses' station and wondered what to do next. The hospital was three-quarters empty. Every patient who possibly could had gone home. For those who remained there were the sounds of individual festivities as each family made a party around their special patient's bed.

These were private parties and he wasn't wanted.

Maybe he could go for a run now, he thought. After all, the beach would be deserted. But he knew he'd be seen—which meant Nell would be offended. To run in solitary state while the rest of the town ate their Christmas dinners would have everyone feeling sorry for him. People would be calling out for him to come and share their dinners, and the last thing he wanted was sympathy.

Why should he want it? His solitude was self-imposed. That was what he wanted. Wasn't it?

Nell would be carving the turkey by now.

What Nell was doing had nothing to do with him, he told himself fiercely. Nothing at all. He'd ring her to tell her he was busy, and then he'd go back to his own kitchen and eat.

His hand wouldn't quite lift the receiver.

OK. He'd eat and then ring, he decided. Then she'd think the medical need had been really urgent—something had happened that meant he hadn't even been able to phone.

But back at his apartment, his ham and the strawberries looked absolutely pathetic.

'Merry Christmas, Sutherland,' he muttered to himself as he stared at the plate of ham he'd cut from Ernest's bone, and he couldn't help thinking that even Ernest would be having a better Christmas than he was.

He was being pathetic. This was what he wanted! He opened a bottle of wine, took his ham and carried it into the living room. Here was Nell's tree, the only thing she'd left for him. His three haemorrhoid angels beamed from the tip, and their smiles mocked him. Fool, they said, and he knew they were right.

'I can't go.'

'You promised you would if you could.'

'So you were stupid. You're getting yourself into deep water, Blake Sutherland.' Heck, he was going barmy here, talking to himself and a bunch of paper angels, but there was no one else to talk to and his need to unburden his soul was overpowering.

'That's what you want.'

'It's not.'

'Well, you could just go out to her place and eat. After all, half your geriatric practice is there. Maybe it wouldn't hurt.'

Maybe.

Maybe he couldn't help himself. Maybe he was going mad, but with a groan he put the ham aside. Sensible or not, he was going to share Christmas with Nell.

Her back was on fire. As the meal continued Nell grew more and more aware of the pain. She'd been trying to ignore it all morning, and while there'd been things to do she'd managed, but now... She'd been on her feet too much, she told herself, and she shouldn't have carried the pudding. Now she was suffering the consequences.

Around her, the meal was everything she'd hoped. The food was fantastic and every person there was aching for a good time. With company like this, her party couldn't help but be a success.

Oh, but her back hurt.

Where was Blake?

He wasn't coming, she thought as the piles of Moreton Bay bugs and oyster shells were cleared and the turkey was carved—and by the time everyone's plates were heaped with the magnificent main course she was sure of it.

No matter. It didn't matter. These were her people and she didn't need anyone else. Hadn't she sworn that when she'd cut up her king-sized quilt?

It was just...her back hurt so much.

'Are you all right, girl?' Grace was looking at her with a strange expression on her face. 'You look...'

'Tired. I'm just a bit tired.' But the pain was like hot knives. Heck, she must have pulled something when she'd lifted the pudding, and she couldn't afford to be sick, she thought desperately. It'd spoil her guests' Christmas. Besides, she'd promised Blake two more weeks of medicine.

'Are you sure?' There was real concern on Grace's face, and Nell dredged up a smile.

'I'm fine. Honest.'

'You don't look fine. You look just how your—' She bit off her sentence, and if she hadn't been concentrating on her back Nell would have probed deeper.

'I'll get the gravy,' she said, realising the jug was still in the kitchen. It'd give her a blessed couple of minutes away to grimace in private, and maybe she could risk taking a painkiller.

'I'll get it.'

'No.' Nell put her hand on Grace's shoulder to stop her rising and she used the hold to lever herself to her feet. She felt somehow extraordinarily heavy. Extraordinarily...

No! Realisation came with her first major contraction. Her waters burst right as the knowledge slammed home. She doubled over with pain, and she cried out with the shock of it. And a dozen of Sandy Ridge's geriatrics were left open-mouthed as their hostess buckled to her knees and stayed there.

CHAPTER ELEVEN

BLAKE walked up the verandah steps, wondering what on earth he was doing. His last two Christmases he'd spent alone. He was accustomed to it. It didn't matter. The celebrations were way out of scale anyway, he thought. Gross commercialisation. He didn't need it.

But his legs kept carrying him forward. Nell's face, disappointed but stoic, was before him. He'd promised. She didn't think he'd come, he knew, and suddenly he wanted to see her face when he walked into the room. Because he knew it'd light up, and those gorgeous green eyes would smile a welcome and she'd make room for him by...

He was being a romantic fool! But his step quickened, nevertheless, and by the time the front door was flung wide he was almost running.

And so was Ethel. She burst out of the front door like a cannonball and when she saw Blake she almost fell into his arms—which was quite something as she weighed twenty stone.

Blake gasped and caught her—sort of—and she looked at him as though she couldn't believe he was really there.

'Oh, Dr Sutherland.' She was so desperate she could hardly get the words out. 'The phone's not on here yet, and I was just running next door to phone you.'

'I said I'd come.' Surely there had been no need for such urgency.

But it seemed there was. 'Come quick.' She hauled herself out of his grasp and grabbed his arm, dragging him into the hall. 'Quick. Dr McKenzie's having her baby on the dining-room floor.'

* * *

170

It wasn't quite as bad as that.

By the time he reached her, they'd carried Nell into the main bedroom and laid her on her grandparents' big bed. Now she lay wide-eyed with fright, gripping Grace's hand like she was drowning, and when Blake pushed his way through the crowd around the bed she gave a sob of sheer terror and clutched him, too.

'It's coming. Blake, my baby's coming, and it can't. I'm only thirty-four weeks. It'll die. Blake, stop it. I need a salbutamol drip. I need… Dear God, I don't know what I need. Oh…' Her voice tailed into a moan as the next contraction hit.

'Can someone fetch my bag?' Blake tossed his car keys to where at least eight senior citizens crowded around him. Grace seemed the most competent of the lot of them, and the most concerned. 'Grace, can you stay?' He glanced at the sea of elderly faces, each capped with a gay Christmas hat and each looking equally worried and agog. 'Everyone else, I suggest you finish your Christmas dinner while you wait for news of what's happening. I'm sure that's what Dr McKenzie wants.'

What Dr McKenzie wanted didn't include a baby, but that was exactly what she was getting. Blake did a swift examination and all it told him was that they were far too late to get her to the hospital. They were too late for anything but delivery.

'How sure are you of your dates?' he demanded, cutting through Nell's mist of pain and fear with his curt command.

Nell caught her breath on a sob and tried to make herself think. 'I'm…I'm sure.'

'Why are you sure?'

'I dated it from last menstruation.'

'You had a normal period?'

'I don't know. I guess.' She was panting with effort, and a sheen of sweat covered her forehead. 'I must have. It *was* a period. Richard and I were arguing. Maybe…'

Maybe if she'd been emotionally upset she wouldn't have noticed if it had been much lighter than usual!

'You didn't have an ultrasound.'

'No, I...' She bit her lip on pain. 'It was all such a mess. I didn't.'

'So you're not absolutely sure.'

'I must be.' It was a wail. Another contraction rolled through, and Blake winced. They were less than a minute apart—and the head was crowning already!

'OK, Grace, we need lots of hot soapy water and as many towels as you can find. Can you ask Ethel if she can use my car phone to ring the hospital? Tell the nurses what's happening, ask them to send a midwife and tell them to put the Blairglen neonatal team on standby.'

In the face of this crisis Grace was swift and incisive, dropping her years like magic. 'You want them to come at once?'

'The midwife, yes, but the neonatal team, no.' The Blairglen neonatal team flew anywhere in the district to take premature babies back to the city for specialist attention, but... 'I'm not convinced this is early.'

'It's early.' Nell almost yelled. 'It's six weeks early. Blake, stop it.'

'If I stop it now you'll have a baby half in and half out,' Blake told her, and he grinned. 'You've learned breathing techniques?'

'No. Yes. Ow...'

'Breathe, Nell,' he told her. 'Concentrate.'

'I don't want to concentrate. I don't want a baby.'

'You know, I'm very sure you do.' He took her hand, and forced her terrified gaze to meet his. For a moment, mid-contraction, he had her complete attention. 'Nell, by the look of it you're having a normal delivery and a normal baby. That's what you want, isn't it?'

'I... Yes. Oh, Blake...'

'Then what are we waiting for?' he asked. 'To have your baby in your own home, with all your friends... And on

Christmas Day to boot.' He waited until the next contraction came through and his hands held hers all the time, imparting strength.

'OK, Nell,' he told her softly, but there was still strength behind the words. 'You have me and you have Grace. And we both love you and won't let anything happen—to you or your baby. Do you trust us?'

Her attention was caught. She looked up into his eyes and took a searing breath, and he felt her body relax. He felt the terror dissipate. Resolution came to take its place. 'Yes…' It was a breathless whisper but it was enough, and Blake's smile encompassed her as a great hug might have.

'OK, Dr McKenzie, I believe we'll try for the full catastrophe. Grace let's go for it. Nell, I'm afraid the time for talking is past. Shut up and push.'

'Why should I shut up?' It was a hint of the old Nell, belligerent and bossy. 'Why should you—?'

The next contraction hit.

She shut up and pushed.

And ten minutes later, before any nurse could arrive and before any more preparations could be made other than boiling water and warming towels, Blake lifted a tiny bundle of baby away from his mother.

Swiftly he cut the cord, checked the baby and discovered a perfect, near full-term baby boy. For some reason he was close to tears. Why, for heaven's sake? He'd delivered babies before. But he'd never delivered Nell's.

Forcing himself to be practical, he wrapped the infant in a warmed towel and handed him to Grace. After coping with the afterbirth, he washed his hands in some of the gallons of hot water—good grief, the back-up team had boiled enough to bathe an elephant—and then he moved to Nell's head, gripped her hands and held hard.

As the baby had cannonballed its way into the world, Nell had slumped back, exhausted beyond belief. Now her eyes had closed. The baby had arrived like a steam train and Nell was bordering on shock. Not many first babies arrived as hard and as fast as this one, and the shock to Nell's body must be massive.

He needed to set up a drip. She could use some fluid. But first...

'Nell?' It was a whisper. He lifted her wrist to find her pulse steady and strong, and he felt better for it. 'Nell,' he said again, and this time it was a command.

She opened her eyes, but they were full of fear. Full of pain. She was bracing herself for the worst. 'Oh, Blake. Oh, dear God...' Her voice cracked on a sob. 'Is it...is my baby dead?'

'Give her the baby, Grace,' Blake said, and Grace smiled her joy. She came forward, knelt by the bedside and held out the tiny, warmly wrapped bundle for his mother to see.

'Look, Nell,' Blake ordered softly. 'See your son.'

And he was just perfect. He had huge eyes, just like his mother's, already wide and wondering, and showing not a hint of distress. And he had a mass of burnt red hair—just like Nell's.

And just like...Grace's?

Grace's eyes were swimming with tears, and Blake grinned. This felt good. It felt right, and more and more he figured what he suspected was possible.

'He's a perfect baby boy,' he told Nell, and he stroked a finger across her cheek to collect a teardrop. 'Just perfect. Ten fingers. Ten toes. Everything. I'd say he might be a week or two early, but certainly no more. And I'd guess he's about six pounds. He's small enough so you haven't even torn. So...'

The temptation to stroke her cheek again was irresistible, and he did just that. 'Perfect,' he whispered, and maybe he wasn't just talking about the baby. But somehow he hauled himself back on track. 'A perfect little boy. What are you going to call him?'

'What...?' Nell was so dazed she could hardly speak. Grace manoeuvred the bundle into her waiting arms, and

Nell held him close and gazed down at her baby in awe. 'Oh,' she said on a sigh of discovery. 'He looks like…'

'He looks like his mother,' Blake said, and grinned. A perfect birth—a perfect baby—meant doctors were superfluous. He was superfluous. But he didn't feel superfluous. He felt fantastic! 'He looks like you. And…' He cast an odd glance up at Grace, but he was still sure he was right, and more and more this seemed the right time to tell her. 'And he also looks like your grandmother.'

'My grandmother.' Nell was exploring every last feature of her little son's face, and she was awed and wondrous. 'Oh… You knew my grandmother. But he doesn't look like her.' Her brow furrowed, unable to make the connection.

There wasn't one. 'I don't mean your grandmother who died,' Blake told her, and it was too much. Hell, both women were close to tears, and here he was ready to join them. He knew this was none of his business but he was going to do it anyway. 'I mean your living grandmother. The lady who's just given you your son.'

'My grandmother…' Nell was so confused that she cuddled her son for about five minutes before speaking again. Grace and Blake were content to wait. And watch. After one startled glance, Grace had opened her mouth and shut it again, leaving it to Nell to figure things out. Finally she thought it through and tried again. 'Grace…' Nell's eyes lifted to the elderly woman by the bed. 'You mean Grace is my grandmother?'

'I mean Grace, and I'm right, aren't I, Grace?' Blake demanded. When the old lady couldn't speak he drew her to sit on the bed beside him. Grace was weeping openly now, tears forming rivulets down her weather-worn cheeks. 'Nell, Grace is certainly your grandmother. Your mother loved Grace's son, Michael. Michael died before they could be married, but you're the result.' He smiled and looked down at the wrapped baby in Nell's arms. 'So this little boy is Grace's great-grandson.'

'But…how did…how did you know?' Grace seemed almost as confused as Nell. Almost as shocked.

'I guessed,' Blake told her. 'I knew something had happened to your Mike, and when your husband was dying he told me that Mike had got a girl into trouble. He told me Mike wanted to marry her but the girl's parents wouldn't hear of it. They sent the girl away to stay with her aunt and they wouldn't give Mike her address. She came back, though. When Nell was three months old she returned. Mike would have married her in all honour—even though they were just kids, they were desperately in love, and you both supported him, but he was drowned just before she came back. So Nell's mother returned to nothing—just her parents' awful judgement.'

'Oh, Nell…'

'You wanted to keep the baby, but Nell's parents told you that you'd already destroyed her mother's life with your kindness. They denied the baby was Mike's, and they locked you out.'

'We wanted so much…' It was a thready, broken whisper, but Grace was looking straight at Nell. 'So much… Nell, your mother was such a lovely girl. Just like you. Laughing. Happy. Despite her awful parents. She was like a daughter to us, so much so that we didn't realise until too late that she and Mike… I mean, we'd thought of them as almost brother and sister…'

'And you never told Nell.'

Still Grace was talking to Nell, her voice a shamed whisper. 'We couldn't. We knew there'd be a riot if we told you when you were a child, and then you left. And when you came back I was too ashamed. I should have made a bigger push to keep you. But our loving your mother destroyed her, so we couldn't do…we couldn't do the same to you.'

'You don't destroy someone by loving them.' Blake couldn't help himself. His chest had expanded by about six notches and he felt like having a weep himself. 'Nell, your nether regions are looking great. Your baby's looking great. Your grandmother's looking great. How's that for an instant family? What more do you want?'

And Nell looked up at him in wonder. So much had happened so fast. He'd given her the world. Her baby. Her grandmother. It was wrong to want more. But...

'I want *you*,' she whispered.

And then, as he stood stupidly by her bedside, she managed a smile, albeit a shaky one.

'I love you, Blake Sutherland,' she told him, and her voice was sure and strong, a declaration for the world as well as for herself. 'And I'll love you for ever.' She smiled and smiled, her eyes misty with tears of joy, and she held her baby close. 'You're right. You don't destroy someone by loving them. How can you? You can only give and give, and hope and hope. Like I'm hoping now.'

But, despite her joy, her eyelids were drooping with exhaustion. 'Go and eat your Christmas dinner,' she ordered them both. 'Because my son and I intend to sleep.'

It was a riot of a Christmas dinner. Blake and Grace emerged to cheers all round and tears and hugs, and you would have thought it was Blake who was the father the way this crazy lot of elderly folk reacted.

And he didn't mind at all. He felt... He felt terrific! For some reason he felt like a vast weight had been lifted from his shoulders, a weight he hadn't known he'd been carrying.

'I want *you*.'

The words drifted over and over in his mind—in his heart—and he barely heard what everyone else was saying.

'I want you.'

Then Ethel carried in the pudding—and what a pudding! It was the mother and father of all puddings. They'd flamed it, and two of the old men carried it from the kitchen as a ball of blue-gold fire. He'd be treating them for burns next, he thought. Ralph had Parkinson's disease, for heaven's sake—he normally shook all over—and here he was bearing flame, but he didn't even look like dropping it.

They put it in front of Blake. 'You do the honours, Doc,' they told him. 'Doc McKenzie should be doing it but she's got herself otherwise occupied.'

So he sliced the pudding and loaded his portion with brandy sauce and whipped cream and ice cream—and then a bit more brandy sauce for good measure. And then a bit more, because he felt just fine.

Finally they were gone. The table was cleared, the refrigerator stocked with enough leftovers to last for days, the washing-up had been done and the town's elderly folk, Wendy, Jason, Kyle and Christy made their way shakily home.

Jason was back on his bike but the rest of them were walking, which was just as well, given the amount of brandy sauce consumed. Only Grace remained, settling herself on the porch swing and smiling and smiling, like all her Christmases had come at once. Nell was her family—her grandchild—and her time for claiming her had come, but she was willing and wanting to share.

'She should be stirring,' she told Blake, looking at her watch. 'It's about four hours...'

'She might sleep around the clock.'

But Grace wanted a happy ending here, and she wanted it fast. The writing was on the wall, but if Blake was allowed to leave... He'd haul himself back into his shell, she thought, and it might take Nell months to get him out again. Grace had the greatest confidence in her granddaughter, but if she could help, then she would.

'I'm sure you should check her obs,' Grace said to Blake, and she grinned. 'I started nurse training once, you know, before I decided I was born to be a fisherwoman, and I remember that patients weren't allowed to sleep for more than four hours. They might get the idea that the medical staff weren't necessary—and that would never do, now, would it?'

'No, indeed.' Blake sounded bemused. He'd sounded bemused since he'd delivered the baby, Grace thought, and she was pleased by it. He was nicely off balance and she intended that he stay that way.

'And it'd be even worse if *Nell* found that you were unnecessary.'

'Grace…'

'Go in to her,' Grace told him, and gave him a push bedroom-wards. 'And, for heaven's sake, do what you want to do. It's time you looked out for yourself for a change. Give the girl what she wants most for Christmas—and get yourself what you want most into the bargain.'

'I don't—'

'You do, you know,' she said wisely. 'Now, go.'

He did. Blake paused at the bedroom door and he looked across at the great bed where Nell was sleeping and he felt his heart lurch within his chest. She was curled up like a kitten.

Or· maybe not a kitten, he thought as he watched her. Maybe she was more like a fiercely protective mother cat, her arms curled around her bundle of baby and her face resting against the soft fleece of her baby son's wrapping.

She'd had such a hard time… Her short-cropped curls were clinging damply to her face. Her skin was far too pale, and her freckles stood out far too clearly. She looked about ten!

No! A surge of longing so fierce rose inside him that it threatened to overwhelm him. She wasn't about ten, he thought savagely. She was a grown woman—she was every inch a woman—and she was so desirable…

He felt his hands clenching into fists, and his nails were digging into his palms. Dear God…

Nell opened her eyes and she smiled, and as she did so, knowledge slammed home like a thunderbolt. He'd been so afraid of exposing himself to pain again—of loving as he'd loved Sylvia. But this wasn't like that. It wasn't in the least like that. This wasn't a love that exposed one to pain. It was no bitter-sweet barb, waiting to hurt him and waiting to hurt others with it.

It was a different sort of loving—the right sort. It was infinitely precious, infinitely tender and infinitely wonderful. It was love as he'd never loved in his life before.

'Nell...' And all the joy of the day was in his voice. After all, it was Christmas. The time of giving.

He'd already given, he thought dazedly. His heart was hers. It was just up to Nell to accept.

'You said... You said you wanted me,' he managed in a voice that was so unsteady he could hardly comprehend it was his.

'Did I?' Her eyes were wary.

'Yes.'

'You can never depend on what a woman says in labour.'

'So you don't want me.'

'I never said that.'

Hmm.

'Are you hungry?' he asked, and he smiled at her. And such a smile... It was all Nell could do not to gasp.

'Um...maybe.'

'There's Christmas pudding and brandy sauce.'

'How about if I just have brandy sauce?'

'You can have anything you damned well want.'

'Including you?'

That set him back. He stared and she smiled across at him, but her eyes were suddenly unsure. 'I guess,' he said. 'Nell...'

'You gave me my grandmother,' she said softly. 'And my son.'

'You know where the brandy sauce recipe came from?' he asked, because the tension was unbearable and he had to break it somehow. 'From Grace. We figured out what had happened. Your mother used to sneak over to visit them on Christmas Day and she wrote down the recipe. It's like a final piece of evidence.'

'I don't need evidence to know I'm Grace's granddaughter,' Nell said softly, but her eyes were still on his face and her attention was only half on what she was saying. The rest was devouring the way Blake was looking at her. 'I guess from the time I came back to town, I sensed that I was loved.'

'By Grace.'

'Who else would love me?' But her voice was strained, and he couldn't bear it. Not now. Not when the joy of the world was in his heart.

'I would.'

Silence. 'Blake, you don't have to. Just because I...'

Still he didn't move. 'Just because you what?'

And in the end it was easy. 'Just because I love you,' she whispered, and the whole world held its breath.

And that was enough for him. He was across the room in seconds, stooping and gathering her into the safety of his arms, her tiny son cocooned between them both. 'Nell. My love...'

And then there was no need for words. He was kissing her and kissing her, tenderly at first, wondering, but then more urgently, his kiss a claim and a giving all on its own.

'My Nell...' Finally he broke away—an inch, but no more. Just enough to get the words out.

'You can't...' She gazed up into his eyes, and her whole body trembled.

'What can't I do?'

'You can't love me.'

'Watch me.'

'But I'm your Christmas present.'

'So?'

'I'm only yours for four weeks.' But she was smiling now as he put her away from him and held her at arm's length, and the trembling had ceased. What she read in his face was fine by her.

'When I was two,' he said softly, smiling and smiling, 'I was given a fire engine for Christmas. It was a particularly splendid fire engine.'

'So?' She was smiling so much she could hardly speak. Between them lay her tiny son, just hours old, and Blake looked down at him and his smile encompassed him as well. Answering an unspoken question.

'I'm thirty-four years old,' Blake said softly. 'I've kept my fire engine for thirty-two years and it's still going strong. I might get it out and play with it this very night just to check it's still in working order for one young man who might have a use for it someday.'

'I don't understand,' Nell whispered, but she did and her heart was singing.

'It's simply that I keep my Christmas presents for a very long time,' he told her, and his hands held her and his eyes caressed her face. 'Thirty-two years for my fire engine is the record, but I'm working on it. I reckon fifty's a better bet. What do you say, Nell McKenzie? Will you be my Christmas present for fifty years?'

'Fifty years!'

'What's wrong with fifty years?'

'Just that it's not nearly enough,' she said strongly, and she put her hand around his head and found his mouth with her lips. 'Oh, Blake, my darling, merry Christmas. For now and for ever.'

CHAPTER TWELVE

'NOT again?' Blake groaned as he opened the door. 'Jason Gunner, you did this to us last Christmas.'

'Last Christmas was the bike.' Jason stood on the front porch and grinned, blood dripping from a very impressive cut on his elbow. 'This year we got a trampoline.'

Blake sighed as Nell emerged from the kitchen to see what was happening. One very small boy crawled determinedly behind her—where his mum went, Michael went—and Ernest brought up the rear. 'Nell, look what we have here. It's Jason.'

'Well, I'm not stitching you on the bathroom floor,' Nell said sternly. 'Look what happened when we did it last year.'

'Hey, you're only four months pregnant this time.'

'It's pregnant enough not to take any chances,' Nell told them. 'Take him into the kitchen. I'll move the turkey from the table.'

'I'll move the turkey,' Blake growled, but he was caressing his wife with his eyes. 'You're right. We're taking no chances.'

'If I can lift Michael then I can lift a turkey.' Nell hoisted her one-year-old into her arms and hugged him. 'And you'd best hurry. With a birthday and Christmas on the one day, we have a heap of celebrating to do.'

'Let me take him.' Grace came through from the kitchen, wiping flour from her hands. She took her great-grandson into her arms and held him close, their copper heads blending together as she planted a kiss on his grubby cheek. 'Michael Blake Sutherland, what have you been up to?'

183

'He's had his fire engine in the sand pit,' Blake told her, and Nell smiled fondly at the pair of them.

'You realise nothing Santa can give him this Christmas can ever come up to the standard of your thirty-three-year-old Christmas present. Your fire engine's the best.'

'No,' Blake told her, and his arm came around his wife's waist and hugged hard. 'It's not the best Christmas present. Last year I received a wife and a son. What could be better than that?'

'A trampoline,' Jason said promptly, and glared at them both. 'Aren't you going to fix my elbow? I'm dripping.'

'So you are.' Blake grinned. 'If I didn't know you'd deserved it, I'd be worried. But come along.' He steered the nine-year-old kitchenwards. 'Let's get this turkey off the table and you on it.'

'Hey, I haven't started the brandy sauce yet,' Grace called as both doctors disappeared toward the kitchen. 'You be quick.'

'We'll be the fastest stitchers in the West,' Blake called back. 'If brandy sauce is at stake... How many eggs are we putting in this year?'

'A dozen.'

'It's not nearly enough.' And as he reached the kitchen door he paused, his arm around his wife. Both of them looked back at Grace and they smiled.

'Our family's extended, and then some,' Blake told Michael's great-grandmother. 'I want enough brandy sauce to feed all Sandy Ridge and a few more besides.'

'How many have you invited?' Nell asked, startled.

'Twelve for Christmas dinner, but afterwards...'

'Afterwards?'

'Afterwards everyone who loves us will be here to sing carols. So we need to be ready.'

'Everyone who loves us?' Nell grinned up into her husband's face. 'Oh, for heaven's sake, Blake Sutherland, stop looking smug. You look like the cat that got the canary.'

'I'm not. I'm the Blake that got Nell.'

He stooped, and she succumbed to his kiss for an instant and then pushed him away, laughing. 'Blake, Jason's waiting. Blake, you can't kiss me like that in front of the children. Blake!'

'Well, you will wear those overalls and you know they always do things to my insides. And, besides, that's what you get for hanging mistletoe.'

'There's no mistletoe here.'

'Mistletoe's somewhere and mistletoe's infectious,' Blake said softly, cupping his wife's hands in his palms and stooping towards her once again. 'As a medical condition, I'd say it's extremely infectious and it lasts a very long time. Fifty years or more. As diseases go, it takes the cake.'

'There's no cure?'

'Just brandy sauce to keep it fed,' he said softly. 'And a baby or two. And you. Who could ask for more than that, my love?'

'Hey, remember me,' Jason said indignantly, and Blake grinned and waved his hand at the boy.

'Join the queue,' he told him. 'This doctor's busy. He's dealing with a very urgent Christmas present—in fact, it's so urgent it's left over from last year. And he always treats emergency cases first.'

'Always?' Nell whispered as Blake's lips claimed hers once again.

'Always.'

For ever.

'Nell, shall we give them our recipe?'

'But it's a family secret.'

'They *have* just read our story and it *is* Christmas. The time of sharing.'

'And I guess we've so much to share. Grace and Michael and you and me—and our own special Ernest and a new little life on the way. You've talked me into it, my love. So…Merry Christmas, everyone. From Blake and from Grace and from Ernest and from me. With love.'

BRANDY SAUCE

1 egg, separated
120 g / 4 oz / ³⁄₄ cup sifted icing sugar
125 ml / 4 fl. oz / ¹⁄₂ cup whipped cream
45 ml / 3 tablespoons brandy

Beat egg white until stiff. Gradually add icing sugar, a tablespoon at a time. Fold in whipped cream and beaten egg yolk. Flavour with brandy to taste. Chill.

Multiply the recipe as many times as you like.

Enjoy!

Instant Father Christmas

by

Josie Metcalfe

CHAPTER ONE

'IT CAN'T *still* be snowing!' Livvy groaned over the drifting sound of Christmas carols when she glanced out of the window on her way back to the ward.

'Don't you believe it,' croaked Aled Parry, his voice almost non-existent as he fought the bug going the rounds in the hospital. 'I don't know who put in the special request with the Almighty for a white Christmas, but he's certainly delivering a lot of it! It looks as we're going to be properly snowed in—and on Christmas Eve, too.'

Livvy scolded, 'In fact, you shouldn't be here at all. You've come back to work far too soon, if you feel as bad as you look.'

'Whereas you, Livvy Jones, look as if you're absolutely blooming,' he said with heavy-handed gallantry, the musical drift of his Welsh accent only just discernible through his sore throat.

'If you mean blooming enormous, I'd agree.' She smoothed one hand over the prominent bulge of her pregnancy with a grimace as they made their way along the corridor. 'I look like a beached whale.'

'If the other whales look as sexy as you, I don't know why there hasn't been a whale population explosion.'

'The only explosion around here will be mine if I don't get to a bathroom soon,' she grumbled. 'Now that the head has engaged it feels as if my bladder has been squashed to the capacity of a thimble.'

'Well, I'm just hoping you don't decide to go into labour any time in the next week,' the young registrar retorted in his painfully scratchy voice. 'The whole hospital's in absolute chaos with the flu epidemic. It was bad enough with it being Christmas week, but then this freaky snow coming so early…'

'That's why Duncan French made the decision to call in the mums who were very close to delivery,' Livvy pointed out with a wry thumb at herself. 'Although it isn't far as the crow flies, some of us live in very isolated areas. If we were cut off from the rest of the world by snow and then went into labour we could end up with a disaster.'

'Well, I want it to go on record that I don't approve of you working,' Aled said firmly. 'You stopped work over a month ago and you're supposed to be on maternity leave, waiting for your own delivery, not helping us out here.'

'I *am* on leave. I wouldn't be here if it weren't for the danger of being isolated,' Livvy reminded him, swatting at a bunch of festive balloons as she passed. 'Anyway, apart from looking as if I've swallowed a very large watermelon, I'm feeling fine. I certainly couldn't sit around, twiddling my thumbs, while the department's so busy and short of staff.'

'As long as you leave all the heavy work to the rest of us and keep your feet up as much as possible,' he warned with a shake of a stern finger as he paused beside her outside the toilets. 'Say your prayers that the next two days are utterly peaceful and remember… I'll be keeping an eye on you.'

Livvy heard his raw cough, receding along the corridor as the door swung closed behind him, and winced.

'If you're still on *your* feet,' she muttered as she made a dive for the nearest cubicle. She knew he should really have taken several more days off work before he returned, but the staffing levels were becoming desperate, especially as the epidemic was causing more and more of the vulnerable surrounding population to be admitted for care.

Not that she minded spending her time on the wards—far from it. It was lovely to be surrounded by the hustle and bustle of the wards after the enforced peace and quiet of the last few weeks since she'd stopped work.

She'd been employed on this combined unit for over six months before she went on maternity leave, dividing her time between the maternity section on one floor and the obs and gynae on the next, and it had come to feel more like home than her own home did.

Livvy thought of the tiny cottage she'd left late yesterday afternoon, picturing the tiny artificial tree sitting forlornly beside the fireplace and the meagre pile of presents underneath it—mostly gifts for the baby from her colleagues.

Knowing that a couple of them had half promised to visit over the holiday period, she'd bought a packet of baubles and tinsel, but it had hardly seemed worth the effort of doing any more decorating than that when she would probably be the only one to see it.

The unhappy shadow of loneliness started to encroach and she deliberately pushed it away.

Livvy certainly hadn't intended to become a single mum, but as that had seemed to be the only choice open to her for her baby's sake she would make a darned good job of it. Next year she would have her baby's first

Christmas to celebrate, and with two of them everything would be different.

She couldn't prevent a quick mental image of Daniel's face, flashing across her mind's eye, a wicked twinkle in his eye as he stole a kiss under the mistletoe last year, and her heart clenched.

Most of the time she could force herself to stop thinking about him, but she knew that was mainly because, since she'd moved to Bryn Madoc Memorial, she never saw him any more. If this baby she carried was born with her own blue-grey eyes and blonde hair everything would be all right. If it had inherited Daniel's blue-eyed, dark good looks it would be so much harder to forget the person from whom they'd been inherited.

She tugged her outsized uniform smock over the bulge and when she smoothed her hand over it was rewarded by a hefty kick.

'Hey, you!' she murmured softly as she ran her finger over the outline of something pointed and bony. 'All the books say you should be moving around a lot less by this stage, but I suppose they forgot to tell you that!'

She was still smiling at the energetic contortions going on inside her as she returned to the maternity ward to check up on her charges.

'Anybody had their baby while I was gone?' she asked when she joined the group congregated in the chairs surrounding the television set at one end of the ward, and received a chorus of groans in reply.

'It's obvious you didn't either!' quipped Megan Williams, one of the older women waiting more or less patiently for something to happen. Two of the group had come in yesterday afternoon, apparently in the first stages of labour, but nothing much had happened since they'd arrived.

In more normal circumstances they would be on their way back home by now to wait for further developments, but the weather being what it was…

'Where have all the men gone?' Livvy asked when she realised belatedly that it was just the women left on the ward.

'They decided they wanted to watch the TV action adventure film, starting in a few minutes, so they've gone to find another set in the visitors' waiting room,' Megan explained.

'So, what are you watching here?' Livvy angled herself so that she could focus on the screen, surrounded by a forest of Christmas cards, and saw characters in Regency period dress.

'My Christmas present,' said Alwyn Morgan, the youngest of the group, around whom the rest of them had gathered.

She was the only one actually lying on her bed because of the monitor leads, snaking away from the belt around her to the blinking box of technology on a trolley beside the bed.

Livvy stifled the grin that tried to surface when she saw the big tinsel bow decorating the top of the high-tech pale grey box. That was probably Megan's doing, she thought as she glanced around at the glittery additions that had appeared all around the room since the bubbly woman had arrived this morning. Tinsel and baubles seemed to be dangling from anything that had stood still long enough.

'It's the film of Jane Austen's *Pride and Prejudice*,' she explained with a cheerful grin. 'My husband, Phil, brought the machine from home when he brought my things in, but the men didn't want to watch it with us— probably couldn't stand seeing us drooling over Mr Darcy.'

Livvy joined in the laughter. 'I wasn't certain he was the right actor for the part when I first saw it,' she commented, remembering how she'd always imagined the character as somehow leaner and more aristocratic-looking…more like Daniel…

She dragged her thoughts away from forbidden territory.

'I thought the same, but he grew on me,' said Megan, and for a moment Livvy thought she was talking about Daniel.

'He certainly looks like the sort of man a woman could depend on,' Nerys Owens added with a dreamy expression on her freckled twenty-something face, her eyes riveted to the screen. 'He seems like the sort of man who doesn't fall in love easily, but when he does you know it'll be for ever.'

Livvy joined in the renewed laughter but hers had a hollow ring. She'd once thought the same about Daniel, but had learned the hard way how wrong she could be.

'Well, if you're all quite happy drooling over Mr Darcy, I'll take myself off for a quick trip round the rest of the department. There'll be someone in Sister's office if anyone needs anything before I get back.'

'You're still hoping you get to do another delivery before you have to go through it yourself,' Megan taunted with the experience of a couple of previous deliveries of her own behind her. 'All book-learning, you. About time you took your practical exam!'

There was genuine laughter on her face when Livvy

left the maternity ward to go and check up on the other patients, and her heartache at the memory of Daniel's betrayal had eased a little as it was pushed to the back of her mind by the work in hand.

She waited under a bunch of balloons for the lift to take her to the next floor, silently groaning when she remembered how easily she had once run up and down the stairs. Sometimes it felt as if she was never going to be able to see her feet again...

By coincidence, she'd been at the hospital yesterday for what she had hoped was her last antenatal check-up before her baby was born. The weather had already been turning bad when she'd driven in and when the met. office had predicted worse her obstetrician had decided it would be safer for her and her baby if she abandoned her isolated little cottage and stayed at the hospital.

She'd argued that her due date was still ten days off but Duncan French had been adamant.

'You can always occupy yourself by criticising your erstwhile colleagues,' he'd suggested, and Livvy had brightened.

'If you're going to call in all the mums most likely to deliver you're going to need extra hands,' she'd commented with subtle guile, knowing that her wistfulness would be obvious.

For a moment it had looked as if he'd been going to object to the mere idea of her helping out in her advanced stage of pregnancy, but at the last minute he'd laughed.

'You wouldn't be able to sit still if I chained you to the bed, would you?' he said in resigned tones. 'Well, as long as you're only an extra, unofficial member of staff and don't have sole responsibility for any ward in particular...'

'I could act as a sort of liaison between the two wards, helping out where necessary,' she volunteered eagerly, her crossed fingers hidden in the voluminous folds of her maternity smock.

He sighed heavily.

'At least there'll be people around to keep an eye on you, in spite of the flu cutting a swathe through the staff,' he grumbled.

At this time of year Livvy knew that it was hospital policy to try to send home everyone who was fit to go so that they could spend Christmas with their families. Theoretically, this also had the effect of allowing as many staff as possible to have some time off.

Unfortunately, this year everything had descended into chaos with the empty beds in both the maternity and obs and gynae wards now filled with the full-term patients they'd called in as a precautionary measure.

It wouldn't have been so bad if the snow still falling steadily outside had waited to arrive until the worst of the flu epidemic had passed, but on Christmas Eve? Now they faced full wards in almost every department and barely enough staff, and there was little prospect of either situation changing.

Still, the work Livvy was doing, although necessary in the circumstances, had been uneventful.

So far this had meant making a circuit of each area for a supervisory chat with the nurses, and a more social visit with each of the patients while she updated their charts.

At first she had worried that the staff might have resented her presence, but so far they'd all been delighted to welcome her back.

'Hi, Livvy. No problems here—apart from lack of bed space. Any minute now we're going to have to start making a waiting list,' called Staff Nurse Sue Tarrant when she caught sight of Livvy making her ponderous way along the corridor.

'Waiting list?' Livvy questioned. 'Since when? I thought we were keeping pace with things.'

'We've had a call to say that a young woman, visiting relatives in the area for Christmas, has gone into labour three weeks early. She should be here within the hour to take up the last available bed.'

'Will we have any of her antenatal records?' Livvy worried aloud, focusing on the problems she could do something about rather than the ones she couldn't.

'The hospital is contacting the place she was booked to attend and they'll be doing a computer transfer.'

'Well, keep your fingers crossed that both arrive in time and in the right order,' Livvy said fervently. 'I don't really want to be in the position of delivering someone without any idea of their past history.'

'I'll keep you posted,' Sue promised. 'Shall I let you know as soon as she arrives?'

'Please.' Livvy frowned slightly, mentally sorting through the things she would have to do before the woman arrived. 'In the meantime, I'll make certain the computer knows we haven't got any more space up here and check that the delivery suite is ready.'

'I know she's only three weeks premature but do you think we ought to make certain there's a crib ready in the special care baby unit?' Sue suggested.

'That was going to be my next port of call,' Livvy

confirmed wryly. 'So far we've only got word of mouth telling us she's three weeks early. I'd rather be prepared for every eventuality than have to do everything in a panic if we find she's really three *months* prem.'

'Don't even think it!' exclaimed Sue. 'That's the stuff of nightmares, especially with the numbers we've got in the hospital at the moment. How are they doing downstairs?'

'Nothing was moving when I left there a few minutes ago, apart from a bit of heavy breathing as they settled down to watch Mr Darcy in *Pride and Prejudice*.'

'Mmm! I know what you mean. What that man does for a wet shirt ought to be illegal!' Sue said with a laugh and a wiggle of her eyebrows. 'Unfortunately, all quiet a few minutes ago doesn't mean anything with full-term mums.'

'Especially when they hear about the one coming in,' Livvy pointed out. 'Sometimes the fact that one of them is in labour seems to trigger others off!'

'As long as it doesn't have the same effect on you, or we *will* be stuck! You know that Amy's been feeling a bit rough since she came on duty today?'

Livvy's heart sank with dread.

Amy Aldarini was the most senior and most experienced midwife on duty, and if she went sick at the same time as several of their patients went into strong labour at once...

Livvy drew in a deep breath and rubbed her hands over her face.

'I refuse to think about it,' she said firmly. 'It's just sheer bad luck that the flu jabs we had don't seem to be fully effective against the strain that's hit us. Usually, enough of us can keep going to run things more or less smoothly but, coming on top of the snow...'

'Forget about that for now,' Sue advised. 'I'll give her a gallon or two of orange juice to bump up her vitamins while you check that everything's ready for the lady on her way in.'

'That's always supposing she gets here if the roads are as bad as the reports suggest,' Livvy said. 'She could end up having it in a police car if they get stuck somewhere.'

'Wouldn't be the first one,' Sue said with a farewell wave, resignation in her voice.

Livvy stepped out of the lift and saw the member of staff in question, walking towards her around the corner.

'Amy, Sue told me you weren't feeling too well. How are you now?' she asked, noting the other woman's pale face with trepidation. Her pallor hardly went with the red tinsel bow pinned to the front of her uniform.

'Awful, if you want the truth,' her colleague admitted honestly. 'The only good thing about it is that I'm not going down with flu so I won't be infecting anyone and you won't be losing me halfway through my shift.'

'Are you sure? Everyone's been dropping like flies.'

'I can be absolutely certain because I've just had the result of a pregnancy test,' she said a little smugly after a quick look around to see who might be listening.

'Congratulations!' Livvy said with an answering grin and a quick squeeze of her slender arm. 'I know you and Antonio were hoping to start a family fairly soon.'

'At our age we haven't got as much time to waste as other newly-weds,' she said candidly. 'In fact, once I passed thirty-four I had finally resigned myself to remaining single. Now, within the space of three months,

I've met the man of my dreams, married him and we're already starting a family!'

Happiness absolutely radiated out of her willowy frame and Livvy had to squash down a quick surge of envy. Once she'd thought that she had everything, too, and within just a few short weeks everything had fallen apart...

'As long as you're certain that everything's OK?' Livvy prompted when she'd dragged her thoughts ruthlessly back to the present.

'As OK as they can be when I turn green at the slightest thing,' Amy complained. 'I was hardly a week pregnant when I started feeling queasy, and if it lasts right up until the usual three months I'll have faded to a shadow.'

'Don't make me jealous,' Livvy joked as she glanced pointedly down at her non-existent waistline. 'But seriously, make certain you take the time to raid the biscuits. The tin is usually half full of the plain ones that everyone else leaves till last, and it's amazing how much nibbling on them can help.'

'I've been too worried about being sick to try it, but if you recommend it I'll give it a go. I've been telling expectant mums to do it for years but I didn't know whether it was one of those old wives' tales. Anyway, I was feeling too green to dare.'

'It's one of the ones that seems to work, at least it did for me. In the meantime, have you heard about the prem. mum on her way in?'

'When? Whose is she—one of mine?' Amy asked, referring to the new system Bryn Madoc Memorial had begun of assigning each pregnant woman to a particular midwife.

'No. She's a complete stranger on a visit to her husband's relatives in the area for Christmas. We're waiting for her antenatal notes to be transferred from her own hospital.'

'Let's hope they arrive in time to do some good, then,' Amy said with her fingers firmly crossed. 'The delivery suite's all ready to go. Do you want me to check up on the special care baby unit, just in case? It was cleaned from top to bottom first thing this morning after little Stephen Fisher was transferred to the special cardiac unit in Cardiff, but I could just cast an eye over it to make certain we're ready for every eventuality.'

'Please. That would be great,' Livvy said with a grateful smile. 'Everything's in such a muddle, with both the obs and gynae *and* maternity wards full of pregnant mums. With any luck, the snow will be short-lived and the highways authorities will be able to clear the roads so everyone can go home in a day or so. I'll be happier when everything's back in order again.'

'I'm just glad we were able to send the last lot of mothers and babies to spend Christmas at home or there'd really be standing room only. Let's hope the last thirty-six hours without a delivery isn't the lull before the storm,' Amy said, crossing her fingers again. 'It will probably be a very jolly Christmassy atmosphere today and tomorrow with the number we've packed in, but if they all decided to go into labour at the same time...'

'Bite your tongue!' Livvy exclaimed. 'Don't even think it!' She gave a theatrical shudder then looked at her watch. 'I'm going to have to dash to the toilet again before I make my way back down to Pat. In spite of what I said, I've got a funny feeling about a couple of the mums down there.'

'Just tell them to keep their legs crossed!' Amy joked frivolously.

'That won't work for them any more than it would for me,' Livvy pointed out as she set off rapidly towards the ladies' toilets, cursing that second cup of tea.

She smiled wryly. Over the last few months she had come to know, almost to the last pace, exactly how far she was from the nearest toilet at any given moment. She'd known dogs to take less notice of trees than she did of the hospital's public conveniences...

'Sister!' called Megan Williams, surreptitiously beckoning her over almost as soon as Livvy appeared in the doorway of the maternity ward.

'Problems?' Livvy asked quietly, picking up an air of tension about the usually upbeat woman. 'Are you feeling all right?'

'It's not me, it's Nerys,' the older woman murmured under the cover of the video, still playing on the television. 'She hasn't said anything but I've noticed that she's glancing at the clock about every ten minutes and her breathing alters. She's due for another one in the next couple of minutes if I'm right.'

Livvy surreptitiously watched the younger woman under the guise of watching the film and saw what Megan meant.

'Well spotted. Have you ever thought of becoming a detective?' she joked. 'She probably doesn't want to say anything until she's certain it isn't another false alarm,' she continued calmly. 'Shall I leave you to keep an eye on her for me? I don't want to put any stress on her if she's coping all right.'

'There's plenty of time before the rest of the group needs to know what's happening,' Megan agreed, apparently delighted to be asked to help but concerned about her young charge. 'Poor kid. I can remember how scared I was with *my* first. My aunties had fed me on a solid nine-month diet of childbirth horror-stories before I got to that stage.'

'At least she's got someone like you to give her confidence,' Livvy said, watching the freckled face grow paler as Nerys closed her eyes and concentrated on her breathing. She carefully looked away before the young woman's eyes opened again. 'Just call me if you notice anything you think I should know.'

'You'll be doing your round of the charts in the near future, anyway,' Megan said. 'I'll tip you the wink if she looks like she needs you and she's too shy to say anything before then.'

Livvy gave her shoulder a silent squeeze and left the group to their appreciation of Mr Darcy's aristocratic charms.

She made her way towards Sister's office, suddenly conscious that all the charging around she'd been doing seemed to have given her an ache low down in her back. What she needed was a few minutes with her feet up and with the hospital central heating roaring away to combat the bitter cold outside, she was desperately in need of another cup of tea. She was too thirsty at the moment to care about the resulting trips to the bathroom.

'Is the kettle on?' she asked as she joined Pat Lersh out of hearing of the musical accompaniment to the video being played at the other end of the ward.

'Are you gasping?' Pat said with a grin as she reached across to flick the switch. 'The air in here is very dry when the heating's turned up so high.'

Livvy glanced up at the clock, having to peer at it

through the dangling strands of tinsel. 'Is that really the time? Where has the morning gone? Don't tell our nice young Dr Parry, but it's been several hours since I last put my feet up.'

'Aled? Is he here?' Pat said in a studiously nonchalant voice totally at odds with the quick blush staining her pale skin.

'Not yet,' Livvy said, stifling a grin of amusement at the staff nurse's poorly hidden attraction. The two of them had been warily circling each other for a couple of months, now, with neither of them apparently willing to make the first move. 'But you can bet he'll appear as soon as I do something he disapproves of. He's just waiting for a chance to make me take things easy.'

She squirmed awkwardly in her seat to settle the lumpy cushion in just the right place in the small of her back, hoping it would relieve the niggling ache she'd developed.

'You must admit, it isn't very often that the nursing staff are more pregnant than the patients,' Pat pointed out with a laugh as she handed Livvy a steaming mug and held the open biscuit tin towards her.

Livvy sipped appreciatively, before cradling the mug gingerly on top of her bulge and slipping her shoes off to wriggle her toes.

'Oh, that's good,' she sighed as she tipped her head back. 'Just to sit back and relax peacefully with a cup of tea I haven't had to make for myself.'

She'd barely finished speaking when the phone rang and she groaned when her young colleague silently deferred to her to take the call.

'You answer it, Pat. You're officially on duty.

Besides, I don't want to heave myself out of the chair yet.'

'Maternity. Staff Nurse Lersh,' Pat responded smartly, the smile on her face evident in the tone of her voice.

As Livvy watched it was replaced by a frown of concern.

'She's arrived? Yes. We've been expecting her to—Oh. Another one? But we haven't got any more—' The person on the other end was obviously interrupting her every time she spoke. 'Have you checked with Obs and Gynae? I thought they had a couple of spare places.'

Without needing to ask, Livvy knew that someone was in search of a bed and, having recently spoken to Amy, knew what the answer would be.

The full capacity of each ward under her overall supervision was actually greater than the number of patients currently in them, but there were only so many qualified staff fit to take care of the necessary nursing duties. If they were forced to take in more than the safe limit it could be a recipe for disaster, especially if any more of them went into labour during the next few hours. They already had one lady on her way in, and now Nerys was having contractions.

Pat finished the call and put the phone down with a grimace, but before she could tell Livvy the bad news there was the sound of rapid footsteps, crossing the ward towards them. There was a tap on the door and it was hesitantly pushed open halfway.

'Is Sister there?' puffed Caroline Woolford, one of the ladies who had come in as a false alarm earlier that morning.

She caught sight of Livvy. 'I'm sorry to disturb you, Sister, but Megan said her waters just broke.'

'Tell her I'm on my way,' Livvy said, and threw an exasperated smile towards the nervous first-timer as she started to struggle out of the squashy upholstery. 'At least, I will be if this chair ever lets me escape!'

'I think we spoke too soon,' Pat said as she offered both hands to pull Livvy to her feet. 'Everything's suddenly getting far too lively. That call was to tell us that there are two patients on their way up to us.'

'Two?' Livvy was dismayed but her mind quickly started computing the extra arrangements they would have to make, from checking linens to ordering extra food.

'One of them we were already expecting—the lady visiting family in the area. She's going upstairs. There aren't any hospital notes yet but, apparently, she *is* only three weeks early and hasn't progressed very far so we might be lucky.'

'And the other one?' Livvy prompted.

'She's down in Casualty. Part of a wedding party involved in a road accident. She's about two and a half months pregnant and worried about a miscarriage. Aled's just seen her and told them to send her up. He wants her to have a scan and be kept under observation for a while.'

'Poor woman,' Livvy murmured as one hand smoothed protectively over her own baby. Her situation might not be ideal but she would be devastated if anything were to happen to deprive her of her child.

'Would you like to ring them upstairs to see if they can take both of them?' Pat suggested. 'If Nerys and Megan are both in labour we're going to be pushed if we've got a miscarriage on our hands as well. That's without the mental trauma to the patient when she's threatened with losing her own baby while surrounded by full-term mums.'

'I think you're right. It'll be harder for us to cope with a third mother—the holiday visitor—in labour, but at least upstairs none of them are already in labour.'

Livvy reached for the phone but it rang under her hand.

'Maternity. Sister Jones,' she said automatically. Pat waved to catch her attention and pointed to the ward to let her know where she was going. Livvy nodded and turned to concentrate on her call as Pat left the room.

'Hello, Livvy. Sue Tarrant here on Obs and Gynae,' said the voice on the other end. 'Any chance you could take a couple of bodies down there or can you spare one of your nurses for a couple of hours? Our holiday visitor has just arrived up here and her contractions have just speeded up to four minutes and it looks like two more of our ladies are in labour.'

'Oh, glory be! Sorry, Sue. I was just about to phone to ask you the same thing. I've just had a threatened miscarriage arrive, one of mine is having regular contractions and another has just had her waters burst. It looks as though we're both going to have to muddle through. I'll check to see if we can borrow some willing hands from elsewhere but I think it's pretty much the same situation right through the hospital.'

Sue groaned.

'All we can do now is keep our fingers crossed that they all have relatively short straightforward labours and we'll be all right. Have you been in touch with Duncan?'

'That's the next job on my list,' Livvy said, hoping the consultant was still in the hospital. He lived fairly close by and had been known to dive off home for a couple of hours to eat a home-cooked meal or catch up on sleep. She dialled and crossed the fingers of her free hand that he'd decided to brave a hospital meal this time. It looked as if they were going to need him today.

No one seemed to know where Duncan French had gone so Livvy was forced to try to impress on the frazzled voice on the other end of the phone the urgency of getting in contact with him.

She'd just got hold of Sue and passed on the news when she heard the ward doors lock back to announce the arrival of the new patient. 'Got to go, Sue. The patient's arrived and I need to get her settled down and calm as soon as possible. Keep me posted.'

Livvy tugged the hem of her smock down over her bulge as she walked across the room towards the door, her eyes quickly scanning the figure in the wheelchair.

What she could see of her was swathed in one of Casualty's blankets, the folds clutched around her by a slender hand, wearing a stunning set of rings.

The rest of her was half-hidden behind the man who was bending over her solicitously, his short, dark hair a stark contrast to her slightly bedraggled honey-gold curls.

'Hello, I'm Sister Jones,' she said, and the man straightened to his full height beside the wheelchair and turned to face her as the two of them looked in her direction. 'I'm sorry, but we don't yet know your... name...'

Her voice trailed away in disbelief, the words trapped in her throat as she recognized the man who had been pushing the chair.

Pain clenched around her heart like a tight fist as, for the first time in nearly seven months, she met her husband's clear blue eyes.

CHAPTER TWO

'DANIEL,' she mouthed silently, her eyes widening in disbelief as she helplessly catalogued the lean elegance of his dark good looks.

If she wasn't mistaken, he was wearing the same classic dark suit he'd worn to their wedding, the fit across his unexpectedly broad shoulders just as perfect as ever.

But it was his deep blue eyes that drew her attention back, and when their gazes meshed again she completely forgot how to breathe as her heart leapt into her throat.

He had always had that effect on her, from the very first time they'd met on her first day on the maternity ward at St Augustine's...but there was no time to think about that now, not when his unsmiling face was filled with a mixture of indecipherable expressions.

'Livvy?' he questioned hoarsely, his eyes going from her face to the blatant evidence of her advanced pregnancy and back again in open disbelief.

For just a moment she found herself regretting the fact that she hadn't informed him she was expecting their child but then his companion spoke and the regret was wiped out by a familiar bitterness.

'Daniel? Shouldn't I be having this test?' prompted the woman seated in the wheelchair between them, her hand still visibly trembling from the aftermath of the accident as it came up to grasp Daniel's. 'How quickly will they be able to tell if the baby's all right?'

When she saw the familiar way the other woman drew

Daniel's attention Livvy suddenly realised where she'd seen her before.

'Alice Webster,' she murmured as the events of that dreadful day seven months ago assailed her. *This* was the woman who'd been responsible for the destruction of her marriage. *This* was the woman who had stolen Daniel away…who had given birth to his…

'Jones now,' she corrected Livvy, looking up at Daniel with a smile full of happiness in spite of her bedraggled state. 'It's Alice *Jones* as of ten o'clock this morning.' She held up her other hand to display the gleaming ring on her finger.

The emotional blow was so fierce that Livvy swayed and had to take one staggering step back before she realised that she'd done it. It was Daniel's quickly outstretched hand that jerked her back into control before he could touch her.

'Well, Mrs Jones, if you'd like to come this way.'

Livvy managed to choke the words out, but wasn't capable of saying any more so she turned on her heel as quickly as her bulk would allow and led the way towards the other side of the ward and the waiting bed.

She was able to distract herself for a moment by busily checking that the bed was ready and drawing the curtains around to provide a little privacy.

Unfortunately, that didn't take nearly long enough for her to regain her equilibrium but far too long when she measured the endless aeons she seemed to be spending in close proximity with Daniel and his new wife.

It was raw torture to watch the caring way he helped the shaken woman out of the wheelchair and onto the bed. She could remember only too clearly what it had felt like to be cradled in the powerful warmth of his arms and had revelled in the way he'd seemed to delight in taking care of her.

When she heard him asking the *new* Mrs Jones if she needed any help to take her clothes off Livvy knew she couldn't stand watching them together any more, especially when he made a light-hearted joke about their clothing being full of confetti and rice.

'I'll leave you to get settled while I fetch a file for Mrs Jones,' she said, all too aware that her voice sounded strained. Before either of them could comment on her abrupt departure she had whisked the curtain closed behind her and was hurrying as fast as she could manage towards the office.

'How *could* he?' she muttered fiercely under her breath as she paced awkwardly between the desk and the filing cabinet. 'How could he have come *here*?'

The words seemed to linger in the close confines of the room and she was tempted to giggle hysterically when she heard how ridiculous they sounded.

As if Daniel had *chosen* to have an accident on his wedding day just to upset her! As if he had thought about her at all in the last seven months! He certainly hadn't bothered to let her know that the divorce had been finalised, leaving him free to marry the mother of his son. And now, if all went well in spite of the accident, there was to be another child...

She wrapped her arms as far as they would reach around her own precious baby. The painful sob trapped in her chest was fighting to escape but she couldn't afford to let it happen—if she started crying now she probably wouldn't stop for days.

She managed to fight off the press of tears but she

couldn't stop the memories crowding in on her...the precious memories of the first time she'd met Daniel.

She had been part way through her nursing training at St Augustine's and it had been her first day on Maternity, with Mr den Haag due to arrive on his rounds at any moment.

There had been some sort of mix-up in a message to Housekeeping and they had run short of bed linen. As the newest member of staff, Sister had sent her at the run to collect an armful of freshly laundered sheets. It wouldn't have done for the ward to be untidy when the consultant arrived.

Not that Mr den Haag had been any sort of an ogre—quite the contrary. Sister had been at great pains to tell her that he was such a genuinely caring man that everyone automatically wanted to do their best for him.

The lift had been full of patients on trolleys so she'd been forced to gallop the long way up the stairs. She had just been hurrying round a corner in the corridor with her arms full of freshly laundered sheets when she'd ploughed straight into an immovable object.

'Careful!' The slightly husky tenor voice carried the lilt of laughter as his lean hands steadied her.

She looked up into eyes the same clear blue as an early morning summer sky and was lost.

'I...I'm sorry,' she stammered, feeling the heat of embarrassment spread up her throat and into her cheeks.

'I'm not,' he murmured softly, making no effort to release her even though she was no longer in any danger of falling or dropping her load.

He wasn't holding her arms tightly but she was strangely aware of each of his fingers as they wrapped warmly around her. Her pulse began to race as an extra surge of adrenaline flooded into her system but she was unable to drag her eyes away from him.

'Staff Nurse Pickering?' called a voice from somewhere a million miles away and the spell surrounding her was shattered.

'Y-yes, Sister,' she stammered, wrenching her gaze away. She tightened her grasp around the pile of linens and took a couple of shaky steps back so that he was finally forced to release his hold on her.

To her annoyance she still seemed to be able to feel the warmth of his hold on her arms several hours later when it was her turn to go to the canteen for her lunch break.

Confused by her juvenile preoccupation and annoyed that she'd found her eyes scanning every new person she met in case it was *him*, she made herself join a table full of nurses from other departments.

She had just made the conscious decision that if she was going to be able to keep her mind occupied she had to make an effort to join in with the usual round of gossip and chatter when she caught sight of him at a table on the other side of the room.

Once again she found herself unable to look away from him, but this time he was unaware of either her presence or her avid scrutiny, and she was far enough away to dare to take her time about looking at him.

Her pulse skipped when she saw that he was every bit as good looking as she remembered, his dark hair neat in spite of its tendency to curl and his face alert and intelligent as he spoke to his companion.

As she watched he gestured with one hand to emphasise a point, and she felt a sharp spiral of awareness when she remembered the gentle strength of those long fingers wrapped around her arms.

He laughed and she saw his teeth gleam whitely against the healthy tan of his face, his cheek-bones lean and angular under the harsh artificial lighting.

There'd been no time in their brief encounter for her to even glance at his identity tag. He could have been anyone from a student to a phlebotomist to a consultant.

Now that she saw him sitting with a colleague she could see a stethoscope stuffed in the overloaded pocket of his white coat and could read the word 'Obstetrics' on a small reference book tucked in behind it.

Remembering the direction from which he'd been coming, everything she'd heard on the ward this morning fell into place.

'Is that Dr Jones?' she interrupted to ask her closest neighbour with a shaky attempt at a nonchalant nod in his direction.

'Where?' her neighbour demanded, and openly stared around the rapidly filling room before she followed Livvy's gaze and spotted him at the table on the other side. 'Yes. That's him,' she confirmed with a feline purr of approval in her voice. 'Mr den Haag's new registrar. Totally gorgeous but totally unavailable.'

'What do you mean, unavailable? Is he married?' Livvy asked as her heart made a stupid dive towards the floor. For some reason she was unable to make the attempt at sounding casual even though there was no logical reason that the answer should matter to her one way or the other.

Even so, she was overcome by the irrational disappointment that she hadn't met him sooner—before he'd met his wife—because there was no way she could even contemplate a relationship with someone in his position. The idea of breaking up another's marriage was anathema to her, especially after the nightmare of her own father's infidelity and her parents' subsequent acrimonious divorce.

'Being married doesn't seem to stop *some* of the doctors tomcatting around,' her neighbour commented darkly, almost as if she had somehow picked up on Livvy's thoughts, 'but, no, he isn't married and isn't likely to be.'

'Why not? Is he homosexual?' Her eyes feasted on his lean good looks and mourned their loss to the gene pool if they were never to be passed on to his children.

'Good God! Gay?' her neighbour scoffed in disbelief. 'Does he look gay to you?'

Livvy watched him for a moment as he chatted and laughed with his male companion but there was nothing obvious in his body language to give her any clues as to his orientation.

'I've no idea,' Livvy said weakly as a measure of relief trickled through her. 'I haven't met enough to know.'

'Well, take it from me, he's far from it! But he's such a wary beast that I doubt anyone will ever entice *him* into the trap.'

The loud disbelief in her voice must have reached the other side of the room because as Livvy watched he glanced idly in the direction of their table. Suddenly his attention sharpened and she knew that he had recognised her.

It was an uncanny replay of the events in the corridor. As soon as his eyes met hers she was powerless to look

away in spite of the fact there was the whole width of
the busy room between them.

Livvy was oblivious to the movement of the others
around her as they grumbled their way to their feet and
set off back to their wards. All she could see was the
pair of clear blue eyes, gazing at her with disturbing
intensity while he sat clasping his forgotten cup between
his hands.

His companion must have said something to break his
concentration because for a few seconds he glanced
away from her.

She was still sitting mesmerised by him when his eyes
found her again, and her breathing stopped entirely when
he stood and began to cross the room towards her.

'Daniel,' he said succinctly as he sat down in the seat
opposite her, his eyes taking inventory of every feature
before they returned to mesh with hers again.

'Livvy,' she whispered in reply, knowing somehow
that was all the introduction necessary between them.

She was almost afraid of the intensity of the emotions
overwhelming her. It couldn't be possible that he was
touched by the same madness—not someone as wary as
he was reputed to be—but he was equally silent and
seemed equally strangely content just to be close.

'I'm sorry.'

As if someone had snapped their fingers, he suddenly
switched his gaze from her face towards the latest group
to come into the room and she saw the skin darken over
his lean cheeks. 'It was very rude of me to stare at you
like that.'

With a lift of her heart Livvy realised that he *was*
feeling just as disconcerted by events as she was and she
wanted to chuckle with delight. She'd never felt this

sense of total connection with anyone in her life and knew that only total honesty would do.

'In which case, you'll have to accept *my* apologies, because I was staring, too,' she said quietly, and was helpless to stop her lips curving into a happy smile.

When he turned his blue gaze back to her she could see that her candour had surprised him, but then she saw understanding dawn and his answering smile begin in his eyes.

'Sister?'

A worried young voice dragged her away from memories of happier times and drew her eyes to the doorway to see the uncertain expression on the face of the young nurse standing there.

'I'm sorry to disturb you, Sister. I've helped Mrs Williams into a dry nightdress and made her comfortable but I think you need to come and have a look at her. And she said to tell you about Mrs Owens—that her contractions are only four minutes apart and she's beginning to get a bit anxious and—' She paused to gulp in a much-needed breath and Livvy held one hand up to stop the flow of words.

'In other words, all hell is breaking loose out there?' she asked with new purpose in her voice.

'Something like that, Sister,' the younger woman agreed with a nervous grin.

'Well, then, we'd better see if we can do something about sorting them all out.'

She glanced down at the empty case notes in her hand and held them out, glancing at the young woman's name badge as she handed them over.

'I'm sorry, Cherry, I don't recognise you but, then,

I've been away for a month. Have you worked on Maternity for long?' Livvy asked, wondering just how much help the rather nervous-looking youngster was going to be. If she was likely to fall apart at the slightest thing she wasn't going to last long on *this* ward, especially the way things were...

'This is my first week,' Cherry replied, her head coming up and her shoulders squaring in a very satisfactory way. 'I'm sorry if I seemed a bit of a wimp a minute or two ago but when I got to the office door just then, for one awful moment I thought you were in labour, too.'

There was still a trace of panic in her voice and Livvy couldn't help laughing.

'Don't get me wrong,' Cherry added in a hurry. 'I love the work up here and I've been coping well so far, but there are so few staff and so many patients and I'm so far off qualifying as a midwife that I know there's no way I'm ready to cope with a delivery on my own yet—especially a midwife's baby!'

Livvy laughed at her fervent addition.

'Well, Cherry, if we all keep our fingers crossed it won't come to that—but I can't promise! In the meantime, there's a new patient just getting settled into the bed with the curtains drawn. She's about three months pregnant and she's been in a car accident. Could you get her preliminary details before the technician comes up to do the ultrasound? She's a bit shaky so if you could take her a couple of cups of tea.'

'A couple?' Cherry queried in surprise.

'One for the shock and the other one to make sure her bladder's nice and full for a successful scan,' Livvy explained with a wicked smile, remembering the discomfort of it when she'd had her own scan.

She stood perfectly still for several seconds after the young nurse had set off on her task and massaged her aching back while she gathered her thoughts.

Yes, it had been a shock to be confronted by Daniel like that, but she couldn't afford to allow it to scramble her head. She might not be on duty *officially*, but over the next few hours she could end up with several women relying on her skill to help their precious babies out into the world. From now on she was going to concentrate on the job in hand. There would be plenty of time to mourn the loss of her love when he and his new wife were gone and *she* was back home in her own little cottage. This was no time to fall apart.

'Phone for Duncan French,' she muttered to herself as she leant forward to dial, not daring to sit down in case she couldn't get up again. 'I hope to goodness he's on his way...if the switchboard even remembered to page him. If Amy's busy upstairs then I'm going to need all the help I can get down here,' she continued under her breath as she waited for the call to connect.

A couple of minutes later she put the phone back down and, in spite of the danger of not wanting to stand up again, sank weakly onto the corner of the desk.

'I don't believe it!' she whispered, her voice rising to a squeak. 'I do *not* believe it!'

'What?' demanded a horribly familiar voice at the door, and she swivelled awkwardly to see Daniel enter the office.

It was like their first meeting all over again as her eyes were captured by the intensity of his and every rational thought disappeared under an avalanche of breathless attraction.

'What don't you believe?' he repeated, his dark brows

drawn into a frown, and just that suddenly the spell was broken.

'Not that it's any of your business, but I've just been told that the consultant had a fall on the ice in the car park this morning and he's got a Colles' fracture,' she retorted waspishly, needing to take her frustrations out on somebody. 'At this very moment he's in the plaster room, being immobilised up to his elbow.'

'Not Duncan French?'

'Yes, Duncan French,' she snapped, horribly conscious that she sounded rude and shrewish. 'He's the only consultant who matters at the moment.'

'Why did you need him? Are you having problems?' he demanded, his eyes flicking briefly to her own obvious pregnancy.

'Problems?' Livvy laughed shortly but it was a sound without humour as she raised one hand and began counting off on her fingers.

'*One*, it's snowing outside and we've got two wards full of full-term or ''at risk'' pregnant women who have been called into the hospital in case they go into labour while they're cut off by snow.

'*Two*, it's Christmas Eve and we're down to the bare minimum of staff because of a flu epidemic.

'*Three*, there are two women upstairs in Obs and Gynae in the early stages of labour with a midwife who is in the throes of morning sickness.

'*Four*, there's one woman down here on Maternity hooked up to a foetal monitor and two in labour, one with her waters already broken.

'*Five*, a few minutes ago we had another woman arrive in advanced labour. She's a visitor to the area and until the antenatal notes from her own hospital get here we'll be working blind. She's had to go upstairs because there isn't anywhere else for her to go.

'And then there's your…' She paused, unable to force the word 'wife' past her lips. How could she think of the other woman as Daniel's wife when, until just a few moments ago, she had believed that *she* was still married to him.

She started again.

'*Six*, there's the victim of the car crash, waiting for the technician to arrive to do an ultrasound scan to check that the baby's all right.'

'What about the registrar?' he demanded, and she could see from the familiar intent expression on his face that he was already assimilating everything she'd told him and was cataloguing the priorities and implications. 'We saw him in Casualty not long ago when he was called down to look at Alice. Won't he be coming straight back up here?'

'He probably did, unless Casualty had another patient for him to see.'

'Well, then…?' He paused expectantly.

'He's having to spread himself very thinly at the moment, and they won't all fit in the delivery suite at once,' Livvy explained with dwindling patience. 'Apart from that, he's already been on duty for twelve hours and the poor beggar's only just getting over his own bout of flu. He shouldn't really be back on duty yet.'

He gave a nod as if everything was now clear and his chin lifted in the way that told her that, having absorbed all the data, he had come to a decision.

'In that case,' he announced briskly, 'it looks as if it was your good luck that our accident happened in your catchment area because you just acquired another pair of hands.'

'We...what?' He couldn't be saying what it sounded like. Was Daniel suggesting that he stepped into Duncan French's shoes during the emergency?

She should be delighted that they were acquiring the services of such a well-qualified doctor in their hour of need, but all she was aware of was the way her heart sank.

Surely, after all her efforts to remove herself from the heartbreak of his presence, she wasn't going to end up working beside him again, the way they'd worked together at St Augustine's? That might be just too much to bear in her present fragile emotional state.

'I read a piece of research that suggested that women's brains shrank during pregnancy,' Daniel commented pointedly, breaking into her thoughts. 'I discounted the theory at first, but you could make me reconsider. You weren't this slow on the uptake before. What do you *think* I meant? You're short of senior staff in the department and, apparently, in the middle of a minor population explosion. It should be obvious that I'm offering to pitch in and help.'

Just the thought of spending the next few hours working with him was enough to short-circuit her brain so she concentrated on his inflammatory comment.

'I've always thought that women's brains shrink *before* they get pregnant or they'd never put themselves through it,' she retorted sharply, taking the brake off her tongue as she glared up at him.

Her pithy reply made one corner of his mouth lift in a familiar lopsided grin before his eyes fell to the evidence of her own pregnancy and all humour fled.

For just a second she thought she recognised pain in his eyes as he visibly gauged how far along her condition had progressed, then they darkened. Again, a complex mixture of expressions followed each other across his face and again she thought she recognised pain amid anger, frustration, suspicion and disappointment.

She knew he wanted to ask questions and knew he was going to demand answers but she also knew she wasn't ready to give them to him—not while her emotions were still so much in turmoil.

Knowing it was cowardly to run away from the situation, she turned towards the door before he could frame his first words.

'I'll send someone to find you a white coat,' she began, hoping to sound brisk and efficient but aware that she more than likely sounded as if she was gabbling in her hurry to escape. 'Then, if you would like to join me out in the ward, I'll be checking up on the patients.'

She reached the open doorway and was taking her first shaky breath of relief when his voice reached her.

'Olivia.'

It was just her name, but spoken just that way in his unmistakably husky voice it was enough to stop her in her tracks.

She reached out one hand to grasp the wooden frame as her knees turned to silly putty, not daring to do any more than turn her head to look over her shoulder at him.

'Sooner or later, we need to talk,' he said softly into the silent room behind her.

Livvy nodded just once, knowing he was right.

He needed to know that she wasn't going to try to make trouble between him and his new wife, especially while the distressed woman's pregnancy might be at risk.

She wasn't happy about the way her own marriage to Daniel had ended, but after what she'd seen in her own parents' marriage she'd always believed that a man couldn't be 'stolen' unless he wanted to be.

Daniel's marriage today made it obvious what his choice had been.

But while her pride insisted that she should concentrate on walking away from him calmly and firmly she couldn't quite subdue the little voice inside that was trying to warn her that his words could have equally been a simple statement or a veiled threat.

Thank goodness she was going to be too busy to think for the foreseeable future, Livvy thought wryly as she worked her way systematically round the ward again.

She'd never understood why one woman going into labour seemed to trigger others into following suit, but the phenomenon was certainly in full force at the moment, both here and upstairs.

'Well, Megan, how's it going?' Livvy asked as she perched one hip on the edge of the bed. The tinsel wound around the frame of the headboard shimmered with the movement, sending coloured flashes across the wall to join the rest of the festive decoration, but her patient was quite oblivious.

She'd had a feeling that things had started progressing when the older woman had given up marching up and down the ward between contractions and had opted to make herself comfortable instead.

'It's just about reached the moment where I'm ready to castrate my husband if he even *thinks* of coming near me again,' she muttered through gritted teeth, her eyes

squeezed tightly closed as she tried to block her surroundings out and concentrate.

Livvy waited for the contraction to ease, one hand
gently resting on the bowling-ball hardness of the
woman's belly while she tracked its progress.

'I must be mad!' Megan panted when the pain's grip
eased slightly. 'What on earth could ever make this agony worthwhile?'

'Oh, I don't know,' Livvy mused aloud, taking the
rhetorical question literally. 'Probably that very first second you get to hold your new baby and count all the
fingers and toes.'

Megan chuckled weakly and ran shaky fingers through
her limp hair to take it off her sweaty face.

'You're right, dammit, but just at this moment I wish
you weren't, especially when I know I've still got a lot
of this to go through. It would be nice to put all the
blame on someone else— then I could suggest they went
through this for me, too!'

'Do you need anything for the pain?' Livvy offered,
not wanting to see anyone suffer unnecessarily.

'It's not too bad at the moment,' Meagan answered
stoically, accepting a sip of water with a grateful smile.
'I'd rather wait until a bit later when I'll really need
something.'

Livvy sat with her for a few minutes longer, glad of
the chance to rest while she unobtrusively timed the in-
terval between Megan's contractions. Her own backache
seemed to have gone away for the moment so she was
being careful to pace herself in the hope that it wouldn't
return.

'It might not take quite as long as you think,' she
suggested, glancing at her watch again when a groan

announced the speedy onset of the next one. 'You're progressing quite quickly now.'

Megan pulled a face in reply, obviously not wanting to interrupt her quietly controlled breathing as she rode out the pain.

Livvy heard the phone ring at the other end of the ward and glanced across, glad to see Pat Lersh hurry to answer it so she could keep Megan company a little longer.

A beckoning hand told her that her rest break was over.

'I'm needed at the other end for a minute,' she said as she forced herself to straighten again and tugged on the hem of her smock. Her back twinged briefly, the pain spreading in a broad band across the top of her hips, but it was soon gone. 'Don't forget, if you need anything press your call button or just give a shout.'

Megan gave her a silent thumbs-up sign and closed her eyes to concentrate on her breathing again.

'It's Amy,' Pat said as she passed the phone over.

'Ringing to gloat that you've delivered your first one already?' Livvy demanded as soon as she was connected.

'Hardly!' said Amy. 'Just the opposite, in fact. It's that visitor. I think we've got a big problem here. From what she says, she's carrying twins but it feels like a couple of octopuses with neither head engaged. Has the technician finished doing the ultrasound on your accident victim yet? I need to see what's happening in there.'

'I don't know,' Livvy admitted, but didn't tell Amy that she'd actually been avoiding looking towards the newest patient in the ward. There was no way she wanted to see any more of Daniel and Alice Jones together than she had to.

'Can you find out and let me know?' Amy asked, her voice sounding a little frazzled. 'Or, better yet, send the equipment along as soon as you can—before yours is done, if possible.'

Livvy felt a little guilty that she hadn't followed up on the arrival of the ultrasound technician, knowing that it was her own personal problems that had prompted the neglect.

'Your patient definitely takes priority over mine,' she said briskly. 'I'll check to see where the equipment's got to and send it straight along. If not, I'll phone you with an update.'

She cradled the phone and began to run her finger down the list of numbers to find the right one. Absent-mindedly she began to massage the niggling ache that had appeared in her back again, hoping that it would disappear again as quickly as it had earlier.

There was far too much to do for her to be able to afford to waste any time on her own health, she thought as she found the number she was looking for and began to tap it out. The patients definitely had to come first and, as with triage in the casualty department, the most urgent cases needed attention first, no matter who they were or who they had married...

'What equipment is that?' demanded a husky tenor voice right behind her, startling her so much she nearly dropped the phone.

Livvy whirled as fast as her awkward shape permitted to face its owner, her pulse suddenly racing.

CHAPTER THREE

'You made me jump!' Livvy exclaimed breathlessly, before turning back to complete her call. She felt marginally less vulnerable in Daniel's presence if she wasn't actually facing him.

'Which equipment were you talking about?' he repeated. 'The ultrasound?'

'Yes. I need to find out where it's— Ah! Dewi? This is Sister Jones up on Maternity. When do you expect to reach us?'

She listened to the slightly rambling reply, finding it hard to keep her mind on what she was hearing when every nerve seemed to be concentrating on the fact that Daniel was right behind her.

The technician was full of apologies for not arriving sooner, and Livvy could clearly picture the painfully slender young woman as soon as she heard her distinctive Indonesian accent.

It was a relief, in a way, to have to focus on the fractured English rather than let her attention wander to the fact that her nose was telling her that Daniel was still using the same soap and shampoo he had when they were married.

It would be disastrous if she were to allow herself to think about how familiar it felt to have him standing so close that she was surrounded by the same indefinable mixture of warmth, soap and man that would forever be Daniel.

'So, you're free to come up straight away?' Livvy questioned at last, dragging her attention back to the matter in hand.

'Good,' muttered a masculine voice behind her. 'About time…'

Livvy turned to glare at him and found he was even closer than she'd thought. She drew in a hasty breath to combat the strange light-headed feeling that attacked her and continued what she was saying.

'Don't bother coming here,' she directed briskly. 'Go straight upstairs to—'

'What? No!' he exclaimed sharply, one hand coming out in a silent demand for the receiver.

Undeterred, Livvy half turned away from him so that the phone was out of his reach and continued.

'Sister Aldarini is waiting for you to arrive so if you could get there as soon as possible.'

She paused just long enough for the technician to confirm her instructions then hung up.

'How dare you?' Daniel said, his deadly quiet voice more potent than any shout. 'There's a woman out there in that ward who's still shocked by a car crash and is worried sick that she's in danger of losing her baby. It wouldn't have taken long for the technician to set her mind at rest—or was that why you chose to do it?'

For a moment Livvy was speechless that he could believe her capable of such contemptible pettiness.

God knew she had little enough reason to like the woman, but for Daniel to accuse her of deliberately delaying a test that could set Alice's mind at rest only showed how little he respected her.

She swallowed the bile that rose in the back of her throat and concentrated on the facts.

'No, it wouldn't take very long,' Livvy agreed with a hard-won appearance of control, 'but, either way, even you would have to admit that having the ultrasound half an hour earlier or later won't make any difference to the outcome.'

She clenched her fists, feeling her short nails score the soft skin of her palms as she fixed him with a furious gaze and saw him frown darkly, his blue eyes flashing like steel. He would have interrupted if she hadn't continued heatedly.

'Unfortunately, while *she* just needs to have a little peace of mind, there's a woman upstairs, carrying twins who's already in labour with neither baby engaged, and as her antenatal clinic notes *still* haven't arrived from her own hospital I assumed her case would be *slightly* more urgent.'

There was an awful silence when she'd finished speaking, and as the open sarcasm in her voice echoed and re-echoed inside her head Livvy suddenly wondered if she had gone too far.

It was one thing to defend her decision with carefully reasoned facts, but it was another thing entirely to berate a doctor with such venom.

'You're absolutely right,' Daniel said quietly. 'I had no right to criticise your actions without asking for an explanation.'

Instantly, Livvy was speechless again and very close to tears.

This was the Daniel she had fallen in love with—an honest man incapable of duplicity, a man who wasn't afraid to admit to a mistake or make an apology if he found himself in the wrong.

What had happened to change him? They had been

so happy until the older woman had come into their lives. What had been the attraction? What hold had Alice Webster had over him that he would break his solemn promises to Livvy?

'Amy will send it straight down as soon as they've finished scanning the mum upstairs,' she finally managed through the tears thickening her throat, using the pain of her nails still embedded in her palms to maintain some semblance of calm. 'In the meantime, I think it might be a good idea if you went along to the delivery room in case the poor woman needs surgical intervention.'

He nodded soberly then one eyebrow lifted in his own familiar way.

'Don't tell me that this is one of your "feelings",' he teased quietly. 'When we worked together at St Augustine's I came to dread the times you started a sentence with "I think it might be a good idea if you...". It usually meant that there was a complication about to happen.'

Livvy pulled a face.

'I can't help it,' she protested. 'When Amy said it felt like two octopuses I had a sudden mental image of how difficult it was going to be to untangle the two of them between contractions and still end up with two healthy babies.'

'As usual, I will bow to your intuition,' he said with a quickly sketched salute. 'If she does need help it's better to do it before all three of them are in distress.'

'Good luck,' she murmured as he turned towards the door, a sudden flood of memories of all the difficult cases he'd successfully rescued briefly softening her attitude towards the new Mrs Jones. 'Shall I explain to...to

Alice why there's been a delay?' With the best will in the world, she couldn't force herself to call the woman his wife.

'That would help to set her mind at rest,' he accepted. 'We still haven't heard how my father's doing in surgery so it would be one less pressure.'

'Your father? In surgery?' Livvy parroted, aghast. 'What's the matter with him?'

She'd really liked her former father-in-law and had admired the way he had steadfastly loved and cared for his severely disabled wife.

The last time she'd seen him had been several months after the poor woman's death when he'd still been struggling with very mixed emotions. She'd known that he'd been consumed with grief that he'd lost her and that he'd felt guilty for his relief that her suffering was finally over, but she'd always believed that there'd been something more, eating away at his soul.

She'd always thought that he would have loved to have had a large brood of children instead of a single son, and had hoped her marriage to Daniel would provide him with several grandchildren to spoil to his heart's content.

Unfortunately, it was just hours after she found out that the first of those children might be on the way that she had also found out about Alice Webster. Livvy had confronted him, but when Daniel had refused to tell her what had been going on between himself and the older woman their marriage had fallen apart.

'My father was injured in the accident,' Daniel was saying, dragging her attention back to the present day. 'The car hit a patch of black ice hidden under the snow and spun out of control. His side of the car took the impact when it slammed broadside into a lamppost. Orthopaedics are trying to put his hip and thigh back together but I've no idea yet how successful they're going to be.'

Livvy cringed. She wanted to express her sadness that the kindly man had been injured, particularly when it had happened on what should have been such a special day, but before she could speak the phone rang.

'Sister Jones,' Livvy said promptly, and frowned when she heard Amy's voice on the other end.

'It's a hopeless malpresentation,' she heard her colleague say rapidly, barely taking the time to introduce herself.

'The two of them look almost as if they're lying across each other, belly-to-belly, with their arms and legs wrapped around each other. The one closest to the vagina is lying transverse so the other one can't present for delivery.

'There's no way we're going to be able to deliver them normally, I can't find Aled anywhere and there's no room in Theatre even though I have managed to find an anaesthetist still on his feet.'

From the sound of it, this was the sort of case that could go wrong in a hurry—the sort of situation that could cause nightmares—but Livvy had no doubt that Daniel could deal with it.

She covered the mouthpiece just long enough to relay the information to Daniel and, as she had anticipated, he swiftly agreed with her feeling that surgical intervention was probably the only viable option.

'Amy?' she said, returning to the call. 'Get everything prepped and ready because help will be with you in about two minutes.'

'Two minutes?' squeaked Amy in disbelief. 'In that case, Superman must have just flown in because I know Duncan French isn't fit for duty and they haven't been able to get hold of anyone else.'

'Not quite Superman, but near enough,' Livvy joked with a grin. 'Now get on with it because when he gets there to look at the ultrasound he won't want to hang about.'

She put the phone down and turned to Daniel.

'She's got the anaesthetist standing by and the technician's there with the ultrasound. Is there anything else I can tell you?'

'Well, I'm disappointed to hear that you don't believe I'm Superman,' he joked, then continued more seriously, 'But I knew that your intuition about an impending problem was probably right on target so I'm not surprised. Just for the sake of argument, tell me what you think.'

'It sounds to me as if you're going to have to do a Caesarean in the delivery room,' Livvy said succinctly, subduing the leap of pleasure his words of praise had caused. 'With the ultrasound showing one twin lying transverse so neither of them can be delivered normally, you haven't really got any option, and there isn't time to wait to transfer them up to Theatre even if there was one free.'

'As I said, that intuition of yours...' He allowed the sentence to die away with a wry smile. 'You'd better point me in the right direction so I can scrub up.'

'Better than that, I'll show you,' Livvy said, leading the way out of the office. 'I'm probably going to be involved in another delivery by the time you're free to come back and I need the ladies' room before I can contemplate that. Anyway,' she added honestly, 'I'd like a quick look at that ultrasound myself. If I remember rightly, the presentation Amy described only happens in about five per cent of deliveries involving twins.'

By the time Livvy had made a detour to tell the new Mrs Jones the bare bones of why her ultrasound would be a little delayed, and had made herself comfortable, Daniel had scrubbed up and was gowned and gloved and ready to start.

'Let's see what you've got,' he prompted, and Amy recited the latest observations of each of her three patients while Dewi ran the ultrasound again.

There was silence for several moments while he concentrated fiercely on the shadowy outlines, obviously making certain that he had the babies' internal geography right before he started.

'Please, Doctor, are my babies all right?' whispered the patient when he turned towards her again, her pale, terrified face gleaming with perspiration under the bright lights as she hung onto her husband's hand.

'Mrs Simpson, from what I can see, your two look absolutely perfect. The only problem is that you've already taught them such good manners that each one is saying, "After you," "No, after you," and neither wants to be first out into the world.'

The young woman couldn't help a giggle of relief at his nonsense and she glanced up at her husband.

'We both wanted to see them being born, but now it looks as if we're going to miss it.'

'I'm afraid there isn't time to give you an epidural to allow you to be awake for the delivery, not without risking the babies—'

'No,' her husband interrupted fiercely. 'We're not going to do anything to risk harming the babies. God willing, we'll have them for the rest of their lives, so the first few minutes aren't that important.'

'What he means,' his wife butted in before Daniel could comment, 'is that he's terrified that he'll pass out if he sees any of the gory stuff.'

Livvy saw the look of male understanding Daniel exchanged with the bashful father-to-be.

'I know what you mean,' Daniel said with a grimace. 'This childbirth stuff isn't nearly as interesting for us men as starting the babies off.'

'Well, we can both enjoy that bit,' Mr Simpson agreed. He got an embarrassed dig in his ribs from his wife but it didn't stop him from continuing. 'I just don't like the idea that Jill's going to go through such pain and I can't do anything for her, and as for cutting her up—'

'I've got a suggestion,' Daniel said, butting in before he could go into any more graphic description. 'I know your wife isn't going to be able to be awake for the babies to be born, but if we rig up a screen so you can't see the grisly bits you could sit up by her head. Then we can pass you each of the babies as soon as they're born so you can tell her all about them when she wakes up.'

Mr Simpson looked doubtful but his wife had a newly hopeful expression in spite of the fact that another painful contraction was starting. Livvy could see that she was willing her husband to agree to Daniel's plan.

'You're sure I wouldn't see anything gory if I stay here with her?' the young man demanded, obviously needing reassurance.

'Scout's honour,' Daniel promised, raising one gloved hand, and the deal was struck.

Livvy would have loved to have stayed to watch Daniel operate the way she had when they'd worked together at St Augustine's. She remembered only too clearly how exciting it had been to work with someone of his expertise, but there were other patients back on the ward she had to supervise.

With a cheerful wave and good wishes she left the room, glancing back briefly through the window to see Daniel's face settle into familiar lines of concentration as he signalled the anaesthetist to begin.

'Sister. Thank God you're back,' Pat Lersh said fervently almost before the doors had swung closed behind her. 'I just rang through to find you and they told me you were on your way. Mrs Williams's baby suddenly seems to be in a hurry to arrive.'

Livvy changed direction and made straight for Megan's bed.

'Staff Nurse says you're trying to catch us on the hop,' she said cheerfully as she reached her bedside.'

'I don't know about that, but things certainly seem to have speeded up in the last ten minutes,' she agreed. 'I'd be delighted, except no one seems to know where to find my husband. He's always been at work when I've gone into labour with the other babies and he's missed every one of them coming. This time, because he's already at the hospital, I thought he'd be able to see one of them born—especially as it might be his last chance.'

The last pointed words were forced out through gritted teeth as the next contraction took vicious hold of her.

Livvy spoke calmingly to her until the pain began to fade, telling her that they would transfer her to the labour suite as soon as she caught her breath, but barely had that contraction eased than it was replaced almost immediately by the next one. Things had certainly been moving quickly since she'd gone up to the delivery room to have a look at Mrs Simpson's ultrasound.

'I want to push,' Megan gasped desperately. 'Is it time yet or will I hurt the baby?'

'Don't push until I've had a chance to check you inside,' Livvy ordered as she hurriedly pulled the curtains around to give some semblance of privacy. It didn't look as if there was going to be time to move Megan out of the ward before this little one arrived in the world. 'I must make certain that you're fully dilated or you could damage yourself inside so pant like a dog during your contraction.'

Livvy turned to ask Pat Lersh to fetch a sterile obstetric tray but the staff nurse had obviously anticipated the request and was already standing there with one in her hands.

'Well done,' Livvy murmured as she broke the seals on the package and carefully unfolded it so that she only touched the outside. 'Could you pour the povidone-iodine scrub over my hands…?'

With a speed born of long practice, Livvy thoroughly cleaned her hands. They all chuckled when she donned the sterile apron, which had no chance of reaching around her waist, but it was more important that she pulled on the gloves supplied in the tray.

'If you can raise your hips for a moment,' she prompted, and slid a sterile towel underneath, without touching either her patient or the bedclothes.

She draped a second towel flat across the bed under

Megan's thighs and draped sterile cloths over her abdomen and each thigh.

'Now we just need to find Mr Williams or he's going to miss the show.'

'Again,' Megan Williams panted. 'Could someone check the smokers' lounge to see if he's there? He gave up a couple of years ago when our last one was born, but if the other dads are smoking...' She ran out of breath, wincing as Livvy began her examination.

'All right, Megan,' Livvy said as she straightened, hoping that the twinges in her own back would ease before she had to do anything more involved than examine her patient. 'Everything's fine in there so next time you get a contraction you can start pushing.'

'You mean now?' the older woman joked wryly on a quick gasp of breath before she closed her eyes tightly and bore down.

Matters seemed to move very quickly after that and the baby's head was already crowning when there was the sound of hurrying footsteps approaching the curtain.

'Can I come in?' said a male voice in a harsh whisper, and Livvy suddenly realised how quiet the ward was. Someone must have turned the video off because she couldn't hear the soundtrack of *Pride and Prejudice* playing any more. There was just the sound of Christmas carols, drifting in from somewhere along the corridor.

'Of course you can come in, you daft beggar,' muttered his wife. 'Better late than never.'

'Am I too late, then?' he demanded, disappointment clear in his voice as he fought his way through the curtains, while trying to shove beefy arms into a gown and tie on a mask at the same time.

'Just in time,' Livvy reassured him, and directed him

to the other side of the bed. 'If you sit beside Megan you can hold her hand.'

He sidled around the end of the bed and Livvy saw him glance tentatively towards his wife and do a double-take.

'Hell, love, I can see the head!' he exclaimed, then blushed furiously. 'Sorry for swearing, Sister,' he muttered, and slunk into the chair.

'Don't worry about it,' she said with a grin. 'The baby isn't far enough out yet to hear you.'

Megan gave a snort of laughter but it was cut off by the start of the next contraction.

'Earn your keep,' she muttered as she groped for her husband's hand and squeezed it tightly.

Within minutes the head was delivered and after a few seconds' pause—while Livvy checked that the cord wasn't around the baby's neck—it took just one more sustained push for the shoulders to appear and the slippery bundle slid out into Livvy's hands, already objecting noisily.

'It's another boy!' exclaimed Mr Williams in awe as he caught his first glimpse of the squirming infant.

Livvy chuckled heartily.

'I think you're boasting again,' she teased as she moved aside the thick umbilical cord draped between the baby's legs and revealed the distinct lack of male appendages. 'You've got a daughter.'

'At last!' Megan breathed, a beatific smile flooding her face as Livvy lay the baby across her stomach to check the baby over and take care of the cord. 'I'll have someone to take *my* side in family arguments for a change.'

Livvy knew that Meagan had three boys already and

that the most important consideration was that the baby should arrive healthy, but she also knew how much Megan had been hoping that this one would be the little girl she'd yearned for.

After making sure that the baby's airways were clear and totting up an excellent Apgar score, it was a real delight to wrap her in a towel and give the proud new parents a few minutes to savour their delight.

Megan automatically offered the infant her breast and the picture of contentment was complete.

'Shall I take Dad to get his new daughter cleaned and dressed while you take care of Mum?' Pat offered behind Livvy when she saw her finish recording the time of birth and the five-minute Apgar score.

'If Megan can bear to let go of her,' she teased, her eyes pricking as she saw the utter delight in the way Megan was examining the miniature perfection of each tiny finger and toe.

It was a very proud father who gingerly scooped his baby daughter up, then settled her comfortably into the crook of his arm before he made his way towards the opening in the curtain.

When he emerged into the ward there was a spontaneous round of applause and various shouts of congratulations from the rest of the patients and their visitors.

'Anyone would think *he'd* done all the hard work,' Megan grumbled as renewed contractions heralded the expulsion of the placenta, but Livvy could see from the smile on her face that she was far too overjoyed for it to be anything more than a token complaint.

'It's certainly the most public delivery I've done so far,' Livvy said, as she massaged the flaccid abdomen gently over the fundus to help the expulsion of the afterbirth. 'I wasn't aware of it at the time, but the rest of the ward must have been able to hear every word in here.'

'My God!' Megan whispered, looking stricken, her concentration completely diverted from what Livvy was doing. 'Did I use a lot of bad language?'

'Not a bit of it, in spite of the fact you didn't want any pain relief,' Livvy assured her with a grin as she finished tidying everything away and made her patient comfortable. She'd been delighted to confirm that Megan hadn't torn at all. 'The whole thing happened so quickly and, anyway, you didn't have any breath to spare for swearing.'

'You're not joking. This was the quickest of any of the babies. If you could guarantee that they'd all be this easy, I wouldn't mind having a few more.'

'You're talking about having more of them already?' demanded her husband, as he carried their new daughter through the curtains, this time wrapped in a soft pink blanket. 'Just over an hour ago you were threatening to dock my tail if I came anywhere near you. That's why I ran away to hide!'

'I'd only want another one if I could be sure it would be another girl,' Megan pointed out, her arms already reaching for her precious daughter. 'They seem to be much easier to give birth to than the boys were and it would help to even up the teams at home.'

Her work finished for the time being, Livvy offered the two of them the option of leaving the curtains closed.

'I'd rather show her off,' Megan said with a happy grin so Livvy drew the curtains back and carried the debris away, leaving the two of them to field all the comments from the surrounding beds as they admired their new treasure.

More than one of the mums-in-waiting voiced their jealousy that Megan's waiting was over, but a quick glance to one side as she walked the length of the ward reminded Livvy that not everyone was thinking similarly.

In spite of her personal animosity towards the woman, she couldn't help feeling a twinge of sympathy for the new Mrs Jones as she lay waiting to find out whether the fragile life inside her was going to survive.

'It must be so hard for her, listening to all this, while her own baby's at risk of dying,' she murmured to Pat Lersh as she finished writing up her notes on the delivery. 'If the whole department wasn't in such uproar she wouldn't have to be in here with mums and babies.'

'It will be even worse if she does lose it and still has to stay in here,' Pat said quietly. 'We'll just have to cross our fingers for her.'

The phone warbled and Livvy went to reach out for it, but her arm just wasn't long enough from that side of the desk with her prominent bulge in the way.

'If you went on a diet I'm sure it wouldn't take you long to get rid of that fat you've accumulated around your waist,' Pat teased as she lifted the receiver and passed it across.

'Cheek!' Livvy complained before she put it to her ear.

'Two boys,' announced Daniel without preamble. The husky tenor sounded like rich brown velvet and she could sense his smile of delight even over the phone. 'Mother and babies doing well.'

'And Father?' Livvy prompted, remembering how nervous the poor man had been.

'Coped beautifully,' Daniel confirmed. 'We've even chased a camera up and managed to get a photo of him, holding the two of them. He hasn't stopped smiling yet.'

'Well, we haven't been idle in your absence,' Livvy pointed out. 'Mrs Williams is now the proud possessor of a little daughter.'

'Wonderful. Tell her I'll be in to see her as soon as I can. I want to wait with Mrs Simpson until she comes out of the anaesthetic so I can set her mind at rest about the operation.'

'How long before you want to move her back to a ward—only I've been wondering whether it might be better to have all the post-delivery mums in the same place?' Livvy asked, mentally planning how many beds they would have to move.

'She can stay here for a bit of peace and quiet until the room's needed for the next delivery, but unless there are any particular problems, having the two wards mixed, I think it would be better to leave well enough alone. The mums in labour have collected their own cheering squads around them and it seems to be creating a good atmosphere.'

Livvy had to agree with him. They could always review the situation later if necessary. Everything seemed to be happening in a topsy-turvy fashion today.

Ideally, when Megan had been ready to deliver, she should have been moved into the specially equipped room so that everything would have been ready to hand if an emergency had developed, but the second stage of her labour had happened so fast she'd been lucky that there had been time to draw the curtains around.

Livvy was hardly surprised when she looked at the watch pinned to the front of her uniform and realised that she'd missed out on mid-morning teas and coffees. The morning had been so full of activity that it seemed as if hours had passed.

'I don't think I've ever seen an atmosphere like it,' Pat commented, as she grabbed a couple of biscuits and settled herself on the corner of the desk with the large mug of coffee she'd made to keep Livvy company. 'The whole ward is buzzing with adrenaline.'

'Well, you must admit, it has been an exciting morning,' said Cherry, her eyes shining. 'I never realised that things could be so dramatic. I thought it took hours and hours of waiting around for the contractions to finish doing their job, and then ages more while the mum slowly pushed the baby into the world.'

'Well, you've learnt an important lesson, then,' Daniel said as he walked into the room, the sound of his voice shocking Livvy's pulse into double speed. 'With pregnant mums, you always have to expect the unexpected.'

'A couple of the men looked a bit green around the gills when they realised they were going to be eavesdropping on the birth,' Pat commented with a grin.

Livvy was following the conversation with half of her attention while her eyes followed Daniel as he poured himself a drink and turned to lean easily against the edge of the desk. As she watched, he casually crossed his long legs at the ankles and wrapped his free arm around his lean waist to provide a prop for the other elbow.

'It's one thing to see a sanitised video of edited highlights of a birth at the antenatal classes with a midwife explaining everything,' he commented with a grin.

'Their imaginations must have been doing overtime this morning when they only had the soundtrack running.'

Livvy joined in the laughter. She'd been too busy, concentrating on the job in hand, at the time to think about the other people surrounding them and what they would be hearing.

'You should have seen the grin on Mr Williams's face when everybody applauded,' Cherry added. 'He looked proud enough to burst.'

'By the look of things, we're going to be seeing quite a bit of that look around today, with the number of women already in labour upstairs and down here,' Daniel said as he ran his fingers through his hair and absently ruffled the dark strands.

Livvy recognised the unconscious gesture and only just managed to hide a bittersweet smile behind her coffee-mug.

Soon after their first meeting she'd noticed that whenever he'd taken off one of those dreadful 'paper knickers' hats after an operation he'd always had to lift his hair off his head where it had been flattened.

So many little mannerisms she remembered from their time together, so many little things that tugged at her heartstrings.

Most of all, she'd always loved his open delight when he'd been able to hand a healthy new baby to its mother, and had daydreamed about the time when it would be his own child he was holding—*their* child.

Livvy rested her hand on top of the pronounced bulge of her advanced pregnancy and tried to subdue the sudden surge of sadness.

The last couple of hours had brought back some of her pleasure in working with the man who used to be her husband. It was hard to make herself remember that he had a new wife now and she was still waiting for the ultrasound to confirm the safety of her second pregnancy. That was absolute confirmation that the best of her dreams would never come true.

She'd had no idea what had been ahead of her when he'd asked her to marry him. She'd believed that he had meant the promises they'd made to each other, that he'd been an honest man who would have kept his word.

Where had her famous intuition been then?

CHAPTER FOUR

'WILL you marry me?'

Livvy's heart leapt when she heard the husky words. She had never dreamt that Daniel was going to ask her, not when they'd known each other for such a short time.

'Oh, Daniel,' she breathed, as she looked at him across the secluded restaurant table, knowing that her feelings for him must be displayed on her face. 'Are you sure?'

'I was sure the first time I met you,' he murmured, his voice strangely fervent as he leaned closer so that only she could hear his words. He caught her hand and held it between his and she felt surrounded by his lean strength and infused with his confidence until she was certain she was invincible and dared to reveal her own feelings.

'I felt as if I'd found the other half of myself,' she admitted. 'Being with you felt so right that it seemed as if we must have known each other for years.'

And it *still* felt like that weeks later, with the certainty that he was the only man for her growing with every day.

From that first collision in the corridor to the meeting in the staff dining room and every time they'd been to- gether since, it was as if there was a special connection between them. For the first time in her life she knew she had met someone she could trust with her heart and soul.

'Yes, Daniel, I'd be delighted to marry you,' she said, and happiness burst into full bloom inside her.

'When?' he demanded, and the hint of relief she detected in his voice told her that until she'd answered he hadn't been absolutely certain that she'd accept.

'When do you think would be best? In the summer?' she suggested, suddenly imagining Daniel standing tall beside her as she wore a traditional flowing white dress. In her mind, the two of them were surrounded by sunshine and flowers and happy laughter.

'In the summer?' he echoed hollowly, his straight brows creasing into a troubled frown. 'That's months away. Why so long? Arc you having second thoughts? Or are you afraid you're going to have them?'

'No. Not at all. I just thought... Well, it would give us time to get everything organised and make decisions about where we're going to live and...' When she realised that her explanation hadn't changed his expression she ground to a halt and turned the tables. 'When did you have in mind?'

'Saturday,' he said, without a second's hesitation.

'*Saturday?* But...but, it's Tuesday today, and...' She was so stunned her brain refused to form the words to tell him how impossible his suggestion was.

Daniel didn't have that problem as he hurried into details. 'You could go out tomorrow to find a dress while I book a room at one of the local hotels for a celebration meal with our friends. Then we'll have two days free to pack your things up and move them to my flat ready for Saturday. What else needs doing?'

'Well...' Livvy was completely at a loss and her thoughts were whirling around in her head far too fast for her to catch any of them and examine them closely.

Why was he trying to arrange everything so quickly?

This was going to be one of the most important days of their lives. Didn't he want to take the time to get everything perfect?

They'd never even mentioned the topic of marriage before so she had no idea about his feelings on the subject. Perhaps he didn't feel the same way as she did about the solemnity of the step they were contemplating. Perhaps, in this divorce-prone society, he saw it as a fairly temporary situation and not worth a great deal of fuss...

'Olivia?' The way his husky voice sounded when he said her name always sent a shiver up her spine, and she tried to shove all her misgivings to the back of her mind as she met his intent gaze.

'Why do you want to get married so soon?' she challenged softly, mindful that they were surrounded by other diners in the softly lit room.

'Because I love you and don't want to wait any longer than we have to,' he said, his blunt words sending a thrill right to her core. She would defy any woman to hear those fervent words, without melting.

It wasn't just the words that affected her, though, but the utter conviction in his eyes and on his face.

'You mean, you don't want to wait because you want to become more...intimate? Is it because we haven't... haven't slept together?' she asked, remembering snippets of articles she'd read in magazines from time to time.

The two of them hadn't made love yet, but their kisses and caresses had been growing ever more passionate so that sometimes it had been hard to draw back from the brink.

Was it true that men couldn't survive very long without the physical release of sex? To her knowledge, gleaned from the highly efficient hospital grapevine, in all the time he had been working at St Augustine's Daniel had avoided any relationship that might have ended up in bed.

Silently she berated her own ignorance of such matters.

What did she know about the needs of a virile man such as Daniel? Perhaps if she'd bothered to accept more invitations during her teens and early twenties she wouldn't be left, wandering about in the dark like this.

'We haven't slept together, but we haven't slept apart either,' he said, one corner of his mouth curving up wryly. 'At least *I* haven't slept. Not since I met you. I just lie there, thinking about you. About how glad I am that we met.'

He paused and by the time he began again she was surprised to see that a flush of embarrassment had darkened his cheeks.

'I'd never believed that I would ever find anyone who would mean as much to me as my career, but you mean more.'

At his stark admission Livvy's heart leapt again, but before she could comment on his intrinsically private revelations he was speaking again, his words hurried, as if he was trying to distract her from his unaccustomed candour.

'Not that I expect to get any more sleep once we *are* married,' he pointed out with a wicked gleam in his eyes. 'In fact, *sleeping* together will probably be the last thing we do, at least until we collapse with exhaustion.'

The distraction was complete.

'Daniel!' she exclaimed, her own cheeks burning as her imagination suddenly filled with erotic images of the two of them entwined on a bed, naked…

She shook her head to try to dispel such ideas until a more appropriate moment, glad that he couldn't read her mind.

She heard him draw in a sharp breath as she shook her head, then he dragged his eyes away to gaze fiercely at the table decoration of fragrant freesias for several long moments before he met her eyes again.

'I'm sorry, Livvy, that was very selfish of me,' he said quietly, his voice low and slightly uneven as he sought her gaze again. 'Would it spoil it for you if you couldn't have a big traditional wedding? I'd never really thought about it before, but I suppose that's what little girls grow up expecting.'

Livvy caught a fleeting glimpse of uncertainty in his eyes but it was swiftly hidden. She'd seen that expression several times in the last few weeks and had thought how incongruous it seemed in such a confident, self-reliant man.

It wasn't until she suddenly remembered one late-night conversation over tepid cups of coffee in the nurses' home that she began to understand the reason he wanted their marriage to be sooner rather than later.

They'd had an unusual case on the ward that day. An older woman, close to the upper end of her child-bearing years, had given birth to a baby she'd conceived for her daughter.

It had been an entirely do-it-yourself surrogacy arranged between the woman, her daughter and son-in-law, and Livvy's first reaction had been one of distaste.

It wasn't until she had spent some time in the delivery

room with the struggling older woman that she had heard about the daughter's earlier successful but very aggressive treatment for cancer which had left her unable to have any children of her own.

The joyous scene when the unusual family group had welcomed their baby into the world had affected Livvy deeply, especially when she learned that 'Grandad', whom the little boy was to be named for, had fought a losing battle with cancer, dying just weeks before the longed-for child was due.

Livvy had shed a few tears when she'd told Daniel about the family's background, marvelling that they'd found some way to create happiness out of so much tragedy.

Daniel had held her quietly, one arm around her shoulders as they'd monopolised one end of the settee in the dimly lit nurses' home lounge.

He'd been silent for a long time after she'd finished speaking, but she'd grown accustomed to that, happy to be with him without feeling the need to fill every second with meaningless chatter.

'I'll probably lose my mother first,' he murmured softly, and surprise robbed her of speech.

In spite of all the things they'd shared with each other in the days and weeks since they'd met, he'd said so little about his family that she'd begun to think he was all alone in the world.

'She's been confined to bed for years now, and just gets steadily worse,' he continued, threading his fingers between hers and bringing them up to his face to rest against his lips as if he wanted her help to stop any more painful words escaping.

'And your father?' she prompted softly, needing to hear the worst before she dared to offer sympathy.

'Inside, he's been dying by inches for years because he can't do anything for her. He feels so guilty because he's a doctor and the one person he most wants to be able to help is the one he can't...'

'How long has she been ill?'

'I can hardly remember a time when she was well. I can remember far enough back that my father was helping her to walk to the bathroom and then, eventually, having to carry her. Now he has to do everything—feed her, wash her, brush her hair.'

'But...doesn't he have any help, and...and what about his career?'

'He has some help, but he's cut his work down to part time so that he can be with her as much as possible. He says that the biggest tragedy is the fact that until fairly recently her mind stayed as sharp as ever but was trapped in a body that was bent on self-destruction.'

'He loves her,' Livvy said quietly, not having to make it a question.

Daniel gazed at her intently and she could see from his expression that she understood many of the things he hadn't voiced.

'Yes, he loves her,' Daniel said, pain making his voice even huskier than usual. 'And he tells her that he regrets the fact that they waited several years before they married when they could have spent that time together, and it's killing him that he knows he's going to lose her...'

Suddenly she understood the real reason behind his apparent headlong rush to get married. His own parents had enjoyed so few years of happy marriage before his mother's health had begun to deteriorate. As a consequence, he seemed to have developed a keener appreciation than most of how fleeting happiness could be.

Apparently, he'd coped with the idea of heartbreaking loss by keeping any possible entanglements at arm's length. Now, having decided to take the plunge, he didn't want to make the same mistake as his parents.

Livvy drew a swift breath for courage and offered her heart to him with her smile.

'Will you come shopping with me for my dress?' she asked softly. 'I'm off duty tomorrow afternoon.'

He gazed at her in silence for several seconds, his eyes probing hers deeply as if he needed to read the meaning behind her words in her soul.

Then he gave her an answering smile, the expression like the sun coming out after a long cold winter.

'Just tell me where and when,' he agreed, his hands capturing hers again in a fervent squeeze. 'If I have to get Mr den Haag to cover my shift for me in person I'll be there.'

So many of their colleagues were marrying at that time that it seemed as if they were always being invited to registry offices, churches or receptions.

'Our wedding was the best,' he growled huskily in her ear part way through the long weekend they'd managed to scrounge for a honeymoon.

They were submerged up to their necks in a gently bubbling Jacuzzi and Livvy wondered if she was ever going to be able to summon up the energy to move.

'Why?' she asked, replaying the events of their day and remembering the way it had been organised on a shoestring and all at breakneck speed.

In the last couple of months they'd been to some very

elaborate ceremonies and some very lavish parties to celebrate the marriages of some of their colleagues, while
theirs had been neither elaborate nor lavish.

'Simple. It was the best because this time I got to take
the bride to bed,' he declared wickedly as he swept her
up in his arms.

Totally ignoring her squeals of delighted surprise and
the torrents of water cascading across the floor, he carried her back to a circular bed as big as a helicopter
landing-pad and demonstrated the concept to their mu-
tual satisfaction.

A dragging ache in her hips and low down in her belly
drew Livvy back to the present, and she found Daniel
gazing at her with his straight brows drawn into a frown.
The vivid memories were still reverberating through her
head as she met his gaze.

He hadn't slept with the bride *this* time, she realised
with a fierce stab of something suspiciously like relief.
At least...not yet. There'd been no time between the
wedding and the accident.

A further thought tightened new bands of misery
around her heart. The fact that the two of them hadn't
had time to consummate their marriage could hardly
make a difference when the bride in question was already pregnant with their second child. He obviously
hadn't wanted to wait for their wedding night...

'Are you all right, Livvy?' he asked, drawing everyone's attention to her.

Hastily, she tried to compose her expression. Had her
thoughts been spread across her face for all to follow?
The sudden flush of heat in her cheeks told her she was
blushing hotly and she silently cursed.

Why was she still reacting like a teenager, for heaven's sake? She was a grown woman, due to be a mother in a couple of weeks, not some sixteen-year-old ninny. At least the turmoil had taken her mind off her aches and pains.

'I'm fine...really... Just enjoying getting my feet up and relaxing.'

If anything, his frown grew fiercer.

'You shouldn't be here in the first place,' he declared hotly. 'I don't know what your obstetrician was thinking of, giving you permission to go back to work this far into your pregnancy.'

Pat laughed, drawing the focus of his attention away from her, and she gave a silent sigh of relief.

'If I know Livvy, I don't think Duncan French had much to say about it,' she said with a wry chuckle. 'In fact, I think it's probably less wearing on Livvy, *and* the rest of us if she's kept busy. You wouldn't like to see what happens if we try to make her sit and twiddle her thumbs when there's work needs doing. Especially when we're in the sort of mess we are at the moment.'

'You don't need to tell me how stubborn the wretched woman can be,' he growled. 'There is a good reason why we're both called Jones.'

'You're *married*!' Cherry squeaked, breaking the startled silence and gazing from one to the other in amazement.

'Not any more,' Livvy tried to say, but her words were irretrievably lost under Daniel's deeper voice.

'Nearly three years ago,' he confirmed, 'so you can't tell me much about her that I don't already know.'

Livvy was still so surprised that he'd mentioned their now-defunct marriage that she hardly contributed to the flurry of questions and exclamations that followed the revelation. She was hardly able to concentrate on the answers he gave as she waited for him to mention their divorce and his recent remarriage…but he never did.

Was it out of deference to her heavily pregnant state that he left her colleagues thinking they were still married or was it simply because he was more preoccupied with her present state of health in a more immediate way?

He continued speaking politely enough but Livvy knew, from the way he kept glancing at her, that he was still far from happy with the situation.

There was an air of determination about him when their coffee break was over that told her that their threatened discussion wouldn't be long in coming.

'Could I have a word?' he said just as Livvy was waddling in Pat's wake to make her way out to the ward.

Drat, she thought, silently bemoaning the fact that she wasn't fast enough on her feet these days to get away from him.

She'd been hoping that they'd have had a positive result from the new Mrs Jones's ultrasound before he cornered her. Once he knew that their second child was safely on the way she reasoned that he'd be less likely to want to interfere in her plans for *her* baby.

'I know you said you were fine in front of your colleagues, but are you sure?' he asked quietly, with every evidence of concern. 'You haven't got much colour in your cheeks.'

The question was so unexpected that he completely took the wind out of her sails, and she sank back against the edge of the desk, suddenly needing the support.

She'd been ready to argue till her last breath if he

tried to tell her what to do or made any demands con-
cerning the baby.

She'd begun to think that he'd never really cared for
her—after all, it had been seven months since she'd last
seen him and he'd made no attempt to see her in the
interim. He hadn't even bothered to contact her to let
her know that they were divorced.

Now, against all her expectations, his first concern
was for *her*.

'I'm fine, really,' she murmured round the lump in
her throat as sweeter memories assailed her.

This was the caring Daniel she remembered from the
early days, and her heart ached anew for all they'd lost.

'If you need to rest you've only got to grab one of
your colleagues,' he pointed out earnestly. 'It's obvious
that they all care about you. Any one of them would be
only too willing to do all the leg-work for you.'

'I know,' Livvy said with a smile. 'They're a smash-
ing bunch. The trouble is, everything's so topsy-turvy at
the moment that everyone's running just to stand still.
Mostly, I'm spending my time going round talking to
the patients to reassure them that everything's under control. I've also been acting as an unofficial liaison between the two wards because, with a mixed population,
we're having to share resources.'

'And the delivery you did this morning?' One dark
eyebrow rose to accentuate the pointed question.

'That wasn't work—that was the icing on the cake,'
Livvy said with a beaming smile. 'She's an experienced
mum who knew exactly what to expect, and everything
happened so quickly and so smoothly that I was little
more than a spectator.'

'Hmm. That's the first time I've heard *that* excuse for

a pregnant woman to do exactly what she wants whether she should or not!'

Livvy chuckled, marvelling how the atmosphere between the two of them could change so quickly.

She knew that he would never be reconciled to the fact that such a heavily pregnant woman was actually working to help others deliver their babies, and would probably be keeping a close eye on her, but at least he wasn't glaring at her any more. Perhaps now would be the time to have their discussion about—

'Sister!'

Cherry's voice preceded her and something in the tone alerted Livvy that their brief spell of calm was coming to an end.

Had she ever been that young and eager? Livvy found herself thinking as the fresh-faced young woman almost bounced with excitement at the door, her strictly non-regulation red and white pixie hat flopping from side to side.

'Yes, Cherry?' she said, subduing the grin that wanted to appear and turning it into a patient smile.

'It's Mrs Owens, Sister. We've been timing her contractions and I think you ought to check her. They're getting very close together.'

'Thank you, Nurse,' said Daniel, as he held out both hands towards Livvy to pull her to her feet. 'We'll be there as soon as we can.'

'We?' Livvy panted indignantly as she straightened her smock and tried to ignore the warmth in her tingling hands where he'd grasped them. 'You don't need to wait for me. I can get there under my own steam.'

'All right. Have it your own way,' he said, with both hands held up in submission as he turned to walk away.

Livvy couldn't help the chuckle that escaped her when she heard him muttering on his way out, knowing he was doing it deliberately just loud enough for her to hear a litany that started with 'independent' and progressed through 'stubborn' and 'pig-headed' before he was out of hearing range.

She was still smiling when she joined him beside Nerys Owens's bed, just in time to see him work his familiar magic on the apprehensive young woman.

'Everything's going beautifully,' he told her reassuringly. 'In fact, I think you're just about ready to transfer to the luxury accommodations along the corridor. Christmas carols and decorations will be thrown in free.'

The young woman frowned briefly before her face cleared.

'Oh, you mean the delivery room!' she exclaimed, and flicked a glance towards her equally young-looking husband. 'Is it really time?'

Livvy saw what Cherry had meant when she'd said some of the fathers-to-be in the ward had turned green during Megan Williams's delivery.

'Mr Owens might need to be re-christened Kermit before the morning's over,' she warned quietly as Daniel joined her at the end of the bed.

She saw the assessing gaze he trained on the young man's colour and the nod that told her he'd understood what she'd meant. Her gaze lingered for a moment on his profile and she visually traced the slight bump on the lean perfection of his aristocratic nose.

She couldn't help remembering the day he'd received that bump and the fact that he'd blamed it on her.

It had only been a couple of days after their first meeting when she'd heard from one of the other nurses that he was a member of the hospital's rugby team—well, he was partly Welsh *and* a doctor so it had been almost expected of him.

Never having dated much, she'd never developed an interest in the game—hadn't even realised that the hospital fielded a team.

Having heard that he was playing, that afternoon had found her making her way towards the cheers and jeers of the supporters as St Augustine's had taken on a team from one of the London hospitals.

One minute the game had been in full flow, with two sets of mud-caked men charging towards her end of the pitch flinging the oval ball apparently indiscriminately from one to the other. The next minute there had been an almighty crash and a tangle of arms and legs as the figure at the head of the pack had been brought down.

It hadn't been until the unknown nurse beside her had exclaimed aloud that Livvy had realised that Daniel had been the man at the bottom of the pile of heaving bodies, and it hadn't been until later that evening when he'd been nursing his broken nose that he'd blamed her presence for distracting him and causing the disaster.

'Right, Mr Owens,' Daniel said briskly, snapping Livvy's attention away from its preoccupation with his profile. 'If you'd like to come with me a minute, we'll let the nurses get your wife organised.'

Livvy spared the two of them a glance as Daniel led the terrified father-to-be away, and she couldn't help comparing Mr Owens's slight, almost boyish frame with Daniel's far more imposing height and breadth.

'Where is he taking John? He will bring him back in time for the baby to be born?' Nerys demanded with renewed panic in her voice.

'Don't worry, he's taking him along to the delivery room to put a gown on. He'll look like one of the television doctors by the time we get there,' Livvy joked as she set her patient's mind at rest.

Her own mind was a different matter.

It had taken Nerys Owens's question to make her realise that she and Daniel had automatically slipped into their seamless routine of working together, with hardly a word needed for each to know what the other meant.

How many times in the past had he drawn a nervous father aside for a surreptitious pep-talk? All she knew was that those he spoke to usually sailed through their wives' deliveries, if not enthusiastically then at least supportively, adding to the special atmosphere surrounding the miracle of birth.

She didn't doubt for a minute that he would work the same magic on John Owens and that in a few days the Owens family would leave the hospital, wondering what on earth they had ever worried about.

In the meantime, she needed to organise Nerys Owens's speedy transfer to the delivery suite just as soon as she made certain that Jill Simpson had been safely removed to her bed on the ward upstairs.

It was in the middle of this organisation that Dewi finally arrived with her trolley full of equipment to run the ultrasound test on the new Mrs Jones.

CHAPTER FIVE

LIVVY was pulled two ways.

Of course she wanted to be there for the ultrasound and wanted it to show that the baby was fine.

That would mean that she could look forward to Daniel taking Alice away so that she wouldn't have the woman's presence on the ward as a reminder of everything that had gone wrong in her life.

Unfortunately, it would also mean that Daniel wouldn't be there any more, and that was something she didn't want to think about.

At least when they were busy it was just like when they had worked together at St Augustine's before her world had fallen apart. If she concentrated on the minute-to-minute events of their time together she could almost forget the dreadful seven months in between, as if they had been nothing more than a shadowy nightmare.

Livvy gave herself a mental shake and set about organising Nerys Owens's transfer along the corridor before she joined Dewi and Alice Jones behind the curtains drawn around her bed. Silently, she made herself a promise that as soon as the test was over, and Alice Jones had been settled down, she would hurry along to see if she could be there for Nerys Owens's baby to arrive.

That always supposed that the ultrasound gave good news. If not, she might find herself in the uneasy position of having to offer comfort and consolation to the one person in the world to whom she didn't want to speak.

'I am so sorry you have been kept waiting so long,' Dewi was saying as she began to unravel the electrical connections from several strands of multicoloured tinsel and prepared to set everything up. 'It must be so uncomfortable, having to wait so long.'

Livvy had to hide a grimace of her own when she thought about how long it had been since she'd sent the two cups of tea to this patient. She would have had difficulty waiting five minutes after drinking that much, let alone...

'After I was told to go to the pregnant lady I was called back down to Casualty to scan a patient with the kidney stones so I have come back to you as swiftly as it is possible.'

Alice Jones lay quietly as the torrent of words poured over her, her face white with tension as she gazed intently at the screen when the first indistinct images appeared, and Livvy couldn't help feeling sympathetic.

No matter what the woman had done, Livvy couldn't wish the baby any harm, especially as it would be so closely related to her own child.

'Ah, now, look at this,' Dewi said, as she drew the probe smoothly over the well-oiled skin and the image on the monitor grew more distinct. 'I am seeing where your little one is situated inside you and if you will be so good as to look just here...' she reached out to point at the screen with one slender finger '...you will see the rhythmic pulses of your baby's heart.'

'The heart is still beating?' quavered the poor woman lying flat on the bed. 'My baby's still alive?'

Livvy had to bite her lip to control its quiver when

she heard in her voice just how much Alice Jones wanted her baby to live.

As she lay there, helpless, bruised and obviously afraid, Alice looked every one of her years. Nearly ten years younger, Livvy was consumed with jealousy when she wondered just what Daniel had seen in the woman that he had so easily abandoned his wife for her.

Was it the fact that Alice had borne him a son when he and Livvy hadn't intended starting their family yet? Had he felt morally bound to give her and her child the support of his name? If he'd known that Livvy, too, was carrying his child, would he have stayed with her?

'Yes, your baby is still very much still alive,' Dewi assured her as she programmed the machine to make a copy of the scan. 'If you will like, I will give you the picture so you can look at it and one day you will like to show to baby when it is big.'

'Oh, thank you so much. I would like a picture, then I can show it to the baby's father.'

Livvy saw her peering at the technician's name-tag with a slight frown.

'Your name is so unusual,' Alice said, relief obviously making her relaxed enough to make conversation. 'What part of the world did your family come from?'

'We come originally from Thailand where my father was with the diplomatic corps. When he had the posting to come to England he is bringing his family with him and I am staying here to learn about Western medicine before I go back to do the same thing in the big new hospital near to our home.'

'And how do you pronounce your name? What is the correct Thai way?'

'Davey,' Dewi said with a giggle. 'It makes me sound like a boy in your country.'

'Oh, but what a coincidence!' the older woman exclaimed. 'That is the name I gave my son!'

Livvy didn't know how she'd got out of the cubicle. Had she just rudely barged her way out through the curtains without a word or had she actually managed to make her excuses before she'd hurried across the ward and into the nearest staff toilet?

'Davey,' she whispered when she'd shut herself in a cubicle and leant weakly back against the door. 'She called their son Davey...'

The only person she'd ever discussed baby names with had been Daniel, and they'd laughingly decided that in honour of his father their hypothetical son would one day be called David.

'How *could* he,' she moaned in anguish, the tears starting to trickle down her cheeks. It had been one of the few consolations left to her that, whichever sex their child turned out to be, she would be able to give it the name Daniel had helped her to choose.

How could she do that now when he'd given that name to his other child first?

The trickle of tears became a torrent as she remembered that dreadful day seven months ago, the day which had been the beginning of the end of her happy marriage.

It had been no more and no less hectic than any other day in St Augustine's busy Maternity department until Miss Webster had been brought in.

She had been full term and already in strong labour when she'd arrived, and as Livvy's previous patient had just delivered a healthy daughter and been settled into the ward she'd been free to attend to the unexpected intake.

It had appeared that, although she'd been resident in the area, Alice hadn't been attending the antenatal department at the hospital so she hadn't met any of the midwives.

Having settled her into bed, Livvy had sat down with her to ask the questions that would form the basis of her case notes.

There hadn't been enough time to build up any sort of bond of trust between them before suddenly the woman had gone into transition and had rapidly entered the second stage of labour.

'Where's Daniel?' the woman demanded in a panic-stricken voice as she resisted all Livvy's efforts to calm her down and get her to concentrate on her breathing. 'He said he'd be here when I needed him. Where is he?'

'Did you let him know you were in labour?' Livvy prompted, wondering who the elusive Daniel was. Miss Webster definitely wasn't married, according to her hastily taken details, so perhaps he was the baby's father? Or perhaps a supportive friend?

'He works here,' she said shortly as she panted for breath between contractions which seemed to be almost continuous now. 'He's Daniel Jones…the gynaecologist and obstetrician. Please…will you call him? Quickly. Tell him I need him…'

Livvy was too surprised to do anything else, her hand reaching out automatically for the phone to arrange for the switchboard to page him.

So far there had been nothing in the progress of her patient's labour that made Livvy think that they were going to need Daniel's help. But perhaps her patient knew something she hadn't told her, and if it helped her to calm down it was worth the call.

Even so, it was nearly half an hour before Daniel arrived, the Caesarean he was performing in Theatre necessarily taking precedence over Miss Webster's needs.

When Daniel finally entered the room his eyes had gone to Livvy first to find out what the problem was, but as soon as he began to speak her patient recognised him.

'Daniel… You came,' she said, and burst into tears.

Livvy felt almost invisible as she continued to manage the older woman's labour while her husband focused entirely on talking to their patient to calm her down.

He chidingly bullied her into concentrating on what her body was trying to do and gently encouraged her to push just one more time.

When the little boy was safely delivered and Livvy wrapped him up to hand him to his mother for the first time, it was to Daniel that the proud new mother held up the little scrap for inspection, for all the world as if he were the father.

'Look, Daniel,' Miss Webster crowed as she unwrapped the tiny mite just far enough to examine his fingers and toes. 'He's even got the Jones toes.'

Livvy froze in the act of writing her notes and turned in disbelief to gaze at the tiny feet.

As if in slow motion, she watched Daniel lean forward to look and saw him smile his slightly lopsided smile— the one that always made her breath catch in her throat and her heart skip a beat with anticipation when directed at her.

This time it chilled her to the marrow.

'They're just like yours, aren't they?' Alice Webster

crooned as she stroked the strangely curled little digits with a gentle finger. 'You said they were inherited from your father's side of the family and now they've been passed on to my baby.'

Livvy could barely remember the rest of that shift. It was lucky that Alice Webster had been the last of her patients because she must have moved through her remaining duties like an automaton.

The thing she could recall with nightmare clarity was the terrible argument that had exploded between Daniel and herself when they'd reached the flat that evening.

It hadn't seemed to matter what she'd said or how often she'd asked—he had utterly refused to tell her anything about Alice Webster's place in his life.

The argument had raged intermittently for several hours, but when she'd seen that adamant look come into his eyes she'd finally realised that he wasn't going to change his mind.

'I gave her my promise,' he repeated stubbornly, as if that was the last word on the subject.

That only incensed Livvy even more.

'You made some promises to me, too,' she pointed out, feeling the ominous prickle behind her eyes and silently cursing her recently discovered pregnancy for messing with her emotional control.

What disastrous timing. How could she share her momentous news with him when there was so much ugliness between them?

'Do your promises to her take precedence over the ones you made me?' she demanded, blinking furiously so that not a single tear should fall.

'I promised to love, honour and cherish you,' he said

in a voice grown even huskier after a night without sleep and a day full of arguments.

'And *do* you?' she challenged bluntly. 'How can you honour me when there's a child in St Augustine's that shares a remarkable resemblance to you, even down to an inherited deformity?'

As ever, he set his mouth in a stubborn line, asking only that she trust him.

She had no option but to share their bed that night, going to sleep as far away from him as she could manage with her back firmly turned towards him.

She woke up the next morning to find Daniel's arms wrapped around her, her head pillowed on his shoulder, the way it had been right from the first night of their marriage.

For a moment Livvy smiled as she savoured the happy intimacy and shifted the position of her head slightly so that she could look at her sleeping husband.

'Don't go yet,' Daniel murmured sleepily, his voice a sexy growl as he tightened his arms around her and rubbed his beard-roughened cheek over the top of her head. 'I missed this last night.'

Those few words were enough for her to remember the black cloud hanging over her happiness and she rolled swiftly across the bed.

It might have been the sudden movement or the gut-wrenching disappointment when she remembered his adamant refusal to tell her what was going on but, whatever was the cause, she suddenly had to run to the bathroom to endure her first racking bout of morning sickness.

It was the last straw.

*　　*　　*

From a distance of seven months, Livvy looked back at her last-ditch demand that he talked to her and his continued refusal, then her hasty search for another job and somewhere to live before her own pregnancy became obvious.

When even those drastic methods hadn't changed his mind her heart had finally shattered and she'd contacted the first firm of solicitors she'd come to for advice about divorce.

She'd only been back once, for Sarah Jones's funeral just weeks after their separation.

During the journey, she decided to make certain that she spent her time close to her father-in-law. She'd been worried that Daniel might try to corner her and she couldn't have borne it if he compounded his father's unhappiness, by creating a scene.

As it was, she needn't have worried.

'Livvy. Thank you for coming.' Daniel greeted her at the church, sparing her no more than a brief nod before he welcomed the next group of mourners behind her.

It was the same at the house.

'May I take your coat?' he asked when she entered the spacious hallway, his voice no warmer than if they were strangers, then he directed her into the lounge as if she'd never been in the house before.

To give him the benefit of the doubt, it didn't look as if he'd slept properly for weeks, his eyes dull and darkly shadowed and his face quite grey with exhaustion.

She paused in the doorway to look back at him, and just for a crazy moment she was swamped by compassion. He looked so…so lost and alone, and all she could think of doing was wrapping her arms around him to offer comfort.

For just a moment she wondered if she'd made a terrible mistake in leaving Daniel. She still loved him as much as ever, and although there was yet little outward evidence, she was now carrying his child while he seemed far from happy.

What if she'd jumped to conclusions and there was a perfectly rational explanation for everything that had happened?

Once again her mind was buzzing with possibilities.

Had that woman, Alice Webster, been some unacknowledged relative of Daniel's father that her child had inherited the same curled toes that she'd teased Daniel about?

Was she, perhaps, an illegitimate daughter whose presence had to be hidden while Sarah Jones was alive?

Perhaps, now that circumstances had forced them to meet, they should pause in their headlong rush to destroy the last bonds between them. Perhaps she should take this opportunity to sit down with him and talk everything over. Perhaps, now, he would be ready to tell her the reason for all the hurtful secrecy.

At that moment, the front door opened again to admit another mourner. Indecisive, Livvy hovered for a moment, waiting for Daniel to direct her through to the other room, but as soon as he helped the newcomer off with her coat she turned into his arms and rested her head on his shoulder.

With a gasp of shock she recognised Alice Webster.

Without a second thought she whirled and made her way to her father-in-law's side and there she remained, steadfastly ignoring the fact that Daniel stayed out in the hallway with the woman.

*   *   *

In some ways, those events seemed to have happened to a different person in another lifetime, but just at the moment it felt as if the wounds were fresh and raw.

Was her life going to be one long round of meetings with Daniel in which she got to see him just long enough to remember everything she was missing before Alice Webster stole him away again?

She hiccuped twice in quick succession and scowled at the resulting kick the baby gave her.

'There's nothing like a swift reminder of the facts of life,' she muttered as she blew her nose and emerged from the toilet stall to soak a paper towel with water and hold it to her burning eyes.

What had she been thinking about?

This time would be the last her path would be crossing Daniel's. Now that she knew he'd married Alice and their union was to be blessed with a second child she would have to forget all those hopeless little fantasies about her handsome husband coming to find her and swearing he'd loved her all along. It just wasn't going to happen.

She drew in as deep a breath as the restrictions on her ribs would allow and glared at her reflection in the mirror over the basin, deliberately ignoring the smiling Santa someone had stuck in each corner.

Her eyes were red, her nose was shiny and her silvery blonde hair was starting to straggle untidily around her face like a limp dishmop.

'Tell me, madam, how does it feel to be Mrs Goodyear Blimp?' she asked, then pulled a face as she tried to lean a little closer while she fiddled with her hair to neaten it.

Thank goodness there were only two weeks left to her

due date. She didn't know if she could put up with much more of this.

Suddenly the girdle of muscles around her uterus tightened and she had to grip the edge of the basin while she concentrated on her breathing, waiting for the pain to die away.

She'd been experiencing Braxton Hicks contractions for some weeks now but that was the heftiest one yet. All she hoped was that all the practising her body was doing would lead to a comparatively quick and easy birth when the time came.

'Speaking about when the time comes,' she muttered, hearing footsteps hurrying past the door as she straightened her shoulders and gave her back a rub, 'I should be out there, seeing what I can do to help. That'll keep my mind off my own problems.'

It was only a small pep-talk, but if she was lucky it would work just as well as Daniel's did on the expectant fathers. They went in the delivery room as trembling mice and came out as confident fathers. Quite a transformation...

Her own was less obvious, but would have to do. The trick was to let people see what they wanted to see, and in her case that was a pregnant nurse in control of herself and her destiny with plenty of time and energy left over to help others along the way.

'And it's all done with mirrors,' she whispered as she made her way towards the delivery room. At least she could console herself that she was going to be the one to give Daniel the good news about the baby.

'Livvy?' Pat called before she'd gone more than a dozen paces.

She sighed, suddenly feeling more than a little weary.

'More problems?' she asked when she saw the sheets of paper Pat was brandishing.

'Luckily, not this time.' She turned the top sheet so that Livvy could read it. 'The notes from Mrs Simpson's own antenatal hospital finally arrived.'

'Do I say better late than never?' Livvy asked wryly. 'Is there anything there we need to know about for her post-operative care?'

'As far as I can see, everything was perfectly straight-forward until the twins got themselves into the wrong position,' Pat offered. 'Certainly nothing major.'

'I'll take these and show them to Daniel before I put them with our notes,' Livvy said, and set off again towards the delivery suite.

With a swift detour to don gown and gloves, she reversed through the swing doors to enter the room, and in spite of her determination her heart stammered in her throat when the first thing she heard was Daniel's voice.

'You're doing beautifully, Nerys,' he said with a world of encouragement in his tone. 'John and I can see the baby's head now.'

'And it doesn't take after your grandfather,' quipped the young man, proving conclusively to Livvy that Daniel's man-to-man words of wisdom had worked their miracle again. 'Girl or boy, it's got a lovely head of hair.'

'Good. You'll have something to grab hold of to pull it out, then,' grumbled the young woman, her freckles more obvious than ever under the clinically bright light. 'I don't want to do this any longer.'

Daniel must have caught sight of Livvy out of the corner of his eye because suddenly he was looking straight at her with a wicked twinkle in his eyes above the top of his mask.

'Sister, if you'd managed to push your baby that far out, would you want to stop now?' he demanded.

'I'd certainly find it difficult to walk around or sit down,' she retorted with a wink for the exhausted young woman. 'Especially when the baby's head is so close to coming.'

'Is it really close?' Nerys pleaded tearfully, turning automatically to the other woman in the room for reassurance. 'It feels as if I've been doing this for hours and getting nowhere.'

'Do you want to see?' Livvy offered, and took the couple of steps necessary to locate a mirror left in the room for that specific purpose. 'If John can support your shoulders for a minute…'

She held the mirror between the young mother's spread knees and tilted it in approximately the right direction.

'Can you see now?'

'Tilt a bit more, please. Oh!' The exclamation emerged on a soft breath as she caught her first sight of her baby, the dark head of hair already visible as the head crowned. 'It's nearly here,' she whispered with reverence in her voice as she looked up at her equally young husband. 'The baby's nearly here…look.'

There wasn't time for any more conversation as the next contraction began to take hold of her and Livvy put the mirror aside again to take up her position on the other side of Daniel.

This time Nerys pushed with a will, barely stopping to draw in another breath as she strained to push her baby into the world.

Each time a contraction faded she asked one of them for a progress report until it was easier for Livvy to keep the mirror to hand.

It wasn't long before there was the sharp sound of a baby's cry in the room and Daniel was presenting the couple with their son to the soft strains of 'Unto us is born a son' in the corridor.

'Oh, he's so beautiful,' Nerys sobbed happily as she cradled her noisy infant. 'Absolutely perfect.'

'And with a perfect set of lungs,' Daniel murmured in an aside to Livvy, making her chuckle.

Their laughter was interrupted when Amy Aldarini stuck her head around the door and gave the two of them a sharply speculative look.

'Have you lot nearly finished in here? I've got another one coming to the boil upstairs.'

'Hello, Livvy,' Amy said.

Knowing the efficiency of the hospital grapevine, Livvy was suddenly aware of the significance of the thoughtful expression in her colleague's eyes and was forced to make introductions. 'Amy Aldarini, Midwife, this is Dr Daniel Jones, Obs and Gynae. We shouldn't be more than a quarter of an hour or so. Will that do?'

'Should do fine unless Mum had dynamite with her breakfast,' Amy quipped with a grin. 'Catch up with you later...' She disappeared again.

'Speaking of breakfast,' Daniel murmured beside her, 'is there any chance that I could grab some food? We never got to the wedding reception and I'm starving.'

After the light-hearted banter of the last three-quarters of an hour his words were like a shower of icy water.

To cover her sudden shock Livvy made a show of consulting the watch pinned to the front of her smock, but it took several seconds before she could focus on the numbers.

How could she have let herself forget that the two of them were no longer married colleagues, working at the same hospital with an enviable record for delivering healthy babies to happy parents?

Daniel was no longer her loving husband but, as of this morning, now belonged to Alice, the new Mrs Jones.

'If you like, you could go now,' she said coolly, glancing in his direction without actually looking at him. 'I could finish up in here. Oh, by the way, the technician finally made it up to the ward to do the ultrasound. It doesn't look as if the baby has suffered any ill-effects from the crash.'

There was a strange silence in the room and she could almost feel him frowning at her changed attitude, but she resisted the temptation to look at his expression as she turned away to gather up the used instruments.

'Livvy?'

There was an air of strain in his husky voice but she couldn't let it affect her.

'Yes?' she replied with all the nonchalance she could muster.

He paused, obviously expecting her to turn and face him but she steeled herself not to.

He'd always been far too perceptive where she was concerned, and there was no way she was going to let him know that his defection could still hurt her this way. Nor did she want to reveal that having to pass on news about his new wife and baby was like having to drive a dagger through her own heart. She'd never felt such jealousy before, and wasn't proud of it now.

The more time she spent with him and the more often

she feasted her eyes on him the harder it was going to be to shut him out of her mind when the snow cleared and he was able to take Alice away. It was better—for the sake of her sanity, if nothing else—if she started to push him away now.

'I just wanted to say thank you,' he said quietly, his voice telling her he was far too close for comfort, 'for letting me know about Alice and the baby. Now all I have to do is find out whether my father's out of Theatre so I can let him know.'

CHAPTER SIX

DANIEL followed the directions and found himself outside the doors of the surgical ward.

Until he'd actually rung through to find out how his father was faring under the orthopaedic surgeon's knife he hadn't realised how many hours had passed since the accident.

His first inclination when they'd all arrived at the hospital had been to stay near to his father until he knew how the operation had gone.

His father's injuries had looked horrific, even to someone who saw the gorier side of life on a daily basis, and the fact that it was his father's bone Daniel saw sticking out through lacerated flesh made it worse than ever.

By the time they'd been transported to hospital logic had kicked in and Daniel was able to admit that, now they were running fluids into him to replace the oceans of blood he seemed to be losing, his father's injuries weren't actually life-threatening.

Logic also told Daniel that because Alice had remained conscious throughout the horrors of the crash and their slow extraction from the shattered vehicle her need for support and patient understanding was actually the greater.

Poor Alice.

This certainly wasn't the wedding day she'd hoped for. First, the unexpected weather front, dumping inches of snow, and then the disaster of the accident.

97

It was bad enough that his father might be incapacitated for months while his hip mended, and would require a great deal of patient handling if he wasn't to explode with frustration at being confined. That was going to cause a great deal of stress all round.

Then there was the possibility that Alice might lose the baby.

No wonder she had wanted to cling so closely, barely letting him out of her sight. The fact that little Davey had escaped the crash virtually unscathed, and was now more or less happily settled in the children's ward for observation, had been the only piece of good news Daniel had been able to give her.

It had been almost a relief that he'd had the excuse of staff shortages in the department to allow him to occupy his hands and brain, otherwise he would have been close to cracking too. It wasn't as if he could actually do anything to help her, in spite of the fact that this was his speciality.

He relived the moment when he'd looked up from pushing Alice in the wheelchair to find Livvy, standing in front of him.

He'd nearly lost it then.

He'd known that she was working at Bryn Madoc Memorial and had thought that he was prepared to see her but all his mental lectures about staying calm and civil if he bumped into her had vaporised in an instant.

'Bloody woman,' he muttered forcefully, quite startling a passing orderly who gave him a wide berth on his way into the department.

Why hadn't she contacted him to let him know she was pregnant? Not only did he have the *right* to know that he was going to be a father but she should have known that he would *want* to know.

His heart clenched with the knowledge of all the weeks and months he had missed of his child's development. He didn't know the simplest things.

How long had it been before she'd realised she was pregnant? Had she been very sick? How many weeks had it been before she'd felt the first faint fluttering movements deep inside? Did she know what sex the baby was? Had she decided what names she was going to use?

He felt the frown pleat his forehead when he remembered the names they'd joked about using for their hypothetical children, and his quiet dismay when Alice had chosen the same name for her son. Had Livvy been disappointed too? Did she even know?

God, it had been an awful seven months since she'd left. Everything that could have gone wrong seemed to have done so.

First it had been his mother's death and the inevitable emotional, practical and legal aftermath. It had hardly been surprising that his father had relied so heavily on him during those initial weeks as a mixture of guilt and relief had warred for supremacy.

He'd longed for the comfort and security of having Livvy waiting for him when he got home, the only person he'd ever felt comfortable about confiding in.

Unfortunately, apart from her fleeting presence at his mother's funeral, when he'd been barely holding himself and his father together, she seemed to have disappeared off the face of the earth, and Daniel honestly hadn't had a minute free to find her.

At first sight, tracing her hadn't struck him as a dif-

ficult task because he'd believed that she'd stayed somewhere in the vicinity of St Augustine's.

When he'd realised that she'd resigned her post he'd
widened the area of his search to other maternity wards,
gradually going further and further afield.

Daniel's pride had hurt that he'd had to ask around,
but once he'd discovered that apparently none of her
former colleagues at St Augustine's had a forwarding
address he became really concerned.

It had been a chance comment of his father's when
Daniel had asked him about his conversation with Livvy
after the funeral which had prompted him to search the
other side of the country.

Daniel had just tracked Livvy down to Bryn Madoc
Memorial and had been making plans to confront her
when Alice had surfaced in his life again and everything
had been thrown into turmoil once more.

'Excuse me, sir. Are you waiting for someone or are
you lost?'

The security guard's polite enquiry suddenly made
him realise how long he'd been standing outside the
ward. No wonder the poor man thought he was behaving
suspiciously.

'I've been gathering the courage to visit my father,'
he said, stretching the truth more than somewhat. 'He's
just come out of surgery after a car crash this morning.'

'Ah, well, it's understandable that you're a bit nervous
about it if you're not used to being in hospitals,' the
guard said kindly. 'If you go straight through the doors
you're bound to see one of the ward staff and they'll
take you to see him if he's allowed visitors yet. I hope
he's doing all right.'

Daniel didn't correct the man's misapprehension. The

thought of what he would say if he knew he'd been talking to a doctor was the one thing that lightened his mood.

He was aware that the smartly uniformed man stood and watched him through the tinsel-framed safety-glass panels in the door until he reached the door of the ward sister's office and stuck his head in.

'Probably thinks I'll chicken out,' Daniel muttered under his breath before he knocked on the open door to attract her attention.

It only took a moment to tell her who he was looking for and confirm that he'd come to the right place.

A brief mention of his professional qualifications gained him a host of details about the success of his father's operation and its favourable prognosis, and was the open sesame to an immediate visit.

'Daniel,' his father croaked as soon as he appeared by the bedside, his eyes popping open almost as soon as his son reached him.

'I should have known you'd be too stubborn to stay asleep when they want you to,' Daniel teased gently, and pulled up a chair beside the bed.

'Any news?' his father prompted, his free hand reaching across to grasp Daniel's fiercely.

Daniel returned the pressure and gazed down at their clasped hands. Until that moment, he hadn't really noticed just how much alike their hands were and that thought prompted a critical examination of the man lying helpless in the bed in front of him.

His father certainly wasn't looking his best so soon after a major reconstructive operation, but he was still a very good-looking man. If Daniel wore half as well he would be able to count himself lucky, especially if his life was filled with the sort of anguish his father had been forced to endure year after year.

'Daniel, for God's sake,' his father broke in, his face deathly pale and sounding quite frantic, 'tell me what's happened?'

'Sorry, Dad,' he apologised, suddenly realising that the staff probably hadn't had the chance to tell him how things had gone. 'They think the operation was a complete success. They've managed to plate and screw you back together and within just a few weeks you'll be able to—'

'Not *me*,' his father interrupted, dragging his hand away to flap it dismissively. 'What about Alice and the baby? And Davey? What's happened to them? Oh, son, I feel so guilty. If only you had been driving.'

'Hey, Dad, calm down.' Daniel grabbed for his father's hand again and squeezed it tightly between his own. 'It probably would have happened anyway, given the road conditions. Alice is fine—they all are.'

'You're sure? Absolutely sure?' he demanded.

'Absolutely,' Daniel repeated. 'She's had the ultrasound and all is well. The heart is beating strongly. And Davey's got the nurses wrapped round his little finger already. The children's ward will never be the same.'

'Thank God,' his father breathed, and as he finally relaxed back onto the pillows the colour began to seep into his cheeks. 'I was so afraid I'd killed them.'

Daniel spent a few minutes reassuring his father that all was well, but his concentration was divided. He was talking about Davey and Alice and the growing hope that the baby she carried was unaffected by the crash, but all the while he had an urgent need to bring the conversation round to Livvy.

Finally he saw an opening and took it.

'The sister who organised the scan was Livvy,' he said, barely aware in his preoccupation that he was being so blunt until he saw his father's eyes narrow with speculation.

'You mean we ended up in the same hospital?' he asked with a rusty chuckle. 'Well, at least it saved you a journey. You mentioned that you were thinking of paying her a visit after the wedding.'

'Did you know she's pregnant?' Daniel demanded, this time remembering just in time to keep his voice down out of deference to his surroundings and his father's temporarily fragile state of health, but his soft voice was definitely at odds with the way he was feeling.

Livvy had obviously let slip enough details during their conversation after the funeral for his father to be able to direct his search towards Wales. If she'd also told him about the baby and his father had kept the information to himself...

'Pregnant?' the older man exclaimed, clearly shocked. 'Good God!'

'It looks as if she's nearly full term, but due to a flu epidemic causing shortages of staff, and that bloody snow, she's actually still working.'

His father was silent for long moments, lying with his eyes closed, and Daniel felt his frustration growing when he realised that the poor man was in no fit state to be badgered. Now that his mind had been set at rest about Davey, Alice and the baby, he probably wanted nothing more than to sleep off the rest of his anaesthetic.

'You're as protective as ever,' his father growled softly as he opened his eyes the merest crack. 'You're obviously still smitten so what are you going to do about it?'

Daniel didn't bother to contradict him. He knew it wouldn't do him any good. The wretched man was far too perceptive, even when he was doped up to the eyeballs on analgesics.

'I don't know *what* I'm going to do yet, but one thing is certain—no child of mine is going to grow up without knowing its father.'

As soon as Livvy arrived back on the ward she noticed the air of suppressed excitement building while the other patients waited for Nerys and her new baby to return.

'Having several babies arrive so quickly is making them all very hopeful,' she commented wryly as she supervised the distribution of the meals around the ward.

'You mean, the rest of them are hoping they're going to cough and, hey presto, there's a baby!' Pat Lersh said with a laugh.

'If only it *was* that easy!' Livvy groaned. 'The more I think about it the more I feel like asking for an epidural or even a Caesarean!'

'Chicken!' Pat taunted. 'You're one of the professionals. You can't afford to let the side down. Anyway, you're luckier than most. Your husband is in the trade, too, so you'll get preferential treatment.'

'Ha!' Livvy snorted inelegantly.

She swiftly suppressed the stab of discomfort at the reminder that Pat believed she and Daniel were still married. She was going to have to explain all that misunderstanding at some stage, but wasn't in any hurry to do it now. There were too many ears about and the whole thing could end up being very embarrassing, especially with her replacement lying in the bed on the other side of the room.

'You're joking, of course,' she grumbled in answer to Pat's teasing. 'If there are several of us in labour at once you know darn well that the professional will be left to get on with it because she knows what's happening, whereas the poor ''amateur'' needs all the help she can get!'

'You could be right,' Pat conceded with a laugh. 'You'll just have to time it right.'

'Talking about timing,' Livvy said, determined to change the direction of the conversation, 'has there been any sort of update on the various Christmassy events for the people stuck here over the holiday? I know there's supposed to be a carol concert this evening and Christmas dinner tomorrow midday, but what about Father Christmas visiting the wards?'

'As far as I know, the choir—in its much depleted form—will be paying a brief visit to each ward some time during the evening. There was a message a little while ago, asking for volunteer voices to swell the ranks, so if you've got any sort of a voice…?'

Pat left the question hanging tantalisingly in the air and Livvy pulled a face. Her participation would depend on how busy the ward was this evening so it was better if she didn't make any promises. Anyway, she could use the fact that she wasn't *officially* staff at the moment as a get-out clause.

It wasn't that her voice was bad—in fact, it was a lot better than most—but in an area of Britain noted for superlative singing she was hesitant to put herself forward.

Now if it had been Daniel they'd been asking, that

was another matter. He might be only half-Welsh, but he seemed to have inherited all of the genes for musical ability with a beautiful rich tenor voice.

Her thoughts switched instantly to the first time she'd heard him, the day they'd decided to start decorating the living room of the flat.

She'd honestly thought he'd put a CD on to listen to while he worked, and had wondered whose voice it was, sending shivers up her spine—until she'd walked in the room with a reviving tray of coffee and had realised the voice had been his.

Once, she'd made the mistake of letting him know the effect it had on her. After that, he'd often teased her, by singing brief snatches of romantic arias as a prelude to snatching her up in his arms and rushing her, shrieking and laughing, to the bedroom.

'As for Christmas meals,' Pat continued, dragging Livvy's attention back to her immediate surroundings, 'you'll see in a few minutes that we usually have something festive with the evening meal, such as mince pies, but, regardless of snow and flu epidemics, there'll be Christmas dinner with all the trimmings tomorrow at midday just after Father Christmas does his rounds.'

'Pretty much the same whichever hospital you're in,' Livvy commented, hoping the flush her heated imaginings had brought to her cheeks could be attributed to anything but their real cause.

'Under more normal circumstances,' Pat continued, apparently oblivious to Livvy's heightened colour, 'on our ward it usually means that the younger relatives can be here for the handing out of gifts and then can go home for their own lunches. That leaves the possibility of another quieter visit later in the day for the adults.'

'But with all that snow out there, who knows what's going to happen?' Livvy pointed out. 'Some visitors might not dare make the journey.'

'And others might get stuck here,' Pat added darkly.

'Well, it's obviously a matter of wait and see while we get on with the routine stuff,' Livvy concluded as she tried to make herself comfortable enough to sit down to eat. As a patient, her meal was being delivered to the ward, but she'd opted to eat it in Sister's office to keep Pat company.

It felt quite strange to be caught halfway between being a member of staff and being a patient, she thought as Cherry brought in the tray. Officially, Livvy was supposed to be sitting out in the ward with the rest of them to have her meal, but as the unofficial liaison between the two wards she needed to be in close contact with the telephone and computer links to the rest of the hospital.

'At least we're warm and dry and well fed,' she added cheerfully, breathing in the savoury smells as she lifted up the plate cover.

She caught her breath suddenly as another contraction gripped her, but when she remembered to relax it was fairly easy to weather it. It was all good practice for when the real thing happened.

'Are you all right?' Pat asked with a note of concern in her voice, and Livvy suddenly realised just how sharp-eyed the young staff nurse was.

'Braxton Hick's contractions,' she explained offhandedly as her breathing returned to normal. 'They've been happening quite strongly for several weeks now. As they're intermittent I never know when to expect them and they sometimes catch me out.'

'You're sure that's what they are?' Pat demanded suspiciously. 'You're not in labour, are you?'

'No such luck.' Livvy laughed. 'I've got two more weeks to go, and knowing my luck, I'll end up carting this lump around right till the last possible minute. I've almost forgotten what it feels like to be able to bend in the middle or catch sight of anything below the Plimsoll line!'

Just then the phone rang and Pat reached out to answer it.

'Maternity. Pat Lersh,' she said, then listened for a minute, her expression growing darker by the second.

'Yes. She's here. I'll pass you over,' she said swiftly, waiting just long enough for Livvy to put her meal aside before she handed her the receiver. 'It's Amy.'

'Livvy here,' she began, but Amy wasn't waiting for social chit-chat.

'Can you come to the delivery suite straight away? I can't get hold of Aled and I've got a problem,' she said succinctly.

'Of course. I'll be with you in...' Livvy stopped speaking when she realised that Amy wasn't listening any more.

The swift cutting of the connection brought home to her just how urgent the matter must be, and that was enough to get her out of her seat and on her feet, pregnant or not.

'See if you can get hold of Daniel,' she suggested, wondering where he'd disappeared to after Nerys's baby had arrived.

Her heart sank at the thought that her attitude towards him in the delivery suite after the Owens baby was born might have made him change his mind about staying around. If, as Amy said, she couldn't get hold of Aled then Daniel was their only hope if there was a mother or baby at risk.

A sudden thought struck her and she called back over her shoulder. 'Check to see if he's gone to get something to eat, or he might be visiting his father up on Orthopaedics.'

Within a couple of minutes Livvy was once more swathed in an ill-fitting gown and pulling on gloves as she reversed through the swing doors.

'Amy,' Livvy called softly when she saw her bending over her patient to speak to her.

'Thank God you're here,' Amy whispered when she'd made her excuses for a second and hurried across to speak to Livvy.'

'I've got a shoulder dystocia and I'm going to need some help. I've assisted several, but I've never had to do one myself. I know the delivery usually needs more than one pair of hands but there's always been an obstetrician in the unit before. I tried external over-rotation of the head but it didn't free it. I can't get it to budge.'

Livvy drew in a breath and released it in a silent whistle of dismay. She would far prefer it if Daniel was to turn up at any second, but they couldn't afford to wait.

Her first glance at the patient had told her that the woman was very overweight, a factor which was often contributory in such cases. She also seemed to be totally alone.

'No partner?' she murmured softly.

'Works away from home and out of contact at the moment. We're all she's got,' Amy replied succinctly. 'I couldn't believe it when the head delivered safely then everything came to a halt. Those shoulders are well and truly stuck. I'm just amazed how calmly she's taking it.'

'OK,' Livvy said, and shrugged her own shoulders right up to her ears and circled them back down again to relax her muscles. 'Let's have a look.'

'This is Jo Moffat,' Amy said, beginning with basic introductions. 'Jo, this is Livvy Jones. She's a midwife and she's going to have a look at you.'

Amy added an aside to Livvy. 'I told Jo that her baby must have Arnold Schwarzenegger's shoulders, and we were having a bit of difficulty turning them to the right position so they can be pushed out.'

'And I told her I hoped that meant it was a boy, 'cos I certainly don't want a girl with Arnie's shoulders,' the patient joked bravely around the Entonox mask.

'Well, we aren't going to find out the sex of the baby until we get that bit out on view,' Livvy pointed out. 'If you'd like to take a couple of deep breaths through the mask to take the edge off the discomfort, I'll just see what I can feel. Whatever you do, don't push.'

'I'll tell you what you'll feel—a quart stuffed into a pint pot,' Jo Moffat grumbled, but she quickly complied with the encouragement to breathe in the gas.

It didn't take long for Livvy to complete her examination, and the only good thing she could see was that the internal presentation seemed to be the same as a couple of previous cases she'd had a hand in delivering—literally.

'The first thing I want to do is get some more pain relief into her so she'll relax,' Livvy muttered softly when she compared findings with Amy, one ear tuned to the way their patient was panting her way through a contraction. 'As soon as I went to examine her she tensed up and we're going to need every millimetre we can get if we're going to pull this cork out of the bottle.'

'We're also going to need a larger episiotomy, aren't we?' Amy asked.

'I've got small hands so we could keep that possibility in reserve,' Livvy suggested. 'I don't like cutting any more than I have to. For now I want to get the analgesic into her and see if we can rotate the baby far enough to get that anterior shoulder out from behind the pubis, without fracturing the clavicle.'

It didn't take much encouragement to get the patient to breathe steadily and deeply to build up the amount of pain relief in her system when Livvy explained what they were going to be doing.

'There isn't room for the *baby* in there,' Jo squeaked in horror. 'How do you think you're going to get your hand in as well?'

'Not my *whole* hand,' Livvy pointed out.

'I bet it'll feel like it,' Jo muttered, and took her first deep breath.

As Livvy prepared to slip her fingers past the baby's vulnerable neck she could hear the echo of Daniel's voice inside her head.

He'd been in the delivery room with her the first time she'd faced a case of shoulder dystocia, and he'd said then that to cope with it you needed either long, strong fingers and a lot of luck or slender agile fingers and a lot of luck.

He'd had the long, strong fingers and she'd had the slender, agile fingers, and between the two of them they'd made an almost unbeatable team.

'Why did this happen?' Jo panted between deep

draughts of gas. 'Is the baby too big? Should I have had a Caesarean?'

'There can be several reasons,' Livvy said, the words interspersed by pauses as she concentrated on what she was doing.

'Usually, as the baby's head starts to come out it will begin to turn so that the shoulders are at the right angle to fit through the space in your pelvis. If that doesn't happen and the baby is coming down the passage fast he can hit a roadblock with his shoulder. With the contractions pushing him from behind, he gets stuck so he can't turn.'

It was difficult to maintain her explanation while she tried to manipulate the wedged baby into a more helpful position. The thing that kept her talking was the fact that she could feel through the pressure on her fingers that when Jo was busy listening, instead of talking, she was breathing in enough gas, and concentrating on Livvy's voice allowed her body to relax.

There was the sound of hushed footsteps behind her and the familiar rustle of a gown. She knew it couldn't be Amy coming towards them—she was standing close by, supporting the baby's head—but it could have been almost anyone else, including Aled Parry or the anaesthetist.

It was the tingle of awareness which travelled through her that told Livvy that Daniel had entered the room and was now standing right behind her.

'How's it going?' he murmured softly, his husky voice sounding strangely intimate in the clinical surroundings.

Livvy closed her eyes as a mixture of relief and pleasure swept through her and kept them closed to force herself to maintain her concentration. It was amazing how much more heart his presence had put in her, but she couldn't afford to be distracted by his nearness.

'It's not…yet!' she muttered briefly through clenched teeth as she struggled to get just a bit more leverage. She certainly wasn't ready to call it quits. 'I can't quite get… Ah! Got it!' she crowed suddenly as something shifted. 'Now I just need to rotate the shoulder and… That's enough of the happy gas, Jo. I need you to give me a big push,' she ordered as she guided the little shoulder. 'One really big one now.'

It was obviously a relief to the poor woman to be able to obey her body's instincts again because she complied willingly.

This time the effort produced movement and, as if there'd never been a problem, one large baby boy slithered into Livvy's hands and let out an indignant bellow.

'It's Arnold all right,' Amy announced with a burst of laughter as she took over the care of the baby. 'The equipment isn't quite the same size yet but it's all there.'

'Delivered through a moderate-sized episiotomy *and* with no broken clavicle,' Daniel said softly. 'Well done.'

'I'd begun to wonder if we were going to have to push the head back up and go for a Caesarean,' Livvy admitted quietly. 'I actually gave in and tried to break the clavicle at one point, but the damn thing wouldn't go.'

'Congratulations on your persistence, then. Yet again you proved my adage.'

'I'm just glad that I got a lot of the luck to go with my slender fingers,' Livvy said, letting him know she remembered what he'd told her.

'Well, I definitely think that success deserves to be

celebrated with a cup of tea,' he announced, and gestured towards the door.

'Sister?' called a voice behind them. 'Wait a minute.'

Livvy turned to see a happily tearful new mum holding her precious son.

'I just wanted to thank you,' she said. 'I know I was joking and everything, but I was so afraid that he was going to die before you got him out.'

'In that case, you should really be thanking Dr Jones here because he's the one who taught me to get that sort of cork out,' Livvy teased lightly. 'He taught me the right way to do it, and also that you don't give up until you've succeeded.'

'In that case, thank you both.' Jo smiled, her eyes glittering with the threat of more tears. 'I've decided I'm going to call him David.'

Livvy knew her smile had dimmed but she had to say something. Was *everyone* calling their son David?

'I've always liked that name,' she said with a lightness she didn't feel. 'I think it will suit him better than Arnold.'

They left the room and Daniel stripped his own disposable gown off then took Livvy's from her.

'It's time you were off your feet,' he announced, and ushered her out to the corridor. 'I saw you wincing when you were up to your elbows on that job so your back's probably killing you.'

'You won't hear me arguing with the prospect of getting my hands on a cup of tea and putting my feet up,' she said, as she revelled in his protective arm around her back.

Self-sufficiency was all very well, but it seemed like years since anyone had taken care of her. Since she'd known the pleasures of a good partnership it was bliss to have someone who wanted to make certain that she put her feet up and... Her happy thoughts ground to a halt as she realised where they were leading.

There was no point in deluding herself with an impossible happily-ever-after scenario when she'd already lost him.

In spite of the euphoria of the successful delivery, she was in a rather more sober frame of mind when he pushed open the door to the ward.

Unlike Daniel. He seemed positively full of the joys of...well, hardly spring, with all that snow outside.

It must be the good news that Alice and the baby were going to be all right. Either that or he'd had good news about his father.

She turned to ask him if he'd been in contact with the orthopaedic ward just as they stepped into her own domain.

'Hey, Doc. Look up,' called a male voice from about halfway along the room, obviously one of her ladies' visitors.

Automatically, Daniel brought the two of them to a halt just inside the doorway and looked up at the sprig of green taped to the lintel.

'Good idea,' he called back with a wicked chuckle. 'Can't miss out on a kiss. Bound to be bad luck.' And before Livvy realised what he intended to do, he'd leant forward swiftly to brush his lips over hers.

Livvy gasped in horror, her eyes immediately flying towards Alice Jones's bed.

She was even more horrified to see that she was looking their way and couldn't have missed seeing what Daniel had done.

CHAPTER SEVEN

'WHAT do you think you're doing?'

Horrified and embarrassed beyond belief, Livvy tried to extricate herself surreptitiously from Daniel's grasp but he easily prevented it, by tightening his arm around her.

While the infuriating man just laughed down at her from his six-inch height advantage the room filled with a chorus of whistles and cheers, but when it looked as if he was going to do it again Livvy knew she had to call a halt.

'Stop it!' she hissed, and managed to jab him in the ribs with her elbow.

'Oof! What was that for?' he demanded, trying hard to look injured, but Livvy knew he was just playing to the gallery.

'Behave yourself. Alice can see what you're doing,' Livvy said as she hurried towards the office to hide the fierce blush of mortification that heated her cheeks.

'So?' he challenged with another wicked grin as he followed in her wake. 'As far as I know, there's no law against kissing under the mistletoe or half the fun would disappear out of Christmas.'

'But you're married!' she objected, knowing that *she* certainly wouldn't have wanted to see him kissing an ex-wife if their positions had been reversed.

'So?' he repeated. 'Most of the people in the ward are married, too, and as at least half of them are pregnant

116

they weren't seeing anything new. Anyway, as a married man, I can tell you that I heartily approve of kissing, whether under the mistletoe or anywhere else.'

She remembered it well, damn him, Livvy thought as she recalled the heady days of their marriage when he'd found any excuse to practise the art.

But that didn't mean that he could continue now.

'Well, you'll have to learn self-control, then, won't you?' she snapped, turning on him clumsily and blocking his path into the office. There just wasn't enough space in there for her to share with him while he was in this strangely ebullient mood.

What on earth had got into him? Had he had good news about his father?

'Have you checked up on your father yet? I presume he's out of Theatre?'

As a distraction, the topic worked perfectly.

'He's out and has already been taken up to the ward,' he told her, obviously delighted. 'When I visited, they told me he'd been plated and screwed in multitudinous directions to hold everything in position, but the operation had gone well. I was actually able to speak to him for a little while.'

'He was awake enough to speak to you?' Livvy was amazed. His father had probably been under anaesthetic for anything up to four hours—maybe more, depending on the mess the surgeon had found when he'd got in there. 'He must have phenomenal powers of recovery.'

'I think it was fear and guilt that brought him round so soon,' Daniel said soberly. 'He thought he'd killed Davey, Alice and the baby.'

'*He'd* killed them?' Livvy frowned.

'He was the one driving the car when it went out of

control so he blamed himself. When I saw how much the weather had deteriorated during the ceremony I *did* offer to play chauffeur but that would have meant one car having to be retrieved later.'

Livvy didn't quite understand the logistics of the problem, but it wasn't that important.

'I suppose the BMW was written off in the crash,' she ventured, mourning the loss of the first car they'd chosen together—the most luxurious one she'd ever driven in.

'Not at all,' he said with a frown. 'It was Dad's car that crashed. I was following a little way behind and saw it happen. I was able to alert the emergency services on my mobile phone.'

'But…' There was definitely something here that didn't sound right. 'Why wasn't Alice travelling with you?'

'That's what I suggested—the BMW's a far more comfortable car than Dad's old Volvo, but he insisted that he wanted to drive her to the hotel for the reception and the baby seat was already strapped in.'

He suddenly clicked his fingers.

'Oh, Lord! I remembered to tell Dad that *she* was all right but I forgot to tell Alice about Dad's operation,' he groaned. 'I'm going to find my neck in a noose.'

Before Livvy could say a word he was gone, hurrying towards Alice's bed.

There was an awful fascination in watching the way he sat himself down on the edge of the mattress and cradled one of Alice's hands in his while he spoke earnestly for a moment.

From her vantage point at the end of the ward Livvy could see his heart-stopping, caring smile as he passed on the good news to Alice.

It was painful enough to see the two of them together, but it was the way she suddenly wrapped her arms around his neck and pulled him towards her for a heartfelt hug that tied Livvy's throat in a knot and wouldn't let her breathe.

It was just sheer bad timing that made her next Braxton Hicks contraction arrive at that precise moment, and if she'd had enough breath she'd have been hard-pressed not to shout out.

Carefully, she propped her hips against the desk and gripped the edge with white-knuckled hands as she concentrated, focusing all her thoughts on staying as relaxed as possible while she controlled her breathing.

'Wow, that was the strongest one yet,' she muttered, releasing a deep breath of relief as it began to fade. 'If they're just the practice runs, I'm certainly not looking forward to the real thing.'

She straightened and rested both hands on the full curve of her swollen belly, stroking it gently.

'At least you're being a little quieter at the moment, aren't you, monster? Did someone finally make you understand that you're not supposed to be so energetic by this stage?'

'Uh-oh! She's started talking to the filing cabinet,' Pat teased as she entered the room. 'That kiss must have scrambled her brains completely.'

'Don't mention it, please,' Livvy groaned, embarrassed all over again. 'Wretched man. Has he forgotten that I have to work here? It'll be all round the hospital in no time and I won't be able to look anyone in the eye.'

'It certainly will be all around the hospital if I have anything to do with it,' Pat confirmed with glee. 'Just wait till I see Sue and Amy. Fancy you working here all this time, without even mentioning that you were hiding someone as gorgeous as him at home. You're a real dark horse.'

'Uh, Pat,' Livvy began, knowing the time had come to explain about the divorce.

In view of her obviously pregnant state, she'd been avoiding any mention of it—after all, what were the chances that any of the staff would ever meet Daniel?

She'd hoped quite desperately that he would have come looking for her when she'd disappeared out of his life, but when even her appearance at his mother's funeral hadn't prompted a visit that hope had died. Especially when she'd seen Alice's arrival at his father's house.

The trouble was, how was she going to tell Pat about her divorce and the circumstances surrounding it, without revealing Alice's part in the events of seven months ago? Could that be termed violating a patient's privacy?

'Actually, Livvy, I came in to ask if you could be persuaded to join the group going round singing,' Pat said, and the moment was lost.

'I've done it a couple of years and thoroughly enjoyed it. Once your little one arrives you probably won't want to take the time away from him or her at Christmas so this might be your last chance. Unless, of course, you can't carry a tune in a bucket and would rather not?'

'I'm certainly not operatic standard,' Livvy admitted honestly. 'I hardly like to put myself forward when my only claim to Welsh tunefulness is my name.'

'Not wanting to be rude, but this year they're desperate enough to be looking for quantity rather than quality. Go on. You'll have fun.'

'But what about the patients? I know I'm not officially on duty but—'

'Don't worry about the ward—I can always get the switchboard to track you down if we need you, and Amy's not much more than a quick shout away in the delivery suite.'

'Oh?' This was news to Livvy. 'Has another one of the upstairs ladies gone into production, then? Do you know which one?'

'I don't know her name but she's another experienced mum who's had the last two as easily as shelling peas. Apparently, she's hoping that she'll be able to go home to the rest of the family in the morning if everything goes smoothly.'

'Sounds like she's a glutton for punishment if she wants to hurry back to running the home that quickly,' Livvy said with a worried frown. 'I hope she's not going to be doing too much too soon or both she and the baby could suffer.'

'It's either that or she doesn't want to miss the baby's first Christmas with the family. We could always make her release conditional that her husband did everything for the next few days,' Pat suggested. 'Anyway, I've always felt that there's something very special about babies born at Christmas, especially those born on Christmas day.'

'It could certainly save a lot on presents,' Livvy pointed out, with her tongue firmly in her cheek. 'They'd be able to have Christmas and birthday all rolled into one.'

'Oh, I don't like that idea,' Pat objected, her expression quite horrified. 'Poor little things would miss out on a special celebration every year.'

A movement at the corner of her eye drew Livvy's attention as Cherry hurried through the doorway, once again quite breathless with excitement.

'Sister? I think that jinx of having babies arriving in bunches is working again,' she announced with shining eyes and a broad grin.

'Uh-oh! Who is it this time?' Pat demanded.

'I'm almost certain Alwyn Morgan's just started labour. I was right beside her when the monitor went off.' Cherry turned to go back to the ward then spun back with words bubbling out of her, her pixie hat flopping wildly.

'I'll admit I wasn't looking forward to being on duty over Christmas because I thought I would be missing out on all the excitement of the celebrations at home, but this has been so much better than I expected. Things have been almost non-stop for hours!' She threw them a final infectious grin and bounced out of the room.

'Were we ever that young and enthusiastic?' Pat demanded in the wake of her departure, and Livvy groaned.

Then they both stayed still and listened, their heads up like animals trying to pinpoint an elusive sound.

At first all that could be heard was the chaotic mixture of noises in the ward, with voices tumbling over each other as they vied for supremacy with the television and Christmas carols.

They smiled simultaneously when they suddenly heard the distinctive electronic sound of the monitor cut through the rest.

'Thank goodness for that,' Pat said, voicing Livvy's equal delight. 'The poor girl was beginning to get very depressed that it was taking so long.'

'Well, it was bad enough, having to be confined to bed for months so she didn't lose the baby,' Livvy pointed out, grateful that there hadn't been any similar problems with her own pregnancy. 'Once the ultrasound confirmed that the baby was fully developed and they took her off the drugs she obviously thought she'd automatically go straight into labour.'

'Perhaps she should have watched Mr Darcy sooner,' Pat joked. 'He obviously got her hormones stirred up and got things moving.'

Livvy chuckled at the idea then heaved herself up off the edge of the desk again, silently groaning at the resulting backache as she started to make for the door.

'Oops! Time for a quick detour to the toilet,' she announced wryly when other pressing needs made themselves known. 'I'll meet you by Alwyn's bed in a few minutes.'

Unlike the last few mums, Alwyn's labour progressed very slowly and steadily, and as none of the others in the ward seemed to be going to start anything interesting Livvy finally made the decision to join the ragtag choir for their trip around the wards.

'Here, you can borrow this cloak,' Amy offered.

Livvy took a closer look at the woman making the offer and saw how tired she looked. It couldn't be easy for her to cope with this level of pressure and responsibility while she was feeling less than a hundred per cent. Livvy could remember vividly how drained she'd felt during the all-day nightmare called morning sickness.

Still, with Alwyn's slow progress the only one to

monitor, perhaps Amy would be able to catch her breath a bit.

Amy had arrived soon after the debris from the meal had been cleared away to report the birth of a rather small but otherwise perfectly healthy baby girl, and found Livvy, preparing to set off.

Now she was holding out one of the traditional heavy nurse's cloaks that was a thick navy fabric on the outside and lined with bright scarlet.

'We usually turn it inside out to give everything an extra Christmassy feel,' Amy said. 'You'll probably find that when you join the rest of them you'll also be given a length of tinsel to put in your hair, like an angel's halo.'

'As long as they don't expect me to sit on top of the Christmas tree,' Livvy warned darkly.

The two of them glanced down at her ungainly shape and burst out laughing at the idea.

The tour was due to begin in the main reception area of the hospital, and there was already a small crowd of porters, Casualty staff and patients gathered as Livvy stepped out of the lift. One of the group was just checking the tuning on his guitar as Livvy nervously walked across to join them.

'Oh, good. Another volunteer,' announced a voice and Livvy felt her face heat furiously when everyone turned to look at her as she scurried to hide herself in the edge of the group.

At least she could console herself that her borrowed cloak went a long way to camouflaging her rather distinctive shape. She doubted they'd ever had a heavily pregnant member in their choir before. Hardly the traditional image of ethereal heavenly hosts...

Amy had been right about the tinsel, too, and Livvy was just trying to use one of her hair clips to get the wretched thing to stay on her head when someone stepped up behind her and it was taken out of her hand.

'Allow me,' said the slightly husky tone of a familiar tenor voice, and she turned to look up into the well-remembered blue of Daniel's eyes.

Silently she relinquished her hold, unable to prevent her fingers brushing his as she handed him the clip. Then she had to stand still while he stood behind her to twine the strands around her head in the form of a coronet.

Just the touch of his fingers against her head while he carefully skewered the strands in position was enough to send shivers of awareness to every extremity.

Her pulse began racing and her skin almost seemed to tingle with the heat she could feel radiating from his body, so that all she could think about was how close he was standing. It didn't help that he didn't say another word, making absolutely no effort to break the silent cocoon that seemed to surround them.

When he'd finished the task she managed to find her voice to thank him, but when she would have moved away to put some distance between them he caught her elbow and drew her attention to the small sheaf of papers he retrieved from his pocket.

'I've got the words of all the songs so you'd better stay with me to share,' he suggested. His advice was logical enough but the expression in his eyes carried more than a hint of challenge.

Livvy didn't know if she was up to it, not with her emotions in such turmoil after the events of the last twelve hours.

With the memories of a similar event last year so clear

in her head she didn't know if she could endure a whole evening with their heads bent together over the same sheet of paper, and she glanced around for some reasonable form of escape. When she realised that the majority of the choir had already paired up she was left with little alternative but to agree.

She didn't voice her reservations but he must have known, otherwise why did his actions seem so deliberate when he made concentration so difficult by pressing his shoulder so closely to hers?

Then, when he changed sides and wrapped his free arm around her waist, she honestly didn't know whether to give up the attempt at singing and go back to the ward or simply wallow in the unexpected guilty pleasure.

It was all so much like Christmas Eve a year ago that she didn't know whether to laugh or cry.

For a while, as they worked their way through the repertoire of songs and moved their way from ward to ward, Daniel was able to concentrate on his singing.

When they'd started off in the children's wards with 'Rudolph the Red-Nosed Reindeer' and 'Jingle Bells' he'd been afraid that she was going to insist on treating him the same as any other member of the choir. He'd been reduced to deliberately using his possession of the song sheet as an excuse to stand close to her.

It didn't take long before he recognised from the raised colour in her cheeks that his ploy was working, that she'd been forced to acknowledge his physical presence beside her, and he stepped up his campaign by curving one arm around her.

He tried to do it casually so that she wouldn't balk at the implied intimacy, but inside he yearned for her to accept the gesture as it was really meant—that she could use his body as a source of comfort and support the way she had a year ago.

Unfortunately for his peace of mind, as the evening wore on her proximity began to have its usual effect on him and he found himself less and less able to control his response to the woman beside him.

After seven months of separation, having his arm around her was like offering a sip of water to a man dying of thirst.

At first he tried to blame his discomfort on the elusive flowery scent that wafted over him whenever they leaned closer to read the words of unfamiliar verses.

He had no idea what it was called, but it was one that would always remind him of the steamy air she'd left behind when she'd finished in the bathroom.

Most of all it would remind him of the way his own skin had smelled when he'd joined her in the shower and wrapped himself around her slick, soapy body. He glanced sideways at that body, hidden now under the tent-like structure of her nurse's cloak.

From his observations today of her shape and the way she was moving he was pretty certain that she was close to full term, and that would mean... He did a quick mental calculation and felt a reminiscent smile cover his face. If his mathematics was correct, he had a damn good idea exactly when that baby she was carrying had been conceived.

His body reacted predictably when he remembered that it was just such an occasion in the shower that could have been the culprit.

After several days when their shifts had left them with little time together he'd made a special effort and had actually been able to leave the hospital on time, knowing that they'd been invited out that evening.

He'd arrived home with time to spare and had surprised her in the bathroom, getting ready to go out to their colleagues' engagement party.

No matter how stern he was with himself while he stood surrounded by a dozen or so complete strangers he couldn't help the mental images unrolling in his mind like an X-rated film as he remembered the alternative way that evening had been spent.

Without saying a word to alert her that he was there, he'd stripped his own clothes off his heavily aroused body and had joined her behind the recently installed opaque glass screen.

Her eyes had been tightly closed against the sting of shampoo and she'd squealed with shock when he'd wrapped his arms around her slender body and pulled her against him from head to toe to possess her with a ravenous kiss.

The body leaning against him now wasn't the same slender one he remembered from that memorable night, but somehow the full, blatantly fertile curves she'd developed since then only served to attract him more. Until he'd seen her body shaped by his baby growing inside her, he hadn't realised how much he'd wanted to see her this way.

He had to pause in his singing to clear his throat, amazed and horrified to realise that his thoughts had actually brought him to full arousal.

Was he some sort of pervert, for heaven's sake, to be lusting like this after a heavily pregnant woman?

No, he decided resolutely, he was just a man attracted

to a woman regardless of her physical appearance...or was it that?

He cast her several sidelong glances before he shook his head firmly.

No. In Livvy's case he was attracted to her because she was Livvy. Whether she had the figure of a slender sprite or the quintessential earth mother was immaterial.

He drew in the next breath to continue singing 'Once in Royal David's City' and sighed heavily instead.

He certainly hadn't expected to be pitchforked into this sort of situation when he'd decided to confront Livvy. He needed to talk to her but with the siege atmosphere in the hospital it had been all too easy for her to avoid him.

He pressed his lips together when he thought about how badly he must have hurt her.

He couldn't believe that she'd moved so far away— to Wales, for heaven's sake. It was hours by road from St Augustine's and almost impossible by train.

The only reason he could think of was that the idiot woman had chosen to move here in the belief that a Jones would be able to disappear for ever in a country full of Joneses. And, because he hadn't been in contact with her in the months that had passed since she came here, she must have convinced herself that he didn't care enough about her to look very hard.

He had a horrible feeling that it was going to be an uphill task to persuade her otherwise.

The fact that he'd finally tracked Livvy to this hospital at the same time as he was in the middle of organising the wedding nearby had seemed the height of serendipity. The location had been suggested by his father so that they could combine it with a visit to their few surviving relatives—those same relatives who hadn't even been invited when he'd married Livvy because he couldn't bear to wait to make her his.

As soon as the ceremony was over this morning he'd had every intention of asking Alice to release him from his promise and then he'd be free to search Livvy out and make his long-overdue explanations.

What a fool he'd been to allow Alice to come between him and Libby. He'd known all along that his blonde-haired sprite was the best thing to have happened in his life and he'd been stupid enough to give someone else the power to spoil it.

Well, enough was enough.

He loved Livvy as much as ever and wanted her back—*needed* her back in his life or it wasn't worth living.

He'd spoken to Alice to pass on the good news about Davey and his father's operation and at the same time had told her his decision. He'd deliberately left her little option, but she'd finally agreed to release him from his promise.

Now all he had to do was persuade Livvy to hear him out and he might stand a chance of getting his life back on track. He wasn't going to let himself think about the possibility that he'd lost her trust for ever. That was a prospect that had kept him awake for more nights than he cared to think about.

There was just one more ward to visit after this, the obstetrics ward that Livvy had been spending most of her time in today, and then—

Suddenly, the guitarist began to play the plaintively simple introduction to 'Silent Night' and Daniel's heart turned over.

Instantly he was surrounded by the magic memories of a year ago when the two of them had taken part in a very similar Christmas Eve's tradition at St Augustine's.

Then, as now, they'd been standing in a ward full of mothers and babies, both those already born and those still in waiting, as they'd gathered for the impromptu concert.

Then, as now, he'd had his arm round her shoulders as they'd shared the song sheet.

He hadn't realised until then just how beautifully the tone of her voice blended with his, and when he'd begun to sing the harmony to her melody their voices had blended and twined so seamlessly that it had been enough to draw the soul out of his body. If only that harmony could once more extend into their lives as well.

For just a moment when the familiar notes sounded he'd felt her stiffen within the circle of his arm and knew that she was remembering too. But then she relaxed again and when they began to sing it sounded to his hopeful ears as if she was letting the words and music come from her heart.

Livvy could feel the tremor in her voice as she joined in with the familiar words of the first verse of 'Silent Night', the memories sharp enough to cut her like a knife. But suddenly it was as if the last year had disappeared and all she knew was that she and Daniel were together, their voices blending effortlessly.

She was so wrapped up in the song that she didn't see Daniel make any signal but when the second verse began and she realised that theirs were the only voices left singing, she faltered. Her eyes flew up to his as uncertainty struck, but when she met his steady blue gaze and realised that he was willing her to continue what else could she do?

Once more he sang the harmony to her melody, the simple tune taking on an unearthly poignance in the quiet of the dimly lit ward.

She barely noticed that the rest of the choir joined in for the final verse, her heart too full of the realisation that one song could be the focus of everything that had changed in her life. Since the last time they'd sung it together she'd become pregnant and carried the child to within a few days of term, but she'd lost the man who had fathered that child.

She might try to tell herself that she couldn't keep looking back over her shoulder, that she must move on with her life, but with his clear blue eyes fixed intently on hers she had to admit to herself that he was the only man she would ever love.

The carol came to an end and after several seconds of appreciative silence there was a swift burst of applause.

At first Livvy was oblivious to it all, with Daniel smiling down at her and holding her snugly at his side as though she belonged there.

Suddenly Livvy couldn't take any more.

'Excuse me,' she whispered, taking him by surprise when she turned away as swiftly as her ungainly shape would allow and broke his hold on her. 'I've got to go.'

A group of patients was converging on their little choir with smiles and words of praise but she couldn't bear to stay, taking advantage of the temporary mêlée to make her escape.

CHAPTER EIGHT

'Livvy, wait!'

The sound of Daniel's voice, following her along the corridor, was enough to lend wings to her feet.

In spite of the fact that her traitorous body decided to try to break her in half with another clenching spasm of pain she forced her feet to move a little faster.

She knew it was going to take him a few minutes to fight his way out of the surrounding throng but he could move so much more quickly than she could. It wouldn't take him long to catch her up.

The lift doors closed behind her with a soft sigh and she gave a sigh of her own as she leaned gratefully against the antiseptic-smelling wall and waited to be delivered to the floor below.

Heat surged up into her face when she thought about the spectacle she'd made of herself just now. She'd been tricked into partnering her less-than-perfect voice with Daniel's for that impromptu duet in front of all those people. Heaven knew, that was embarrassing enough when she thought that she was going to have to face all her colleagues within the department, knowing they'd heard her make a fool of herself.

It was all very well Daniel trying to tell her that she had a lovely voice, but she knew he was just being kind. Her mother had been the one with the voice in their family and she knew she could never compare.

The worst part was knowing that everyone on the

ward and in the choir had been watching the two of them, and when she'd looked up at him they must have been able to see the besotted expression on her face. What made it worse was that once she'd met his gaze she hadn't been able to help herself.

Once they'd started singing that carol her brain seemed to have switched to automatic pilot, completely ignoring the fact that she was no longer married to the man. When she'd seen the warmth in his eyes she'd been helpless and unable to look away.

There was a soft jolt as the lift arrived and she stepped out into the corridor, the contraction beginning to die away now.

As she unfastened the ties of the borrowed cloak and slid it off her shoulders her feet automatically took her towards the ward. After all, she thought wryly, where else could she go?

It was Christmas Eve and outside was the perfect illustration for a million Christmas cards, with the snow lying deep and crisp and even.

Knowing the narrow road that led to her cottage, there was no way she would be able to get there by taxi, and she wasn't exactly in the right physical shape to walk the distance even if a taxi driver could be persuaded to take her as far as the end of her turning.

As she folded the heavy cloak over her arm tiredness suddenly overwhelmed her and she had a mental image of the hospital bed reserved for her on the ward.

What a relief it would be to curl up under crisp sheets and shut her brain down for the night. It was all very well wanting to keep her hands and mind occupied to stave off boredom, but eventually she was going to have to admit that a nearly-nine-months pregnant woman just didn't have the same reserves of energy.

As she pushed the ward door open all eyes turned towards her and she suddenly remembered that the choir still had to come here to sing.

'They're here!' called Megan Williams as she settled herself back against a bank of pillows with her precious daughter cradled in her arms.

'They're on their way,' Livvy corrected, while her brain frantically tried to think of somewhere to hide out until it was all over. She could hardly spend the next half hour in the bathroom or someone would come looking for her, thinking she was in labour.

'All that standing around was killing me so I ducked out,' she added by way of explanation.

'Oh, Sister,' breathed Cherry in obvious relief as her head popped around the corner from Sister's office. 'I was hoping it was your voice I heard. I've been trying to track you down.'

Livvy silenced a groan and straightened her shoulders.

'What did you want? There aren't any problems, are there?'

She glanced quickly around the ward but everyone seemed to be happily waiting for the choir to arrive.

'It's Mrs Morgan—you know, the one on the monitor,' Cherry said, nodding towards the far corner. Livvy suddenly noticed that the young woman wasn't there any more and neither was her tinsel-decorated box of technology. 'Pat was keeping an eye on her and now she's taken her along to the labour suite. She asked me to get hold of you and send you along.'

'Are you all right here?' Livvy demanded, worried that she was leaving such a novice in nominal charge of the ward, but her brain was already whirling with all the potential problems that could be happening in the labour suite.

Alwyn Morgan's labour had been progressing slowly when she'd left the ward but there'd been nothing to worry about on that score. Had something gone wrong?

'Provided no one gets so excited, listening to the choir that they instantly jump to second-stage labour I'll be all right,' the younger woman said with quiet assurance. 'Anyway, I can always shout for help, can't I?'

'Good girl,' Livvy said with a tired smile, appreciating the youngster's steady confidence. 'I've got a feeling you're going to do well on this ward.'

She hurried towards the labour suite, taking with her the memory of the glow of pride that had lit the young nurse's face.

'I felt like that, too, once upon a time,' she muttered, scowling along a corridor that seemed to stretch into infinity. 'About a million years ago before I started carrying an elephant around as a fashion statement.'

'Talking to yourself is supposed to be the first sign of madness,' Pat commented through her smile of relief when Livvy came through the door.

'I've moved on from there to full-blown paranoia,' Livvy informed her grimly as she fought with ties that barely met around her middle. 'I've started answering myself, too.'

A sudden sound made her look up and she met the eyes of the understandably nervous expectant father who now looked quite horrified.

For a moment she was hard-pressed not to laugh aloud but she wasn't certain that she would be able to stop if she did, and that would probably have sent him over the edge too.

It was all very well for hospital staff to joke among themselves that they had to be mad to work here, but when you were waiting for expert help for your wife, you obviously didn't want to know that.

'Don't worry, Mr Morgan,' she said calmly. 'It's the night before Christmas and everyone's allowed to talk a bit of nonsense.'

He tried to find a smile but it was a weak one.

'Now, Pat,' Livvy said in an undertone as she joined her on the other side of the monitor. 'What's the problem?'

'Mum seems fine, but I'm beginning to get worried about the baby,' Pat admitted. 'Each time she has a contraction the baby's pulse drops. For the last half hour it's been a steady downward graph.'

Without having to make a list, Livvy knew there could be several reasons for those findings. Some pointed to danger for the baby and some to danger for mother *and* baby, but none of them were good.

'Have you managed to get hold of anyone?' she asked while the possibility of a hasty Caesarean section loomed large in her mind.

'I paged Aled Parry and he was here within a quarter of an hour, but when he got here he looked more dead than alive so I sent him away again,' Pat said, her more than professional concern for the reserved resident obvious even over her concern for her patients.

'I know he's only just recovering from that flu bug and I told him earlier that he sounded dreadful,' Livvy agreed.

'With Duncan French's broken arm putting him out

of commission, and Simon away on holiday and uncontactable, Aled was intending to work straight through the forty-eight hours of Christmas.'

'That's taking devotion to duty rather too far when he's not well himself,' Livvy said. 'Especially when we've got a well-qualified captive replacement available.'

She sent up a mental sigh of resignation as she lumbered heavily across to the phone.

She'd been hoping to keep out of Daniel's way as much as possible for the next twelve hours while keeping her fingers crossed that Alice would be ready to be released tomorrow. Now she was going to have to search him out and ask him to cast a professional eye over yet another patient.

'Obstetrics. Cherry Watts speaking,' said the voice in her ear, and before Livvy could say a word she heard the sound of voices in the background raised in song.

That answered her first question—the choir had arrived.

'It's Livvy Jones here, Cherry. Is Dr Jones with the choir?'

'Yes. Well, no. He arrived on the ward with them, but he's not with the choir exactly,' she floundered.

'Damn. Where's he gone, wretched man?' Livvy muttered as she heard a scuffling sound on the other end of the line.

'And I love you too,' Daniel quipped, the sudden sound of his voice in her ear nearly causing her to drop the receiver. 'Do I take it you want me?'

She could hear the laughter in Daniel's voice but she wasn't smiling.

Yes, she wanted him—would always want him—but that didn't mean she could have him.

'I've got a patient here I'd like you to have a look at,' she announced, trying to ignore his suggestive words. 'Foetal pulse and b.p. dropping,' she added cryptically in case the parents were listening.

'I'll be with you in a minute,' he said briskly, suddenly all business, and the line went dead.

Livvy turned back to the other occupants of the room and this time, with the major weight of the patient's welfare lifted off her shoulders, her smile was genuine.

'Please, Nurse, what's going on?' young Mr Morgan asked as he held his wife's hand in a vice-like grip. 'I can see the numbers for the baby are getting lower. Does that mean he's dying?'

Livvy's heart clenched with dismay. Did he really think that they would stand by idly while his baby slowly died? Sometimes ignorance could be very cruel and the only remedy for that was to explain a little of what was happening. She would keep it simple, knowing that too much information could be just as frightening.

'The numbers you're watching on the monitor are telling us that each time Alwyn has a contraction the baby's blood pressure is going down a bit and his heartbeat slows.'

'Is that dangerous?' demanded Alwyn, her eyes huge in her face. 'It must be or you wouldn't be worried about it, would you?'

'It *could* be dangerous if we didn't check why it was happening and do something about it,' Livvy confirmed. 'As it is, Dr Jones will be here any minute to check things over. He's an obstetrician and gynaecologist, the same as Duncan French.'

'Is he good?' demanded Mr Morgan, and Pat chuckled.

'Good enough to marry,' she said with a grin. 'He's Sister's husband, too, so she knows him well.'

Now was not the time to correct Pat about her marital status— she certainly couldn't do it in front of worried parents-to-be—but soon she was going to have to set her colleague straight.

Anyway, at that moment Livvy heard the swing doors open and she looked up just in time to see Daniel enter the room.

Not wanting to stand too close, she retreated from Alwyn Morgan's side and stood against the wall, gratefully leaning back to try to relieve the nagging ache in her back. She watched Daniel's easy manner as he greeted the frightened couple, knowing that he could set their minds at rest if anyone could.

He accepted Alwyn's notes from Pat and slowly read the résumé of all the problems she'd had over the last two years.

Livvy knew the file started with the two miscarriages she'd endured at about the ten-week mark. When this, her third pregnancy, threatened to go the same way six months ago she'd been brought into hospital for correction of a diagnosed progesterone deficiency and monitoring.

While he was reading, Alwyn had another contraction and Livvy saw him add the latest read-out figures from the foetal monitor to the file.

He put the notes to one side without comment and turned to Alwyn to begin a thorough examination, taking the time to explain at each stage what he was looking for and why and always keeping his explanations clear and simple.

When he eventually straightened and stood frowning for a moment, Livvy wasn't in the least surprised that neither Alwyn nor her husband interrupted his thoughts. They had obviously decided to trust the man implicitly in spite of the fact that they barely knew him.

She remembered the feeling well.

Right from the first time she'd met Daniel, when they'd survived their collision in the corridor, she'd known that he was going to be something special in her life—she'd never have agreed to marry him so quickly if that hadn't been the case.

She had known him for just a few weeks before she had taken a chance, trusting him enough to place her heart in his keeping.

Shelving the painful memories of the way he had broken that trust, Livvy forced herself to concentrate on the situation in front of her.

During his examination of Alwyn she had realised that Daniel had virtually ruled out the possibility of a detached placenta because Alwyn's blood pressure remained within normal bounds. If she had been haemorrhaging that would have been a different story.

'I think we've got two possibilities,' he announced at last, carefully including the baby's parents in the discussion. 'Either the cord's got itself somewhere it shouldn't so that every time there's a contraction it gets squeezed and starves the baby of blood or your little one's just getting tired of the labour taking so long.'

'Can you do anything—speed it up, perhaps?' Tom Morgan demanded bluntly, and Livvy couldn't help but admire his determination.

'What I propose doing is keeping an eye on Alwyn and monitoring her closely through the next few contractions. If the blood pressure doesn't drop any further then we can assume that the baby's holding his own. If that's the case, and providing everything doesn't take too long, labour can continue normally.'

'And if it doesn't?' Alwyn prompted, one hand resting protectively on the covered mound that hid her baby.

'If the blood pressure continues to fall then we might not have time to wait for a normal labour. We might have to get the baby out by the quick route.'

'You mean operate?' Tom Morgan asked, his voice rather unsteady at the prospect.

'At this stage it's just a possibility,' Daniel said. 'Whatever happens, we don't want the baby to be at risk. You've both gone through too much to get this far for us to take any chances now.'

The young father turned to his wife and they shared a wordless communication for several long seconds before he turned back to face Daniel.

'OK,' he said simply. 'We trust you to keep the baby safe.'

For a moment Livvy had to blink rapidly to clear the sudden threat of tears from her eyes. It was a testament to Daniel's obvious honesty and concern that the young couple had so readily placed the life of their precious child in his hands.

She tried to straighten away from the wall and when she was suddenly gripped by another pain she couldn't help gasping aloud.

All eyes were turned on her as she tried to control her breathing and the pain.

'What's the matter?' Daniel demanded as he strode

towards her, his straight brows drawn down fiercely over his nose. 'You've been on your feet far too long, you silly woman.'

'Stop fussing,' she hissed between gritted teeth, hating the fact that she wasn't coping very well while he was watching. 'It's just a Braxton Hicks contraction.'

'She had another one earlier,' Pat volunteered.

'How much earlier?' Daniel demanded, one lean hand now resting on Livvy's belly to monitor the progress of the contraction.

'Several hours ago—sometime this morning,' Pat supplied, and Livvy didn't correct her. There had been several in the interim, but if she told Daniel that he'd probably jump to the conclusion that she was in labour and handcuff her to a bed.

'How long until she's full term?' he asked, once more directing his question to Pat.

'Still several weeks yet,' Pat told him, and Livvy gave a mental sigh of relief when he nodded his acceptance. If he'd known that it was now just under two weeks she had a good idea that there was no way he would let her out of his sight until either Aled Parry or Duncan French were fit for duty again or Simon was back from his holiday. He certainly wouldn't be letting her help out on the ward no matter how short of staff they were.

She drew in a deep breath as the contraction faded and slowly became aware that his hand was still resting on the full curve of her belly.

Once it was obvious that the pain had gone she expected him to take his hand away and turn back to their patient, but he didn't move away, standing quite still in front of her.

'Daniel?' She looked up at him, feeling a frown pleating her forehead when she found him staring at his fingers curved over the front of her smock.

She could feel the heat of his hand travelling through the layers of material to reach her tautly stretched skin, and when his fingers spread as if he was trying to encompass the child within, she looked up, needing to see his face to try to divine his thoughts.

Her breath caught in her throat when she saw the expression in his eyes. He looked so sad and suddenly she knew that he must be thinking about how much he had already missed of his baby's life.

As if he'd just noticed where his hand was resting, he abruptly snatched it away and grasped her firmly by the elbow instead.

'You'll be all right in here until I can get this woman off her feet, won't you?' he asked Pat as he started to lead Livvy to the door, pausing just long enough to strip off their disposables with practised efficiency.

'No problem,' Pat agreed with a wry lift of an eyebrow for Livvy when she briefly met her eyes.

'You don't want two of them producing in here at once,' said Tom Morgan, obviously much chirpier now he understood what was going on with his wife.

Livvy objected to having decisions made for her like that and wasn't very keen on being manhandled along the corridor, but as the ultimate object was to get her to relax a bit and as she *was* feeling a bit the worse for wear it wasn't worthwhile saying a word.

Daniel paused for a moment when they entered the ward, finding several members of the choir standing in a knot making their last farewells as they admired the new babies.

Changing direction, he led her towards Sister's office and drew her to a halt beside the desk.

'Tea? Coffee? Water?' he asked, one hand reaching out to check the level of water in the kettle before he switched it on.

'There should be some juice left in the fridge,' Livvy said as she perched on the edge of the desk and surreptitiously tried to rub the ache in her back.

She watched him crouch down in front of the compact fridge to find the container, the muscles bunching in his thighs reminding her of the first time she'd seen them naked. Well, if you could call caked in mud on a rugby pitch naked, she amended. Because he was nearly six feet tall he had long legs but his choice of sport meant that his whole body was well muscled and fit.

He straightened easily and she was forced to drag her eyes away quickly in case he turned and caught her ogling him.

'Were you very sick?' he asked suddenly, the question seeming to come from nowhere as he stood facing her across the room. He appeared to have completely forgotten the carton of orange in his hand as he gazed intently at her.

'Morning, noon and night,' she admitted with a grimace. 'I couldn't stand the smell of bacon or cigarettes—still can't—and I couldn't bear the taste of coffee.'

'That must have made waking up in the morning a problem,' he teased, his expression lightening as he referred to her former habit of setting the coffee-maker on a timer before she went to bed so that it was ready for her first thing.

'Luckily, once I got to three months I could have the

odd cup again but only if it was heavily diluted with milk.'

'What about now?'

'About the same—that's why I've switched to juice or milk. I'm hoping my taste buds will go back to normal once the baby's arrived—at least when I stop breast feeding.'

It had been a throw-away comment but when his eyes suddenly focused on the relevant portion of her anatomy it was as if he'd reached out and touched her.

Livvy felt her nipples react to the visual stimulation and as they were so sensitive these days, anyway, just the friction of her plain cotton maternity bra made them feel as if he'd caressed them through the finest silk.

Afraid that he might notice the physical evidence of her reaction, she tried to disguise it by folding her arms nonchalantly but only succeeded in pulling her smock tight and making her condition look more obvious.

It wasn't as if there was anywhere for her to put her folded arms, with the newly lush curves of her enlarged breasts almost meeting the top of her bulge.

She huffed out an exasperated breath.

'I'll be so glad when this is all over,' she grumbled uncomfortably, remembering how he used to enjoy stroking her and praising her dancer's legs and slender body.

His blonde haired-sprite he used to call her... There wasn't anything very sprightly about her now.

'I didn't realise how clumsy and ungainly I would end up,' she said almost apologetically, suddenly realising just how much her body had changed since he'd last seen her. 'I feel like one of those hot-air balloons, only twice as large and ten times as heavy.'

'You're beautiful,' he exclaimed huskily, his eyes still roaming over her from head to foot, almost as if he was eager to discover her new shape. He seemed especially fascinated by the full curves so poorly disguised under her smock.

She made a wordless sound of denial even as her eyes widened in surprise when she saw the tide of dark colour wash over his cheeks.

He glanced down and didn't seem to know why he had the carton of juice in his hand. He passed it from one hand to the other, focusing on it intently as if he needed something to occupy his hands while he came to a decision.

Suddenly he looked up at her again with a new determination in his expression.

Almost absent-mindedly he put the carton aside and took the half-dozen paces that brought him in front of her.

'You are, you know,' he said earnestly, softly, his hands hovering for a moment before he placed them gently on her shoulders. 'I don't think I've ever seen your skin more radiant or your face more serene. You almost glow with it.'

'Daniel…' She didn't really know what to say. He seemed so sincere, as if he really cared about her, but if that was the case, why had he—

'Oh, Livvy, I've missed you,' he whispered, his voice huskier than ever as he angled his head and brought his lips to meet hers.

For a moment Livvy was transfixed by the heated awareness that flashed through her at the contact.

Helpless to resist when it was what she'd been craving for seven long months, she found herself parting her own lips to admit his sleekly questing tongue and instantly met it in a dark, hidden duel.

She felt more than heard his rough groan of appreciation as it rumbled from his body into hers, and she slid her hands up his arms and over his shoulders to clasp them in the thick softness of his hair in her need to deepen the kiss.

She was completely oblivious to her surroundings, her senses aware only of the fact that she was once again paired with the other half of her soul when he pulled her up from the edge of the desk and into his arms.

The sudden crushing pressure of her pregnant body against his lean strength was shocking in its impact and she wrenched herself away from him.

'Daniel!' she gasped breathlessly as guilt poured through her to dampen her desire. 'We…we shouldn't be doing this. It…it isn't right!'

'I admit it isn't quite as easy as it was when there were just the two of us to consider,' he said teasingly, his voice gravelly with arousal as he glanced down at the protrusion beneath her smock.

'That's just the point,' she snapped, wishing she could just abandon all her principles. How could anything that felt so right be so wrong? 'It's not the two of us any more. There's Alice to consider.'

'Alice?' he repeated with an absent frown as he tried to gather her close again, his eyes intent on her lips. 'What on earth has she got to do with anything?'

'What has she…?' Livvy shook her head in disbelief, trying to ignore the way her whole body was throbbing with denial. It would be so easy to give in to what Daniel wanted because she wanted it too. The trouble was, she wouldn't be able to live with herself afterwards.

'Daniel, what's happened to you?' she demanded as she braced her hands against his chest and glared up at him. 'You used to believe that it was a mark of a man that he kept his word, but in the last seven months you seem to have done nothing but break it, first to me and now with Alice.'

His head came up in surprise and he blinked as if he were surfacing from a deep dive.

'What are you talking about, Livvy?' he demanded, clearly confused. 'What on earth has *Alice* got to do with anything between *us*?'

Livvy drew in a deep breath and started again.

'Daniel, you're a married man and you made certain promises,' she began, only to have him interrupt almost immediately.

'I remember vividly,' he agreed, with a wicked gleam in his eyes. 'I promised to love you and honour you and worship you with my body.'

He reached for her again, his head tilting and his lips already parted in anticipation as they approached hers.

'But that was before the divorce,' she whimpered, as she fought the need to give in to the pleasure she knew he was offering. 'You're not free to love me any more.'

He stopped moving, seemingly turned to stone as he stared at her in stupefaction.

'Divorce?' he repeated in disbelief. 'What divorce?'

'Our divorce,' she said, trying to sound firm. 'The one you had to get before you could marry Alice this morning—unless you're into bigamy.'

The silence seemed to go on for ever as he gazed at her, his eyes boring right through to her soul.

To her utter mortification he suddenly threw his head back and roared with laughter.

'Marry Alice!' he exclaimed, having difficulty saying the words because he was laughing so hard. 'I couldn't marry Alice if I wanted to because I'm still married to you.'

CHAPTER NINE

LIVVY stared at Daniel, hurt beyond belief that he could be treating the situation so lightly.

'Daniel, she told me herself,' she pointed out, furious that she couldn't control the quiver in her voice and the tremble of her lips. 'You were there and you certainly didn't contradict her.'

'What? When?' he demanded, clearly shocked. That had certainly wiped the laughter off his face.

'When you brought her up to the ward this morning,' she reminded him, the scene all too vivid in her memory because that had been the moment when all her dreams of happiness had died. 'She showed me her ring and told me she was Mrs Jones now. She said you were married this morning.'

'Oh, Livvy, no. You misunderstood what she was saying,' he began, with a horrified expression on his face, only to be interrupted by the phone.

He paused to glare at it, obviously wanting to continue the explanation now that he'd started, but the ringing was imperative and he was forced to turn away, cursing in an exasperated mutter as she reached out to silence the noise.

She knew how he felt.

How could she possibly concentrate on a telephone call when her whole future might be hanging on a thread? How could the whole world not go into suspended animation to give Daniel and herself time to—?

'Livvy, it's Pat. Is Daniel there?'

As soon as she heard the urgent tone of Pat's voice she knew that her own problems were going to have to wait.

'Not good?' she asked.

'Getting rapidly worse,' Pat confirmed succinctly, her voice low-toned enough to tell Livvy that she was trying not to let the young couple overhear her talking. The pregnancy had been a nightmare for them almost from the beginning and they'd weathered it very bravely. It would be heartbreaking if anything went wrong at this stage.

'He's right here. I'll hand you over,' Livvy said and twisted clumsily to hold the receiver out to Daniel.

'It's Pat. The baby's not doing well,' she warned him, then stood with her hands clenched as she listened to his rapid-fire questions.

She didn't need to hear the answers to know what he was hearing. All she had to see was the rapidly darkening expression on his face.

Putting aside her own feelings of sympathy for the young couple, she deliberately switched her brain to thinking about what needed doing. If Daniel had been on the staff here he would have known all the channels. As it was, she was going to be his link between what needed doing and how to achieve it.

By the time he'd put the phone down she'd composed a mental list.

'Caesarean?' she asked, almost certain of the answer.

'Labour has speeded up nicely but the baby's pulse rate is going down alarmingly. How do I get hold of that anaesthetist?'

Livvy's hand was already reaching for the phone. She

knew from what Amy had said that Antonio was staying on call for the duration as well. As the phone began to ring she crossed her fingers childishly and sent up a little prayer that he wasn't already involved in an operation.

'I'll be in the delivery suite,' Daniel said, just as the click at the other end told her the call had been answered. She held up a hand to signal that she'd heard him.

She glanced over her shoulder just in time to cast a longing look at him as he went striding out of the door, and felt a pang of frustration.

They'd been in the middle of one of the most important conversations of her life when all this had blown up in their faces. How long would it be before they could finish?

'Aldarini,' said the voice in her ear as Antonio answered his pager, and instantly her brain switched into work mode.

It took less than five minutes before she put the phone down for the last time and hurried out of the room to deliver her messages in person.

'All arranged,' she announced in quiet triumph as she stuck her head through the swing doors.

Daniel was standing by Alwyn's side, speaking softly to the young woman and her husband, and she knew that he would have spent the time she'd been making her calls explaining what he was going to do and trying to reassure them of their baby's safety.

Livvy just had time to notice that he'd taken hold of the young woman's free hand and patted it gently before he made his excuses and came across to her.

'What have you got?' he demanded briefly, his tension showing in his slightly clipped tone.

'I've got a fully equipped and fully staffed theatre free right now and the anaesthetist is already on his way up to join you there.' Livvy grinned, pleased with the success of her efforts.

'Brilliant!' he said, with relief in his answering grin, and he suddenly leaned forward to bracket her face between his palms and deliver a brief but noisy kiss.

'Daniel!' she squeaked breathlessly over the sudden thundering of her pulse.

'You deserved it for getting everything organised so quickly,' he said unrepentantly, a wicked gleam in his eyes.

'Well, damn!' said Pat with a laugh. 'If I'd known there was a reward like that in the offing I'd have made the phone calls myself!'

Livvy was laughing at Pat's nonsense as she made her way back to the ward but her lips were still tingling from their contact with Daniel's.

Wretched man. It wasn't fair to do things like that when they hadn't finished their discussion.

She had to admit that her heart was immeasurably lighter, though, because, in spite of seven months of pain and disillusionment, deep down she'd discovered that she still trusted him. She'd known from the first that he was a man of honour and integrity so how had everything got in such a mess?

Was it all her fault for not trusting him implicitly? His, for not being open enough to explain what was going on? Both?

She sighed heavily and tried to reach back with both hands to massage the ache that had been gripping her back at intervals all day. She was beginning to feel very tired and very old, especially with all these Braxton

Hicks contractions. She hadn't realised they were going to happen so frequently or be so painful.

The next two weeks weren't going to be much of a picnic if things were going to continue this way—it already felt as if she'd been pregnant for a couple of years.

As she entered the softly lit ward she noticed that most of the patients had settled themselves in their beds to sleep or read with their nightlights on. There were just a few hardy souls left gathered round the low murmur of the flickering television set.

She glanced at the watch pinned to the front of her smock and saw with surprise that it was already ten o'clock. Where had the day gone? Christmas Eve was almost over and Christmas Day would soon be here.

Still rubbing at her back, she wandered across to the window and pulled a corner of the curtain just far enough to see outside.

The sky was mid-winter dark but the layer of snow on the ground lent everything an unearthly glow. Usually the Mynydd Du, the Black Mountains, were completely invisible at night, disappearing into the darkness, but tonight was different.

It had stopped snowing at last and the sky had cleared just far enough to allow the moon to appear. Its soft radiance was reflected back from the snow-covered crags and peaks, giving them a strangely ghostly appearance against the dark of the sky.

Closer to home the security lights dotted along the paths crossing the hospital grounds poured circles of buttery yellow onto the carpet of white, making it look more like a soft warm blanket than a layer of cold wet snow.

Enough of the warmth of the room behind her had escaped through the curtains to start melting the snow on the window-sill outside, and she grimaced at the thought of days of dirty grey slush while they waited for the thaw.

That had been one item on the news tonight which had received a cheer—when the weather forecaster had promised an early thaw to this unseasonably early snow-fall.

There would undoubtedly be more before the winter was over but as she would be on maternity leave by then with any luck all the severe weather would be over before she was due to return to work.

Although *where* she would be working then was something she didn't dare think about until she and Daniel had found time to finish their interrupted—

Livvy gasped, dragged back to the present moment by the rapid onslaught of the strongest contraction yet. For nearly two minutes she was forced to grip tightly to the edge of the window-sill while she concentrated on re-laxing and controlling her breathing.

Resting her forehead against the chill of the window helped a little but it still seemed like for ever before she was able to straighten again and let the curtain drop back into place.

She was almost holding her breath as she walked slowly and carefully across the ward and into Sister's office, still stunned by the enormity of her realisation.

'I'm in labour,' she whispered, as if saying the words aloud would make them more valid. She spread her hands wonderingly over the taut bulge under her smock. 'The baby's really on its way.'

She gave a slightly breathless chuckle as she tried to work out exactly how *long* she'd been in labour.

Now that she knew that it hadn't been Braxton Hicks

contractions she'd been experiencing, she realised that it was quite possible that things had started slowly some time this morning and had gradually been speeding up all day. Those last two had been only twenty minutes apart, though, the time noted by sheer accident, so that meant things were beginning to get more serious.

It looked as if she was going to have a Christmas baby after all.

She glanced around the small, functional room distractedly, suddenly impatient for things to happen. As a first baby it could be hours yet, and in the meantime she knew she wasn't going to be able to rest much and certainly knew she wasn't going to be able to sleep—even if she hadn't been in labour, the thought that Daniel would be returning as soon as he'd finished delivering Alwyn's baby would have kept her awake.

She contemplated perching herself on the edge of the desk again but her back ached and she knew she needed the comfort of a real chair for a while. If all the births she had witnessed were anything to go by, it would be soon enough that she would be forced to be up and walking about again.

She lowered herself gingerly into the chair, this time making certain that the cushion was placed just right to support the hollow of her back before she tilted her head and tried to relax.

It wasn't long before a sudden thought struck her and she felt a wide smile creep over her face.

Daniel was actually going to be with her for the birth of their child.

That was something she'd dreamed about during the last seven months while she'd longed for him to come to her and demolish the walls that had grown up between them, but as the time had dragged on without a word from him she'd finally given up hope.

Now he *would* be the first one to hold the baby they'd made together, the one to take it from her body and place it in her arms, the one to marvel with her at the perfection of the tiny fingers and toes and feathery eyelashes.

'Olivia?' said a husky voice near her ear, and she didn't have to open her eyes to know who it was. Only Daniel had ever said her name in exactly that way.

'Daniel,' she murmured, and turned to look at him.

'If you need to go to sleep you'd be better off in bed,' he pointed out gently, smoothing back a straggly tendril of hair to hook it over her ear. He ran the back of his finger down her cheek and Livvy felt her eyes widen as his darkened with awareness.

'I was waiting for you to come back,' she murmured, glad that he hadn't arrived a couple of minutes earlier when she'd been puffing her way through yet another contraction.

Suddenly she remembered where he'd been.

'Alwyn's baby!' she exclaimed, struggling to sit up. 'What happened? Is he all right?'

'He's fine,' Daniel assured her with a grin. 'Perfect, in fact, according to his father.'

'What was the matter with him?' Livvy demanded, remembering the worrying drop in pulse rate with every contraction. 'What did you find when you got in there?'

'He'd managed to wrap the cord round his neck since his last scan—twice!'

'So every time a contraction pushed him a bit further along the birth canal it was getting tighter and tighter and he was getting strangled?' she guessed. 'Poor little boy.'

'It certainly didn't stop him yelling his head off as soon as it was removed,' Daniel pointed out. 'Young Mr Morgan looked quite shell-shocked when he realised there wasn't a volume control on his new toy.'

Livvy chuckled with him, loving the happy expression in his eyes. He was always so genuinely pleased with every baby he delivered. It would be interesting to see how he reacted when this one was born.

She drew in a slow breath and prepared to make the momentous announcement that she was finally in labour. She was looking forward to watching the expression on his face change.

Would he be pleased? Of course he would. He was one of that rare group of men who genuinely loved children rather than tolerated them.

Would he panic because it was *his* child on the way? Maybe. But very few people knew him as well as she did and they probably wouldn't know how to tell. He certainly hadn't seemed in the least bit worried when Davey had been born but, then, he'd only arrived right at the very end of Alice's labour. Perhaps going through it once before would make it easier for him this time.

In the end she had taken so long to start speaking that he beat her to the punch, his voice dragging her away from her convoluted thoughts.

'Livvy, how on earth could you believe that I'd divorced you and married Alice?' he demanded bluntly, and the ocean of quiet hurt in his voice nearly drowned her.

'I sent you the papers,' she reminded him sadly, remembering how angry and unhappy she'd been then. She'd hoped that receiving them would jolt him into seeking her out. 'Or rather the solicitor did.'

'And I tore them up and threw them in the bin—where they belonged.'

'But I didn't know that—you never told me,' Livvy pointed out defensively. 'And when you came here with Alice and she said that she was Mrs Jones and that you'd got married this morning what else was I supposed to think?'

'Well, you should certainly have realised that your solicitor would have been in contact with you to tell you when the case was going to court. How did you think a divorce was conducted?'

'I've got no idea,' she snapped, feeling stupid. 'I've never had one before.'

'Well, you haven't had one this time either,' he said firmly. 'Your name is still Mrs Jones and you're still married to me.'

'But what about Alice?' Livvy persisted. 'She's got that beautiful ring and there *was* a wedding this morning, and what about the baby she's carrying? And there's her little boy, Davey, and your toes and…and…'

'Hey! Hey! Stop and take a breath!' he advised, his tone suddenly teasing as he reached out to grab the straight chair from behind the desk to position it closer to her.

'First things first,' he began with new purpose in his voice. 'Alice *did* get married this morning and she *is* now called Mrs Jones, but you paired her with the wrong man—she married my father.'

'Your father!' Livvy choked in shock. 'But he only lost your mother a few months ago and they'd been married for years.'

'Married and not married,' Daniel pointed out sadly. 'He loved her dearly and cared for her right to the end, but theirs hadn't been a real marriage for a very long time.'

'But Alice?' she questioned. 'How does she fit into all this? And little Davey?'

'Alice was helping Dad to nurse Mum. Inevitably, they ended up spending a lot of time together and they just fell in love.'

'So Davey's *his* son…your half-brother,' she said incredulously. 'And the new baby too?'

'Both of them,' Daniel said, his expression half pride, half bemusement. 'He always wanted a lot of children but I never expected him to start producing the rest of the crop when his oldest was old enough to be producing his own.'

Livvy was silent for a long time while she tried to assimilate everything he'd told her. There was almost too much of it for her to be able to sort everything out in her head.

She had never for one moment considered that Daniel's father could be involved. Although he had warmly welcomed her into the family when she and Daniel had married, and was outwardly a very friendly person, she had recognised a deep well of reserve inside him. He was the last person she would have suspected of conducting an extra-marital affair.

Still, with what Daniel had told her about his parents' marriage, perhaps it wasn't so strange. Even the most reticent of men must have a need for human companionship and physical contact. With the best will in the world, poor Sarah Jones hadn't been able to provide that for years.

Anyway, when she thought about it further, perhaps she should have suspected something like this. After all,

Daniel was so much like his father that she could understand any woman finding him attractive. She'd certainly been bowled over by Daniel—from the first moment she'd met him.

The thing that had really thrown her onto the wrong track had been Daniel's reticence, the way he had refused to explain what was happening. If he had only told her there would have been no need for all this unhappiness.

'What I don't understand is why you didn't explain all of this seven months ago,' she complained bitterly, getting right to the heart of the matter. 'I asked you and asked you to tell me what was going on and all you would do was tell me to trust you. Was it all some elaborate sort of test?'

'God, no!' he exclaimed, and leaned forward to catch her hands in his, holding on tightly in spite of the fact that she tried to snatch them away. 'I wanted to tell you but Alice had sworn me to secrecy.'

'Sworn you to secrecy?' she said in astonishment. 'Why, for heaven's sake?'

'Because she didn't want my father to know that she was pregnant.'

'Why on earth not?' she demanded, exasperated. 'If she loved him enough to go to bed with him what on earth made her think that he wouldn't stand by her when she was pregnant with his child?'

'Firstly, and most importantly, because he was still married to my mother at the time,' Daniel said, staying calm in spite of her anger. 'Alice knew that he would never divorce my mother—she would never have thought of asking him to. But she also knew that it would break his heart to find out that she was pregnant and that he couldn't do anything for her. That's why she wouldn't even let me tell you.'

'But...' Livvy blew out an exasperated breath. She could see Alice's reasoning even though it all seemed very over-dramatic in hindsight. What she wanted to know was how Daniel had become so involved in the situation.

She was just about to ask when he began speaking again, obviously feeling she needed to know some of the background.

'By that time she'd been working for him, and with him, for nearly four years. She would have known better than anyone else how little he was getting out of the marriage and knew how trapped he must be feeling.'

'But he loved your mother,' Livvy objected, remembering the tender, unselfconscious way Daniel's father had fed his helpless wife and read to her from the paper, never once allowing a hint of impatience to colour his voice.

'Yes, he loved her, but it had become more like the protective love of a parent for a child because, really, that's what she'd become. His love for Alice must have taken him completely by surprise after all those years because it was the passionate love of a man for a woman. The age difference between them wouldn't have made the situation any easier for them either.'

'By that time they must both have known that your mother wasn't going to live much longer. Couldn't Alice have told him about the baby on the understanding that she would wait until he was free before they made a commitment? Why did she come to you?'

'She wasn't going to tell him at all,' he said quietly,

releasing her hands and straightening to lean back in the chair.

He rubbed both hands over his face and she could see how deeply weary he was. It must have been such a strain for him, and it obviously wasn't over yet.

She could see from his turbulent expression that he was still fighting demons, and when his gaze dipped to the evidence of the child they had created she realised that he thought she had done a similar thing. Where Alice had concealed her pregnancy from Daniel's father—for whatever reason—she had done the same to Daniel.

In her case, she knew that she hadn't wanted to use her pregnancy to make Daniel feel he had to stay with her, not when she'd believed he'd rather have been with Alice. It had broken her heart to lose him to the other woman that way, but simple pride hadn't let her use the baby to blackmail him into staying.

That reasoning couldn't be the same in Alice's case.

'I still don't understand why she didn't want him to know. You said they were in love and that he's always wanted more children. Surely she would have been giving him everything he'd wanted after half a lifetime in a relationship that was going nowhere.'

'It was because she felt she would be using the baby almost like blackmail,' he said, his words an uncanny echo of her own thoughts a moment ago. 'She knew him well enough to realise that as soon as he found out about the baby he would insist that they got married but she couldn't bear for him to feel that she'd used the baby to trap him.'

He leaned forward again, his expression intent as he tried to make her understand.

'Think about it, Livvy,' he said persuasively. 'She'd seen the way Dad had been trapped for years in a sterile prison, and just when his freedom was in sight—when it looked as if Mum was finally going to be released from her own earthly prison—Alice found out she was pregnant.'

Livvy was silent, his words suddenly making sense.

If she was honest she would probably have made the same decision—in fact, the more she thought about the similarities in their situations the more she realised that she had.

'I understand,' she murmured softly, sadly. 'I can see why she made the decisions she did and I know the thoughts that were going through her head but... I thought you didn't love me any more. I thought you loved her and that the two of you had already started your family.'

'So when you decided to go it was your choice, but it was partly because you thought I'd made *my* choice— that I'd chosen her,' he elaborated, proving that he was just as quick at following verbal clues as she was once they were on the same wavelength.

'I thought that if you really wanted her then I would only be wasting my time if I tried to hold onto you,' she agreed, feeling once again the deep well of unhappiness that had accompanied her on her journey west.

She gave a wry smile, knowing there was no humour in it. 'Mind you, I was also telling myself that if I went away it would make you think seriously about what you really wanted, and if you missed me enough you would leave her in spite of the fact that you'd had a baby together, and come for me.'

'And then I *didn't* come for you,' he said quietly,

reaching for her hand and threading his fingers between hers. 'You couldn't have known that Mum was going to die so soon or that there was going to be a big reorganisation in the department at the hospital to cover Mr den Haag's lecture tour.

'It meant that within days I was absolutely inundated with work at the same time as I was trying to sort out reams of family business.'

'Oh, Daniel,' she murmured, sorry now that she hadn't been there for him when he'd needed her support.

'I was also in contact with Alice and Davey to make sure that she was coping with single motherhood without any friends or relatives to fall back on,' he continued, his remembered frustration clear in his voice.

'I knew she didn't have any family and because she insisted that I keep my promise I couldn't ask anyone else to help out. For weeks before the baby was actually born I was the only one she had to call on for help.'

Hence her insistence on Daniel being there for her son's birth, Livvy thought, remembering how she'd been dreading her own baby arriving without the comfort and support of having Daniel at her side.

She still couldn't understand how the situation had gone on for so long, without her noticing that Daniel was preoccupied with Alice's concerns. But, then, he had also been spending more time visiting his rapidly weakening mother and giving his father some respite from his lonely vigil at her side so perhaps it wasn't so strange.

'All the time I was trying to get her to see that Dad really needed her,' Daniel continued. 'Especially when Mum died. He was absolutely gutted that he'd lost both of them, and that was without knowing that Alice had been carrying his baby. I persuaded her to come to the funeral in the hopes that when she saw him she would change her mind, but she dug in her heels at the last minute.'

'Oh, Daniel, I'm sorry,' she whispered, suddenly overwhelmed by the thought that instead of easing Daniel's problems by going away, she had actually added to them. 'You must have been at your wits' end, trying to sort everything out.'

'And then you had to move to Wales,' he said in disgust. 'What on earth possessed you? Do you have any idea how difficult it is to do any research about medical personnel in an area that far away from St Augustine's? I could hardly jump in the car and spend a quick half-hour on it.

'Do you have any idea how many nurses there are named Jones? Do you have any idea how long it takes to extract their department phone numbers out of personnel departments and then to contact all of them to find out if they're *my* Mrs Jones?'

He glared at her but it wasn't anger she saw in his eyes but the painful echo of…what? Fear?

Livvy was still trying to work it out when he started speaking again, this time his voice strangely unsteady.

'Do you have any idea how frightened I was that I had lost you?' he demanded softly as his hands tightened around hers, his eyes darkened by strong emotions. 'Or how I would have felt if I never saw you again?'

Livvy felt her eyes burn with the press of tears and had to swallow hard as she blinked to force them back.

As she gazed at his dear, handsome face and saw the evidence of the torment his love had put him through, the bands of mistrust around her heart shattered and her own love burst free.

He must have seen the turbulent emotions in her face because suddenly he leapt out of his chair and pulled her to her feet before he gathered her into his arms, protruding stomach and all.

'God, Livvy, I've missed you,' he whispered fervently, as he held her tightly and her head came to rest naturally in its usual place on his shoulder, with his hand stroking her hair. 'I've missed everything about you, you know. Your smile, your laugh, your special perfume even when you aren't wearing any. Everything…'

His head angled towards hers and he met her lips in a kiss that started off sweetly tentative but swiftly escalated to nuclear meltdown.

They were both breathing heavily when he tore his mouth from hers.

'This is impossible,' he groaned as he glanced wildly around. 'Anyone could come in here.'

'And probably will,' Livvy added, only realising the double meaning to their words when she heard his hoarse chuckle.

'I hope that's a promise, Livvy. For God's sake, where's the nearest place we can be alone together? A broom cupboard would do.'

'Daniel, we can't—'

'Pat told me that you've still got a couple of weeks until the baby's due,' he broke in persuasively, a wickedly arousing gleam in his eyes as his fingers began exploratory forays over her shoulders and down towards her tingling breasts. 'That's only two weeks to make up for seven months without the sexiest pregnant woman in the world. It couldn't possibly be enough to make up for all that time without you, but we could do our best to catch up.'

'Yes, but—'

There's less time than you think, she thought as her uterus began to tighten ominously again, but for a few seconds desire overrode the escalating pain.

Yes, she wanted to be alone with him, to make love with him, but she didn't think it was advisable or even possible while she was in labour.

'And you know as well as I do that making love in the last few weeks of pregnancy helps to ripen the cervix.' He continued to argue eloquently as he covered her face with kisses and slid his hands down the length of her back to palm the curves of her hips. 'It could actually be good for you.'

'Oh, Daniel,' Livvy whimpered helplessly as her body clenched tightly with a combination of desire and her strongest contraction yet, then felt a strange release of tension.

She buried her face against his shoulder and moaned, half in laughter and half in frustration.

'Oh, Daniel, I'd love to go with you to the nearest private place and make mad, passionate love—I'd even be willing to make do with a broom cupboard—but I think my waters just broke.'

CHAPTER TEN

LIVVY cradled the precious bundle in her arms and glanced over her shoulder at Daniel.

'Does he know we're coming?' she demanded, suspicious of the barely contained glee in his expression as he pushed the wheelchair towards the entrance of the orthopaedic ward.

It seemed awfully early to be going visiting. Daniel probably wouldn't have been allowed to do it if he wasn't a doctor and she wasn't a member of staff.

Breakfast was hardly over but from the moment the main lights had come on in the ward it had been filled with a real air of excitement.

It wasn't just because it was Christmas Day but also because once the curtains had been drawn back everyone had seen that the snow had virtually disappeared overnight and several patients had been told they would be allowed to go home today.

As for the rest, they now knew that the roads would be clear enough for their families to be able to visit them so everyone was feeling much happier.

'He'll know we're coming soon enough,' Daniel said with a grin as he expertly reversed through the swing doors and swung her gently back to face the room.

The first person she saw on the other side of the room was Alice, who was sitting on the chair tucked closely beside the bed, her hand tightly held by the man she was visiting.

Perched on the edge of the bed between them was a young child who bore a startling similarity both to the man confined to the bed and the one behind her, pushing the wheelchair.

'Hello, Dad,' Daniel said softly when the older man didn't seem to have noticed their arrival at the end of his bed. He apparently only had eyes for the radiant woman by his side and the bonny young lad propped between them.

'Daniel?'

The older man's expression was startled and only grew more so when he recognised the person sitting in the wheelchair at the foot of his bed.

'Livvy? Is that you?' he demanded, a beam of pleasure filling his face. 'What on earth are you...?'

He paused, doing a visible double-take when he saw what she was holding in her arms.

'My God! Is that *yours*? Daniel told me you were pregnant but when did that happen?'

Daniel laughed at his less than elegant speech.

'It certainly is ours, *Grandad*. Born just a minute before midnight.'

David Jones still didn't seem to be able to take it in, his eyes going from one face to the other almost as if he expected them to disappear as quickly as they'd come.

'Until Daniel told me yesterday, I didn't even know Livvy was pregnant,' he complained to Alice, sounding almost bewildered. 'I know I was pretty much out of it on anaesthetic but I'm sure I hadn't heard that the two of them were together again—not that I knew why they parted in the first place.'

'That makes three of us,' Daniel muttered in an aside

to Livvy, who couldn't help the wide smile that spread over her face.

'We're definitely together again,' she said, reaching up one hand to weave her fingers between Daniel's. 'We just thought you'd like to meet the latest addition to the Jones family.'

'*He* just wanted a chance to crow,' Daniel's father accused wryly. 'Did you hear the emphasis he put on the word *Grandad*? And here I was congratulating myself that people would think I was just a youngster to have such a pretty wife and several small children.'

'Several?' Alice echoed, trying to sound horrified. 'The last I heard it was just one-and-a-bit children, and I've got the ultrasound picture to prove it.'

'So far,' David agreed with a roguish look which was uncannily like his oldest son's.

'You do realise that you're going to be crossing the generations over with this next one,' Daniel pointed out. 'By the time your second one is born it will already be an uncle or aunt to ours.'

The situation sounded so strange that they all laughed.

'So, what did you have?' David prompted. 'I've an idea that Alice already knows because she's been in a funny mood ever since she brought Davey in to visit.'

Alice shared a secretive smile with Livvy. Everyone on the ward had found out the sex of the baby within seconds of the birth but she'd obviously decided to let Daniel break the news to his father.

'It's a girl,' Daniel announced with a besotted grin as he turned to lift his daughter carefully out of Livvy's arms.

He turned to carry her round the end of the bed for

inspection with all the confidence of a man who knew that he would meet with approval.

Livvy hid her amusement when she saw the extra care he took as he held their child. No one would have guessed, from the exaggerated precautions he was taking to support her head as he handed her over to his father, that he was well accustomed to dealing with tiny babies…but, then, this really was the first one that was *his*.

'Have you decided yet what you're going to call her?' David asked, glancing up at them briefly as he stroked one petal-soft cheek with a gentle finger.

Daniel had returned to Livvy's side and threw a quick look at her, as though he was waiting for her to answer, but she gestured for him to do it, tightening her hand around his in loving support.

'We thought we'd like to call her Sarah—after Mum—if you've no objection?' he suggested softly.

Silence surrounded their little gathering for several long seconds while David looked searchingly from one to another, ending up with Alice.

As Livvy watched, she saw the silent communication that passed between the two of them and it was Alice who answered.

'That's a lovely idea,' she whispered as she reached out to stroke a gentle hand over the silky blonde wisps covering the new baby's head. 'A beautiful name for a beautiful baby, and one that will help to keep all the good memories alive.'

Young Davey chose that moment to try to wriggle off the bed and Alice had to grab him before he nose-dived towards the floor.

In the ensuing exclamations and laughter conversation became more general, encompassing the possibilities of transferring David closer to home—preferably to St Augustine's, where Daniel would be able to help Alice with visiting—and questions about Livvy's plans for returning to work.

'We haven't got that far yet,' Livvy confessed honestly. 'It's a bit of a long story, but the only thing we're certain about at the moment is that I'll be going back home with Daniel as soon as I'm released from here.'

'Well, with Daniel as your doctor, you can virtually sign your own release,' David pointed out with a chuckle as he relinquished his hold on his first grandchild with every evidence of regret. 'I'm not going to be quite so lucky. Our honeymoon is going to have to be put off for the foreseeable future—and just when we'd persuaded my cousin to take Davey on for the duration!'

'Theoretically, Livvy could be released today as her labour was so perfectly straightforward, but it's not quite as simple as that,' Daniel said, and explained briefly about the staff shortages on the obstetrics and gynaecology wards.

'One down with flu, one with his arm in plaster and another on a skiing holiday?' David said. 'I bet the last one is kicking himself. He could have had free skiing in his own back garden and saved himself a lot of money.'

'Well, he's not due back for another four days, and as I'd already arranged to take some time off from St Augustine's I thought I might as well pitch in at Bryn Madoc,' Daniel explained. 'At least it means I'll be able to see something of Livvy at the same time.'

'It's not quite the same as being at home, though,' Alice pointed out. 'There'll be no privacy at all.'

'There's always the broom cupboard,' Daniel said with an attempt at a straight face, but Livvy knew the colour that surged up into her face had given her thoughts away when David's eyebrows shot up towards his hairline.

'We'd better take Sarah back to the nursery or we'll be in trouble,' she pointed out hurriedly, before Daniel's father could comment on the cause of her embarrassment. His thought processes certainly weren't being slowed down by anaesthetic today and he was intelligent enough to make a fairly accurate guess.

'Lord, yes,' Daniel agreed when he glanced at his watch. 'I've got to track down that wretched Santa suit before I can give out the presents on the ward.'

Livvy couldn't help chuckling at the idea of Daniel disguised under pounds of padding and a full white beard, but she knew that the mums who were expecting their young families to visit were delighted by the idea.

When they were travelling back up in the lift she tried to scold Daniel for mentioning the broom cupboard but he silenced her with a sizzling kiss.

'We never even got as far as the broom cupboard so don't take away my fantasies,' he murmured. 'Now that you're off limits for a while they're all that I've got.'

Livvy's brains were so scrambled by his kiss that she couldn't reply, but as the doors opened just then to reveal a group of people waiting to enter the lift, it hardly mattered.

There would be time enough to remind him of all the things they *would* be able to do when they didn't have an audience.

Their return to the ward coincided with the arrival of a whole group of relatives, including Megan Williams's little boys.

For a while the three of them were overawed enough by their surroundings to stay quietly by her bed, but it wasn't long before they became brave enough to start exploring the ward and introducing themselves to all the other patients.

Livvy had settled herself back into bed and was eagerly waiting for Daniel to return from his 'duties' as Father Christmas on the ward upstairs when the two bravest of the sturdy imps reached her.

'You're not fat,' announced the older of the two. 'Didn't you get a baby?'

'Yes. I had a little girl,' Livvy said, side-stepping the issue of size. She'd been amazed and delighted when she'd sneaked onto the scales this morning to find that she was going to have to lose less than four pounds to get back to her pre-pregnancy weight. She'd been convinced when it felt as if she left dents in the floor just by walking, that it was going to be a great deal more than that.

Unfortunately, most women weren't nearly so lucky...

'Oh!' said young Master Williams in tones of commiseration. 'We had a girl too.'

Livvy didn't know how she stopped herself laughing. The poor lad had made it sound as if he equated the arrival of a baby sister in the family with the offer of a plate of snails for breakfast.

Daniel's reaction had been very different when their daughter had been born late last night.

Her announcement that her waters had broken had stunned him, but not nearly as much as the realisation, when he'd looked down at his shoes, that he was just as drenched as she was.

'Livvy!' he'd exclaimed, his ardour definitely damp-ened. 'I've heard of pouring cold water on an idea but this is going too far. If you didn't want to come in the broom cupboard with me all you had to do was say so!'

Livvy had already been chuckling so hard at his ex-pression that the contraction had completely robbed her of breath.

By the time she'd been able to speak again he'd found a wheelchair and grabbed Cherry to take her off to get rid of her wet clothing and put her in a gown.

The young nurse had been strangely quiet while she'd helped Livvy make herself comfortable, but she'd waited until the relative quiet between contractions before she'd dropped her bombshell.

'I'm having second thoughts about my speciality,' she announced, hardly able to meet Livvy's eyes.

'Oh, Cherry, why?' Livvy demanded. 'You've got good instincts, you're calm and steady with the patients and you've coped marvellously with everything that's happened over the last couple of days, even though it's been chaotic.'

'That's partly why,' she said quietly. 'The last couple of days have been fantastic, with everything happening at once, and I've thoroughly enjoyed myself. But I think it mightn't be so interesting when everything gets back to normal and it's all peaceful and well organised.'

'Normal? Peaceful and well organised?' Livvy chuck-led breathlessly, trying to relax and control her breathing as the next contraction roared towards her like an ex-press train. 'You must be joking! This *is* normal for a maternity ward!'

'What? But...' Cherry was clearly at a loss.

'Think about it,' Livvy gasped. 'No one has yet found

a way of persuading babies to arrive to order… There are no neat lists of operations… You never know when the next mum is going to arrive in labour, day or night… Or if there are going to be half a dozen at once… Or how long each one is going to take… Disorganised chaos every time…' she finished with an agonised groan.

'And she loves every minute of it,' Daniel announced as he joined them, this time dressed in a baggy pair of blue theatre scrubs.

'Delivering other people's babies,' Livvy pointed out through gritted teeth, 'is much easier than do-it-yourself…'

Cherry laughed, her eyes once more bright and enthusiastic as she gathered up Livvy's clothes into a large damp bundle.

'I can see I shall have to do a rethink—about my career *and* my thoughts about having babies of my own,' she announced as she disappeared out of the swing doors.

'How is it going?' Daniel asked as he blotted the sweat off Livvy's face and stroked the clinging hairs away to make her comfortable.

'I'd rather be in the broom cupboard,' she muttered crossly as he held some water for her to take a mouthful. She'd only had a sip when she was seized with the uncontrollable urge to push. 'On second thoughts, what you were suggesting we did in the broom cupboard was what got me into this situation,' she said, her voice rising rapidly like a kettle coming to the boil. 'If you so much as mention broom cupboards again I'll—'

'Livvy?' Daniel said sharply, cutting her off in full flow.

'Yes?' she snapped, glaring up at him, uncomfortably aware that she was behaving like a shrew.

'Shut up and push.'

Livvy could laugh about it now, especially as Daniel had threatened to tease her about broom cupboards for the rest of her life.

The rest of her life... She gave a happy sigh. It seemed impossible that so much had changed in the space of a day.

Yesterday she had been alone and lonely with only the prospect of the birth of her baby in the New Year to look forward to. Today she was the mother of a perfect baby girl and had the absolute certainty that she was never going to be alone or lonely again.

Guiltily she realised that her lack of interest in their conversation had prompted Megan Williams's sons to move on to more interesting people.

She was just looking around the ward to see where they were now when a commotion just outside the doors to the ward drew everyone's attention.

'Ho! Ho! Ho!' said a voice as the doors slowly opened.

'It's Father Christmas!' exclaimed one of the junior Williamses in a piercing whisper when he caught sight of the familiar red-clad figure in the doorway.

Livvy threw him a quick glance and saw that the little child's eyes were almost standing out on stalks with excitement, and his brothers were just as amazed.

She looked back in time to see Daniel appear, his shape so completely disguised that if she hadn't known it was him under the suit there would have been no way of telling.

This was a Father Christmas with a difference, though. Instead of the traditional sack of brightly wrapped parcels slung over his back, this Father Christmas was carrying a double armful of babies.

'Wow!' breathed another junior Williams, every bit as awed as his brothers. 'He's giving out *babies* for presents!'

There was a ripple of laughter around the ward, including one from Father Christmas himself as he made his way to Jo Moffat's bed.

'I've got two presents for you,' Father Christmas announced. 'Baby David is the first one.'

He leaned forward so that Jo could lift her little boy out of his hold and cradle him in her arms. She obviously hadn't understood what he'd meant about two presents because she was looking up at him with a puzzled frown.

'You'll have to look towards the door for your second surprise,' he prompted.

Jo's head swung towards the doors, now framing a rather rumpled-looking man, and she burst into tears.

'In case any of you are wondering,' Father Christmas announced to the rest of the room, 'her husband has managed to get some leave to be with her for Christmas.'

He moved out of the way to allow husband and wife to embrace around their new son and moved on to Nerys Owens's bed.

Nerys and John didn't need any special gifts—their baby was obviously all they wanted as the proud new father perched on the edge of the bed to share a cuddle.

Alwyn Morgan was almost as overwhelmed as the Williams children, still hardly daring to believe that her baby really was alive and safely in her arms.

'Now, then, who have we here?' Father Christmas asked as he arrived at Megan Williams's bed.

In the time that it had taken him to work his way round there, the two boys had hurried over to station themselves beside their father and their younger sibling.

'This is the Williams family, Father Christmas,' Megan announced seriously.

'Well, then, this must be your special delivery,' he announced as he handed over Megan's precious daughter, all snugly wrapped in a pale pink blanket.

'We got a *girl*,' the oldest boy whispered loudly to his father. 'I wanted Father Christmas to change it for a boy but he only had girls left.'

Livvy could see that Daniel was fighting laughter but the rest of the ward was free to chuckle aloud.

She straightened as he settled his final delivery securely in the crook of his scarlet-coated arm and set off towards her, only to veer towards the door.

'Hey! Was that a spare one?' called a sharp-eyed child. Livvy didn't see which one it was—she was too busy watching to see what Daniel was doing with their daughter.

He paused in the doorway to reach up over his head and grab the mistletoe, then turned to make his way towards her.

'What's he going to do with that?' demanded the same little voice.

Livvy didn't bother to listen to the explanation. She *knew* what Daniel was intending to do with the mistletoe—giving himself an excuse to kiss her in front of all these people.

'Ho! Ho! Ho!' he said softly as he reached her side. 'And have you been a good girl?'

'Of course I have, Father Christmas,' she answered demurely.

She nearly burst out laughing when he leaned closer to mutter, 'Unfortunately... But I hope you'll do better next year!'

He carefully transferred Sarah to her arms and ostentatiously held the sprig of green leaves and waxy white berries over the baby's head.

'Happy Christmas,' he said as he placed a whiskery kiss on the soft curve of the baby's cheek.

He looked up to meet Livvy's eyes and his softly loving expression darkened and suddenly became heated.

'And a very happy Christmas to you, Livvy,' he murmured as he leaned towards her. 'I love you.'

At the very last moment, when his raised arm clad in voluminous red hid their faces from the rest of the room, he tugged his beard out of the way and their lips met.

Without a word their mouths spoke of happiness and for ever, gradually extending the vocabulary to include desire and searing passion, but once again it was the piercing whisper of a little boy that brought everything back to earth.

'What's Father Christmas doing?' he demanded, and Daniel groaned softly into Livvy's mouth as he was forced to bring their kiss to an end.

'He's giving her a kiss to wish her a happy Christmas,' Megan Williams explained simply, then, obviously knowing her son well, she added, 'It's all right. She's Mrs Christmas.'

Livvy hid her burning face against Daniel's shoulder, certain that her cheeks must be the same colour as his coat.

'Hey, how did I do on my first foray as Father

Christmas?' Daniel asked, his beard once more in position. 'I thought it would be a good idea to get some practice before Sarah's old enough to be critical.'

'You were the perfect instant Father Christmas,' Livvy teased.

Daniel's gaze fell on their daughter, sleeping peacefully between them.

'Instant father, too,' he murmured. 'I didn't have time to get stage fright or have second thoughts.'

'A bit like the way you do most of the really important things in your life,' she pointed out. 'You proposed just weeks after we met, but I bet you never thought you'd manage one day of father-to-be before the big event.'

'There are certainly *some* advantages,' he agreed, 'but next time can we do things the traditional way, with a nine-month lead-in?'

'Next time?' she demanded. 'You can mention next time when it's less than twelve hours since I went through agony to bring this one into the world.'

'Ah, but remember how much fun we had, putting her there in the first place,' he murmured, the wicked twinkle in his eye nothing to do with cuddly old Father Christmas.

'Go and take your clothes off and we'll talk about it when you come back,' she prompted, needing to see her beloved Daniel beside her when he was saying such outrageous things.

'If I took my clothes off now *everyone* would have something to talk about,' he said gruffly, but he slid off the edge of the bed and surreptitiously rearranged his robes. 'I'll be back in a few minutes with the rest of the children's presents—the dads left them in a pile in the corner by the lift—but I've been asked to do the ceremonial turkey-carving a bit later on so we're not going to have much time together.'

Livvy knew hospital life too well to complain, but she would have liked their first day together with their new baby to have had a little more opportunity for privacy.

It wasn't until just before he was due to carve the turkey for lunch that Daniel, in his own persona, handed her a plain white envelope with a whispered, 'Happy Christmas.'

Intrigued, Livvy untucked the flap and drew out a single sheet of hospital stationery and a key.

'Oh, Daniel,' she squeaked when she'd read the contents. 'When?'

'The administrator said he can have the flat ready for me to move into by this evening,' he explained. 'I went to ask him if there was anywhere I could lay my weary head, in between delivering all these babies, and I just happened to mention that my wife was on the staff here and that she'd just had her first baby unexpectedly early and—'

And they've found you somewhere to stay while you're helping out,' Livvy finished.

'Actually, it's somewhere for *us* to stay,' he said with a flash of that familiar grin. 'I just couldn't wait any longer to have my instant family all to myself.'

'You may have been an instant Father Christmas and an instant father,' Livvy began softly, sliding her fingers between his so that the key was enclosed between their palms, 'but from now on we're going to work hard to make certain that it's going to be for-ever-after love and happiness.'

'That's a promise,' Daniel said, and leaned forward to

brush a chaste kiss over her lips. He had to draw back in a hurry when a horrified whisper pierced the general hubbub of the ward.

'Mummy! He's kissing Mrs Christmas!'

A Baby of Her Own

by

Kate Hardy

For Gerard,
Chris and Chloë with all my love.

CHAPTER ONE

'INCEY wincey spider climbed up Amy's arch; down he came, to make our Amy laugh!'

Sam Taylor stopped dead in his tracks. He knew that voice, and it shouldn't have been singing nursery songs. He strode to the doorway of the small room—a room that was really a quarter of one of the bays in the paediatric ward, partitioned off to give more flexibility when it came to isolation nursing or a parent needing privacy—and leaned on the jamb, watching the young doctor who was playing her own version of Incey Wincey Spider with the toddler in traction in the cot, wiggling her fingers up the traction arch and then letting them drop down onto the little girl's tummy.

Her blonde curls cascaded over her shoulders, hiding her face from Sam's view, but he had no doubt she was smiling. Just like the red-headed toddler lying on the iron-framed cot in front of her, flat on her back with both legs in plaster. The ties that bound the child's legs to the traction arch were gradually moved lower and lower down the arch so her hip joints were pushed back into their proper place as her legs were stretched out.

Why was his registrar playing with a sick child when there were notes to be written up and a ward round to finish? Particularly when they were so short-staffed, thanks to the virus that had decimated the ward. Play was fine in its place, but they just didn't have time for it right now.

He cleared his throat. 'Dr Price. A word, please?'

She looked up instantly and her green eyes widened as she saw the grim expression on his face. 'Of course, Mr Taylor.' Jodie gave the consultant a brief nod, then turned back to the little girl. 'I'll see you tomorrow, Amy.' She gently touched the tip of the child's nose, the gesture telling in its affection. 'Big smile?'

'Yes, Doc-a Dodo,' the little girl lisped, doing her best to give Jodie a smile, though clearly disappointed that she was going to lose her playmate.

Satisfied that the child was happy to be left, Jodie joined Sam at the door.

'There's still half a round to do,' he pointed out tightly.

'I know.'

His steel-grey eyes narrowed. She *knew*, and she was leaving all the work to others? 'And you're playing with Amy Simcox.'

She nodded, seemingly unconcerned. 'Apart from the fact that plenty of studies show how play helps children to recover faster, it's my day off.'

Sam flushed at the double rebuke. 'I see. Well, I'm sorry, Dr Price. Though if you wore a white coat like the rest of us,' he continued, his voice very soft and very dangerous, 'maybe it would be easier to tell when you're off duty.'

It was her turn to redden now; with her fair skin, she flushed spectacularly. Literally to the roots of her hair. 'In my experience, small children are scared enough when they come into hospital. A white coat's just another barrier for the kids *and* their parents to overcome.'

'And how do the parents know you're who you say you are?' he countered silkily. 'Anyone could walk around here with a stethoscope slung round their neck and a clipboard under one arm—' just as she casually floated round the ward '—and say they're a doctor.'

'True.' She gave him an impish grin that riled him even more. 'But they don't have one of these.' She fished her hospital ID badge out of the pocket of her trousers.

He ought to remind her of her position as a junior doctor, Sam knew, but a glint in her eyes warned him she was expecting something of the sort. He couldn't be more than six or seven years older than she was, but she made him feel as if there were a whole generation between them.

'So what are you doing here on your day off?' he asked. 'Showing your dedication to the ward?' Hoping for a quick promotion, perhaps? Though that was unfair. She didn't seem the type to trample on others on her way to the top. Her dedication and enthusiasm were above question, yet Jodie Price always had time for people.

'Actually, I'm just playing with little Amy.' She bit her lip. 'Poor kid. As if it isn't bad enough being in traction at the age of eighteen months, just when she's getting used to walking, it's made worse by her father being "too busy" to visit her and her mother bursting into tears every time she sees the little one.'

'And?' he prompted, seeing the glint of tears rather than defiance in her eyes. Doctors were taught from the word go not to let themselves get so emotionally involved that it affected their judgement—but sometimes a case really tugged at your heartstrings and you forgot to be sensible.

'Her mother's convinced it's all her fault that Amy's hip joints haven't formed properly. She had three glasses of champagne on her wedding anniversary, when she was pregnant.' Jodie grimaced. 'I've told her it's not her fault, that clicky hip's fairly common in babies who were breech presentation, particularly girls. It should have been picked up even before Amy's six-week check, anyway, rather than Mrs Simcox asking her health visitor why Amy wasn't walking at sixteen months when all her peers were, then us finding out at referral that the baby had clicky hip. But she still blames herself, so little Amy doesn't get many visitors.

'I'm not saying her parents should *live* here,' she went on, lifting a hand to forestall any comment he might make. 'Parents who stay during the day need to go home at night for a proper rest—which they wouldn't get here, with monitors beeping all over the place. But I do think that a child who's stuck in one place and is old enough to talk needs a bit of company. The nurses are brilliant with her but they're overstretched.' The generous mouth thinned. 'So I've just been spending a few minutes talking to her and playing with her in my lunch-hour or before I go on duty.'

'And you do that for all your patients?'

Jodie lifted her chin, and Sam realised for the first time that she was only a couple of inches shorter than he was. Around five feet ten in the flat shoes she was wearing.

'For the ones in need, yes,' she stated defiantly.

'It can't go down very well with your boyfriend.' Why on earth had he said that?

She coloured. 'No. It didn't. Still, you have your round to finish, Mr Taylor. I won't hold you up any longer.'

It didn't. Meaning the boyfriend was history? He suddenly realised she was staring at him, expecting an answer. 'Oh. Yes. Goodnight, Dr Price.'

Sam continued on his rounds, carefully writing up his notes on each case, but he couldn't shake the image of the fair-haired junior doctor from his mind. Crazy. Even if he had been interested in another relationship—and his marriage to Angela had put him off that idea for good— it wouldn't be with Jodie. Being the subject of the hospital grapevine wasn't something he wanted to repeat. He'd been there, done that and worn the T-shirt when Angela had left him for another man.

Besides, Jodie really wasn't his type. Casual, breezy, and way too confident for a young doctor in her position. She still had a lot to learn, about life as well as medicine.

But…

No buts, he told himself firmly. He didn't even want to be her friend, let alone anything else.

So why ask her about her boyfriend, then? a little voice in his head queried wickedly.

Slip of the tongue.

Freudian slip, more like, the voice continued. *She's beautiful, clever, fun. And you want to—*

Shut up. I've got a job to do.

He forced himself to concentrate on his rounds; then, just as he was about to leave the ward, he heard her laugh. A laugh that made him yearn, for a brief second, to have been the one who'd put a smile on her face.

'See you tonight at Mario's, Jodie,' Fiona Ferguson, the ward sister, said. 'Eight o'clock sharp.'

'I'll be on time,' Jodie promised with a grin as she sat on the edge of the desk, swinging her long legs.

'As if. You doctors are all the same, thinking that time and tide and pizza will wait for you,' Fiona teased. 'Well, if you're late, we'll just eat your share of the dough balls.'

'You wouldn't do that to a poor, starving junior doctor,' Jodie retorted, wringing her hands theatrically and laughing. 'Not where Mario's dough balls are concerned…'

'Want to bet?' Fiona threatened, laughing back.

'Still here, Dr Price?' Sam asked, sauntering up to the nurses' station.

'Oh— Mr Taylor.' Jodie's smile dimmed at the implied rebuke. 'I'm sorry. I was just…' Her voice tailed off. What was it about Sam Taylor that unsettled her so much? She'd never had a problem with her seniors before. But he was reserved to the point of being unreachable. In the six months he'd worked with them he hadn't once yet socialised with the staff on the ward. No wonder they'd nicknamed him Mr Frosty. She didn't think it was just professional distance either.

The man, she decided, needed bringing out of himself. 'Why don't you come with us tonight?' she suggested on impulse.

'With you?' He looked blank.

'To Mario's.' The way he was looking at her, she thought crossly, anyone would think she'd suggested a date, a candlelit supper for two. 'There's a crowd of us going. It's a regular thing. On Thursday nights, they have a jazz band playing—not heavy stuff, more your Nick Drake jazz-folk sort of thing—and they do the best pizza in the city. The risotto's good, if you don't like pizza.' So he couldn't use that as an excuse.

'I—'

'Eight o'clock. And we don't talk shop *all* night.'

Excuse number two neatly sidestepped, he noticed with sudden amusement.

'And partners are welcome.'

Circumventing excuse number three? Or was she fishing to see if he was involved with someone? No. Of course she wasn't interested in him. She'd made it clear it was a group event which happened every week. 'I—'

'Good,' she said, before he could think up a valid reason to refuse. 'See you there, then.' She gave him directions to the restaurant. 'It's the little Italian place with a green sign outside—just ask for the hospital table when you get there. They'll know who you mean. Bye, Fi,' she called to the sister. And then she was gone in a swirl of soft hair, brightly coloured tunic top and black trousers, leaving Sam staring after her and Fiona with raised eyebrows.

When Jodie had changed into an elderly pair of leggings and swapped her loafers for a pair of trainers, she fastened her hair back into a ponytail, shrugged on her waterproof jacket and headed for the bicycle sheds in the far corner of the hospital car park.

What *had* she done? Jodie asked herself as she unlocked her bike, slid her handbag and document case into the waterproof carrier on the rear wheel and started cycling home. Fancy inviting the ward's newest consultant to their crowd's usual Thursday night gathering! He'd think she was trying to curry favour. Or, worse, that she was trying to net herself a husband with a prestigious job and a good income.

And she didn't fancy Sam Taylor. Not at all.

Though he was attractive enough, if you liked the strong, silent type. Tall, dark and intense. Grey eyes that reminded her of a rainy Wednesday morning, lonely and forgotten. She preferred the athletic type. Blond and suntanned, rather than that fine, pale skin. Curly, unruly hair, not straight and brushed back neatly from his face. Someone who wasn't too serious, saw the sunny side of life. With a mouth that smiled a lot and crinkles round the eyes—and she liked cornflower blue eyes.

Oh, stop thinking about it! she told herself, skidding to a halt outside her house. He probably wouldn't even turn up.

CHAPTER TWO

HOWEVER, when Jodie arrived at the small Italian restaurant at a quarter past eight—'just in time for the last garlic dough ball,' as Fiona commented with a grin—Sam Taylor was sitting at one end of the long table. Opposite the only spare chair, she realised with dismay. Wearing plain black trousers and a matching cotton round-neck sweater—trust him to do the Man in Black routine.

And it looked even better on him than she would have guessed.

Ignoring the rapid pounding of her heart, she sat down and gave him her most professional smile. 'Hi. So you made it.'

He nodded.

Not going to make it easy for me, are you? she thought crossly. 'Has everyone ordered?'

'Yes, and we ordered for you,' Mick Salmond, one of the few male nurses from the paediatric ward, told her. 'Your usual. Margherita with mushrooms, black olives, Dolcelatte and avocado.'

'Cheers. You're a mate.' She wrinkled her nose at him. 'Avocado? On *pizza*?' Sam lifted one eyebrow.

For the first time, Jodie saw amusement in his eyes. And suddenly that rainy Wednesday morning was gone: in its place was a sultry silver. And although his mouth wasn't smiling widely—just a tiny lift at one corner—it had lost that vulnerable look. Instead, it looked… kissable.

Her mouth went dry. No. Absolutely not. No way was she going to start thinking of Sam Taylor in those terms.

Drop-dead gorgeous or lame duck? That was what her brother would have asked if she'd told him she'd been stupid enough to invite the consultant on their Thursday night pizza run—reasoning that either Sam was drop-dead gorgeous and someone had dared Jodie to do it, or he was another of Jodie's lame ducks. Earlier today, she'd have said lame duck. Now she wasn't so sure.

To cover her confusion, she nodded to the jazz band, a trio of singer-pianist, double-bass player and drummer, who were setting up for the night's session. 'They're very good.'

'So I've been told.'

She grabbed a bottle of red wine from the table and poured herself a glass, then took a large sip. 'Mmm, that's better,' she said in satisfaction.

'It's the one you discovered last month,' Fiona told her. 'The Sicilian job.'

'Trust a woman to find a wine that tastes of chocolate,' Mick said, rolling his eyes. 'It was on the "Specials" board. "Red wine with a chocolate finish." And *she* was in charge of ordering, that night, so we didn't get any choice.'

'Come on. You know you like it. Anyway, red wine and chocolate are good for you. You've read the studies in the *Lancet*.' Jodie grinned broadly.

General hooting greeted her words.

'And then there's that study on pleasure. People who enjoy themselves have better immune systems. It's all to do with SIgA.'

'Enough of the lectures, Jo-jo.' Mick ruffled her hair. 'And, please, don't anyone mention the P-word.'

'The P-word?' Sam asked, mystified.

'P-l-a-y.' Mick spelled it out in phonics, amusing Jodie even more. 'She's writing some article or other for the *British Medical Journal* about the importance of play in paediatrics, how it helps children get better.'

'So that's why you spend all your free time on the ward, playing with certain patients?' Sam asked.

She flushed. 'Yes. No. I just enjoy my work, that's all.'

The pizzas arrived, diverting everyone's attention. Jodie had eaten three mouthfuls before she realised that Sam was staring at her. 'What?' she asked.

'I can't believe you're actually eating that.' He made a face.

'Don't knock it until you've tried it.' Jodie cut another piece, making sure there was a slice of avocado on it, and speared it with her fork. 'Here,' she said, reaching over towards him.

Again, there was that silvery glint in his eyes and he bent his head to taste the pizza, his gaze locking with hers. Jodie's mouth went dry again. She hadn't eaten since a snatched half a sandwich for lunch, so the wine must have gone to her head. What *was* she doing, feeding him from her fork? And what must he think of her?

Embarrassed, she almost snatched her hand back.

'Better than I expected,' he said.

She could feel her face burning. Was he referring just to the pizza, or to her, or to the evening? And, come to think of it, why was he here? True, she'd pretty much steamrollered him into it on the ward—but he could have just not turned up and made an excuse the next morning.

Jodie decided to take refuge in her pizza. Maybe when she had some good, solid carbohydrates inside her, she might start thinking more clearly.

'What made you decide on ... startling her into looking up at ...

'I like children,' she said simply ...

'But you're not married, not pla ... own?'

Jodie's eyes narrowed. Why was he ... so he could decide not to recommend her for pro... n, since she didn't have any real commitment to her job—she was going to give up work to have kids and waste all her years of training?

No, of course not. He wasn't one of the old school, the sort who couldn't help discriminating against young female doctors. He treated everyone on the ward alike— polite and distant. He was just trying to make conversation. It wasn't his fault he'd touched on her sore point. Three months ago, her ex-boyfriend Graham had told her she spent too much time on her career and he wanted to start a family almost as soon as they were married. Not that he'd actually asked her; he'd just assumed she'd fall in with his plans. When he'd realised she wasn't prepared to give up her job, he'd walked out on her.

'No, I'm not married, and I'm not planning a houseful of kids,' she said tightly, still seething inwardly at the memory of Graham's parting shot that she'd be a lousy wife anyway—she couldn't even cook! 'Not all women want children, you know.'

'Don't they?' asked Sam, his face completely unreadable.

'No. I'm an honorary auntie—well, godmother to my best friend Ellen's little boy, Billy—and that suits me fine.' Actually, that was a bit of a fib. She did want children, just not yet. Not until she'd figured out how to raise a family without throwing away all those years of study-

...and working silly hours. And then there was the small matter of finding a suitable father...

That rainy Wednesday morning look was back in his eyes again. Children were obviously a sore point with him, too, Jodie thought. Not that it was any of her business.

Time to change the subject. 'Why did you decide on paediatrics?' she asked.

'I...' He wasn't going to tell her the whole truth. 'I did a stint in Paediatrics after I qualified. I went to Cardiology after that, then Oncology—but I found that I liked working with children best.' Even though it was like rubbing salt in the wound.

'Cardiology.' She looked thoughtful. 'I nearly did that, too. Because of Sadie.'

'Sadie?'

'My younger sister.' Her green eyes were suddenly sombre. 'She had a hole in the heart. There wasn't anything they could do at the time. She died when she was two weeks old.'

'Was she much younger than you?' he asked gently.

Jodie shook her head. 'I was nearly three at the time. My brother, Matt, was seven, so he remembers more about it than I do. Anyway, when I decided to become a doctor, he was the one who said I should give myself time to find out what I was really interested in, not rush straight into heart surgery or neonatal so I could save future Sadies. We had a huge row over it, but I have to admit he was right.' She smiled wryly. 'He rang me tonight, actually. He's getting engaged—at last. He and Annie have known each other since junior school but they only realised their feelings for each other a month or so back. Now they've decided they've wasted too

much time already, so the engagement party's this weekend.'

'And you're on duty?' Sam guessed.

She nodded.

He tipped his head on one side. 'Can't you swap shifts
with one of the others?'

'Not when we're almost skeleton staff.' She shrugged.
'Ah, well. Matt and Annie'll come up for the weekend
some time soon and we'll have a party of our own. Just
the three of us.'

So the boyfriend was *definitely* off the scene, Sam
thought. Though he wasn't sure if she was upset about it
or not. Jodie had seemed touchy when he'd mentioned
children—maybe the boyfriend hadn't wanted them and
she had.

But he couldn't get involved with her. One, she was a
colleague; two, she was probably on the rebound; and,
three, maybe she'd sort out her differences with her ex
and they'd get back together.

But he couldn't take his eyes off her. Even when they
were both talking to other people, and she'd shifted
places to drink her coffee at the other end of the table
and chat to Fiona Ferguson, he was aware of her. Aware
of every move she made—the way her blonde curls cascaded over her shoulders, the way her bright purple silk
shirt highlighted the intense green of her eyes. Aware of
the curve of her mouth. His body tightened and he suddenly wondered what it would be like to kiss her. To
tangle his fingers in that silky soft hair, to feel her mouth
soften and open under his own, her hands against his bare
skin…

He took a deep breath. Hell. What was it about Jodie
Price that got under his skin? He'd always been so scru-
pulous about keeping work and his private life separate.

Not that he had a private life. Just himself and the cat who'd adopted him when he'd moved to Norfolk. Not the children he'd once expected to have by this age. Not a little boy climbing everything in sight and wanting to help Daddy make a tree-house and listen to his heart with Daddy's stethoscope and go to the park together to sail a model yacht on the boating lake. Not a baby girl just starting to walk, tottering on unsteady legs towards her father with a beaming face and chubby outstretched hands when he walked in the door, greeting him with a loud 'Da-*da*,' and a stream of delighted babbling.

He locked his hands together under the table, squeezing his fingers hard until the physical pain took his mind off his mental torture. Half the conversation tonight had been about children—particular cases on the ward who'd touched everyone's heart—or handing round the latest family snaps to be admired. It was why he always avoided social events at work, so he didn't have to smile and smile and pretend the yawning gap in his own life didn't exist. The yawning gap that even dedicating himself one hundred per cent to his job didn't fill.

He caught himself watching Jodie again. The way she laughed, throwing her head back, her whole face lighting up. The way she looked earnestly at whoever she was talking to, making them feel as if they were the only person in the room. The way her eyes crinkled at the corners...

Oh, get a life, Taylor, he told himself wryly. Nothing's going to come of it. Ever.

When everyone had finished their coffee and gradually drifted home in twos and threes, sharing lifts and taxis, Sam and Jodie were left in the doorway of the restaurant.

'How are you getting home?' he asked.

'Pushbike.'

He frowned. 'In this rain?'

She shrugged. 'It's only about three miles between here and my place. Fifteen minutes, tops, if I catch all the traffic lights on green.'

'But you'll get soaked.'

'It won't kill me. You can't catch a cold from getting wet, Doctor,' she reminded him, wrapping a scarf round her glorious hair.

'Where's your bike?'

'I…er… Why?'

'Because you're going to stop being stubborn, put your bike in the back of my car and let me give you a lift home. It's the least I can do,' he said, making her close her mouth on the argument she'd been about to produce. 'You were kind enough to ask me to join you tonight.'

You plural, not you singular, she reminded herself. 'I…er…' Oh, why was she suddenly so inarticulate?

'Where's your bike?' he asked again.

'Chained to that lamppost,' she said, pointing to the elderly and slightly battered racer she'd inherited from Matt fifteen years before, on her thirteenth birthday, and had liked too much to replace with a newer—or more feminine—model.

'Keys?' he asked, holding out his hand.

She shook her head, unlocked the bike herself, and wheeled it alongside him to his car. 'Are you sure about this?' she asked, eyeing the four-wheel-drive doubtfully. It was big enough to cope with her bike, but it was also pristine. And, judging by the number plate, less than six months old.

'Sure.' He opened the back and hauled her bike inside. 'Hop in.'

Being in an enclosed space with Sam Taylor was a

definite mistake, she thought. It was a big car, but she was still very much aware of how close he was to her. If she shifted her hand less than six inches, her fingers would brush against his. Fingers that were gentle with his patients. How would they be with her?

Stop it, Jodie, she told herself fiercely. And yet she couldn't help remembering the look in his eyes as she'd fed him pizza. She could imagine them lying in the park on a sunny day, with his head in her lap as she fed him seedless grapes and morsels of Brie—and then bending down to kiss the crumbs away from his lips...

That's the last time you ever drink more than one glass of wine in his company, Jodie Price, she warned herself.

Then she flushed as she became aware that he'd been talking to her, and she hadn't heard a single word he'd said. 'Sorry. I was miles away,' she apologised.

'Where do I go from here?' he asked.

He sounded completely cool and calm. Obviously he didn't feel the same pull and she'd be wise to remember that. Dragging her thoughts together, she directed him through the back streets of the city to her small terraced house. He parked the car and hefted her bike down.

'Thanks for the lift.'

'No problem.'

Should she ask him in for coffee? It was only polite, seeing as he'd given her a lift home, but she didn't want him misreading her motives.

In the end Sam made the decision for her. 'Goodnight, Jodie.'

It was the first time he'd ever used her name, and she wasn't prepared for the sudden lurch of her heart. 'Goodnight,' she muttered, not quite daring to use his first name but not wanting to rebuff him by using a more formal mode of address.

She watched him as he drove away. She still knew virtually nothing about him, despite having spent most of the evening talking to him. He was as mysterious and distant as ever. Though there had been a moment when she'd thought she'd come close to breaking through his wall.

Shaking her head, she walked into the house. Maybe he didn't want to be rescued. But that sultry silver in his eyes told her that she couldn't give up. Not yet.

As he drove away, Sam could have kicked himself. Why had he insisted on taking her home? He'd been so close to breaking a personal rule. When he'd taken her bike out of the car, the way she'd looked up at him, her eyes all shiny and her mouth so soft and warm and inviting... His body had been screaming out for him to take her in his arms and kiss her, and to hell with the consequences.

But the sensible side of him had overruled it. Just. Apart from the fact that affairs with colleagues were bad news, he'd sworn he'd never get involved again. Not after his extremely messy divorce.

Come off it. What have you got to lose? Angela's the complete opposite of Jodie, the voice in his head taunted. *Just look at her.*

Angela was petite, slender and well groomed, and she only ever wore little suits teamed with designer shoes, handbag and briefcase, whereas Jodie was tall, curvy and had a much more casual attitude towards clothes. Angela's make-up was always immaculate, whereas Jodie's barely existed—he suspected that the nearest Jodie came to cosmetics was a lip-salve. Angela would never have dreamed of letting her expensive haircut get wet—and if she'd had a bike it would have been an expensive and trendy mountain bike, not a battered, elderly racer.

Maybe that was the attraction: Jodie was the opposite of Angela. No, that was unfair. Jodie was a little like the Angela he'd fallen in love with at university, the young lawyer with a sparkle in her eye and a sense of fun that had stopped him being too serious.

The sparkle that had soon dimmed when Angela had discovered what a failure Sam had been as a husband— that he couldn't give her what she most wanted in the world. And it would be exactly the same with Jodie. It might start out fine, full of love and laughter, but over the months it would change and one day he'd come home to an empty house and an apologetic note. Just like he had with Angela.

Though what was he doing, even thinking about Jodie in those terms? She wasn't interested in him and he didn't have the right to get involved with anyone. Not with his past.

She said being an honorary auntie was enough for her, the little voice reminded him.

Only because her biological clock hasn't started ticking yet.

She was serious. She's dedicated to her career.

Now, maybe. Things change. She's a natural mother. You can see it in her eyes, in the way she acts with the children on the ward.

But supposing—

Supposing nothing. It's *not* going to happen.

CHAPTER THREE

'I'M JODIE PRICE,' she said, extending a hand to the pale-faced woman who was sitting holding a small baby. 'And this is Dr Taylor, who's sharing the assessment clinic with me.' Mr, actually, but she'd learned that it was easier to say 'Doctor' than go through all the explanations about when you got high enough up the career ladder, you swapped Dr for plain Mr or Ms. Worried parents weren't interested in the social niceties: they just wanted reassurance about their sick children. Right now.

She glanced down at her notes. 'This is Harry, yes?'

The woman nodded.

'And he's seven weeks old.'

Tears welled in the woman's eyes. 'He's so small... I thought it was just a cold. And then he couldn't breathe...'

'You're here now and we can help him, Mrs Bartlett,' Jodie soothed, crouching down beside her and focusing on the baby. 'Let's have a look at the little fellow and see what's going on. Can you tell me a bit about his symptoms? When did you first notice he was ill?'

'Two days ago. He picked up his sister's cold—but he wouldn't feed properly yesterday, only took half what he normally has, and he started coughing. Then, today, he was so quiet...I thought I was probably fussing too much but I took him to the doctor anyway—and she sent me straight here.'

'To the paediatric assessment unit. I know, it sounds scary, but you're in the best place,' Jodie reassured her.

23

'All it means is that we're specialists in babies and children, so we'll be able to work out what's wrong with him and how to treat him quicker than your GP can. Now, let's get this vest and nappy off.' She quickly undressed the baby, weighed him and measured his length, and noted the details on his chart. 'He's a lovely big boy, isn't he?'

'Yes. My husband's tall.' Mrs Bartlett gulped. 'He's parking the car. Laura's with him.'

'Laura's Harry's sister?' Jodie guessed.

'Yes. She's three and a half.'

'The perfect age gap. My brother's nearly four years older than me,' Jodie said. 'Young Harry here's going to hero-worship her from the minute he can toddle. I was just the same with Matt.' She put a thermometer under the baby's armpit, and waited until it bleeped, then looked carefully at the reading. 'That's good, he doesn't have a high temperature. Apyrexic,' she said to Sam, who was writing down what she said.

The baby coughed, and gave a hoarse cry.

'Lost his voice, has he?' she asked sympathetically.

Mrs Bartlett nodded. 'He's a happy baby anyway, doesn't normally cry a lot, but now he can't even tell me when he's hungry or wet.'

Jodie replaced the baby's nappy, noting the way the skin underneath the baby's ribs and the base of his throat sucked in sharply every time he breathed. Pretty much a textbook case. 'Tracheal tug,' she said to Sam. She turned to Mrs Bartlett. 'I'm going to listen to his chest now.' She placed her stethoscope on Harry's chest. 'Hmm, he sounds pretty wheezy. Creps,' she said to Sam. 'There are a few bubbles there, Mrs Bartlett—that means there's lots of mucus clogging up the tubes.' Gently, she palpated the baby's abdomen. 'His abdomen's fine.' She took her otoscope, the instrument used for checking the ear canal, and looked in the baby's ears. 'Bilateral wax,' she said to Sam, then turned back to Mrs Bartlett. 'He's got a fair bit of wax in both ears—he's really bunged up with that lurgy, poor love.'

'It's just a cold, then?' Mrs Bartlett looked hopeful.

'It's a little more than that, I'm afraid. There's a rather nasty virus going round called RSV or respiratory syncytial virus. I'll need to take a sample of his nasal secretions to check if that's what he has—all I'll do is put a tube up his nose so we can suck out some of the mucus and send it off to the lab for them to run a few tests. It looks a bit scary but it won't hurt him,' she reassured Mrs Bartlett. 'And then I'll put a probe on his foot so I can make some more checks. The light goes through his foot and hits the probe—again, it won't hurt him, because it's just like having a very soft strap wrapped round his foot—and that helps me measure the oxygen levels in his blood, his pulse rate and his breathing.' She indicated the machine next to the bed. 'It'll probably bleep a lot, but don't worry—these things don't take into account the fact that babies tend to wriggle! The minute they move, the alarm goes off—it'll probably say something like "insufficient light" on the screen, and all that means is that he's moved so the probe needs to be reset.'

Quickly, Jodie took the sample of the nasal secretions, then wrapped the cuff of the probe round Harry's foot. As she'd suspected, his oxygen saturation was a little on the low side and his pulse was rapid. 'Sats eighty-seven in air, pulse a hundred and sixty.' She watched the child's chest rise and fall, keeping one eye on the second hand of the clock as she counted his breaths in her head. 'Resp sixty-five.' She brushed her fingers momentarily against the baby's face. 'You're having a tough time, little one, but hang on in there. We'll sort you out. We're going to admit him for a few days, Mrs Bartlett,' she said. 'All the signs are that he's got bronchiolitis, which is usually caused by RSV. In adults and older children, it just gives you a bad cold and a cough, but in young babies it tends to make them quite poorly.'

'He'll be all right, though?' Mrs Bartlett's eyes were wide with anxiety.

Jodie nodded. 'It's very common—there's often an epidemic between November and March. We've got six babies on the ward with it already, so he'll be in good company.' She gently rubbed Harry's cheek again. 'You did the right thing in bringing him in to us. He hasn't got it that badly, though I should warn you that they often get worse before they get better. He'll be in for somewhere between three and seven days, depending on how he responds to treatment, and he'll be coughing for a good six to ten weeks after he gets home, maybe even until the clocks go forward.'

'So you can do something for him?'

Jodie nodded. 'The problem is that some of his airways are so small—less than a tenth of a millimetre across—so the mucus is gumming him up and making him wheezy. We'll try giving him a nebuliser—that's just a mask with a drug in it—to help widen his airways a bit, and he'll breathe the drug in through a mist of oxygen. That might help him to feed a bit better. We may need to give him some oxygen, too. We'll do it through a tube under his nose, which looks frightening but won't hurt him. And if he's finding it too tiring to feed—bearing in mind he's having a hard time getting his breath, he's only got the energy to take a bit of his usual feeds at the moment—we'll feed him through an nasogastric tube.

What that means is a tube goes up his nose and into his stomach, so he'll get all the goodness he needs without having to work so hard for it.'

Mrs Bartlett looked shocked. 'Can we—can I stay with him?'

'Of course you can. He'll be in a room on his own because the virus is highly infectious and we don't want it spreading to the other children. There'll be a notice on his door saying that he's in isolation nursing, but all that means is that the nurses and doctors will wear a gown and gloves when they come into his room to stop the virus lingering on their clothes or their hands and then spreading to other patients on the ward. This particular virus can live for around twenty minutes outside the body, on clothes, which is why it spreads so quickly.'

'I see.'

'There's a chair-bed in the room, and you'll be able to use the staff restaurant when the public restaurant's closed,' Jodie added. 'And we have a policy of shared care in the ward, so you'll know at all times exactly what's going on, what you can do to help and what we need to do.'

Mrs Bartlett still looked stunned at the idea of her child being hospitalised.

'There's a visitor phone on the ward. Parents and visitors answer it, rather than the ward staff, and that means you can take any incoming calls without worrying that you're stopping important calls coming into the ward. There's a payphone just outside the assessment unit, too, though I'm afraid we have to bar mobile phones because they could interfere with the equipment,' Jodie warned.

Mrs Bartlett nodded.

'Give Harry a cuddle while I finish writing his admission notes,' Jodie said, 'and I'll ask Alice, the dark-haired nurse over there, to take you through to the ward. If your husband and Laura haven't arrived by the time you go, I'll make sure someone brings them through to you.'

'Thank you, Dr Price.'

'That's what I'm here for. Alice will give you an information sheet about bronchiolitis and RSV, which should answer most of your questions.' She smiled. 'I'm on duty later tonight, so I'll see you when I do my round and we can have a chat then if you have any other questions or you're worried about anything.'

When Mrs Bartlett had left, cradling the baby in her arms, Sam turned to Jodie. 'You're good with parents. You explained everything to her without being patronising. Well done.'

'Thank you.' She was surprised at the compliment. He'd barely spoken to her since he'd dropped her home from Mario's the previous week, so she'd been dreading it when she'd realised that he was going to be with her on the paediatric assessment unit shift this morning. She'd expected him to pick up every single fault, however minor. Instead, he'd let her get on with it and had only occasionally offered an opinion, phrasing it more as a question so she could show off her own knowledge of the subject.

'You're a good doctor, Jodie,' he said, surprising her even further. 'Though are you sure about the nebuliser?'

'I know it's controversial and some doctors don't approve of using bronchodilators,' Jodie said, 'but if it helps the baby breathe, that's the most important thing. We'll trial Atrovent and salbutamol, see which one works best for him. Sometimes they respond to one better than the other.'

Sam grinned. 'Yes, Dr Price.'

She flushed. 'Sorry. You already knew that.' Of course

he did. He was a consultant, with a good six years' more experience than her. Trust her to open her mouth and say something so stupid, just when she was trying to prove to him that she could be a cool, calm and rational colleague.

Not to mention proving to herself that Sam Taylor didn't make her hormones run amok.

'I'd always rather you explain yourself than make assumptions,' Sam said gently, as if sensing her embarrassment. 'It leaves less room for errors.'

'Right.'

'What else have we got in?' he asked.

'An asthma attack—when I know the history, I might suggest some skin tests to see if the girl's allergic to cats or dust mites or any particular sorts of food, and I want to check whether the parents smoke round her—plus two rashes and a possible fracture.'

'Lead on, Macduff,' he misquoted with a grin.

Jodie stared at him for a moment, slightly dazed. That grin could only be described as dazzling. What was it about the man? Since Mario's, he'd as good as avoided her. And just when she'd decided that he was remote, glacial and not worth thinking about, he did or said something that made her look again, see him as a man—a very attractive man, at that. Without that wall of reserve, he'd be devastating.

It couldn't work out between them. There were too many barriers, social *and* professional, so why couldn't she stop that voice in her head telling her to go for it?

Not now. They had work to do. 'Let's go,' she said, forcing herself to smile at Sam in her best professional manner.

The voice grew louder over the next week until it was positively deafening. The departmental Christmas party was traditionally held in the middle of December; those who were married came with their partners, but those who were single—which meant most of their ward, as the staff were all fairly young—picked the name of their partner out of a hat, the day before the party.

And Jodie had picked Sam. Completely by accident, but it felt as if fate or some higher power had done it by design. She'd agonised over it for nearly the whole of her shift. Should she give him the option of backing out, or use the chance to break down his reserve? He'd hate it. Hadn't he gone back into his shell since Mario's? On the other hand, it was the Christmas party—and Christmas was a season of magic, when everything could change.

When Sam had finished his ward round, she caught his attention. 'Mr Taylor—could I have a word, please?'

'Of course, Dr Price.'

The formality made her nervous, but she pressed on. 'Um…your office?' she suggested.

'My office,' he agreed.

Sam's office was the same size as that of Lyn Trevor, the other paediatric consultant, but whereas Lynn's desk sported pictures of her husband and children and the walls were decorated with pictures drawn by patients and her own children, Sam's office was completely devoid of personal touches. Not even so much as a pot-plant graced the window-sill and even the Christmas cards were stacked in a neat pile on his desk rather than being on display.

Jodie felt even more daunted. Everything around her screamed, *Keep off! Don't touch!*

He sat down on the swivel chair behind his desk. 'So, what can I do for you, Dr Price?'

She took a deep breath, gathered up her courage and swallowed hard. 'It's about the departmental Christmas party, tomorrow night,' she muttered.

'Yes?'

'I…er…I picked your name out of the hat. It means I'm supposed to go with you.'

Not a flicker of emotion. He was completely unreadable—and unreachable. 'And?'

'I…' she floundered. 'Look, if you'd rather I made some excuse and didn't go…'

'Why would I do that?'

'Honestly, men could be so *dense* sometimes!'

To her shock, he laughed.

'What?'

'I take it you didn't mean to say that out loud?'

Jodie clapped a hand over her mouth, horrified. 'Oh, no. Please, tell me I didn't…' When he said nothing, she closed her eyes. 'I'm sorry. What I meant was—'

'Given that the first half of the party is a revue, and Mr Frosty's bound to have a part in it, you think I'd find it too embarrassing to attend,' he finished.

Her eyes widened. He knew about his nickname on the ward?

He folded his arms. 'Yes, Jodie, I know.'

'I'd see a specialist but there isn't a cure for foot-in-mouth disease,' she said wryly.

'You didn't say a thing this time. You have one of those faces that shows every single thought.' Still, his own expression was unreadable. 'Do I take it you'd rather not go to the party with me, then?'

'I…' She sighed. 'I don't know.'

'Explain.'

'Do you always have to be so, so…' Unable to find

the word she was searching for, she growled in frustration.

That at least raised a smile. 'Difficult?'

'Something like that.' Well, he'd asked. If he didn't like the answer, that was his problem; she couldn't keep quiet any more. 'When you came to Mario's with us, I thought you'd, well, thawed out a bit. And then...'

'Back to Mr Frosty.'

'Yes.' This time, Jodie had the grace to blush. 'I guess Fiona didn't ask you before she put your name in the hat.'

'No.'

'If you'd rather not go, I won't make a big deal out of it.'

'And if I do go?'

'Um, there's the revue.' Jodie winced. She didn't know a huge amount of detail, but what she knew wasn't good.

'Consultants are fair game for sketches. And I suppose it's time the boot was on the other foot.'

Jodie digested his words and then blinked hard. 'You mean—you've acted in a revue?'

He shrugged. 'I think all doctors get involved in some kind of revue at some point. When I was a house officer, I played our senior consultant as God.'

'No.' Without thinking, Jodie perched on the edge of his desk and crossed one long leg over the other. 'Show me.'

'Show you?'

'Oh, come on. You can't feed me a line like that and back off again.'

He shook his head. 'I can't really remember the lines now. It was something about the ten commandments of working on his ward. Thou shalt not drink coffee until thou hast knelt at my feet and worshipped me for five minutes—that sort of thing.'

'Hmm.' Jodie's smile was pure mischief.

'Don't even think about it,' Sam warned, guessing at what was going through her mind. 'Are you in this revue?'

She shook her head. 'I'm a hopeless actor. I just made some of the props—with a bit of help from some of the older children on the ward.'

'Such as Mr Frosty's costume?' he asked.

'I think it's time I left.' She gave him a nervous smile, slid down from his desk and headed for the door.

'Not so fast.'

She stopped with her fingers on the doorhandle.

'Am I picking you up or meeting you here? And what time?'

'I'll make my own way there,' Jodie said. 'It starts at seven in the canteen.'

'I'll see you there, then. At ten to seven.'

'OK.' Jodie left his office, closing the door behind her, and heaved a sigh of relief. It hadn't been as bad as she'd expected…or, now she thought about it, had it? She had her date for the party, but she still had no idea whether he really wanted to be there or not.

'Well, Mr Frosty, if the revue doesn't thaw you out, nothing will,' she said softly to herself.

Sam leaned back in his chair. He was walking on very thin ice indeed. Jodie had even given him the perfect get-out for not going to the party—so why hadn't he jumped at it?

Because you want to see her all dressed up, the little voice in his head informed him. *And then you want to take every scrap of material off her again…*

Do not.

You're in denial—Mr Frosty, the voice taunted him.

Sam groaned aloud. He was going to have an awful lot to live up to—but he was aware that distance wasn't a style the ward was comfortable with. Maybe the party was his chance to show the rest of the team that he had a sense of humour, that he could laugh with them.

How long had it been since he'd laughed? Really laughed? Before Jodie had burst into his life and insisted on him going to Mario's with the rest of the team?

He closed his eyes. Jodie again. Maybe he should have accepted her get-out. He wasn't sure how he was going to cope, dancing with her. Holding her so close and knowing he couldn't have her—ever. It wouldn't be fair on either of them.

He smiled wryly. Who said life had to be fair? Besides, he knew there were people out there far worse off than he was—it was just that, right now, it didn't feel like it.

Tomorrow morning, he decided, he'd have a convenient sore throat. One that got worse during the day so he wouldn't feel up to going to the Christmas party. That way, Jodie wouldn't think he was avoiding the party because of her. She'd still be able to go and enjoy herself, she wouldn't be embarrassed dealing with him at work—and he wouldn't have the torture of wanting something he knew he couldn't have.

CHAPTER FOUR

THOUGH, of course, Sam did nothing of the kind.

Although his path didn't cross Jodie's during their shifts the next day, he could have complained about his 'sore throat' to any of the nurses or junior doctors he worked with, knowing they'd pass the message on to Jodie. But something stopped him and at ten to seven he was striding down the corridor to meet her.

She looked absolutely stunning, Sam thought as he saw her standing by the entrance to the canteen. She'd piled her hair on the top of her head and little tendrils escaped here and there to soften the severity of the style. Her make-up was understated, just enough to emphasise her beautiful green eyes and tempting mouth. And the crimson raw silk shift dress suited her colouring perfectly. Not to mention showing just how long her legs were. She was wearing heels high enough to make her the same height as he was and a smile that made him feel as if a knife had been plunged into his stomach—because the smile was directed at the man who was talking to her. Mick Salmond, a nurse on their ward. The man who knew her well enough to order her pizza for her when she'd been late at Mario's.

And the warmth of that smile… Was something going on between them? He searched his memory. Wasn't Mick Salmond married? What the hell did Jodie think she was doing, having an affair with a married man?

'Dr Price,' he said stiffly, joining them. 'I trust I'm not late.'

'No. I was early.'

'For once,' Mick said, teasing her.

'Huh. I'm not late all the time.'

'Only on a day with a Y in it,' the nurse retorted with a grin.

'Yeah, yeah. Hey, Mick's got some fabulous news.' She dug her companion in the ribs. 'Go on, *tell* him, before I burst.'

'News?' Sam echoed, frowning.

Mick beamed. 'I'm going to be a dad!'

'Congratulations.' Sam forced the word out. Hadn't he come to terms with this years ago? So why could those six little words still hurt him so much, the six words he'd never be able to say himself?

And why was Jodie going to burst? Was *she* the one expecting Mick's baby?

The thought was like a physical blow. He felt winded, sick.

'Shelley's going to make a brilliant mum,' Jodie said. 'And she's asked me to be godmother.'

Shelley? Godmother? The fog cleared and Sam suddenly realised what was going on. Jodie wasn't having a baby. She was just excited for her friends and delighted at being asked to be godmother. So when it came to her own babies, she'd—

'When it's your turn,' Mick said to Jodie with a grin, echoing Sam's tortured thoughts, 'I bet you'll never get any housework or anything done. You'll spend the whole day playing with your kids.' He gave her a sidelong look. 'Observing them at the same time. And you'll write it up as a study paper when they're in bed.'

Jodie rolled her eyes. 'I will not. I'm not that bad, Mick.'

'Yes, you are, Jo-jo. Look at the way you are with the

kids on the ward. You even come in on your days off to play with some of them. You'll be ten times worse with your own,' he teased.

'No, I won't. I'll be just like any other mum.'

'As if!' he scoffed. 'I can see you with half a dozen.'

Jodie chuckled. 'Yeah, right.'

'So how many are you planning?'

She shrugged. 'Depends.' Her face softened. 'One of each would be nice.'

'You mean, so you get to play with the trains *and* the doll's house?' he teased.

'Let's p-l-a-y,' Jodie teased back.

Just like any other mum. The words reverberated inside Sam's head, numbing his senses. *Just like any other mum.* Meaning that Jodie, despite her protests at Mario's, was planning to have children one day. *One of each would be nice.* Taking it for granted that she could have children—and so could her future husband.

'Can't you just see what our Jodie'll be like with her kids, Mr Taylor?' Mick asked, laughing.

'Yes,' Sam said shortly. He could just see Jodie with her arm round a three-year-old, reading him a story and getting him to act out one of the speaking parts while the baby was curled up asleep on her lap. *I'll huff, and I'll puff, and I'll blow your house down...* He could imagine only too clearly the softness in her face, the deep enduring love of a mother in her eyes as she cuddled her children.

A stab of something—pain or envy—lanced through him as he listened to them talking about their future children. It amazed him how easily they could talk about their plans. If anyone had asked him, the words would have stuck in his throat. *I can't have babies. I'm infertile.*

He became aware that Mick was talking again. 'I

dunno who called it morning sickness. Shelley gets it in the evenings.' As if he'd sensed the message behind the sharp look Sam had given him, Mick continued, 'I would have stayed with her to hold her hand and mop her face and what have you, but she wanted me to video the revue so she doesn't miss out on it.'

'Indeed,' Sam said brusquely.

'Mick wr—' Jodie stopped abruptly, suddenly realising she'd been about to blurt out that Mick had written the revue. 'Shall we go and sit down, Mr Taylor?' She didn't quite dare use his first name. Not when he was back in Mr Frosty mode. And why the sudden freeze? Something was obviously bugging Sam...but what?

I'll be just like any other mum... One of each would be nice...

The words echoed round and round in Sam's head as if his mind were stuck on continuous-loop replay, and he couldn't stop it, even though it was torture. And the dreams he'd started entertaining about Jodie crumbled into dust.

He sat locked in misery until he realised that Jodie was shuffling in her seat, looking distinctly nervous. Then he realised why: the revue. It had been going on for ten minutes and he hadn't even noticed.

He forced his attention to the stage. Yes, there was Mr Frosty: a consultant in a formal suit, a white coat and a snowman's head, with an expressionless mouth, large grey eyes and a big carrot for a nose.

Stuart Henderson, one of the senior house officers, was playing Mr Frosty and had Sam's mannerisms down to a T. Sam found himself laughing at the way various nurses pretended to be overcome with heat and Mr Frosty cooled them down by blasting snow at them. Jodie visibly relaxed when she saw Sam laugh. He found himself relaxing, too. Maybe he was reading too much into all this, overreacting. Hadn't Angela always said he was too serious?

Finally there was the pièce de résistance—something Jodie obviously hadn't expected, by her gasp of surprise followed by a giggle—the pantomime dog. One of the auxiliaries had made herself up like an English springer spaniel and trotted onto the stage, dropping a ball on the patient's bed and saying, 'Let's play!' She bounded up to every other actor on the stage—'doctor' and 'patient'—saying, 'Let's play! It's good for you. Let's play!'

'Hoist with your own petard?' Sam whispered in her ear.

'Deservedly.' Though she didn't look cross or embarrassed by the lampooning—just amused. In her shoes, Angela would have stormed off in a huff.

When the revue finished, Sam gave some of the loudest applause. He also collared Mick when they'd both helped to shift the chairs out of the way of the dancing area.

'I…er…hope you weren't offended,' Mick said, shuffling his feet slightly.

'If it weren't for your impending fatherhood,' Sam said coolly, 'I'd be suggesting that you consider a change in career.'

Mick looked completely crestfallen, and Jodie—who'd joined them and had overheard Sam's comment—was clearly about to jump to his defence when Sam added, 'Your comic timing's brilliant and you've an eye for detail and mannerisms. But nursing's a steadier job than scriptwriting, so I'd stick with the day job for now. Besides, we'd all miss you too much on the ward if you went off to London.'

Mick stared at the consultant, open-mouthed. 'For a minute there, I thought you were going to...' He tailed off awkwardly.

'Freeze you?' Sam gave a rueful smile. 'Message received and understood.'

'Thanks for being such a good sport about it,' Mick said.

'Hmm. Well, another lesson's been drummed into me tonight.' With a sidelong glance at Jodie, he explained, 'Play's good for you.'

Jodie's face clashed spectacularly with her dress. 'I'm not really that over the top, am I, Mick?'

The other nurse nodded. 'But the patients love it.' He looked diffidently at Sam. 'And they think a lot of you, too, sir.'

'The name's Sam, not sir,' Sam corrected.

'Sam.' Mick smiled. 'Well, have a good time, you two. I'm off to get some banana and anchovy pizza before I dare go home and show the missus this.' He waved the video camera at them and headed for the exit.

'Banana and anchovy?' Sam and Jodie simultaneously pulled faces.

'Am I really like a spaniel?' Jodie asked Sam.

He tipped his head on one side, considering. 'Well, I don't see any evidence of a wet, shiny nose, big brown eyes, long ears or halitosis.'

Her colour deepened. 'That isn't what I meant.'

He smiled. 'Your enthusiasm keeps everyone going.'

'Oh.' Jodie bit her lip. 'Shall we get something to eat?'

'As long as it isn't banana and anchovy pizza.'

'Definitely not!' They wandered over to the buffet table and helped themselves to chicken satay, tiny bridge rolls and cheese straws. Jodie eschewed the mince pies in favour of chocolate cheesecake, and ate Sam's share as well as her own.

'I had you pegged as a traditionalist,' Sam said.

Jodie grimaced. 'I hate mince pies. And Christmas cake. And Christmas pud.' She screwed up her nose. 'I don't care if dried fruit's good for you, it's revolting.'

Sam's lips twitched. 'So you have chocolate instead?'

Jodie spread her hands. 'Chocolate's actually quite healthy.'

'That report about catechins was referring to top-quality plain chocolate,' Sam said, surprising her. 'And it didn't say you should eat industrial-sized quantities of the stuff.'

'You weren't eating your cheesecake,' she pointed out, 'and it'd be a shame to waste it.'

'Huh.' Sam gave a mock grimace and the corners of his eyes crinkled.

Jodie felt her pulse accelerate and looked away. Not now. No, please, she couldn't develop a huge crush on the man *now*. She was supposed to be getting him out of his shell, that was all. Though a part of her wanted to do much, much, more...

As the band started, Sam looked round and raised an eyebrow. 'Is that Stuart Henderson again, on vocals?'

'And air guitar. A man of many talents,' Jodie said. 'Not to mention a string of nurses desperate for his attention.' She shrugged. 'He's young.'

Sam burst out laughing. 'You're starting to sound like me.'

'You mean, old?' she teased.

'Listen, you, I'd hardly started at infant school when you were born.'

'Uh-huh.' Jodie tapped her nose meaningfully. 'I believe you.'

To his surprise, Sam was thoroughly enjoying himself. How long had it been since he'd had some fun? Excluding Mario's…too long, he thought. When his marriage had disintegrated, he'd buried himself in work and avoided the social side of hospital life completely.

Right now, he wanted to have fun. And if Jodie thought he was an old fogey, she was about to learn something! 'Come on. Let's dance,' he said to her.

'Dance?'

'Move your feet, wiggle about a bit in time to music, that sort of thing.'

Was this really Sam Taylor, Mr Frosty, talking? Jodie thought. But the offer was too good to resist. 'Let's go,' she said, putting her plate down on a convenient table.

Dance. She'd expected him maybe to do what everyone else at the party was doing—as he'd put it, 'move your feet, wiggle about a bit'. But, no, Sam Taylor could *really* dance. When Stuart's band switched to a rock 'n' roll number, Sam was spinning Jodie round and getting her to do all sorts of complicated things that would have had Matt goggling at his clumsy kid sister's performance.

When the music stopped, she was out of breath. And then she became aware that she and Sam were the only two on the floor—everyone else was standing watching them, applauding and cheering. Yet again that evening Jodie's face clashed with her dress, and she retreated to the table where she'd left her plate.

'Come on. Play's good for you,' Sam teased.

'Not this sort of play. I've got two left feet.'

'I didn't notice.'

'You were leading me.' She paused. 'I didn't know you could dance like that.'

'I'm a bit out of practice.'

'Could have fooled me.' If that was out of practice,

heaven only knew what he'd be like when he was back in the swing of things!

'Oh, Mr Taylor…' a breathy voice asserted beside them.

Melissa the Maneater from the neonatal unit, Jodie thought with a sigh, recognising the brunette in the skimpy dress.

'I was very impressed with your…' big pause '…dancing. Could we?'

'I believe I'm Dr Price's partner for this evening,' Sam said, stepping closer to Jodie.

'Jodie won't mind, will you, sweetie?'

It was more of a command than a question. Jodie lifted her hands in surrender. She had to face it: men preferred small and slinky, not strapping and Amazon. In any contest with Melissa, she'd lose. 'Be my guest.'

It was another fast number, and Sam dutifully twirled Melissa round the floor and somehow managed to evade her clutches for the next dance. Jodie merely sat on the sidelines, watching him and wondering what made him tick. One minute he was Mr Frosty, completely unreadable; the next he was shy and retiring; and now here he was, the star of the dance floor. She couldn't work him out.

Four dances later, he was back at her side. 'You're supposed to be my partner for this evening.'

'So?'

'So, dance with me. Come on, Doc-a Dodo. Playtime.'

So he'd heard Amy's pronunciation of her name, a nickname that half the ward staff had adopted. She flushed deeply. 'I—'

'Dance with me, Jodie.' The sultry silver gleam in his eyes made her nod mutely and join him on the dance floor.

She wished she hadn't when the music suddenly turned soft and Stuart started to sing a ballad. Sam drew her closer so that she was forced to put her arms round his neck for balance, and they swayed together in time to the music. She could smell his clean, fresh scent so clearly; the feel of his arms round her, together with the sweet seductive spell of the music, had her resting her head on his shoulder a few moments later.

Sam rested his cheek against her hair. He'd thought this would be a test he couldn't cope with, holding Jodie in his arms. But it was easy. So very, very easy. She felt right; she belonged there. Her skin smelled of honey, and she was warm and soft and sweet and…

He couldn't help himself. Her neck looked graceful and her skin was soft, and he couldn't resist touching his lips to the curve of her neck. And once he'd kissed her there, he couldn't stop. She felt so good. He needed to touch her, taste her. He trailed his lips up towards her ear, soft butterfly kisses, and felt her tremble in his arms.

So she was affected by this as much as he was.

'Jodie,' he breathed softly in her ear.

'Yes?' She lifted her head to look straight into his eyes. Hers were very green and very large, and her mouth was too tempting to resist.

His lips were just millimetres away from hers when the music changed again, to a bouncy, uptempo song. They'd both been in so deep that they hadn't even heard the ballad finish and Stuart introduce the next number. Shocked, they pulled apart and stared at each other. They'd almost kissed—in front of just about all their colleagues.

'Mr Taylor?'

'I, er, yes, Megan.' Sam forced himself to smile at the young nurse who'd interrupted them.

'Could I have this dance, please?'

He looked at Jodie, who spread her hands. 'It's a party. You're meant to dance.'

'Then let's dance, Megan,' Sam said.

Relieved at being let off so easily, Jodie made a quick exit to the loos. She was still shaking from that almost-kiss, and she nearly tripped several times because her knees were still doing jelly impersonations. How could she have been so stupid? Not only had she joined in with the lengthy skit in the Christmas revue, targeting Sam's remoteness, she'd almost let him kiss her in front of everyone—meaning that everyone on the ward would tease them mercilessly for weeks!

What would that kiss have been like? When he'd taken her into his arms, every single nerve-end had been aware of him. She'd felt the lean hardness of his body against hers, been aware of the strength in those arms and yet also the gentleness. Her temperature had risen sharply and the lightest touch of his lips against her skin had sent desire shooting through her. She'd felt her breasts swelling, her body softening with need for him. And if his mouth had found hers…

She leaned against the washbasin, staring at herself in the mirror. Her eyes were over-bright and her lips were red and swollen, as if he'd actually kissed her. And kissed her very thoroughly indeed. 'You look a complete state, Price,' she told her reflection. 'And what *did* you think you were doing?' Though she didn't particularly want to hear the answer to that.

'Are you all right, Jo-jo?' Fiona asked, coming in to find Jodie in a dream.

'Just tired,' Jodie lied.

'Well, that'll teach you to burn the candles at both

ends. Doctors nowadays—no stamina,' Fiona teased. 'By the way, just what did you do to Mr Frosty?'

'Nothing!'

Too swift, too hot a denial, Jodie realised with horror. She'd just made things ten times worse. Thank God Fiona wasn't one of the gossip-mongers, or she'd really have been in trouble.

'Well, whatever you said to him, he's been human tonight. More than just the clever doctor who terrifies the hell out of the staff. If you can keep him out of his shell, Jo-jo, I think we'll all benefit,' Fiona said thoughtfully.

'It isn't up to me.'

Fiona's lips twitched. 'Let's play!'

Jodie laughed. 'I'll never live that down, will I?'

'Not for a while,' the ward sister admitted, smiling.

Finally, Jodie pulled herself together and returned to the dance floor.

'At last.' Sam materialised beside her almost instantly. 'You OK?'

'Just tired,' Jodie said. 'I think I'll call it a night.'

He nodded. 'I'll drive you home.'

She shook her head, mindful of Fiona's comment. Nobody wanted Sam to go back into his shell, but on the other hand she didn't think she could spend much more time in his company without making a complete fool of herself. 'Stay and enjoy yourself,' she said. 'I'll make my own way back.'

'You will not,' said Sam. 'For a start, there's no way you could have cycled in wearing that dress.'

'Taxi,' Jodie informed him. 'I'm just going to call one.'

He shook his head. 'I'm not waiting out in the cold with you when my car's just round the corner.'

'You don't have to wait.'

'Yes, I do. You're my partner for this evening,' he reminded her. 'So stop arguing. I'll drive you home.'

How could she resist? 'Yes, sir,' she said meekly.

He didn't say much on the way out to the car park, and no one commented that they were leaving early— they were all too busy enjoying themselves. Jodie climbed into Sam's car and he drove her home. She noted that he didn't need to ask directions. Clearly he'd remembered the way to her house from Mario's.

When they arrived at Jodie's house, she looked at him. 'Would you like to come in for a coffee?'

His face was unreadable. 'Thanks, but I really ought to be going.'

'Of course.' Jodie hoped that her disappointment didn't show on her face. He was right, anyway. If he came in for coffee and the fire between them started again, and he kissed her, and— She caught her thoughts. No. Not now. Not now, or she'd end up throwing herself at him and embarrassing them both. 'Thanks for the lift,' she said quietly.

'Pleasure.' He paused. 'Jodie…'

Every nerve was suddenly aware of him. Was he going to kiss her? She looked at him, wide-eyed, and her tongue came out to moisten her dry lips.

He was going to kiss her. She could see it in his eyes. Even in the shadowy depths of the car, she could see the sultry silver gleam—he wanted her as much as she wanted him. Now he was going to reach up, cup her face and slowly lower his mouth to hers. He was going to nibble at her lower lip until she opened her mouth and kissed him properly, and then—

'See you on Monday,' he said.

'Right.' She banked down the intense surge of disappointment. How stupid could she get? Of *course* he hadn't been about to kiss her. That almost-kiss, before, had been in the heat of the moment. They'd been in the middle of a party, with soft music playing and everyone around them full of Christmas cheer—they'd both been carried away by events around them, that was all. He wasn't going to kiss her in the middle of the street in his car on a freezing cold night.

Or anywhere else, for that matter, or he'd have taken up her offer of coffee.

'See you,' she said, trying to sound as neutral as possible. She climbed out of the car and closed the door very carefully—although she felt more like slamming it, she didn't want Sam to think her a sulky, childish brat.

Sam waited in the car, watching until she'd unlocked her door and was safely inside. Then he closed his eyes and rested his head on the steering-wheel. He'd been so close to losing his head. He'd wanted to drag Jodie into his arms and kiss her senseless. He could still remember the feel of her skin against his mouth and it had taken all his will-power to refuse her offer of coffee. If he'd accepted, he knew he'd have spent the rest of the night in her bed, their bodies tangled together even in sleep.

Even the thought of it made his body ache unbearably. There was still time to change his mind. All he had to do was walk down the short path to her front door. Say he'd love a coffee, if the offer was still open. And then hold her again, hold her and kiss that soft, warm, inviting mouth...

But what then? He had a nasty feeling that one night with Jodie wouldn't be enough. He didn't have the right to ask her for more—and she deserved more. A lot more. From someone who'd be able to offer something better than a short affair or long-term misery. He couldn't offer her a future—not the future she wanted, anyway. She wanted a normal life with a normal husband. Which meant not with him. And there was no point in starting something he couldn't finish.

From now on, he was going to stay out of her way.

Thus resolved, he straightened up, started the engine and headed for home.

CHAPTER FIVE

SAM was definitely avoiding her, Jodie thought. Maybe she'd scared him off—maybe he'd thought 'coffee' had been a euphemism for sex and that was why he'd refused.

Her skin heated. She'd actually meant just coffee—but, yes, she'd wanted him to kiss her as well. And if she was honest with herself, she'd wanted more than that. Much more.

She still did.

She growled at herself. She really had to stop daydreaming about him. Yet, now she knew what it was like to be held in her arms, she wanted it to happen again. And again.

Three days later, after discussing the problem with her best friend Ellen and a large box of chocolates, Jodie decided to leave it until after Christmas to tackle Sam. She'd be working over the holidays, so she wouldn't have time to start brooding about him, and then she was off to stay with her family. When she came back from Yorkshire, she'd see how the land lay.

In the meantime, she concentrated on her job. Amy Simcox was back in for her check-up, and this time Jodie was relieved to see that Amy's mum had pulled herself together.

'Doc-a Dodo!' Amy greeted her with a beam. 'Mummy, look, is Doc-a Dodo!'

'Hello, Amy.' Jodie ruffled the little girl's hair and sat down on the edge of the bed. 'So how are things going?' she asked Mrs Simcox.

'The surgeon says she's going to be fine—the X-rays show the operation was a success, so he isn't going to have to put her in traction again.'

'That's good.'

'And she can have the plaster off for Christmas.' Mrs Simcox blinked away tears. 'It's the best Christmas present I could have asked for. Thank you so much.'

'Hey, I didn't do much.'

'You spent a lot of your time with her, talking to her. That nice Sister Ferguson told me all about it.'

'It's my job,' Jodie said. 'And Amy's a lovely little girl.'

'Thank you. From the bottom of my heart.'

'Any time. That's what we're here for,' Jodie assured her. 'And I expect you want to be getting home, so I'll say goodbye now. Bye-bye, Amy.'

'Bye-bye, Doc-a Dodo.'

Jodie grinned. 'Everyone calls me that now, you know! Take care.' She squeezed Mrs Simcox's shoulder. 'Everything's going to be fine.'

The next patient on her list was another bronchiolitis victim. Poppy Richardson was the eighth on the ward right now, and she wouldn't be the last. Little Harry Bartlett had recovered well, but Jodie still hated the virus and the deep hacking cough that left the babies exhausted and the parents worried sick.

She put on the gown that hung on the back of the isolation-room door, added a mask and gloves and checked the obs chart. Fourteen-week-old Poppy had been in for three days and was getting worse. The previous night, the nurse had had to put in a nasogastric tube and increase the level of oxygen the baby was being given. Poppy had tried to pull the tubes out, small as she was, so they'd needed to use surgical tape to keep them in place.

Poppy lay in the metal-framed cot, a towel rolled into a horseshoe shape at her feet, to stop her slipping down under her sheet, and a similar one around her head. There was a musical mobile hanging above her—one of the hospital's stock, judging by the non-matching dangling toys and the way the musical box was tied on with ribbon—and either her parents or one of the nurses had tried to make the room more festive by twining bright red tinsel on the metal bars at the head of the cot.

'Poor little love. You're having a tough time, here,' Jodie soothed as she removed the sheet. The little girl's face was red and one of the nurses had stripped her down to her vest to keep her more comfortable in the heat. Yet again, Jodie was annoyed by the way the heating system at the hospital was so inflexible. It was always either too hot or too cold, and it was almost impossible to adjust.

Jodie examined the little body as quickly as she could, then filled in the charts and wrote her plan in the notes. Continue oxygen to keep the sats up; consider a trial reduction tomorrow if the sats stayed above 90; trial of normal feed but use NG if needed to give the baby a rest; check respiration between 30 and 50. Just as she finished writing, the monitor began bleeping. With a sigh, Jodie tucked the folder of notes back in the pocket on the door, refastened the probe and pressed the reset button on the monitor.

'Thanks, Jo-jo,' Mick said, coming into the room. 'These monitors…'

'Yeah.' Jodie replaced the sheet. 'Poor little mite. It's tough on the parents, too, at this time of year.'

'The Richardsons live twenty miles away, and they've

got three-year-old twins. They visit as much as they can, but...' Mick shrugged.

'It's going to be a rough Christmas for all of them. Are you on?'

Mick shook his head. 'I'm doing New Year. You?'

'Yep. Well, I'm single—it's not as important for me to have Christmas Day off as it is for someone with a family.' She gave a dismissive wave of her hand. 'It's only another day.'

'Jodie Price, what *are* you like?' Mick teased. 'Listen to her. "Only another day." It's Christmas, woman.'

'And we'll pull the stops out as usual to make it as good as we can for the patients. I take it Richard's doing his usual stint as the Red-Coated One?'

'Yes, and then it's the buffet for the staff and parents in the evening. Madge is making her sausage rolls.'

Madge was the ward orderly and always reminded Jodie of an old-fashioned housekeeper, plump with grey curly hair, rosy cheeks and a twinkle in her eye. According to all the staff on Paeds, she made the best pastry in the world. She always brought in mince pies and sausage rolls at Christmas, and a plate of old-fashioned lemon-curd tarts when it was a staff member's birthday.

'Yum. Not to mention all the boxes of chocolates from grateful parents,' Jodie said with a smile.

'Which will all be gone by New Year, because the doctors round here are all chocoholics. Or shall we say that one of them in particular is? I bet your pockets are stuffed with wrappers already!'

Jodie cuffed him lightly round the ear. 'Enough of your cheek, Salmond.'

He grinned and did a begging-dog impersonation. 'Let's play!'

'Oh, you!' Jodie couldn't help smiling as she removed

the gown, mask and gloves and moved to the next bay. Two more bronchiolitis patients—there was a definite epidemic this year so it was no wonder that a lot of the staff had also caught the virus, coming down with sore throats and bad colds. At least these two little ones were on the mend and might be allowed home on Christmas morning. Dutifully, she wrote up her notes and walked to the next bay.

Ellie Langton was asleep. Jodie smiled at the eight-year-old and resisted the temptation—just—to smooth back her glossy dark curls. Ellie had been diagnosed with Graves's disease—also known as hyperthyroidism or thyrotoxicosis—two years before. The autoimmune condition meant that antibodies in her blood reacted to stimulate her thyroid gland, which meant in turn that the chemical processes in most of her cells were accelerated. Jodie glanced quickly through the notes. Ellie's had been a classic case—she'd started to become anxious and had had disturbed sleep and nightmares, her schoolwork and handwriting had both deteriorated, she'd had a rapid pulse even when asleep, plus an increased appetite combined with weight loss. She hadn't had the protruding eyes sometimes associated with the condition and her thyroid hadn't been obviously enlarged—the GP had originally suspected a psychological disturbance—but a blood test had shown elevated levels of thyroxine in her blood.

When Ellie had been diagnosed, she'd been given drug treatment to reduce the secretion of thyroxine. She'd tolerated the drug well, but she hadn't been one of the lucky twenty-five per cent who recovered spontaneously within the first two years of drug treatment. As soon as the drugs had been stopped, her condition had recurred, so she'd been given radioiodine. The downside of the treatment was that it destroyed the thyroid gland, so Ellie would have a lifetime of taking drugs to counteract hypothyroidism.

Currently, she was still under observation but there was a more than fair chance that she'd be home for Christmas.

Jodie glanced over the record of Ellie's observations. Yes, she'd definitely be home for Christmas. A miracle, in her parents' eyes: they'd have their daughter home again and well.

Ellie was the last patient and Jodie mooched over to the nurses' station.

'All done?' Mick asked.

She nodded.

'Want to talk about it?'

She shrugged. 'Nothing to talk about.'

'Hmm.' Mick looked as if he didn't believe her, but he didn't press the point. 'Go on, home with you. We'll see you tomorrow.'

'Yeah.' Jodie found it hard to summon up her usual enthusiasm. Maybe the cycle ride home would help. Once the endorphins were flowing, it would help her shake off this sudden dullness...she hoped.

It didn't. And when Christmas Day dawned, Jodie had to admit why she felt so miserable.

Sam.

She hadn't seen him since...it felt like for ever. She assumed that he was away over Christmas, though she hadn't actually checked the duty roster. Christmas on their ward usually meant Lyn would work half-days and be on call for emergencies, so they were covered for senior staff. She and the other junior doctors would do the bulk of the duty.

Sam could have sent her a card, she thought crossly, but he probably hadn't sent anyone on the ward a card. Mr Frosty clearly didn't believe in Christmas. The Christmas party had been an aberration. She was beginning to wonder if she'd dreamed the whole thing.

She did the ward round as usual with Megan and Sheila, wishing various parents as happy a Christmas as possible and delighting others by signing release forms so the children could go home for Christmas. The tinsel-festooned reindeer horns she wore were a hit with all the children, as were the small gifts she gave them wrapped up as crackers—socks for the babies and little tubes that mooed or baaed or chirped when you turned them upside down for the older ones. Particularly when Jodie herself gave a half-decent impersonation of 'Mooey Christmas' or 'Merry Chirpmas' to go with them.

She'd just finished writing up a set of notes when she heard, 'Ho, ho, ho!'

Father Christmas—but the deep voice wasn't that of Richard, the head of Paediatrics. She peeped round the corner of the bay and did a double-take when she recognised the figure in the red costume, white beard and hair.

Since when had Sam been on duty? His name wasn't on the whiteboard near the nurses' station—or had she missed it, subconsciously blocking it out?

'Ho, ho, ho. Merry Christmas, everyone!' He spent a few moments with each child, talking to them and giving them special gifts from Santa. Money collected by the Friends of the Hospital group had paid for each child to have an appropriate gift—a sleepsuit for the babies, colouring books and crayons for the toddlers and a book or jigsaw for the older ones—and every little face had lit up as Father Christmas had swept in. There were gifts for siblings who'd been dragged away from the presents under the tree at home, too, selection boxes of sweets and gift vouchers donated by the local department store. The hospital mascot—a huge bear called Willoughby—would be along later with a bucket of fun-sized chocolate bars, and someone had brought in a CD player with Christmas songs and carols to give more of a party atmosphere.

'Merry Christmas, Sister,' Father Christmas said to Fiona Ferguson at the other end of the ward, and to Jodie's surprise he whipped a sprig of mistletoe from his sack and held it over her.

Mr Frosty, under the mistletoe? Giving Christmas kisses?

No way. She had to be dreaming.

She continued on her rounds, checking observation charts, writing down her findings and reassuring worried parents.

'Merry Christmas, Megan. Merry Christmas, Sheila.' Both were subjected to the mistletoe treatment, and both giggled and kissed him on the cheek.

Just when Jodie thought she'd escaped his notice, he boomed, 'Merry Christmas, Dr Price!'

'Merry Christmas, Santa,' she replied gravely.

He waved the mistletoe at her. 'Come on. Just for Santa.'

His eyes were unreadable, and her knees suddenly turned to water. She couldn't possibly kiss him in the middle of the ward… But if she didn't, it would make her feelings for him even more obvious. Why couldn't he have just left her alone?

'I—I'm in the middle of my rounds.'

'Ho, ho, ho. I'm in the middle of my rounds, too!' Santa informed her.

Sam had avoided her for over a week and now he expected her to kiss him. The nerve of the man! She thought about kicking his shins—but too many people were watching and she was aware of the ever-vigilant hospital grapevine. She didn't want to make matters even worse.

He waved the mistletoe at her again. 'Merry Christmas.'

She gave in and moved to kiss his cheek—except he moved at the same time, turning his face so that she kissed his mouth.

What happened next, she couldn't say for sure, but the next thing she knew one of the older children was whistling loudly and several of the parents were clapping. Jodie's face matched Santa's coat, and Santa's eyes were most definitely silver.

'Happy Christmas,' he said in a strained voice.

'Happy Christmas,' she croaked back, and fled to her patient in the next bay.

CHAPTER SIX

SAM watched Jodie go with dismay. He hadn't intended that to happen. He'd thought maybe a kiss from Father Christmas would break the tension between them and let them return to some sort of friendship…but it hadn't. If anything, it had made the situation a whole lot worse.

Because the minute that his lips had touched hers, he'd been lost. The friendly peck on the lips he'd intended had turned into something much, much hotter. Thank goodness he was wearing the Father Christmas suit and no one could see the effect she'd had on him.

He sighed inwardly. He'd apologise to her later—once he'd worked out what he was going to say. If he went after her now, he'd only end up kissing her again. How could he resist, now he knew what she tasted like? Now he knew how her lips fitted his so perfectly? 'Ho, ho, ho. Merry Christmas, everyone,' he said, and continued with his round, smiling and producing presents from his sack.

'Shouldn't you be having a cold shower instead?' Fiona Ferguson asked, nodding at the mug of tea Jodie was holding.

'Very funny.' Jodie glowered over the edge of the mug.

'Well, you've certainly thawed our Mr Frosty,' Fiona said dryly. 'Who'd have thought he'd take over from Richard as Father Christmas? Much less with mistletoe!'

'He kissed you, too,' Jodie pointed out. 'And Megan. And Sheila.'

'Jodie, sweetheart, hasn't anyone told you there's a difference between a peck and a kiss? We got a peck—and you got one hell of a kiss.'

'It didn't mean anything,' Jodie muttered.

'Didn't it?'

Jodie sighed. 'Not to him.'

'Oh, dear.' Fiona opened a tin of chocolate-covered Viennese biscuits and offered it to Jodie. 'Take several. It sounds as if you need them.'

'I…' Jodie munched on a biscuit. 'I don't know what's going on. First we're friends, then he freezes me out again. He changes like the weather and I don't have a clue what's going on in his head. And now today, he—Oh!' She growled in frustration.

'He's probably as confused as you are, pet.'

'Pet?' Jodie snorted. 'I'm only eighteen months younger than you, Fi.'

'Figure of speech. Jo-jo, why don't you just talk to him?'

'When?'

Fiona shrugged. 'When you've summoned up your courage. Bleep him.'

'And what do I say?'

She raised an eyebrow. 'This isn't like you. You're normally so sure of yourself.'

Jodie made a face. 'Professionally, yes. This is different.'

'You always fight for what you believe in—so why back off now?'

'Because,' Jodie said, 'I don't know what I want—or what he wants.'

'Put it this way,' Fiona told her, 'you were the only one to get a slow dance out of him at the Christmas party.'

'By accident.'

'He spoke to Stuart Henderson before he came to dance with you.'

Jodie blinked. 'You mean, he...?' No. Surely not. Surely he hadn't asked Stuart to play something smoochy so they could dance together cheek to cheek?

Fiona shrugged. 'I don't know. Ask Stuart.'

'And start the hospital grapevine? Sam wouldn't appreciate that.'

'I wouldn't dream of gossiping,' Fiona said, looking askance at the rebuke. 'And you know it.'

'Of course I do—but not everyone's like you.' Jodie took another sip of tea. 'I dunno, Fi. It's all going to go wrong.'

'How do you know until you give it a try?'

'I just do. Can we change the subject?' Jodie ate another biscuit.

'Sure. But you'd be good for each other,' Fiona said, ignoring Jodie's pained look. 'And I still think you should give it a try.'

'I'd better get on with some work,' Jodie said. She drained her tea. 'Thanks for the biscuits.'

'Any time. And you know where I am if you want to talk. Confidentially,' Fiona added.

'Thanks, Fi. I appreciate it. Really.' But right now she didn't want to talk or even think about Sam Taylor.

Jodie decided to avoid Sam completely and slip quietly out of the ward when she'd finished her shift, rather than staying on to have a Christmas drink with the night staff. By dint of rushing to the loo or discussing a patient with the parents whenever she saw him heading in her direction, she managed to avoid him for the rest of the morning and she didn't go for a lunch-break until she was sure that he was back from his and she wouldn't bump into him in the canteen. She just about managed to force down the turkey-and-trimmings lunch, passing on the Christmas pud in favour of a piece of fruit, and she had no idea what she talked about to the others on her table because, despite her determination, she couldn't get Sam and that kiss out of her mind.

He was in the paediatric assessment unit all afternoon, to her relief, as it meant she didn't have to see him at all. Though she should have known that it was going too well, because fate stepped in. Literally. The minute that she finished her last observation and report, she opened one of the double doors to leave the ward and walked straight into him.

'Are you OK?'

She shot backwards as if she'd been burned. 'I'm fine,' she mumbled.

'Jodie, I've nearly finished in the PAU. You were on early as well. I'll give you a lift home.'

She shook her head. 'I've got my bike.'

He sighed. 'It's sleeting out there.' He lifted a hand to forestall her protest. 'Yes, Jodie, I know you're perfectly capable of cycling home, but why freeze when you can stow your bike in my car and be home at the same time as if you'd done it the hard way but still be warm and dry?'

'I…' There was no answer to that. And she had a nasty feeling that he'd make her explain exactly why she didn't want to be anywhere near him if she protested. 'Thanks.'

'I've just got to sort out some paperwork. I'll see you in…' he glanced at his watch '…a quarter of an hour?'

She nodded.

It was more like half an hour, but she hadn't minded waiting. She'd caught up with some of the journals she'd been meaning to read since finishing her paper on the role of play in recovery periods. Plus Fiona had given her a huge handful of chocolates, and she'd steadily munched her way through them to dispel her nervousness.

'Sorry I'm late.'

'No problem.'

'Ready?'

She nodded and put the journals into her bag. 'So how was your afternoon?' she asked.

'Typical PAU at Christmas. Little kids pretending to be grown-ups and taking a big swig of brandy or whatever, then being ill afterwards—worse still, some of the older generation actually give them the stuff in the first place!' He rolled his eyes. 'Honestly. "It was only a little sip, Doctor. I didn't think it would hurt. Not when it's Christmas." They didn't realise that a child has a much lower body weight so one gulp for them is equivalent to a full drink for an adult. And then they get stroppy and start huffing about how it never hurt their own children or themselves, so they don't see why I'm making such a fuss over it.'

'Ouch.'

'Yeah. Well, they won't do it again. Not when they've been forced to witness the resultant stomach pump to get all the toxins out of the child and save it from alcoholic poisoning. And then we have toys with small bits being scattered all over the floor and the baby swallows one or the toddler stuffs it in an ear or up a nostril.' He groaned. 'I hate Christmas.'

She'd already gathered that.

He gave her a sidelong look. 'Sorry. It's just cases like that make me so angry. Children are so precious. Why can't people take more *care* with them?'

'Because there's so much going on at Christmas that half the time they're caught by surprise,' Jodie said quietly as they reached the bicycle sheds.

'I suppose you're right. It still gets to me, though.'

Children. What *was* it about Sam and children? He'd given off all the signs that he didn't want any of his own—and yet any man who reacted like that to the usual Christmas crises really cared about children.

She didn't dare ask him, though: it was too much of a risk, and she didn't want him being Mr Frosty with her again. She unlocked her bike and wheeled it slowly alongside them as she followed him to his car. He hefted it into the back, and she climbed into the passenger seat.

Sam drove to her house in silence, and Jodie wasn't sure how to break it. Finally, he pulled up in her road. 'I'll get your bike out for you.'

'Thanks.'

He vaulted from the car and hauled her bike out from the boot. 'Here you go.'

'Thanks for the lift.'

'Pleasure. And it wasn't out of my way, before you say it.'

They were both aware that they hadn't discussed the subject that had been in both their minds for most of the day, yet neither of them wanted to be the one to broach it.

'I…er… Would you like to come in for a coffee or something?' Jodie said.

'Yes,' Sam's mouth said, ignoring the polite refusal that his brain had intended to make.

Was that yes to coffee? Jodie wondered. Or to something?

He locked the car while she wheeled her bike to the

front door. She unlocked it, turned off the alarm and propped her bike in its usual space under the stairs.

'Make yourself at home. I'll put the kettle on,' Jodie said.

Sam went into the living room. Just as he'd suspected, Jodie was into Christmas in a big way. She might not like mince pies, Christmas pud or the traditional cake, but tinsel adorned the picture-frames, cards were stuck to the walls, and there was a small Christmas tree in one corner—real, he noted with unexpected pleasure, catching its scent—hung with bronze and gold and silver stars. An angel sat at the top of the tree, and there were lights festooned over the branches, although she hadn't switched them on.

There were a couple of framed photographs on the wall—a graduation picture of a young man with fair hair and green eyes who looked so much like Jodie that he had to be her brother, and one of Jodie herself in a gown and mortar-board, sandwiched between a man and a woman with their arms proudly round her, presumably her parents. She had her mother's eyes and her father's smile, he decided. And as for her mouth...

No. He had to stop thinking about that.

More photos were dotted on the mantelpiece and festooned with tinsel, including a formal pose of a baby in a silver frame and a snapshot of Jodie holding the same baby, a milky patch on her shoulder and her face full of laughter. She'd said she had a godson, and she'd be the perfect disreputable 'auntie', no doubt teaching the little boy a stack of silly jokes as soon as he was old enough to remember the punchlines.

She looked a natural mother. She'd *be* a natural mother, he thought, and he took a step back from the mantelpiece. What on earth was he doing? He knew she wanted children one day, so he was the last person she should get involved with.

But he couldn't help himself. Moth to a flame, he thought wryly. And both of them were going to get burned, unless he managed to keep his hands off her. Maybe he should make his excuses. No socialising, no coffee, no—

'One coffee.' Jodie materialised by his side and handed him a mug of black coffee.

'Thanks.' He took a grateful sip. Maybe this would keep his mind on track.

But then she did something fatal. She closed the curtains, switched on the Christmas tree lights and turned off the overhead light. The tree was adorned with what must have been a hundred tiny white lights, which reflected off the stars to make crazy bronze and gold and silver patterns on the carpet.

He looked at the tree, he looked at the angel and he looked at Jodie. Without a word, they both placed their mugs on the low coffee-table, and he pulled her into his arms. This time, without the mistletoe and the Father Christmas outfit to give him an excuse, his lips met hers, brushing them and teasing them until he'd coaxed her mouth open, and then he kissed her properly. The way he'd wanted to on the night of the Christmas party, when she'd been in his arms and they'd both been lost in the middle of a crowd. The way he'd wanted to in the car when he'd driven her home. The way he'd finally done today…

And it was perfect. Her mouth was as sweet as he remembered, pliant against his, and she was kissing him back. Her fingers were twined in his hair, holding him to her, and he could feel her breasts swelling against his chest. The next thing he knew, he'd unbuttoned her shirt and was stroking her soft, creamy skin.

This, he thought, was heaven.

Jodie clearly felt the same, because she was unbuttoning his shirt, running her fingers over his chest. Her lips were red and swollen slightly from being kissed, her glorious hair was loose and mussed and her pupils were huge with desire.

Sam didn't dare speak, afraid of breaking the spell. Instead, he dropped to his knees and kissed his way down her body, reaching behind her at the same time to unfasten her skirt. Things went a little hazy then. The next thing he knew, they were both lying on the carpet, both naked, and every nerve in his body was screaming to be one with her.

He looked at her, all warm and soft beneath him. The lights from the tree glittered above them, making tiny patterns on her skin. She looked, he thought, like an angel. *His* angel.

Her gaze met his, and she nodded in answer to his unspoken question. He shifted slightly, and then at last he was one with her, soaring higher and higher. This was what he'd been born for, he thought. To love Jodie.

Love? The word hit him like a hammer-blow. He shouldn't be doing this. It was unprofessional, it was stupid, it was unfair to both of them—and, God help him, he couldn't stop himself. Not when the hard tips of her breasts were brushing against his chest. Not when her lips were moist and slightly parted, inviting him. Not when her body started to ripple round him, tipping him into his own release...

Jodie was seeing stars. Literally. As she looked into Sam's eyes, she could see the Christmas tree lights casting a halo round his face and their reflections in his silver-grey eyes. She wasn't a virgin—six years of being a medical student and two long relationships since graduation had put paid to that—but she'd never felt anything like this before. As if she were floating in some distant universe, where there were only the two of them and space and sparkling lights.

She shivered, and he began to move. Swiftly, she wrapped her legs round his to hold him where he was.

A slow grin lit his face. 'That, Dr Price, was an extremely wanton thing to do,' he said softly.

'Mmm.'

The grin turned to a chuckle. 'You're purring.'

'Am I?' Her voice was husky, at least an octave lower than usual, and slightly slurred from the passion they'd just shared.

'We're lying on your carpet. I'm heavy. You can't possibly be comfortable,' he pointed out.

She flexed her internal muscles and grinned wickedly as he groaned. 'I'm comfortable enough.' She tipped her head back slightly. 'Very comfortable, in fact,' she added as his body began to stir again.

'Jodie, we—'

'Shh.' She cut off the rest of his words by reaching up to kiss him.

When she'd resolved the situation to her satisfaction, their coffee was stone cold. 'I could make you another, or something,' she offered.

He stroked her face. 'Define something.'

The look in his eyes made her suddenly bold. 'My bed's a bit more comfortable than the floor.'

'Is it, now?'

'And my bath's Victorian. Large,' she said.

'Hmm.'

She nearly added, And it's Christmas. But something stopped her. Despite acting as the ward's Father Christmas that morning, Sam had made it clear that he hated Christmas. She didn't want to remind him any further. Instead, she got to her feet, bent down to take his hand and tugged.

'Pity. I was admiring the view from here,' he said.

She flushed. 'I—'

'And you blush all over. I'll have to remember that,' he added.

She led him upstairs to the bathroom. It was mainly white, with a chequerboard cushioned lino floor and a narrow, deep blue border round the walls. The bath was easily big enough for two, even a couple as tall as Sam as Jodie, and she added liberal quantities of bubble bath to the water, an expensive honey-based one Ellen bought her as an extra treat every Christmas.

Sam soaped her gently all over, arousing her with the sponge and his fingers until she was almost shivering. And then she returned the favour in spades, until he grabbed the soap from her. 'If we don't get out of this bath right now, I'll—'

'Sounds good to me, Doctor,' she teased.

'Right.' He climbed out of the bath and effortlessly hauled her out.

'Put me down! You'll give yourself a hernia!' she shrieked.

'Put you down, hmm?' And that was exactly what he did, letting her slide slowly down his body so she was left in no doubt about his feelings.

'I'd quite like to do the macho thing,' he said, 'and carry you to your room. Except I don't know where it is. And I don't think I can wait much longer.'

In answer, she smiled and twined her fingers round his.

Uncaring of the watery footprints they left on the carpet, she led him to the room at the back of the house, closed her curtains and switched on the bedside light.

She'd always preferred the space of a double bed—her idea of bliss was a lie-in on a day off, propped up with plenty of pillows, with a good book to hand, a cup of weak and very milky Earl Grey tea and soft music playing from the mini hi-fi she kept on her bedside table. Right now, she was glad of the extra space so she'd be able to lie in Sam's arms in comfort instead of them being cramped together in a single bed. And, judging by the look on his face, so was he.

'So this is your lair, Madam Spider?'

'Welcome to my parlour, Mr Fly,' she teased back.

'Indeed.' He lifted her up, pushed the duvet aside and laid her gently on the bed, then joined her. He rubbed his nose against hers. 'Well, Dr Price… Let's play!'

She chuckled, and reached up to pull his mouth back down to hers.

CHAPTER SEVEN

THE next morning, Jodie woke, stretched languidly and turned over with her eyes still closed, half expecting to curl across a warm body. But the space next to her in the bed was empty.

Frowning, she opened her eyes and sat up. She couldn't hear any noises from downstairs, so Sam obviously wasn't making coffee. And the sheet was cold enough for him to have been gone for well over an hour.

She swung her legs over the side of the bed and clambered out. She grabbed her dressing-gown from the back of the door, belted it tightly round her and checked the bathroom. Empty. She almost ran down the stairs. The kitchen was empty, too…and so was the living room.

He'd gone.

She looked round frantically, sure she'd missed something. Surely Sam wouldn't have left without a note—not after the night they'd shared? She went back upstairs. Maybe it had fallen down under a pillow, or underneath the bed… She searched frantically, but she didn't see the sticky note that had slipped down between the bed and her bedside cabinet and stuck to the wood.

He'd tidied up, she noticed—her clothes were stacked in a neat pile on the chair, instead of being the crumpled heap they'd left the night before when he'd made love to her. The two undrunk mugs of coffee had been washed up and dried, and were sitting neatly on the worktop next to the kettle. He'd drained the bath; he'd put the lid back on the bubble bath; he'd hung the towels they hadn't bothered using on the pine towel rail...

How could he have shared a night like that with her and then just tidied up and left—without a word?

Then she caught a glimpse of the clock on her micro-wave. It was one of the few reliable timekeepers in her house and it said half past eight. Maybe he was on duty. Maybe he'd thought she was on a late, had decided not to wake her and was going to ring her from the hospital. But she hadn't told him she was off duty, or that she was spending the next three days in Yorkshire, a five-hour drive from Melbury.

Given that it was eight-thirty now, even if she left in the next half-hour she was going to be late for lunch. Late enough for her mother to start worrying big time. She was half tempted to ring and say she'd be down tomorrow instead, but she knew everyone was expecting her. Maybe she should ring Sam and tell him where she was going. But if he was at work, he'd be right in the middle of the early rounds—and who was to say he wanted to see her anyway? Maybe he hadn't left a note because he hadn't known what to say to her. Maybe he was embarrassed about what had happened between them and regretted it.

She was certainly beginning to regret it.

Oh, what a mess. What a horrible, horrible mess. Pull-ing a face, she showered quickly, breakfasted and packed, then rang home to explain she'd be late before loading the boot of her elderly VW with a suitcase and a pile of presents. Finally, she checked she'd switched off all the lights, set the alarm and locked the door.

Just as Jodie drove off, the phone indoors began to ring. It continued to ring for three minutes, and then there was silence.

*　　*　　*

It was only when she was taking a break at a motorway service station, halfway between Norfolk and Yorkshire, that the thought hit her. She and Sam had been so absorbed in each other they hadn't even considered protection. And they'd made love more than once.

'Oh, my God!' She nearly dropped her cup of indifferent coffee. Rapidly, she did a mental calculation. Her last period had been…when?

A few days ago.

Her cycle was a bit erratic at the moment, but usually it was thirty days. Her most fertile time wouldn't be for over a week. Thank God, she wouldn't have to slope off to the chemist and buy some morning-after pills—particularly as they were at their most effective in the first twenty-four hours after unprotected sex. Today was Boxing Day and finding a chemist that was open wouldn't be easy.

Though that would be a damn sight easier than facing Sam at work. How could she talk normally to him now, remembering how his skin had felt against hers? How could she look into the eyes that she'd seen gleaming with passion and talk about observation charts and clinical symptoms and diagnoses?

Well, she'd just have to. Just like she'd spend three days with her family, as planned, and pretend nothing was wrong.

Sam was in briefly over the New Year, but somehow his path never crossed Jodie's. When he finally spoke to her, a few days later, no one would ever have known how close they'd been on Christmas Day. He'd gone back into his shell, nodding acknowledgements when he was spoken to but keeping every conversation focused solely on work. He didn't even ask anyone about their Christmas; personal details were clearly not wanted.

Mr Frosty was back with a vengeance.

Give up, Jodie told herself. He's a lost cause. And yet she couldn't help wondering why he'd suddenly withdrawn again. She'd thought before that someone must have hurt him really badly in the past, but he'd started to come out of his shell, trust people. OK, so maybe he thought he'd made a huge mistake, making love with her—but why drag everyone else into it? Unless something had happened while she'd been away. Maybe something from his past had resurfaced to haunt him. But what? And why?

There was no point in torturing herself with questions. He'd made it pretty clear that it wasn't any of her business any more—if it ever had been. From now on, it was strictly colleagues. Eventually, she'd stop wishing for something that couldn't be. She'd stop, knowing the instant he set foot in the room, even if her back was turned. She wouldn't hang around in corridors just to hear his voice.

'You're a sad case, Jodie Price,' she told herself crossly, and armed herself with her clipboard, ready to do her rounds.

Sam stared out of his office window, barely seeing what was out there. All he could think about was Jodie. Remembering her Christmas tree, how its lights had cast reflections on every surface. Including her skin.

He sighed. Jodie Price had got under his skin from the moment he'd first met her. His junior reg, who did things her way and to hell with the rules. He'd been exasperated by her—but he'd also been charmed by her impulsive kindness. The way she always stopped to talk to parents, not caring how long she spent with them, until she'd reassured them. The way she'd even tried including him in the departmental outings. And the way she'd opened herself to him on Christmas Day…

The next morning, he'd found it almost impossible to leave. All he'd wanted to do had been to curl protectively round her, hold her close to him, go back to sleep and wake her up later with a kiss. But he'd been on duty and he'd needed to check on his cat Sooty first. When he'd called her from the ward, there had been no answer. She hadn't called him. And she'd been cool and polite with him since then.

She was a bit of a scatterbrain, so she might not have seen his note—even though he'd put it on her pillow, where she'd see it when she woke—but… Oh, who was he trying to kid? Angela had told him the truth, all those years ago. He just wasn't the kind of man women wanted. Too serious, too dedicated to his work—and, worst of all, not able to give a woman the one thing she really, really wanted.

At Mario's, Jodie had been emphatic that not all women wanted children. And yet when Mick had announced he was going to be a dad and had teased her about how she'd be with her own children, she said she'd be just like any other mum. He'd seen the softness in her face as she'd talked about her future children. She wanted a boy and a girl. *One of each would be nice.*

And he couldn't even give her *one* child, let alone two.

He leaned his elbows on his desk and rested his forehead against his clenched hands. How could he go on like this, wanting her and knowing he couldn't have her? And why was he getting so obsessed with her, anyway? He'd spent just one night with her. Plenty of people had one-night stands. Hell, his profession was even renowned for it!

But Jodie wasn't 'plenty of people'.

What a mess. There was no future in a relationship with her, but on the other hand a short fling wouldn't be fair to either of them. True, the affair between them might blow over anyway, for a hundred and one different reasons—but he was beginning to have a nasty feeling that it wouldn't. Jodie reached him in a way no other woman ever had, even Angela in the early days of their marriage.

Which was why he had to do the decent thing and leave. Maybe he could go back to Liverpool, where he'd trained—it was a good five hours' drive from Melbury. Even better, back home to Cornwall, eight hours away. Or maybe he should consider working in the States. Or for a medical charity in some far-flung country, where his skills would be desperately needed and his time would be so filled that he wouldn't even have the chance to think about Jodie Price...

Until he found another job, he'd just avoid her. Then the torture would be over at last and he'd never hear so much as her name again.

A week later Sam's avoidance policy failed because he was forced to talk to Jodie about one of her patients.

'Caitlin Truman.' He sighed and looked at his watch. 'I'm due in clinic at twelve.'

'This won't take long.'

'My office?'

No way did she want to be alone with him in his office. She wanted lots of people round them to remind her to keep cool and professional instead of leaping into his arms and begging him to love her. 'I haven't had breakfast yet.'

He raised an eyebrow; it was just gone half past eleven.

'I overslept and it's been hectic on the ward,' she said, narrowing her eyes. 'My blood sugar's low.' She hadn't even had time to grab a biscuit or a cup of tea. 'I'm sure you don't want me dropping my sandwich all over your desk.'

All over his desk. A tiny tremor ran through him. He could just imagine Jodie spread over his desk, her hair loose and— No. He wasn't going to let himself remember the feel of her skin, the scent of her hair. Do that and he'd be lost. 'Canteen, then?'

'Canteen,' she agreed.

They walked down in silence—not a companionable one either. She bought a cheese salad sandwich and a bottle of fizzy water, while he stuck to a single cup of black coffee.

'Health kick?' he asked, nodding at her tray, before he could stop himself.

'Something like that.' Actually, she just didn't fancy it. 'So. Caitlin.'

He inclined his head.

'I've come across only a couple of cases of scoliosis before,' she said. 'One of them was awful—the little boy caught pneumonia and died, and there was nothing we could do about it.' She took a sip of water. 'I wanted to talk to you about the different options for Caitlin before I discussed them with her parents.'

'What have you told them so far?'

'That she has curvature of the spine—infantile idio-pathic scoliosis—and nobody knows what causes the condition at the moment, though it's thought there may be some genetic involvement.' She took another sip of water and looked back at her notes. 'Some early onset curves resolve spontaneously, but Caitlin's had a second X-ray to measure the angles of the ribs to the vertebrae at the centre of the curve, and it's definitely progressive.'

'Scoliosis is actually more common than you'd think,' Sam said. 'It affects three or four children in a thousand, and one of them will need corrective surgery. If we don't treat her, she may end up being deformed and disabled in middle age.' He paused. 'Single or double curve?'

'Single—to the left, in the region of her chest.'

'How big?'

'Forty degrees.' Jodie took a bite of her sandwich. 'I know it's borderline, but it's definitely a progressive curve, so I thought surgery might be involved. If not, the curve could affect her lung function when it progresses further.'

'And she's how old?'

'Nearly two.'

Sam looked thoughtful. 'It'd be a big operation—a spinal fusion and possibly bone graft.'

'That's where you use stainless-steel rods to fix the spine and stop the curve, isn't it?'

'Yes, but the downside is having a solid spine in that area, so she won't have the full range of movement in her vertebrae.'

'What are the other options?' Jodie asked.

'Keeping a four-monthly check on her to see if it resolves. We could try physiotherapy, or we could try using a spinal brace, meaning that she'd be in plaster for a few months.'

'What do—?'

Jodie was interrupted by the sound of a chair crashing to the floor. They both looked up and, as the only doctors in the almost empty room, rushed straight over to the woman kneeling on the floor beside a small boy.

'It's my Adam—he's not breathing!' the woman cried.

Sam took one look. 'Jodie, we need adrenaline. Now!'

It would be as quick for her to run to A and E as it would be to ring them from the canteen and ask them to bring adrenaline, so Jodie took off at a rate of knots. 'Dr Jodie Price, Paediatrics,' she said, flashing her identity card at the startled receptionist. 'I need adrenaline, a syringe and a space blanket *now*—we've a case of anaphylaxis in the canteen.'

By the time she returned to the canteen, Sam had changed the boy's position on the floor, raising the child's legs to improve the flow of blood to his heart and brain. Clearly his breathing had stopped, because Sam was performing cardiopulmonary resuscitation. He'd just given Adam two breaths, and then he was back to doing cardiac compressions, pressing on the lower end of the breastbone with the heel of one hand. Fifteen of those, and then he'd give another two breaths, Jodie thought, remembering the drill. All the while, Adam's mother was looking on, her face white and her hands shaking. Slow, silent tears were rolling down her cheeks.

'Sam. Adrenaline,' Jodie said succinctly, kneeling opposite him. 'Shall I take over while you inject?'

He nodded, counting the fifteenth compression under his breath, and Jodie took over the routine of giving two breaths and fifteen compressions, while Sam injected the adrenaline.

'Come *on*, Adam. We're not going to lose you!' he muttered.

Jodie kept on with the CPR.

'There are two of us now, so I'll do the cardiac compressions while you do the breathing,' Sam directed.

It seemed to take for ever, but it could only have been a couple of minutes at most before the little boy started breathing on his own again and Sam gave him a second injection of adrenaline.

The boy's mother was weeping quietly. 'Is he going to die, Doctor?' she asked Sam.

'Not if we can help it,' Sam said.

'What's wrong with him? He— We were just sitting there and he…he just collapsed!'

'It looks as if he's had a very bad allergic reaction to something,' Sam explained. 'It's called anaphylactic shock. Has he ever reacted to anything—say, food—before? Had eczema, hay fever, asthma?'

The woman bit her lip. 'He's had a bit of a rash and swollen eyes before.'

'Do you know what caused it?' Sam asked.

The woman shook her head. 'It didn't last that long and, to be honest, I didn't really think anything of it once it had gone.'

'What was he eating just now?' Jodie asked.

'Orange juice and a biscuit.'

'May I?' Jodie gestured to the table. At the woman's nod, Jodie picked up the empty biscuit packet and glanced swiftly down the list of contents.

'It could well be peanuts,' she said, 'though we'd need to do a blood test to check.'

'Is he going to be all right?' Adam's mother asked.

The little boy's breathing was less laboured and his colour was improving, though his face was still swollen. 'I think so,' said Sam. 'We'll need to take him upstairs to the ward to keep an eye on him for a while. We might need to give him some more drugs to help him recover— at least some antihistamines to reduce the swelling.'

'We only came in to visit my mum. She's had her hip replaced. And Adam went on and on about wanting a biscuit and a drink— I brought him down here to give my mum some peace.' The woman's lower lip trembled. 'I never thought this would happen!'

Sam was busy checking the boy's pulse and respiration. Jodie glanced at him, then decided to reassure Adam's mother herself. 'It's fairly frightening to watch,' she said, putting an arm round the woman's shoulders. 'Sorry, I haven't asked you your name yet.' She smiled. 'I guess we were a bit preoccupied.'

'Mrs Kinnerton. Mandy Kinnerton.'

'I'm Jodie Price and this is Sam Taylor,' Jodie said. 'What's happened to Adam is that his body's immune system has overreacted a bit. It's as if his body thinks whatever he's eaten is dangerous, so it releases all sorts of chemicals to repel the ''invader'' and protect the body. Those chemicals sometimes cause a rash and swollen eyes in a mild reaction; in a stronger reaction, like the one Adam's just had, his throat and mouth swell up as well, so he has problems breathing, and his blood vessels widen and so his blood pressure drops. Did he say he felt dizzy, too?'

'He just said he didn't feel very well and…down he went.' Mandy Kinnerton was still shaking.

'When he ate whatever gave him the rash before, did he say his mouth tingled or itched?' Jodie asked.

'I—I can't remember.'

'It's all right,' Jodie soothed. 'We'll sort it all out. Dr Taylor—' again, she avoided the Dr—Mr explanation '—gave Adam some adrenaline. It's a hormone the body produces, too—it makes the heart beat faster. The adrenaline we've given him will make his blood vessels go back to normal, relax the muscles in his lungs again to help him breathe, and stop the swelling around his face and lips.'

'And all this happened just because he's eaten something with peanuts in?' Mandy Kinnerton looked at Jodie in disbelief.

'It's just a guess,' Jodie said, 'but peanuts are one of the most common causes of allergies—around one in two hundred children react to peanuts, though not all of them react quite as strongly as this. Up on the ward, we'll check him over thoroughly and ask you a few more questions, if you don't mind, to find out a bit more about any problems Adam's had in the past and whether he has asthma, hay fever, that sort of thing. Then we'll take a blood test to check what caused his reaction. If I'm right and it *is* peanuts, you'll need to make sure Adam doesn't eat them again, in any form.'

'Not ever?'

'Not ever,' Jodie repeated. 'You'll need to check the labels of everything for peanuts—even peanut oil, so you'll have to be careful when you eat out, too, in case the food's been cooked with peanut oil. In some cases, you might find he has a reaction if he even touches whatever he's allergic to, let alone eats it— I've known cases where someone's eaten peanuts and kissed someone who reacts to them, whose eyes swelled up immediately.'

'It— Could this happen again?'

'Hopefully not, though we can show you what to do if it does. We'll be able to give you an adrenaline pen so you don't have to worry about syringes—it's really easy to use, and you can get practice pens so Adam can have a go on an orange and won't waste the drugs. We'll show both you and Adam how to use it, and you'll need to tell everyone at school and his friends' parents, so they know what to watch out for and can use the adrenaline pen straight away if he does have another reaction.'

'But he is going to be all right?'

'He'll be fine,' Sam said. 'A bit scared after what's

happened and he'll want a big cuddle from his mum, but he'll be fine. We'll just get him up to the children's ward, and Dr Price will sit with you while we admit him.'

'You saved his life,' Mandy said. 'I don't know how I'm ever going to thank you.'

Sam shrugged. 'It's our job.'

She frowned for a moment and then her face cleared. 'Do you work on the children's ward?'

Jodie smiled. 'We do, indeed. We're probably the best people you could have sat near, except for someone from A and E.'

'Thank you. From the bottom of my heart. And no more biscuits for you, my lad.' The sternness of her last words was belied by the slight tremor in her voice.

'Mum...' The little boy reached out for his mother's hand.

'It's all right, Adam. We'll soon have you feeling well again,' Jodie said comfortingly. 'And your mum can stay with you as long as she likes.'

To her surprise, Sam accompanied them back to the ward. Just as he was about to leave again, Jodie excused herself from Adam and his mother for a moment.

'We need to talk,' she said quietly.

He nodded. 'About Caitlin Truman.'

'Not just Caitlin.'

'I don't think there's anything to talk about.'

She flushed. 'I disagree. What about...?' She couldn't quite bring herself to say the words. *What about us?*

Clearly, he guessed what she'd been about to say, because he sighed heavily. 'All right. But not here. And I'm in clinic now.'

'When, then?'

'After clinic. Two?'

She nodded. 'In the canteen?'

He shook his head. 'Take a late lunch. I'll meet you by the river.'

In public—and yet somewhere far more private than Melbury City General. Somewhere they wouldn't be overheard and gossip wouldn't start flying round. 'Two.' She nodded, and turned back to see to Adam and his mother.

CHAPTER EIGHT

At a quarter to two, Jodie headed through the centre of Melbury, trying to avoid the mass of shoppers laden with New Year bargains. It was dry but it was much colder than she'd realised and she shoved her hands deep in the pockets of her woollen coat, wishing that she'd remembered her scarf as well. There was no time to go back for it, though—not if she wanted to meet Sam at two. As it was, she was cutting it fine.

By the river. That could mean anywhere from the bottom of the cathedral close through to the bridge by the train station or even by the ruined fourteenth-century walls. She really should have pinned him down to an exact place.

As she walked down the close, she heard the cathedral clock's melancholy tune and then the hour strike. Two o'clock. Well, Sam knew she was always late. He'd wait for a couple more minutes—wouldn't he?

At the bottom of the cathedral close, she turned left. Luckily, her hunch was right, because eventually she saw him sitting on the wooden bench by the old city walls. He looked tense to the point of being rigid. She'd bet his neck and shoulders ached, but there was no point in suggesting doing something about it. The way Sam was right now, he'd refuse to let her touch him, even impersonally.

Not that she could be impersonal where Sam was concerned. Not now she knew what it felt like to sleep in his arms.

He'd chosen to meet her at a place that always gave

her the creeps, even in the middle of summer. On a winter's afternoon, it was even spookier, the flints pitch black against the sky and the tops of the old towers now crumbled, leaving the insides open to the elements. Looking up through one of the towers of the old city walls was like being in a deep, dark hole from which you knew you'd never escape. But she supposed the place suited Sam's mood: cold and lonely and remote.

'Sorry I'm late,' she said as she reached him.

He shrugged. 'It's not important.'

She sat down beside him. He didn't move a muscle; she sighed inwardly. She was going to have to broach the subject. But how? *When we made love*—well, it hadn't been love on his part, had it? *When we had sex*—no. That made it sound cheap, nasty and meaningless, and it had been far from that. *When we…* What was the point of beating about the bush? If the silence between them stretched on any longer, she'd scream.

'Christmas Day. We didn't use protection,' she said quietly.

He nodded. 'It doesn't matter.'

She stared at him. Was he trying to say that if *he* had made her pregnant, he didn't care? 'Doesn't it bother you that there might be consequences?'

'There won't be.'

'I don't understand.' Her eyes widened. Was he suggesting she should have a termination? But the man who treated children on the ward with such care couldn't possibly want her to get rid of a baby he saw only as an encumbrance—could he? Her stomach clenched. If she was pregnant with his child, she couldn't just snuff out a life and put it down to mere carelessness. Yes, it would be hard, especially if Sam decided he wanted nothing to do with the baby, but she'd keep it.

'Sam, surely you don't—?'

'I guarantee it,' he cut in. 'You're definitely not pregnant, Jodie.'

Was he trying to tell her that he'd had a vasectomy years back? Or was it something else? The bleakness in his eyes made her shiver inwardly. She couldn't begin to imagine what sort of hell he was going through right now. If only he'd let her close enough to take the pain away. 'She must have hurt you very much,' she said softly.

His face hardened. 'Have you been asking questions about me?'

'No. Just making an educated guess,' she said succinctly.

He massaged his temples. 'Sorry. I'm a little…touchy on the subject.' He sighed. 'I owe you an explanation. Jodie, you want a baby, right?'

'No! I'm only twenty-eight,' she protested.

'Not necessarily right now,' he said. 'I mean, at some time in the future, you'll want to have a baby.'

'Probably. Yes.' Surely he wasn't worried about the age difference? He was only six or seven years older than she was. They had plenty of time. 'What's that got to do with us?'

'Everything.' Sam closed his eyes. 'I can't have children, Jodie. Ever.'

So *that* was why he was so *blasé* now about what had happened between them on Christmas Day. He'd known then that there was no chance of her falling pregnant— even if she'd been at the most fertile part of her cycle.

And then it hit her. Sam couldn't have children. So not only was she definitely not pregnant now, but if she spent her life with Sam she'd never have children of her own. Never walk round the supermarket with her hand resting protectively on the top of her bump; never shop together for a cot and a pram and tiny, soft baby clothes; never hold their baby son with Sam's eyes and his slow, sweet smile; never see their little girl pulling herself up on the furniture, gurgling as her father cheered her on and clapped with pride.

Right now, her career was her main focus; but somehow Jodie had always assumed that one day she'd have children, compromising with her partner so she could still work part time but also bring the children up herself and see their first steps, hear their first words, be there to comfort them after a bump or a scrape.

Suddenly, that was no longer an option.

There wasn't a compromise any more, but a choice. Sam or children.

'Y-you can't have children,' she repeated numbly, hoping she'd misheard.

His expression grew bleak. 'Angela was right. I'm not husband material, Jodie. Never was, never will be.'

'Angela?'

'My wife. Ex-wife,' he amended heavily, his shoulders sagging.

She waited, hoping that he'd explain. But he'd retreated back into his shell and was just sitting there on the bench, his face tortured and his eyes despairing. If she said the wrong thing now, she'd never learn the truth. Much as she wanted to yell at him and beat her fists on his chest and do something—anything—to make him stop throwing away their future together, she knew she had to go carefully. The back of her neck felt hot with fear and her hands were shaking. She laced her fingers together and hoped he hadn't noticed the tremors.

'Sam,' she said softly. 'I—I don't understand.'

His face twisted. 'It's not something I talk about.'

Did he think she didn't realise that? She bit back the sharp words. 'Sam. You've—I realise you've been hurt in the past,' she said carefully, stumbling over the words, 'but it doesn't have to be that way. Not with me.'

'Forget me, Jodie. I can't give you a future.'

'I— Sam, I don't want to hurt you, but I...I need to know.'

'All the sordid details?' he asked nastily.

She flinched. 'No. That's not what I meant.'

He closed his eyes. 'I'm sorry. It's just every time I think I—' He stopped abruptly and took a deep breath. 'I had an undescended testicle as a child, and my mother was too embarrassed to talk to the doctor about it, so I didn't have surgery to correct it. I had it removed in my late teens, but it was too late. Angela wanted a baby but...' He shrugged. 'We had the tests and I can't have children.'

Jodie desperately wanted to reach out to him and hold him, but his body language was screaming at her to keep off. 'Oh, Sam, I'm so sorry.' If only his mother had talked to their doctor. Most cases of undescended testicles resolved themselves naturally by around three or four months of age; nowadays, they could be treated by twice-weekly injection of human chorionic gonadotropin, the hormone that stimulated the maturation of the testicles and caused them to move down over the course of several weeks. If that didn't work, surgery was an option. Sometimes there was a hernia accompanying the undescended testicle which needed to be fixed. But if the undescended testicle was left in place, it lost the cells that made sperm, leading to fertility problems and a higher risk of cancer.

'After the test results came back, things were bad between us. It wasn't Angela's fault. I— Well, you know what they call me on the ward. Mr Frosty. I knew how desperately she wanted a baby. I wanted one myself. But I didn't know how to stop us both hurting, so I buried myself in work. I used to work late so I wouldn't have to face her—or the fact I was a failure as a husband. I didn't know what to say to her and I...' His voice cracked. 'I couldn't talk about it. I couldn't comfort her. I couldn't give her what she needed most. So...'

He didn't have to say any more. It was obvious: Angela had left him. 'Sam, it takes two to make a marriage.' And to break it. She reached out to take his hand. 'It's not *all* your fault.'

'Jodie, it's pointless discussing it. I'm not the man you need.' His voice was cold and clipped.

He was hurting as much as she was, she was sure. And she knew she had to be the one to reach out— Sam was way too proud. She didn't dare voice the L-word—she didn't think he could handle it right now—but she couldn't just walk away, letting him think she didn't care. 'Supposing I think you're the one I want to spend my life with?' she asked.

'Then you're mistaken. Very much mistaken.' A muscle clenched in his jaw. 'You adore children.'

'That's why I'm a paediatrician.' And why he was one, too, she'd bet her last penny. He hadn't said as much, but she guessed he'd gone into paediatrics after he'd found out about his infertility.

'It's more than that. I've seen you on the ward, feeding babies and cuddling them and singing them lullabies and playing with the bigger ones—all way beyond your job description. You even do it when you're supposed to be off duty.'

'OK, so I love children.' She shrugged. 'So what?'

'Jodie, you said you wanted children. One of each, you

said. Back at the revue,' he reminded her. 'And I can't give you a child. Ever.' He shook his head in frustration. 'Don't you understand? Whatever you feel about me now—whatever I feel about you—one day, you'll wake up and you'll want a baby. A baby I can't give you. It's corrosive, Jodie, the need for a baby. It burns everything in its path. It'll become the most important thing in your life and you'll grow to hate me because I can't give you what you want.'

'No, I won't.'

Yes, she would. He'd already lived through it once—and he couldn't do it again. He couldn't spend the rest of his life waiting and hoping and praying she wouldn't want a baby and resent him for denying her one, and every day growing more and more scared. Every day knowing that they were getting closer and closer to the point where she'd realise what she was missing out on.

The rainy November look was back in his eyes as he stared at her. 'Can you look me in the eye and tell me it doesn't matter if you don't have children—*ever*?'

'I...' Jodie fell silent. Could she? Right now, she wanted Sam more than she'd ever wanted anything in her whole life. But was it enough—for both of them? Eventually, she sighed. 'I don't know, Sam. I need time to think about it.'

'Exactly. And when you do, you'll realise I'm right. You need someone who can give you what you want.'

Jodie shook her head. 'That's not what I meant. I mean I need time to come to terms with it—I'd always thought I'd have kids.' She swallowed. 'But if we can't, we can't. Whatever happens, we'll still have each other.'

'And you'll miss out on the feeling of your baby growing inside you, the first kick, seeing it move at the scan and hearing its heartbeat on the Sonicaid. Then the moment when you first look at your newborn and realise what a miracle you've brought into the world, then seeing your baby grow up—the first smiles and the first steps and hearing the first words and all the silly, funny things small children say. I can't make you lose all that.'

'It's my choice,' Jodie pointed out. 'And if I choose you—'

'You'll regret it,' he cut in. 'Not now, maybe not tomorrow—but, believe me, the day will come when you'll have this yearning, this hollow in your heart that nothing else can fill.' He didn't even realise he was speaking—the words just forced themselves out as he thought about what had happened all those years ago. 'You won't be able to stop thinking about it. It'll be a physical need. Every time you see someone with a baby, you'll start to shrivel inside, because you know you'll never have that. You'll start asking yourself, Why you? Why can they have a baby and you can't? Every time you see a mother telling off her kids, you'll want to march over and shake her, tell her she should damn well appreciate what she has, because you'd give anything to be in her shoes.'

'How do you know?' she demanded.

Because that's what happened with Angela and I couldn't bear it to happen with you. The words stuck in his throat. 'I just do,' he forced out.

She stared at him. 'So you're going to give up on us, just like that?'

'There is no "us".'

She laughed shortly. 'So you're telling me Christmas Day didn't happen?'

'God, help me, it did,' he said hoarsely. 'I'm a selfish bastard, Jodie. I should have left you alone, but I—I just couldn't resist you. I tried, believe me I tried. I kept telling myself that you were off limits.'

Well, that explained why he'd blown hot and cold on her. Wanting her, reacting with his body—then thinking about it and deciding he couldn't offer her enough so he should stay away from her.

'But once I'd touched you I couldn't help myself. I wanted you so much.'

'You're selfish, all right,' Jodie said. All the anger and hurt and frustration she'd felt since Christmas Day came boiling out. 'Woke up in the morning with second thoughts, did you?'

'What?'

'Christmas Day. If you had time to tidy up, you had time to scribble a note.'

He frowned. 'I *did* leave you a note.'

'Where? Planet Taylor?' she asked nastily.

'On the pillow. Next to you,' he said.

'Saying what, exactly? Wham, bam, thank you, ma'am?'

'No. That I was on early, I needed to check my cat was OK and I didn't want to wake you. I said I'd ring you.'

'Oh, yes?'

'Yes.' He paused. 'And I did, later that morning. You didn't answer.'

'I'd gone to my parents' in Yorkshire.'

They looked at each other for a moment.

'Jodie, I wouldn't have just walked out. Not after...' His voice tailed off.

She nodded slowly. 'So you admit that what happened between us was special?'

He raked a hand through his hair. 'That isn't the point.'

'Isn't it? It wasn't just you, remember. It was *me*, too. I wanted you, Sam. I wanted to make love with you.'

'It was just sex.'

'Like hell it was!' She could tell from the colour of his eyes that he hadn't meant it. He was just trying to put her off him because he was too stubborn to believe she wanted him for himself.

'OK, so it wasn't just sex,' he admitted. 'But we didn't use protection. Doesn't that tell you anything?' He twisted his fingers together in anguish. 'If my condition was different, you could be carrying my child right now.'

Just for a moment, she saw sheer, naked longing in his eyes. Sam wanted a baby, the baby that could never be. And she also knew he'd rather die than admit it. 'It was a safe time of the month,' she said lightly.

'And you knew that at the time?'

For a moment she was tempted to lie. She flushed. 'I...um, wasn't even thinking about it. Not right then.' Protection had been the last thing on her mind. All she'd been aware of had been Sam, and how much she'd wanted to make love with him.

'Exactly. If you were determined *not* to have a baby, you'd have made sure one of us used protection. What we did was irresponsible.'

'Oh, for God's sake! We got carried away—what does that say about us? Just that we're human. OK, we're doctors and we should have known better, but...' She glowered. 'And if you're thinking of STDs, Sam—'

'Of course I'm not!'

She ignored him. 'I don't make a habit of bed-hopping and I don't think you do either. You're making too much of this.'

'I don't want your pity and I don't need it,' he said tightly.

'I'm not pitying you!' she yelled back. Didn't he realise she loved him?

'Jodie, it's not going to work out. Just forget me. I'll be gone soon.'

'What do you mean, gone?'

He stood up. 'What I said. Gone.' He started to walk away.

She ran after him. 'Sam Taylor, don't you *dare* walk away from me! What do you mean, gone?'

'I'm applying for another job.'

'Where?'

'Does it matter?'

'Of course it matters!'

He stopped abruptly. 'Jodie, I'm leaving Melbury—for your sake as well as mine. Don't make this any harder than it has to be.'

'Sam—'

'We've said everything there is to say. One day, when you're happily married with children, you'll remember this moment and you'll know I'm doing the right thing. We don't have a future, Jodie. End of story. Goodbye.'

This time, when he walked away, Jodie stayed where she was, her eyes blurred by tears. She'd put her heart on the line, told him that she wanted to spend her future with him, and he'd rejected her.

Somehow, she had to get through the rest of the afternoon at the hospital. She only hoped she didn't have to consult Sam about a patient today. They hadn't finished their discussion about Caitlin Truman, but maybe she'd manage to persuade the consultant's secretary to arrange an appointment for the Trumans to see Sam directly. And she'd cope with Sam herself *after* today.

Steeling herself, she stood up and trudged back through the cathedral. She heard the mournful five-note chimes that heralded the first quarter hour. A quarter past two. Had it really been just fifteen minutes ago that she'd come hurrying to meet Sam, full of hope that they could sort everything out? It felt like a lifetime away. And the rest of her life stretched out before her, grey and empty without him.

CHAPTER NINE

SAM was nowhere to be seen that afternoon, and Jodie was grateful to leave at the end of her shift. She cycled home wearily, until the blast of a car horn made her realise she'd been distracted enough to swerve off the cycle lane and into the path of the traffic behind her. Shakily, she dismounted and walked her bike the rest of the way home, to be safe.

Life without Sam. It was unthinkable. When she'd thought he'd dumped her without a word, it had been bad enough. But now she knew the truth, that he was ending it between them all because of her biological clock—which hadn't even started ticking yet—it was unbearable.

When she got home, she rushed upstairs to check the bedroom for the note he'd left her at Christmas. This time she searched the room more thoroughly and discovered the sticky note attached to the bedside cabinet, hidden by the frame of her bed. Obviously she'd dislodged it from the pillow in her sleep.

Her eyes pricked with tears as she read it. 'I'm on earlies and you looked too peaceful to wake! I'm going home to check on the cat and I'll ring you later this morning. Happy Christmas. Sam.'

'Happy Christmas.' This from the man who'd admitted how much he hated Christmas.

Happy Christmas.

It was as near as Sam Taylor would get to a declaration of love.

Back then, he'd been prepared to give it a go. If only

she'd found the note. If only she hadn't gone to Yorkshire. If only she'd phoned him on the ward, not caring about what the grapevine would make of it... Maybe then they'd have had a chance.

Now he'd made the decision for them both. Jodie sat on the edge of her bed, drawing her knees up to her chin and wrapping her arms round her legs. Would she really have such a desperate need for a baby that she'd grow to hate him? Would anger and hurt and frustration and resentment replace the longing for his touch? Would they end up trapped in a silent hell of a relationship, where neither dared voice their feelings and both worked late to avoid seeing the other? Was it really a stark choice between having the man she loved and having babies? Was there no compromise, no in-between that would make them both happy?

She shivered. Right now, what she wanted was Sam. She wanted to feel his arms round her, his mouth against hers, his voice whispering in her ear that everything was going to be all right, that they'd find a way to work things out. Together. She wanted to smell his warm, masculine scent; she wanted his skin sliding across hers as he made love with her; she wanted...

But she had a nasty feeling that she was wishing for what she couldn't have.

The next morning, after a sleepless night, Jodie still couldn't answer the questions. Would she want a baby more than anything else? Right now, she couldn't imagine it. But the yearning, the need she felt for Sam, wanting to touch him and hold him and kiss him and lose herself in his body—would the longing for a baby be as strong?

She couldn't predict the future. Nobody could. But if

they didn't give it a try, they'd never know. The problem was trying to convince Sam of that. Stubborn didn't even begin to describe him. And she wasn't sure she was ever going to be able to change his mind.

When she walked onto the ward, she felt sick, but she knew she had to face Sam some time. Maybe if she could make Sam see how well they worked together as co' leagues, he wouldn't leave. And then maybe she'd able to thaw him out again, take it step by step, persu him to give them a chance.

Then she remembered his parting words to her. *We don't have a future, Jodie. End of story. Goodbye.* What could be more final than that?

She took a deep breath. Well, she'd just have to be professional about it. He was her colleague—albeit not for that much longer—and their patients shouldn't suffer because of that.

'Isn't Caitlin Truman your patient?' Julianne, Sam's secretary, asked pointedly when Jodie asked her to set up an appointment for the Trumans to see Sam.

'Yes.'

'Then shouldn't *you* be speaking to them about this?'

Jodie knew that the woman was only trying to do her job—juggle the demands on the consultant's time—but Julianne, despite being only twenty-five, was the archetypal dragon secretary. She even dressed the part, with her hair scraped back severely, little black suits and glasses that just happened to slide down her nose so she could glare over them at any doctor who dared question her authority.

'The parents need information that I don't have and Mr Taylor does,' Jodie said calmly, just about managing to quell the urge to snap at Julianne. It wasn't the secretary's fault that she and Sam had reached an impasse.

'I just feel it's better for them to go higher than me so I want to refer them up.'

'Hmm.' Julianne looked at the computer screen and tutted. 'I'm afraid Mr Taylor's very busy.'

Jodie dug her nails into her palm, but it didn't stop her reacting to the patronising tone. 'Caitlin Truman is potentially a very sick little girl.'

Julianne's lips thinned. 'I can't work miracles, you know.'

'What's the problem?' a voice asked behind them.

Damn. Why had her early warning signal failed her? Jodie wondered crossly. Or maybe that was a good sign. Maybe she was starting the long, long healing process to get over him. She steeled herself and turned to face Sam. 'The Trumans would like to see you,' she said. 'I thought it might be better to transfer Caitlin from my list to yours.'

'I see.'

He really wasn't going to make this easy for her, was he? she fumed inwardly. He could at least do his bit. 'Of course,' she said sweetly, 'I realise you're much too busy to ask you to use this as a teaching case. That's why I've asked Julianne to schedule an appointment for you with the Turners. I'm bowing out.'

If Sam could have waved a magic wand and whisked his secretary to the ends of the earth—if only temporarily—at that moment, he would have done so. He was standing so close to Jodie that he could smell the honey-scented bubble bath they'd used together on Christmas Day. Her face was composed and she sounded completely professional, but her eyes were sending him a completely different message. She was itching to slap his face. Or possibly worse.

He'd been cruel to be kind. If only she knew how much he wanted to touch her. How he wanted to pull her into his arms, hold her close, breathe in that honey scent and feel the softness of her skin against his. How he wanted to kiss her, feel her lips soften under his and part, letting him deepen the intimacy. How he wanted to lose himself in her body, take them both to paradise and beyond.

But it wasn't fair. He could never give Jodie the child she wanted. Right now, she was concentrating on her career. But in five years? Ten? He couldn't go through all that again. Month after month of her trying to pretend not to mind that she wasn't pregnant—month after month of her gradually withdrawing from him, until their marriage was nothing but an empty shell. It wasn't fair to either of them. He had to do it this way until he found another job and they had enough distance between them to forget each other.

Not that he thought he'd ever be able to forget her. She'd haunt his dreams for the rest of his life. Dreams of Jodie, wide-eyed and laughing because she'd felt the little bubbly sensation of the baby's first kick. Dreams of resting his hand on the bump and feeling his baby kick inside her. Dreams of Jodie and a little girl with his dark hair and her green eyes—or a little boy with a mop of blond curls and grey eyes.

Dreams that could never, ever become real.

'Julianne, could you try to fit the Trumans in some time during the next week, please?' he asked.

Julianne gave Jodie a look of sheer dislike, no doubt expecting to see triumph in the young doctor's eyes. But there was no triumph there, Sam realised when he also glanced at Jodie as she muttered her thanks before walking away. Just a dullness, a blunting of her usual enthusiasm. And he knew he was responsible. Yet another reason why he should leave. How could he live with himself if he'd taken away all the pleasure in her professional life, too?

'You're getting as bad as old Frosty-boy,' Duncan, one of the junior doctors, complained a few days later.

'What?' Jodie glared at him.

'Either it's catching or you've got the worst case of PMT I've ever come across.'

'Oh, grow up, Duncan,' she snapped.

'Ooh! Keep your hair on, Jo-jo.'

'There's nothing wrong,' she said tightly.

'If you say so.' He shrugged. 'But you used to be the life and soul of the party. You haven't been to Mario's with us for ages and you never seem to laugh any more. Paeds used to be hard work but fun. Now it's just hard work.'

It won't be for much longer, Jodie thought. Sam's going to leave. And as for me…I don't even know if I want to stay in medicine any more. She shrugged and turned away.

Duncan came over to sit on the chair next to hers. 'Jo-jo, are you all right?' he asked, frowning in concern and clearly regretting the way he'd teased her. 'I mean, I haven't seen you smile for days. It isn't—you haven't had some bad news or anything?'

Bad news. Yeah, you could say that, she thought. The man I love won't take a chance with me. He thinks he knows what's best for us, even though he doesn't, and soon I'm never going to see him again. 'Nothing's wrong,' she lied. 'Just rushed off my feet, trying to sort that paper out…' The paper she'd finished days ago. 'I wish I'd never started it, to be honest.' And she wasn't talking about the paper.

'All work and no p-l-a-y,' Duncan said, spelling it out in phonetics.

She smiled, despite her inner misery. 'Oh, you.'

Duncan smiled back, clearly relieved at seeing his colleague acting more like her usual self. 'Tell you what. I'll cook you dinner tonight, to cheer you up.'

'*You'll* cook?' she asked, shocked. Duncan's culinary skills were reputedly on a par with her own.

'OK, if you don't fancy mushy beans on burned toast, I'll take you out for a pizza,' he suggested. 'Or a Chinese. How about an Indian? Whatever you want. You choose.'

Sam, who'd been about to walk into the room, abruptly turned and walked away as he heard Duncan's words. Yes, he knew that Jodie should find herself someone else—but he couldn't face hearing her accept a date with another man. His self-control wasn't that strong.

It was to face a much harder test within the next two hours.

'Come in,' he called at the slightly timid rap on his door.

When Jodie walked in, it was a full minute before he could speak. He pretended to be finalising some notes while he composed himself. 'Yes, Dr Price?' he asked hoarsely.

She placed a bottle of champagne on his desk. 'From the Kinnertons.'

'The little boy with anaphylaxis?'

She nodded. 'They've had the test results back and it's definitely peanuts. The allergy team's given them a list of things to watch out for and taught them how to use an Epipen. Anyway, his mum just brought this in.' Her voice cracked. 'She said we could share it. I... You did the hard part. I thought you should have it.'

As she turned away, he said neutrally, 'Take it, Jodie. You work hard enough. Perhaps you could share it with Duncan tonight.'

She whipped round. 'What?'

'Aren't you going out with him?'

She stared at him in disbelief. 'How can you even *ask* that?'

'I heard him invite you out.'

Her eyes widened as she digested the message. His voice was neutral but his eyes were far from it: they were a stormy, angry grey. Sam was actually jealous! For the first time in days, a real smile curved her lips. 'Since you were eavesdropping, you should have waited a bit longer, Sam. You'd have heard me refuse. Anyway, I think of Duncan more as the kid brother I never had than anything else.'

'It's really none of my business,' Sam said, backtracking swiftly.

'Isn't it?' Jodie looked at him, noting the high colour slashing across his cheekbones. 'We've been avoiding each other for days—and it's not going to work.'

'How do you mean?'

There were deep shadows under his eyes, too, as if he hadn't slept. As if he'd lain awake night after night, wanting to feel her beside him. Wanting to kiss her, touch her, make love with her, lose himself in the comfort of her body. 'We feel the same way,' she said quietly.

'No, we don't.'

'Prove it,' she challenged.

His eyes narrowed. 'How?'

She circumnavigated his desk and stood beside him. Then she reached out to cup his face. 'If we don't, then it won't bother you if I…' Swiftly, she bent forward and touched her lips to his. Gentle, soft, tiny butterfly kisses.

Sam had intended to stay completely calm and neutral, but his body had other ideas. Before he knew it, he'd pulled her onto his lap, her soft curls were wound round his fingers, and his mouth was urgently, desperately covering hers. The sweetness of her mouth was like a drug, and he wanted more. Much, much more.

Jodie was kissing him back and her fingers were tangled in his hair, urging him on. Sam lost himself in the pleasure of touching her, holding her again. She smelled so good and her skin was so soft, so sweet—he wanted to taste every centimetre of her.

One hand slid under her loose top and his fingertips brushed the skin on her midriff. She arched against him and he unclipped her bra, then moved round to caress the hardening peaks of her breasts. She made a small murmur of pleasure, and he lost it completely. He pushed her top up and bent to suckle one breast. Jodie's fingers were tangled in his hair, urging him on. He turned his attention to the other breast, and Jodie sighed.

'Sam. I need you. Please. Now.' And at least they didn't have to stop because they didn't have a condom, she thought. She didn't want to give Sam the chance to think about what they were doing. If she could get him to follow his heart instead of his head, maybe he'd realise how much she loved him and they could face their future together.

Completely forgetting where he was, and incredibly turned on by the huskiness in her voice, he swept the papers from his desk with one arm, lifted her onto the bare wood and knelt between her thighs.

Jodie sighed with pleasure as he entered her, and wrapped her legs round his waist, drawing him deeper. She cupped his head and gently drew his face down to hers, rubbing her nose against his and then kissing him deeply. Lost and helpless, Sam reacted to her need, deepening his thrusts. His senses were filled by her—the honeyed scent of her skin, the sound of her breathing, the feel of her skin against his, the taste of her mouth under his own—and the sheer, mind-numbing pleasure in her wide green eyes as she reached her climax and held his gaze with her own.

'I love you,' he murmured against her mouth as he fell into the whirlpool of his own release.

A long, long time later, when their heartbeats had slowed down to normal, Sam's mind snapped back into place. They were still entwined, spread across his desk, Jodie's hair fanning out around her just as he'd imagined it. She was stroking his hair—and he was still kissing her, as if his mouth couldn't get enough of hers. And, worse still, he'd just admitted that everything she'd said was true. He'd told her he loved her—even though he knew it was unfair and she deserved better than him.

Where the hell was his self-control when he needed it?

Horrified by his selfishness, he pulled back and restored a rough semblance of order to Jodie's clothes, then his own. Anyone could have seen them making love over his desk. And anyone who walked in right now would know exactly what they'd been doing. Her hair was a mess, her lips were reddened and swollen with arousal, her eyes were glittering and her clothes—despite his best efforts—were distinctly disordered. Heaven alone knew what he looked like. Probably just as bad.

He slumped back into his chair. How on earth was he going to sort out this mess? Where was he going to start? 'Jodie, I'm sorry,' he said softly.

She sat up on the edge of his desk, crossing one leg over the other, and grinned. 'Nothing to apologise for. Sam, you want me as much as I want you. What we just did—'

'Was completely unprofessional,' he cut in. 'We're in my office, for God's sake! Anyone could have walked in.'

'I know that. You know that.' She spread her hands. 'And it didn't stop us, did it?'

'No.' He thrust a shaking hand through his hair. 'And we didn't use protection.'

She smiled wryly. 'No need, is there? And we've already established that neither of us bed-hops.'

'Jodie, what happened—it was completely irresponsible of me.'

'And me,' she cut in. 'We were there *together*, Sam. All the way.'

All the way. He wanted her again, so desperately. He wanted to lock the door and make love to her again until neither of them could even think straight, let alone speak.

But he couldn't. He had to do what was best for her. He shook his head. 'We can't do this, Jodie.'

'Yes, we can. We just need to talk.'

'No. You can't throw your future away like this,' he said doggedly.

'It's my future. So it's my decision,' she pointed out. 'I want you—kids or no kids.' She gave him a confident smile—the young doctor Sam knew so well from work, ready to battle the world and argue her case when she thought she was right.

But this time he couldn't let her win. For her own sake. Somehow he had to get through to her and make her understand what she was proposing to give up. 'Jodie, I've seen the way you are with the kids on the ward. Don't you want to give that love and support to your own child, too? See the first smile, the first steps, hear your baby call you Mummy?'

'Sam, I...'

The hesitation was enough to tell him the truth. Whatever she felt for him, she wanted a baby. A baby he couldn't give her. 'You do. I know you do, Jodie—and you've got so much love to give. I can't let you sacrifice that,' he said softly.

'Then what do we do? Stay apart, both miserable?'

'It'll pass,' Sam said. It would take a long, long time, but one day he'd wake up and he'd stop wanting her. Stop loving her.

And it was precisely because he loved her that he knew he had to give up that love.

'Have you never heard of compromise? There are treatments for infertility, you know!'

He shook his head. 'Not where this is concerned. And if we carry on, we'll both end up hurt.' God only knew why he was talking about future hurt. It already felt like he was slowly bleeding to death, knowing he had to leave her. 'I'm sorry, Jodie. But you're young—you'll get over it. You'll meet someone else, someone who can give you what you want.'

Jodie stared at him for a long, long moment. He thought she was going to argue, but she said nothing— just looked at him. Her eyes were still glittering, but this time with the beginning of tears instead of passion.

'All right, Sam. You've made your point. I give up,' she said quietly, and left the room.

Every nerve in his body screamed to him to go after her, to pull her back into his arms and tell her it was OK, he loved her, he wanted her and somehow they'd make it together.

'Listening to my heart got me into this mess in the first place,' he muttered under his breath. 'I've got to stay away from her—for her own good.'

CHAPTER TEN

IT'LL PASS. Jodie told herself that every time she heard Sam's voice in the middle of ward rounds, every time she had to deal politely and neutrally with him, when all she really wanted to do was to fling herself in his arms and beg him to take a chance.

But two days later, on her day off when she was at Ellen's house, watching *Sleeping Beauty* and eating more than her fair share of the chocolate buttons Ellen had sneaked out of the fridge while Billy slept, she burst into tears. The song about walking with your true love once upon a dream was just too much for her—because that was all she had now. Dreams of what might have been.

Ellen immediately folded her in her arms and let her cry. Finally, Jodie stifled her sobs. 'I'm sorry.'

'I'm your best mate. That's what I'm for.' Ellen gave her a hug. 'It's Sam, isn't it?'

Jodie nodded, and told Ellen the full story.

When she'd finished, Ellen whistled. 'He's stubborn, I'll give him that. But he has a point, Jodie. Remember how I swore I wouldn't have kids until I was at least thirty and had made deputy head?'

'Yeah.'

'And now look at me. Twenty-eight, with a toddler, and I've gone back part time because I couldn't care less about career paths. It's not important any more. When you want a baby, Jo-jo, it takes over your whole life. Everywhere you look, you see babies. And you want one.' She sighed. 'When you get broody, it's almost a physical need and nothing—I mean *nothing*—else matters. Your priorities change, and all you can think of is babies. Could you cope with that, knowing you couldn't have one?'

'I've never had to face it, so I don't know,' Jodie said.

'You can't just duck the issue, Jo-jo. You'll have to face it some time, and it'll test your love to the limits.'

'Maybe.' Jodie closed her eyes. 'I just know that I don't want to spend the rest of my life without Sam. Even if this baby thing hits me the way you and Sam think it will, I can't possibly feel as bad as I do now.'

'Then tell him,' Ellen said.

'I've tried.'

'And since when do you give up on anything, Jodie Price?'

Jodie gave a watery smile. Hadn't she already told Sam that she'd given up on him?

'Tell him, Jo-jo. Tell him how you feel. Tomorrow.'

But Jodie couldn't work up the nerve. Instead, she hid herself in paperwork, writing up case files. At least there was some good news—Ellie Langton's condition was back under control and Poppy Richardson was back home with her family, still coughing but well on the mend. Caitlin Truman's file was on Sam's list now; maybe she could patch things up with Julianne and ask to be kept updated.

She managed to avoid Sam for three days. He was busy with clinics and she volunteered for extra sessions in the paediatric assessment unit, so she didn't have to see him.

Though she pulled herself together and tried as much as possible to be her usual self on the ward, she found it incredibly difficult the day Sam did a teaching round. She and Stuart and Duncan, the three junior doctors in the ward, stood by the bed of Conor Bentley, a six-year-old admitted with suspected myocarditis, inflammation of the heart muscle, the previous day. He was asleep, his long lashes shuttering the stunning navy-blue eyes all the nurses on the ward had admired. Conor's sweet temperament had endeared him to all, but his condition was so serious that he might not pull through.

'OK, let's see what you know,' Sam said. 'Stuart—what are the causes of myocarditis?'

'Bacterial, viral, parasitic and fungal,' he said swiftly. 'The inflammation can also be caused by rheumatic fever, toxins, drugs and hypersensitive immune reactions.'

'Good. It can also be caused by surgery on the heart, some medications and radiation therapy localised in the chest,' Sam added. 'Out of the ones you mentioned, which is rarest?'

'Parasitic—it's most often something like Chagas' disease.'

'Which is caused by?'

'An insect-borne protozoan, often in Central and South America.'

Sam nodded. 'Most common?'

'Viral—which Conor has.'

'Good. Duncan, which viruses are implicated?'

'Coxsackie B—as in Conor's case, when he went down with hand, foot and mouth disease at school. It can also be caused by measles, the flu, chickenpox, the hepatitis virus or adenovirus,' the young doctor answered confidently.

'Good—you've both been reading your stuff,' Sam said, sounding pleased. 'Jodie. How is the diagnosis made?'

'Through observation of symptoms, electrocardiogram

to record the heart's electrical activity, echo—' the ultrasound of the heart known as echocardiography '—which
will reveal an enlarged heart and poor contractions,
though in mild cases both the ECG and echo will appear
normal, angiography and endomyocardial biopsy.'

'And the biopsy is?'

'The removal of a piece of the endocardium, or the
lining membrane of the inner surface of the heart, usually
taken from around the right ventricle. It can determine
the cause as well as verify the disease, and helps us to
monitor potential congestive heart failure.'

'Good. You mentioned observation of symptoms.
Three each, please—Duncan, Stuart and Jodie.'

He'd gone in strict order, youngest and least experienced first. It was only fair, but it felt as though Sam
were picking on her. And she also knew she only felt
like that because of the way he'd rejected her. From anyone else, she'd have taken it in her stride.

'Chest pain, rapid pulse, tiredness,' Duncan said.

'Feverishness, shortness of breath, swollen ankles,'
Stuart said.

'Palpitations, ventricular enlargement, pulmonary
oedema,' Jodie said.

'Good.' He paused. 'Stuart—prognosis?'

'If it's bacterial, it can be cured; if it's viral, it resolves
more slowly. Heart damage is a common result—and because that means the heart can't contract normally, heart
failure can develop.'

'And in this case,' Sam said softly, 'Conor has severe
arrhythmias. We may be talking about a transplant.'

'Do his parents know?' Duncan asked.

'They're coming in to see me tomorrow,' Sam said
heavily.

Jodie knew exactly what was coming next.

'Jodie, I'd like you to see the Bentleys with me.'

Why me? she asked silently. But she already knew: she was good with parents. Especially when it came to a case like this, where the child was so sick that a life-saving operation might be needed. 'Yes, Mr Taylor,' she said dully.

How could he be so dispassionate? Jodie had spent a lot of time sitting next to Conor's bed, playing with his dinosaurs and telling him how clever he was when he told her each of the names, syllable-perfect, what they ate and how they'd lived. It didn't seem fair that the life of a child could hang in the balance. There wouldn't be a dry eye on the ward if a transplant couldn't be arranged—except possibly for Sam Taylor's.

And then, as they left Conor's bedside, ready to move on to the next case, Jodie caught a movement out of the corner of her eye. Sam was touching Conor's cheek with the backs of his fingers, a gesture of tenderness that brought a huge lump to her throat.

So he wasn't completely without emotion, then—just when it came to her. Which didn't make her feel any better. If anything, it made it worse to know that they'd shared something so special and yet it obviously hadn't meant the same to him. When she'd thought he'd said he loved her, it must have been some kind of auditory hallucination. Wishful thinking. Hearing what she so badly wanted to hear. Not the truth.

The next day, Jodie sat in Sam's office with Conor's parents.

'It's serious, Doctor, isn't it?' Mr Bentley asked.

Sam nodded. 'He's a very sick little boy. Unfortunately, the virus he picked up at school is known to cause heart problems in some cases, and Conor's been unlucky.

He may recover in time, but it'll be a limited recovery. If he forgets about his illness and exerts himself too much, his heart might stop working.'

'We've given him steroids to reduce the inflammation of his heart,' Jodie said, 'but there was a lot of damage. He's probably going to need a transplant.'

'You can't give him any other medication?' Mrs Bentley asked.

'I'm afraid not. Some cases can be treated with medication such as digitalis to stimulate a stronger heartbeat, but your son's heartbeat is extremely irregular. We feel a transplant will give him the best chance,' Sam said gently.

'How soon will it happen?' Mr Bentley asked.

'As soon as one becomes available. There has to be a tissue match, or Conor's body might reject the new heart,' Jodie said.

'We'll do anything,' Mr Bentley said. 'Anything. Conor's so precious to us. He's an IVF baby—we tried for years and years and thought it was too late for us. We'd saved up for one more cycle and said that would be the last one, and then we found we were expecting Conor.'

'Please. Don't let us lose our baby. Please. Please. Not now. Not like this,' Mrs Bentley begged, holding her husband's hand so tightly that her knuckles showed white.

Jodie met Sam's eyes and had to blink very hard. Would it be like that for them? Years and years and years of trying for the baby they both wanted so much—and then, when they at last had their precious baby, the risk of losing him…

No. She couldn't think of that right now. She had to concentrate on the Bentleys.

'We'll do our best, Mrs Bentley. He's a lovely little

boy.' She forced herself to smile, even though she felt like crying. 'And I think he knows more about dinosaurs than I ever will.'

'You should hear him about rockets. He's always saying he wants to be an astronaut.' Mr Bentley bit his lip. 'I don't suppose he will now.'

'Having a heart transplant doesn't mean he'll be an invalid for ever,' Jodie said quietly. 'And the surgeons at Papworth are amazing.'

'You won't do it here, then?' Mrs Bentley asked.

Jodie shook her head. 'He'll go to a specialist unit in Cambridge. I know the extra travelling time's going to be a bit of a pain for you—'

'Not where our boy's concerned,' Mr Bentley interrupted roughly. 'Even if he had to go to America—to Australia—we'd be with him every step of the way.'

'I know.' Jodie reached out to take his hand.

'What would a youngster like you know about it?' he asked nastily, pulling away from her. 'Got children of your own, have you?'

Jodie, realising how stressed and frustrated Conor's father must be feeling, didn't take it personally. He was only hitting out verbally at the nearest person, and if that helped him to cope with the situation, she could live with it. Even though he'd opened up wounds that had barely begun to heal. 'No, but I have a godson I adore, and I know how tough I'd find it if he were in Conor's place. And my baby sister died of a hole in the heart when I was younger, so I have a rough idea of how you must be feeling.'

'I'm sorry,' Mr Bentley said, shaking his head. 'I didn't mean to—'

'That's all right. No offence taken,' she cut in gently. 'And we'll do our best for Conor. I promise you that.'

'Thank you.'

'Look, can I get you a cup of tea? There's some paperwork to sort out with Mr Taylor, and I'm sure you could both do with some time to come to terms with it all,' she suggested gently.

'Thank you, love. That'd be nice,' Mrs Bentley said. Her voice was cracked with effort and Jodie guessed that she was trying not to cry.

Again, she inadvertently glanced at Sam. The look on his face was unreadable, but his eyes were definitely Wednesday morning grey. If she hadn't known better, she'd almost have thought he cared.

When Jodie had taken the Bentleys off for a cup of tea, Sam remained in his office, his head in his hands. He'd done the best for his patient's family, asking Jodie to talk to them, but it had been torture sitting there next to her. And then, when the Bentleys had talked about their IVF treatment—before then, he'd managed to avoid looking at Jodie. Just. But he hadn't been able to stop himself meeting her gaze.

A gaze that had said everything.

It could have been them—trying for years and years for an IVF baby. And even if it hadn't worked, they'd still have been together anyway, faced it as a team.

And he'd thrown it all away.

He groaned. She'd meet someone else. A warm, beautiful, bright and funny woman like Jodie—she'd soon find someone who deserved her. Someone who'd love her, someone who'd give her the child she wanted.

If only he could have been that someone.

CHAPTER ELEVEN

TIME for ward rounds, Jodie thought as she glanced at her watch. With any luck, Sam would be busy with a parent or at clinic, so she wouldn't have to face him.

But luck wasn't on her side. Yes, he was at clinic— but it finished at the same time as her ward round. Which meant that he opened the door to the ward and walked straight into her as she was leaving.

'Hello, Jodie,' he said.

'You look like hell.' The words were out before she could stop them.

The corner of his mouth twitched.

She closed her eyes. 'I— Look, I'm not brilliant at tact.'

'Uh-huh.'

At least he sounded amused rather than annoyed. She opened her eyes again. He really did look like hell. There were dark shadows under his eyes and his skin looked almost grey with fatigue and misery. As if he'd been suffering as much as she had, night after night of staring up at the ceiling at three a.m., wishing for what couldn't be. 'Are you OK?'

'I'll live,' he said dryly. 'You?'

To her horror, she found tears welling up. She rushed to the nearest loo and intended to bolt the door against him, but she wasn't fast enough.

'Jodie. Don't cry. Please, don't cry.' He followed her in, locked the door behind him and cradled her in his arms. 'I never wanted to hurt you.'

She simply sobbed against his shoulder.

'Oh, Jodie.' He stroked her hair, holding her close.

'I c-can't do this,' she hiccuped against his shoulder. 'I can't go through every day knowing you're going to leave and I'm never going to see you again.'

'I have to go, Jodie.'

'No, you don't. And I'm never going to feel less miserable than I do now if you leave.'

'You'll get over me.'

She raised a tear-stained face to meet his gaze. 'No, I won't. You're the one I want. I love you, Sam, and I think you love me.'

'Jodie—'

'You said it. In your office. When we...' She swallowed. 'I heard you. I'm sure I heard you. Unless that was just—' her voice wobbled '—wishful thinking?'

He was silent.

So he wasn't denying it. Her heart lifted. Maybe it was going to work out after all. 'I need you, Sam. I want you. I love you. And I don't care about this baby thing.'

'You will.'

'How do you know? You can't predict the future.'

'Neither can you,' he pointed out. 'It's for the best. Trust me—'

'You're a doctor,' she finished bitterly. 'Sam, it's tearing me apart. I can't sleep, I can't eat, I can't think straight. And you look just as bad.'

'I feel it,' he muttered.

'We need to talk.' She scrubbed at her eyes with the back of her hand. 'Not here.'

'Neutral ground,' he said.

'Somewhere quiet, where we're not going to be disturbed.' She swallowed. 'My place, at seven. I'll cook.'

'Jodie—'

'We need to talk. Please, Sam,' she said.

He nodded. 'All right. Your place at seven.'

He wiped away a tear with his thumb, and the intimate gesture almost made her cry again. But she managed to go back to the ward, write up her notes and then head for the supermarket.

I'll cook. Ha. Why had she said that, when she knew she burned everything? For a moment she was tempted to ring Ellen in a panic and ask for help. But then she pulled herself together. The food wasn't that important—the talking bit was far more crucial. And even *I* can bung chicken breasts in the oven, heat up a sachet of sauce and microwave a bag of mixed vegetables, Jodie thought as she stared at the supermarket shelves. Followed by some out-of-season strawberries and luxury praline ice cream, and there was probably something in the wine rack at home that would go with it.

By the time she'd cycled home, had a shower and changed, laid the dining-room table and sorted out what needed to go where and when in the kitchen, it was nearly seven and the doorbell rang.

Sam leaned on the doorjamb, holding a carrier bag and a large bunch of pale delicate orchids.

'Thank you,' she said quietly, accepting them.

'I forgot to ask you if you preferred red or white. So I bought both,' he said, gesturing to the carrier bag.

'Thanks.' She nodded. 'Come in.'

She arranged the flowers in a blue glass jug and put them on the kitchen window-sill. Sam had brought her flowers. Goodbye or hello flowers? she wondered. Her throat tightened and she dug her nails into the palms of her hands to stop herself crying. They were going to discuss this calmly and rationally, like adults—which meant she wasn't going to give in to her feelings and fling herself in his arms and howl her eyes out.

'Wine?' she asked, taking glasses from a cupboard.

'I'm driving,' he reminded her.

'One glass?'

'With dinner.'

Lord, this was impossible. This was the man she loved, the man she was sure loved her—and yet here they were, acting like polite strangers.

'Have a seat. Dinner will be—' she checked the microwave clock '—three minutes.'

'Anything I can do to help?'

Lots. But not in the way he meant. 'It's fine,' she said.

The three minutes felt more like three hours, but at last the vegetables were ready. Jodie dished up the chicken, poured the sauce over it and added the vegetables, tiny new potatoes and runner beans and broccoli florets and carrot sticks. Sam took the plates and followed her into the dining room, where she lit a candle in the middle of the table.

'White OK with you?' she asked, waving the bottle and the corkscrew at him. Being Sam, he'd brought the white wine already chilled.

'Fine.'

One glass, she remembered.

'D'you want me to…?' He indicated the bottle.

'No, it's OK.' She deftly uncorked the bottle and poured them both a glass.

He took a mouthful of chicken. 'This is good.'

'Chiller cabinet,' she confessed. 'I'm…er, cooking's not really my thing.'

There was nothing he could say to that.

They both resorted to concentrating on their food and avoiding the subject they both knew they had to discuss, and the silence grew worse and worse. Why on earth had she suggested this? Instead of making things better, she'd made it a million times worse. The candle had been a mistake, too. The light softened the hard lines of his face and made him look...delectable. That was the only word for it. How was she going to talk rationally to him, argue her case, when her libido sprang into action and turned her mind into soup just because of the way he looked? And if she started thinking about the way his body felt against hers... Bad idea.

She gulped down a glass of the excellent Chablis without even tasting it and poured herself another—then looked up to see the corner of Sam's mouth quirking.

'What?'

'Since when have you needed alcohol to loosen your tongue?'

She flushed. He had a point. And he'd barely touched his own glass. 'All right. Since you brought up the subject, it's time we talked.'

He sat back and folded his arms. 'It was a very nice meal. Thanks.'

She ignored the obvious diversion tactics. 'I asked you here to talk about us. And we do need to discuss it—it's not going to go away. Sam, I can't stand being without you.'

'Yes, you can. I'm leaving soon, and you'll be fine.'

'I won't. And I don't understand how someone so clever can be so—so—so *stupid*!' she burst out.

'Stupid?' His brow furrowed.

'Can't you see what's right under your nose? Sam, you're miserable and I'm miserable. Why can't we be miserable together?'

'Now, there's an offer,' he said dryly.

'Don't joke. Not about this.'

'No.' He paused. 'Let's go for the million-pound question, then. Do you want a baby—and I don't mean right now, I mean at some point in the future?'

Jodie lifted her chin. She'd been asking herself that question for days. Now was the time to be honest. 'Yes. Yes, I do.'

'So that rules me out as your partner.'

'No, it damn well doesn't!' She banged the table and then rubbed her sore hand, angry with herself for reacting so childishly. So much for discussing things rationally, in an adult way. She took a deep breath and began again. 'Sam, just because you have infertility problems, it doesn't mean we can't ever have a baby. There are lots of things we could do. I've been looking into it.'

'Oh, have you?' he asked, his voice dangerously soft.

She refused to be intimidated. 'Yes. I did a search on Medline.' She noted the sudden set look to his jaw. 'Here, before you say it, not at work. And I haven't said a word to anyone else about it.'

He gave her a look as if he didn't quite believe her—they both knew she was quite capable of buttonholing a consultant from Obs and Gynae and asking them about a 'friend's' case.

Maybe she should try a different tack. 'Sam, if you—if you didn't have this problem, if you'd met me and we'd done all the things that normal couples do, maybe even got married and tried to start a family, and then we'd found out I was the one who couldn't have children…would you have walked out on me?'

He just looked at her.

'Would you?' she persisted.

For a moment, she didn't think he was going to answer. Then, finally, his shoulders sagged slightly. 'No.'

'You wouldn't have deserted me,' she said, as if to

confirm his words. 'So why do you expect me to abandon you, just because the position's reversed?'

He shrugged. 'Experience.'

'Angela?'

He closed his eyes. 'Yes.'

She reached across the table and took his hand. 'Sam. Talk to me. Tell me what happened. It's not because I want all the sordid details—'

'I know,' he cut in, looking embarrassed, as if remembering the last time he'd flung that accusation at her.

'Maybe it'd do you good to tell someone,' she said softly, 'instead of keeping all the hurt locked inside.'

Was he going to answer her? Or was he going to refuse to discuss it and walk straight out of the door? For what seemed like hours she really wasn't sure. And then, finally, his fingers tightened around hers.

'I met Angela at university.' His voice was so quiet, she could hardly hear him. 'She was reading law and she was heading for the top—nothing would stand in the way of her career.' His smile held a tinge of bitterness. 'You remind me of her, in the early days—full of life, so sure of where you're going and yet with a sense of fun to stop you being too serious. I'd decided to specialise in oncology, and I was working for my exams. I thought we were happy together.'

And now he'd started talking, it was, oh, so easy to tell Jodie—to explain how the bottom had dropped out of his world and how he couldn't face it happening again.

'And then one day she said she wanted a baby.' His jaw clenched. 'We tried for nearly eighteen months. Eighteen months of using ovulation kits, only making love on the right days, being careful what we did and ate and drank. Eighteen months of her crying every time her period started, asking why we couldn't make a baby when all her friends were falling the first time they tried. Especially when we were only in our mid-twenties, at the peak of our fertility.

'That's when we went for tests and we found out I couldn't have children. She still wanted a baby, more than anything else in the world—so she left me for someone who could give her what she wanted.' His face twisted. 'My failure wrecked more than just two lives, Jodie. She left me for her boss. He was married with children, but I suppose that was part of the attraction. If I'd been the husband she wanted, her boss's family would still have been together now.'

'You don't know that. Maybe…maybe they would have fallen in love with each other anyway,' Jodie suggested.

'Maybe. Maybe not.' He sighed. 'But I'm at least partly to blame. If I'd given her what she needed, she wouldn't have had to look elsewhere.'

'Sam, sometimes you think you're in love with someone, and then you meet someone else and realise…' Her voice faded. She'd thought she'd loved Graham, and she'd been hurt and angry and upset when he'd left her. And yet what had happened between Sam and her on Christmas Day had shown her she hadn't even begun to know what love was. What she had with Sam was something else. Something special. Something she didn't want to lose.

He disentangled his hand from hers, restoring the distance between them. 'So now you know the whole sorry mess.'

She nodded, guessing what was worrying him. 'I'll respect your confidence.'

'Thank you.'

His eyes were definitely Wednesday morning grey

again, and there were finely etched lines of strain around them, Jodie thought. Maybe he was remembering the way Angela had broken his heart, the despair he'd felt when she'd left.

'Sam, I'm not Angela,' she reminded him. 'I'm a completely different person. I want different things out of life.'

'You want a baby,' he said doggedly.

'Eventually, yes.' She looked at him. 'Don't you?'

He flinched. 'Why ask me when you know I can't?'

'What I'm trying to say, Sam, is that it's not just your problem. It's *ours*. So we'll face it together, as a couple. We'll support each other through it and we'll solve it. There are all sorts of things we could do. There's ICSI, for a start.' ICSI, or intra-cytoplasmic sperm injection, was a specialised form of IVF which helped in cases of low sperm count. A single sperm was picked up in a very fine glass needle and injected directly into the egg cell, and the fertilised embryos were then returned to the womb. Jodie had seen figures putting the success rate of the treatment at around twenty-five per cent, which was almost as good as the chances of the average couple conceiving naturally with unprotected sex.

She knew it would be gruelling for both of them— she'd need to take drugs to increase the number of eggs her ovaries released, for the length of the treatment cycle—but it would be worth it to see Sam holding his child in his arms. A little boy with those same beautiful grey eyes and dark hair and beautiful mouth.

'There are all sorts of options,' she repeated. 'All we need to do is talk to a specialist.'

Sam folded his arms. How many specialists had he seen with Angela? His GP, the fertility clinic, the endless tests, the indignity of giving samples…and all for nothing. For one lousy piece of paper that condemned him as forever childless. Sure, medicine advanced quickly—everyone knew that—but it hadn't advanced far enough to help him. And he couldn't face going through it all again, seeing the hope blossom every time in Jodie's face as they started treatment and then die again as yet another cycle passed with no success. And then seeing that hope turn to resentment, dislike, even hate…

Jodie recognised the set look on his face. Mr Frosty again. Was she ever going to thaw him out? She took a deep breath. 'You want a baby—so do I. You want me and I want you. We want the same thing, Sam. So what's the problem?'

'You know what the problem is.' He spoke quietly, normally, and that made it a hundred times worse. If he'd shouted, been hurt and angry, at least he'd have been feeling something, she thought. As it was, he just sounded…hopeless.

'Sperm.'

'What?'

'That's the problem. Sperm.' A tiny little thing that you couldn't even see without a microscope—and it stood between them like a mountain. If it wasn't so tragic she would have laughed at the incongruity. As it was, she was having a hard time stopping herself crying. 'Your turn for the million-dollar question. Do you love me, Sam?'

He swallowed hard. 'Jodie, that isn't fair.'

'It's as fair as your question,' she retorted. 'Do you love me?'

'No.'

'Liar.'

He closed his eyes. 'Jodie…'

'Or maybe you're right,' she said. 'If you loved me,

you wouldn't put me through the wringer like this. You'd give us a chance. Sure, it might not work out between us. It might not work out for a million and one reasons. You might find you can't stand having a partner who can't cook and never tidies up and leaves wet towels on the bathroom floor. I might change my mind and decide I don't want a baby at some point in the future, that I want to be a hotshot consultant in one of the top jobs in the country. I might not even be able to have children. I don't know. But is it really worth throwing everything away for the sake of something that *might* happen in the future?'

'God, help me, Jodie, I do love you,' he said, his voice hoarse. 'And that's why I have to go, why I have to stay away from you. I don't want to see you torn apart the way Angela was.'

Why did everything always have to come back to Angela? If Jodie ever met the wretched woman, she'd want to strangle her for the damage she'd caused to Sam. Could that damage ever be repaired? Could her own love for Sam heal his wounds? More to the point, would he even let her try? She sighed. 'We're back to stalemate again, aren't we?'

'Jodie, I don't want to break your heart.'

'You're doing that already.'

'I'm sorry. I…' He stood up. 'I'd better go.'

'So you're just going to walk out on me, without even discussing it?'

'We *have* discussed it.'

'Hardly.' She walked round the table and placed her hand on his arm. 'Sam, I just don't understand why you won't give us a chance.'

He sighed. 'Because this infertility thing's too big. I've

already wrecked enough lives over it. I don't want to ruin yours as well.'

'It'd be ruined without you,' she said simply.

'We're going round in circles, Jodie, and it isn't helping either of us.'

Her eyes pricked with tears and she tried to blink them back. 'Please, Sam…' His name came out as a wobble.

'I have to go. For both our sakes.'

But it was already too late. The touch of her skin against his was enough to send him up in flames. Unable to help himself, he reached out and tugged her into his arms. The next thing he knew, he was kissing her with a starving desperation matched by her own.

He pulled himself away from her with an effort. 'We shouldn't be doing this,' he warned.

She said nothing, but the look on her face reminded him of the first time he'd made love to her, in the light of the Christmas tree, when she'd looked like an angel. Even with reddened eyes and a face flushed by misery and anger, she was still beautiful. And he wanted her more than ever before. With a muffled curse at his foolishness, his inability to resist her when he knew he ought to give her up, he swung her up into his arms and carried her up the stairs. His feet found the way to her room as if he'd been there a million times, instead of just the once.

Afterwards, he wasn't sure who had undressed who—there was a trail of clothes on the floor that suggested they'd started at the doorway—but, lying there with her in his arms, her head pillowed against his chest and the soft honey scent of her skin and hair in his nose, he felt as if he'd come home.

At least, his heart told him he was home—but his mind told him it wasn't permanent. He didn't want a short, passionate fling. He wanted Jodie for keeps. But it wasn't possible. Whatever she said, he was sure it would be the same with her as it had been with Angela. A beginning full of hope, a hope that slowly seeped away and took their love with it.

Which meant he had to leave. Now.

But she obviously felt him beginning to withdraw, because she tangled her legs between his. 'Sam. Don't go,' she said softly.

'I have to. The cat.' It was an excuse, even though it was partly true.

And she obviously knew it. 'Do you have a cat-flap?' she asked.

'Yes.'

'And neighbours who'll give her a snack if she turns up at their door?'

He laughed softly. 'She's a dab hand at getting what she wants.' Just like Jodie, he thought wryly. She wanted him—and he knew full well he ought to leave now *now*, before both of them got hurt even more. 'Yes.'

'Then she'll be fine tonight,' she said. 'She won't starve and she can go in and out as she pleases. Stay with me tonight, Sam. Go home in the morning.'

His head warned him not to listen, to go now, but his heart made him reach out to stroke her hair, and his mouth refused to form the words it was supposed to say. 'Are you on duty tomorrow?'

'Day off. You?'

Early, his head said. *Tell her early.*

His mouth rebelled again. 'Late.'

'Hmm.'

That sultry note in Jodie's voice made his defences crumble even more. 'There's a very wanton look on your face, Dr Price.'

'Is there, now?' It wasn't really a question. She slid her hand over his chest, her fingers tangling in the dark curls and then moving purposefully lower.

Sam gasped. 'Keep that up and I'll—'

She smiled. 'That's the idea.'

'I can't think straight when you touch me.'

Her smile broadened. 'Good. Maybe you'll start thinking with your heart instead of your head.'

'Jo—'

She cut him off by the simple expedient of kissing him, and he stopped thinking altogether.

CHAPTER TWELVE

THE next morning, Sam woke with Jodie in his arms. It was still early but enough light filtered through her cream bedroom curtains to let him see her face. He watched her sleep, thinking how soft and kissable her mouth looked. And then she moved slightly, murmuring something that sounded suspiciously like his name.

Was she dreaming of him? he wondered. And the way she was smiling in her sleep... It must be some dream, he thought with a grin, to put that kind of look on her face. He couldn't resist bending to kiss the tip of her nose.

She woke immediately and blinked hard, as if adjusting to her surroundings and trying to remember what had happened the previous night. Then her smile broadened. 'Sam.'

'Good morning.'

She reached up to touch his face. 'Mmm. Do I get a proper good morning?'

He laughed, and kissed her. 'Like this, you mean?' he teased.

'You're getting there.' She kissed him back, and Sam's heartbeat accelerated.

Before his mind had a chance to step in and remind him he wasn't supposed to be doing this, he was supposed to be finding a way to let her down gently and bow out of her life, his fingers were stroking her skin, pleasuring them both as she arched up against his touch.

'That'll do nicely, Mr Taylor,' she breathed as he bent to suckle a nipple. 'Very nicely indeed...'

Sam, in turn, sighed with pleasure as he sank into her. She felt so good, so right—as if this was what he'd been meant to do all his life. And although his head was frantically trying to tell him to stop right now and be sensible about things, his body wasn't listening. At all.

They lay curled together in silence afterwards, with Sam's arms wrapped tightly round her. He wanted to stay like this for ever, but he had commitments. That hadn't changed. 'I'd better get up.' He kissed her protests away and gently disentangled himself from her arms.

Jodie snuggled back against the pillows, watching him dress. 'It's only seven o'clock,' she informed him after a glance at her alarm clock. 'Can't you stay a bit longer? Just a *tiny* bit?'

Lord, it was tempting. Sam wanted to crawl back into her bed and never, ever leave it. He shook himself. 'I really do have to go. I'd better check on Sooty. The cat,' he added at her faintly puzzled look. He bent down to kiss her again. 'But I'll be back later.'

'Promise?'

Her eyes were very green. Fear? Worried that his head would take over from his heart again and he'd go frosty on her? He might try, but he'd learned during the night that Jodie Price wouldn't give up until she had what she wanted.

And what Jodie wanted, hard as it was to believe, was *him*.

He smiled. 'Promise.'

Jodie smiled back. Everything was going to be all right, she thought with a leap of joy. He'd finally, finally come round to her way of thinking. The night they'd just spent together proved that. And the future was starting to look distinctly rosy.

But by lunchtime Jodie realised he wasn't coming back. Maybe there'd been an emergency on the ward and he hadn't had a chance to call her first, she thought. He'd probably ring her later. Maybe he'd even come straight round after his shift.

When nine o'clock that evening came and went, she had to face it. Sam wasn't coming back at all. His promise had been like pie-crust—full of air and easily broken.

Unable to bear spending the night in sheets that still smelled of him, she changed the duvet. Then, realising it still wasn't enough—there were too many memories and her double bed suddenly seemed way too big—she made up the bed in her spare room and tried to sleep there.

It didn't work.

She just spent the night awake, wishing she knew what had gone wrong and what exactly was going on in Sam's head.

The following morning, she was on early shift, and she lasted until nearly lunchtime before she walked into Julianne's office.

'Can I help you?' Julianne asked, with her best ask-me-if-you-dare face on.

'I, um, wondered if I could have a word with Sam. About the Bentleys.'

Julianne gave her what Jodie could only describe as a pitying look. 'Haven't you heard? Mr Taylor's away.'

Away? Since when? 'When's he due back?' Jodie asked carefully.

Julianne shrugged. 'No idea.'

'I didn't think he was on holiday.'

Julianne shrugged again.

Jodie gritted her teeth. When she made it to consultant level, she'd insist on having a secretary who didn't abuse her power and make everyone else's life a misery. Someone who realised that other people had a job to do, too. 'So what are the rest of us supposed to do in the meantime?'

'Richard's taking over his cases.'

'Right.' She had to know what was going on. But how could she find out without Julianne suspecting something and spreading rumours? She forced a smile to her face and said casually, 'A bit sudden, isn't it?'

'What?'

'Going away without a word to his firm. Must be difficult for you. Juggling the diary is tough at the best of times.'

Julianne clearly wasn't falling for that one. 'He told *some* of us,' she said loftily.

Sam had been *planning* to go away? He'd known before he'd spent the night with her? He'd promised her he'd be back later—and yet he'd still left. Jodie searched through her memory. He'd said he'd applied for another job, but he hadn't said *when* he was leaving.

And Julianne hadn't said he was going away for ever.

Sam himself had said he'd be back. He'd *promised*. 'Patient?' Jodie asked, hoping Julianne hadn't noticed the slight quiver in her voice.

'Personal reasons,' the secretary said loftily. 'I'm afraid I can't discuss them.'

Personal reasons. Meaning me? Jodie thought wretchedly. He's walked out on me again without a word. This time for good. So much for promises.

'OK. I'll talk to Richard later,' she said, doing her best to appear insouciant. And all the while her heart was ripping into tiny, unmendable shreds.

*　　*　　*

'Sam.' Mary Taylor looked at her son and squeezed his hand, her grey eyes softening. She pulled the oxygen mask from her face. 'My boy,' she gasped.

He stroked her cheek. 'Can I get you anything, Mum? Water?'

She shook her head, the movement clearly an effort. 'Need to talk,' she murmured wheezily.

'No, Mum.' Her sentences were fractured, each word requiring enormous effort, and Sam didn't want her taxing her strength. 'Don't strain yourself. I'm not going anywhere.'

'My fault.'

'Nothing's your fault, Mum,' he reassured her. 'It's pneumonia. Anyone could have got it. And you're in the best hands. You're going to be fine.'

'No. You and Angela. It's all my fault. I should have gone to the doctor's when you were little,' she whispered brokenly.

Sam flinched. 'It's all in the past. You weren't to know. Don't blame yourself, Mum.'

'Have to talk.'

Sam frowned and was about to ask her what she meant, but she drifted back to sleep. He replaced the oxygen mask over her face and sat back in the chair beside her bed, holding her hand and keeping half an eye on the monitor beside her, watching the numbers change in line with his mother's breathing and pulse. Funny to think that just over twelve hours ago he'd been holding a woman's hand in bed. Except it had been his lover's, not his mother's.

He closed his eyes. He really had to ring Jodie. She must have thought he'd run out on her—but when his mobile had rung and the hospital in Cornwall had told him his mother had been admitted with pneumonia and was asking for him, his immediate reaction had been to drop off his key at his neighbour's and ask her to feed the cat, then drive straight up to be at his mother's sick-bed. He'd known his mother had had a flu-like illness a week or so before, but she'd assured him that the warden of the sheltered flats where she lived was keeping an eye on her and she was fine. He knew, however, that bacterial pneumonia could come on suddenly, as it had in his mother's case. Gently, he released his mother's hand and checked her notes again. Respirations rapid and laboured, chest radiograph demonstrating consolidation in the right lower lobe, sputum analysis showing positive Gram stain for bacterial pneumococci, increased white blood cell count.

Which was why Mary was sitting up in bed—to help her lung expansion—plus she was on twenty-four per cent oxygen through a mask and six-hourly antibiotics. She'd be in hospital for a good seven days, he thought. Seven days when he really needed to be here for his mother, plus a couple of days to make sure she'd settled back at home and could manage on her own again, with help from the carers at the complex.

Which made it ten days until he could be with Jodie again.

He'd tried ringing her a couple of times on the way to Cornwall, when he'd taken a break from the eight-hour drive, but she hadn't answered. She hadn't answered during the afternoon either. Maybe she'd gone out some-where—it was her day off after all. If she had an an-swering machine, it wasn't switched on. He only hoped she'd tried ringing him on the ward and they'd told her he'd phoned in and said he'd be away for a few days.

'Mum, I won't be long. I just need to call Jodie,' he told the sleeping woman.

He told the nurse on the desk where he was going, then headed over to the payphone by the visitors' room. A woman with red-rimmed eyes was talking brokenly into the receiver. Not wanting to disturb her by asking how long she'd be, Sam decided to go outside and use his mobile.

The phone rang for three minutes, then a polite voice informed him, 'There is no reply.' And cut him off.

He glanced at his watch. Obviously Jodie was still out. He'd try again later.

Mary's eyes were still closed when he returned to her room, and her breathing was still laboured.

'I've made such a mess of things, Mum,' he told his sleeping parent. 'I've met someone—someone really special. She's a doctor, too. You'd adore her. Her name's Jodie, and she's the most beautiful woman I've ever met. She hardly ever wears a scrap of make-up, her hair goes wild in the rain, she rides this dreadful old boneshaker that her big brother handed down to her years back, and she's got the eyes of an angel.'

He sighed. 'She tried to get me out of my shell. Would you believe, she fed me avocado on pizza? She's got this crazy streak. She's untidy. She's nearly always late. She never wears a white coat when she's supposed to. She drinks frothy coffee but she doesn't like chocolate on the top. She hates dried fruit but she'd live on chocolate if she could. The patients love her, their parents love her, everyone on the ward loves her, and I want her more than anything in the world…but she wants babies. Babies I can't give her. And I don't know where we go from here. She thinks we can get through this together, but I'm not so sure. I want a baby with her, but it just isn't going to happen. Not with me as the biological father, anyway. I've got to accept that. I know there are people much, much worse off than I am, and you can't always have what you want.' He sighed. 'Maybe she's right, maybe there is someone who can help us have a baby. Or maybe not. I don't know.'

He stroked the back of Mary's hand with his thumb. 'I'm no good at talking things through. Patients and their families, yes—I can do that, tell them all the options and help them come to a decision. But when it comes to my own life…I've never been any good at it. Even as a child. I don't know how to do it. I just freeze up and the words I really want to say won't come out. That was half the trouble with Angela. If we'd talked, *really* talked, maybe we could have saved our marriage.' He smiled ruefully. 'I guess you and Dad were like that, too. You never talked—at least, not when I was around. I never told him how much I loved him before he died.' He bit his lip. 'I don't remember him ever telling me he loved me either. But that was Dad. I'm—well, I'm going to try to be different. When you wake up again, I'm going to tell you. I'm going to talk to you about everything. And maybe you can help me find the right words to say to Jodie. Tell her how I really feel.'

He swallowed hard. 'But maybe it's too late for that.'

The minutes ticked by. When it reached half past nine and Mary was still asleep, Sam bent over to kiss her cheek. 'I'm going to try Jodie again now, Mum. I'll be back in a minute.'

This time, the payphone was free. Sam dialled Jodie's number and willed her to answer…but there was no reply. So either she still wasn't back—or she'd given up on him and gone to see Ellen. 'When this is all over, Jodie Price, I swear I'm going to buy you an answering machine and make you use it,' he said through gritted teeth. If he couldn't get hold of her later, he'd have to ring her on the ward and to hell with the grapevine.

Mary was awake again when he returned to her room.

'Sam.' She smiled weakly and removed the mask.

'Mum, put it back. You need it,' he warned.

She ignored him. 'Did you have something to eat?'

He shook his head. 'I went to make a phone call.'

'You have to eat properly.'

He grinned. 'Mum, I'm a doctor. I'm hardly likely to starve myself.' He sat back down by her bed. 'How do you feel?'

'Silly,' she said. 'All this fuss.'

'You're worth it.' He squeezed her hand. 'I want you to get well again. You need to rest.'

'We need to talk,' she said again. 'What happened—you and Angela.'

'It's all in the past, Mum. Please, don't upset yourself. Wait until you're feeling better. We'll discuss it later. Put the mask back on.'

'No. We have to talk now.' She looked hard at him. 'About babies.'

He swallowed hard. 'They're not an option for me, Mum. I'm sorry. And Angela and I—'

'Not Angela. Jodie.'

His eyes widened. 'Jodie?'

'The one who looks like an angel.'

Sam stared at her in shock. Had she heard everything he'd said when he'd been burbling on? 'You mean…you were listening? I thought you were asleep.'

Mary shook her head slowly. 'Just resting my eyes.'

He nodded soberly. 'I guess you know everything, then.'

A tear trickled down her face. 'No good at talking—that's my fault. I never showed you how.'

'It doesn't matter now.' He squeezed her hand. 'I love you, Mum.'

'I love you, Sam.' Her eyes glittered. 'I never told you enough.'

Just as he was about to protest, he remembered how distant his parents had both seemed during his childhood—not like his friends' parents, never wanting to play games or rough-and-tumble. There had been no spontaneous hugs, no embarrassing but affectionate nicknames. He'd just assumed it had been because they were older, from another generation. Or maybe he hadn't been planned and his parents hadn't really known how to respond to him.

It was a sobering thought.

'Does she love you?' Mary asked suddenly.

'Jodie?' He nodded. 'She says so.'

'Then she'll understand about the babies.' Mary squeezed his fingers. 'Talk to her. Follow your heart. It's not too late.'

Maybe. But if he didn't manage to talk to her soon, it would be. Much, much too late.

Jodie didn't answer her phone even at eleven o'clock that night. OK, stop panicking, Sam told himself. She's probably spending the night at Ellen's. Though he couldn't ring her there because he didn't know Ellen's surname, let alone her phone number—there was no way he could find out either. I'll ring again in the morning, he decided.

He did. Still there was no answer.

Which meant he had no other choice. He'd have to ring the ward. He didn't know what shift she was on, but if he rang at two he had a good chance of catching her, whether she was on early or late.

Two o'clock. How was he going to get through the hours until then?

'Explain,' Mary whispered later that morning.

'Explain what?'

'Babies. Why they're not an option.'

He flushed. Talking about something so deeply personal would be hard enough, but to discuss it with his mother, when they'd never really talked about things... Though he'd done it earlier, when he'd thought she'd been asleep. What was so different now? 'Angela and I tried for a long while with no luck. We both had tests and they said I couldn't have children.'

'What about a test-tube baby?'

IVF, in common parlance. He shook his head. 'The problem was with me, not her, so it wouldn't have worked.'

She flinched. 'If I'd taken you to see th—'

'It probably wouldn't have made any difference,' Sam cut in firmly. That wasn't strictly true, but he didn't want his mother worrying about it and setting back her progress. Right now, her own health was more important.

'But they can do more things now, can't they?' she asked hopefully.

'There's AID—artificial insemination by donor,' he said heavily. 'Or adoption.'

She nodded. 'Go home. Tell her how you feel.'

'I am *not* leaving you on your own in hospital, Mum.'

'Go home,' Mary repeated.

Sam folded his arms. His mother might have a stubborn streak, but he'd inherited it. In spades. 'Not a chance. I'm staying put until I'm satisfied you're better.'

Mary sighed. 'Then ring her. Now.'

But when he got through to the ward, Jodie was on her rounds and couldn't be interrupted. Sam almost said, 'Even for an emergency?' But it wasn't exactly that.

Or was it?

In the end, he said, 'No message. I'll try again later.'

The next time he rang, Jodie was on her break and had apparently gone for a walk.

The next, she was with parents and couldn't be disturbed.

Sam gritted his teeth and dialled a familiar number.

'Dr Taylor's secretary,' a brisk voice informed him.

'Julianne, it's Sam. I, um, need a favour.'

'Oh?' Her voice switched from cool and professional to fluttery—or was it just his imagination? Lack of sleep and too much worry, he told himself. Julianne saw him as another white coat, nothing else.

'I need to talk to Dr Price about something and I can't get hold of her.'

'Maybe one of the other doctors can help?'

'No. No, it's—' Sam stopped himself before he said *personal*. 'It's a case she's been dealing with, so she's the one with all the information.' It wasn't an outright lie. He just hadn't said *who* the case was. Himself. 'Could you ask her to ring me when she gets a moment?' He gave her the reception number for his mother's ward. 'Tell her to ask for me.'

'Of course, Sam. Whenever I see her next.'

'Thanks, Julianne.'

'Do you know when you'll be back?'

'Not yet. As soon as I can.' He sighed. 'I'll try to ring in again tomorrow. If anyone needs me urgently, give them this number—but I do mean urgent.'

'Of course. I'll make sure no one disturbs you unnecessarily.'

Sam was smiling when he replaced the receiver. He was aware that the junior doctors called his secretary 'the dragon'—and probably something even more uncomplimentary in private. If he hadn't been her boss, he'd probably be terrified of her himself, he thought wryly. But at least he knew she was efficient. He could trust her to pass on the message. Then Jodie would ring him, he could explain—and, please, God, there'd be a happy-ever-after.

Jodie walked along the corridor to Julianne's office. At the door, she paused, turned on her heel and walked briskly back the other way. There was no point in bearding Sam's secretary in her den. If Julianne did know any more, she wouldn't be telling. For some reason, Julianne seemed to dislike Jodie even more than she did the other junior doctors and was particularly intractable with her.

No, she was going to do the sensible thing. She went to Richard's office instead.

The head of Paediatrics was elbow-deep in paperwork when she knocked on his door. 'Hello, Jodie.' He smiled warmly at her. 'What can I do for you?'

'It's appalling timing, I know, but I need a favour.' She bit her lip. 'I need to take a few days off.'

'Problems at home?' he guessed.

'Sort of.' She sighed. 'Right now, I'm a liability to the others. I'm not thinking straight and I don't want to put a patient at risk.'

He frowned. 'Jodie, this isn't like you. Is there anything I can do to help?'

She shook her head, her eyes pricking with tears. Trust Richard to be kind. But there was nothing anyone could do to help. Not any more. Sam wouldn't let anyone close enough. 'I—I just need a bit of time to sort my head out. A couple of days?'

'Take the rest of the week,' Richard said. 'Go home to your parents. It looks as if you could do with some spoiling, young lady.'

'But with—' she just managed to stop herself saying 'Sam' '—Mr Taylor being away—'

'We'll just have to crack the whip a bit and make Duncan and Stuart work harder,' he told her with a wink that told her he'd do the extra hours himself—Richard never had run the department by imperious demands. 'Lyn offered to do a few more hours if we needed more cover. I'll ask her if she can step into the breach for you. And if she can't there are a couple of others I can try.'

'Thanks, Richard.' She smiled wanly at him. 'I'm sorry, I just…'

'It's OK. Everyone hits a rough patch at some time. We'll all muck in until everything's sorted. Don't worry about it—take your time and come back when you're ready. And if you need to talk about anything, you know I'm here.'

'Thanks.' The lump in her throat prevented her saying any more.

Two days later, Sam realised that Jodie wasn't going to ring him. A day's wait he'd be able to reason round—maybe Julianne hadn't had a chance to see her, Jodie was rushed off her feet on the ward, or she'd been working late and fallen asleep as soon as she got home.

But two days?

Give her the benefit of the doubt, the voice in his head urged. *Ring Julianne. Ask her.*

He did.

'I'm sorry, Sam, I'm afraid I haven't seen her,' Julianne said crisply. 'I think she's away for a few days.'

Since when?

Sam closed his eyes, hoping he hadn't made that last comment out loud. 'Thanks anyway.' He rang off and stared at the receiver. He wasn't aware of any conferences Jodie would have been attending, and he knew he hadn't signed anything to send her on developmental training. And surely she'd have said she had a week off, not just a day, when he'd asked her about her shift that morning?

That morning, which seemed so very long ago now, when he'd woken with her in his arms...

Or maybe she'd changed her duty since then. Since she thought he'd run out on her. And because he'd been so determined to talk to her, tell her how he felt, he'd lost his chance. If only he'd written her a letter, sent her flowers at work—anything rather than leave cryptic messages via his secretary.

Yet he couldn't have told Julianne what it was all about. Jodie needed to hear it from him, not someone else.

Hell, what a mess. How was he ever going to sort it out?

CHAPTER THIRTEEN

'JUST tell her,' Mary said. 'Tell her what you told me when you thought I was asleep. Pretend *she's* asleep, if it helps.'

Sam's face flamed. 'Mum…'

She chuckled. 'I'm your mother, Sam. I might be old and frail, but that doesn't mean I've lost my marbles—or forgotten what it was like, being young.'

'You're not that old,' he said loyally.

'Old enough. And if I hadn't been too proud, too embarrassed to talk to the doctor when you were tiny…' She shook her head, her face crumpling. 'I'll never forgive myself for that,' she choked.

He took her hands. 'Don't, Mum. It was a long time ago, things were different then, and even if you'd taken me to see someone I'd probably still have had the same problem now.'

'Talk to her, Sam. Don't make the mistakes I made all through my life—all through *your* life.'

But I'm the same as you. Frosty when I get scared, Sam thought, and the words just stay inside my head. They won't come out.

'Tell her you love her and if she wants a baby you'll do whatever it takes. Follow your heart.'

And then everything's going to be all right? I hope so, Sam thought fervently. I hope so.

The best part of a week in Yorkshire, being spoiled by her parents and older brother—who, for once, hadn't tried

146

to organise her life or make her talk about what was wrong—restored Jodie to the point where she could cope again.

When she returned to the ward, they were in the thick of things. The bronchiolitis epidemic seemed to have tailed off, with only one or two cases left, but Jodie found herself rushed off her feet with another transplant case, two fracture cases where abuse was suspected, a teenage overdose and a septicaemia case—the parents and carers all needed careful handling or long periods of counselling and explanation from her.

Once she'd have complained—albeit good-naturedly— of feeling drained at the end of her shift. Now she was grateful. Work kept her mind off Sam, who still hadn't returned, and she was too tired to do anything more than fall into bed when she got home at night. And that was just the way she liked it.

Until the day Sarah Ellis was admitted. The same day that Sam came back.

'Hello, Jodie.'

She almost dropped her notes at the sound of his voice. Part of her wanted to spin round and scream at him, demand to know why he thought she'd even be polite to him after the way he'd walked out on her, but the professional part of her won. Just.

'Sam,' she said coolly, not bothering to turn and face him.

'Jodie, I—we need to talk.'

'Not now. I'm with a patient.'

'Who's asleep,' he pointed out.

Jodie shrugged. 'I'm busy.'

'OK. When you're off duty, then.'

She shook her head. 'I don't think so, Sam.'

'Jodie—'

'As you once told me, *it'll pass*.' The sheer bitterness in her voice shocked even her.

He stared at her for a long, long moment.

She turned to face him, hoping that her eyes didn't betray how near she was to tears. 'We're colleagues, Sam. Just colleagues. End of story.'

It was a mistake, facing him. Seeing his face, his eyes that bleak Wednesday morning grey, the deep lines of strain etched into his face. He looked as if he hadn't slept properly for days. Wherever he'd been, whatever he'd been doing, it had taken its toll on him as much as it had on her.

But she couldn't reach out to him. Not now. Not when she knew that it would lead to yet another temporary truce, a truce that would last only until Sam's damaged heart told him to stay away from her again. And then he'd back off, leaving her lonely and aching and miserable with need. She couldn't go through that again.

'You look worried about your patient, Dr Price.'

Dr Price. After what had happened between them it was a mockery. But it was also the best way, she knew. No more hurt. Just colleagues. Keep their distance. Hadn't she told him that herself less than a minute ago?

She handed him the notes.

He read through them quickly, then whistled. 'Sanfilippo syndrome?' Sam looked at the sleeping child, then at Jodie. 'Rare. I'd imagine this must be the first case you've had on the ward.'

Jodie nodded.

'Have you come across it before?'

'No. There was a case in the hospital where I trained, but that was before my time.' She paused. 'I've been reading up on it.' Just like she'd read up on infertility. And this case was just as heartbreakingly hopeless.

'And?'

Clearly he'd switched into teaching mode and was expecting her to recite all the appropriate details. Well, that was something she could cope with. Anything to keep the emotional distance between them. Anything to stop her flinging herself into his arms and begging him to love her.

'It's a mucopolysaccharide disorder, first described in 1963 by Dr Sylvester Sanfilippo and also known as MPS-III; there are four different sub-types,' she recited. 'It's caused by a recessive gene and in the UK it's thought to affect around one in eighty-nine thousand people.'

'And what does that mean for Sarah?'

'She's missing an enzyme so her body can't break down the long chains of sugar molecules used in building the connective tissues. The sugars that haven't been broken down remain stored in the body and cause damage to the cells.' She sighed. 'There's currently a clinical trial in replacing the missing enzymes for MPS-I, but not Sanfilippo. Bone-marrow transplants haven't worked either, so at the moment there's no cure. She might live until her twenties, but probably not much later.'

Sam nodded. 'Symptoms?'

'It will get progressively worse, but we can't really give her parents much advice about which symptoms will occur and when, because some children are affected faster than others.' Jodie thought about what she'd read. 'There are three main stages—Sarah's at stage two. Her parents noticed that she was lagging behind in development, but she was always on the go and needed hardly any sleep. She didn't look any different to her friends— maybe a little smaller—and all preschoolers go through the ''into everything'' stage and chewing their hands, clothes and books. But they couldn't get her to be dry at night or by day—by the age of five, that's pretty rare—and they noticed recently that she's not talking as much as she did. She's very active, restless and what they called "a bit difficult". They wondered if she was hyperactive, but the tests were all negative. Their GP referred her to us and the blood and urine tests show she's Sanfilippo.'

'I had a Sanfilippo patient in London,' Sam said quietly. 'We referred her to Great Ormond Street, and I think we should do the same for Sarah. In the third phase, she'll slow down—she'll fall over a lot and become unsteady on her feet, then eventually lose her ability to walk.' He sat down on the edge of the little girl's bed and stroked her hair. 'Poor kid. She's going to have a tough time. And so are the parents. They'll have to cope with a growing child who's virtually immobile and won't be able to communicate with them.'

'They've got a new baby as well,' Jodie told him. 'They've asked for tests in case he's affected as well.'

'He's probably a carrier,' Sam said. 'There's a two in three chance that siblings of Sanfilippo patients will be carriers.'

'She's only in for tonight. To be honest, she didn't really need to stay in,' she admitted, 'but there was a bed free and I thought the parents could do with some time to come to terms with it. Not to mention get some sleep.'

'How long has Sarah been asleep?' Sam asked.

'An hour or so. Give it another couple of hours, and I think our whirlwind will be back,' Jodie said wryly. 'I've made an appointment for her parents to see a genetic counsellor.'

'Good idea. Do you know which form of Sanfilippo she has?'

'A, I think,' Jodie said. 'I know that B's sometimes milder and sufferers can live a relatively normal life into their twenties.'

'But that's not the case here,' Sam finished for her.

'I just hate not being able to do anything.' The words were out before she could stop them.

'We're doctors, but we're only human,' Sam told her softly. The same soft tone he'd used when he'd told her he loved her.

She forced the thought away.

'Every time I come across a case of, say, leukaemia,' he continued, 'see some bright, happy child that I know won't make it to twenty, I ask myself why I became a doctor, why we don't have a cure yet. And even when we do find a cure, it's going to be too late for that particular patient... I hate that part of our job, too. But we're doing the best we can.'

'Yes.' Jodie thought of the baby sister she'd had for just a few short days. 'If Sadie had been born now, she'd have had much more of a chance, with the medical advances over the last twenty-five years.'

On impulse, Sam reached out and squeezed her hand.

She flinched and pulled away.

'I'm sorry. I shouldn't have...' He sighed deeply. 'Go and get yourself a coffee, Dr Price. I think you need it.'

She forced herself to sound casual. 'Yes, boss.'

Jodie headed for the small kitchen at the back of the ward and put the kettle on. He was right, she knew—she needed a couple of minutes to get her emotions back under control. Emotions that were threatening to run way over the top. She'd been upset enough about her patient, but to have Sam walking back into her life, unannounced, saying they needed to talk...

But the time for talking was past. Long past.

*   *   *

Sam sat on the edge of the little girl's bed, staring at the notes without reading them. Maybe he should have stayed in Cornwall. Maybe he shouldn't have come back at all. Because Jodie wasn't going to give him the chance to explain anything.

He couldn't blame her. As far as she was concerned, he'd walked out on her after promising to be back—and he hadn't even spoken to her in the ten days he'd been away. He could protest his case, tell her how hard he'd tried to contact her, but she'd already judged him and passed sentence: deportation from her life.

But he was sure he'd seen something in her eyes when she'd looked at him. His mother's words echoed in his mind. *Tell her you love her... Follow your heart.*

And if she wouldn't talk to him, well, there were other ways.

'For me?' Jodie stared at the florist in surprise. It wasn't her birthday. Who on earth would send her flowers?

Her lips thinned as the answer hit her. Who else? 'Thank you, but I can't accept them,' she said tightly.

'I've got to deliver them, or my boss'll have my guts for garters,' the girl said, looking worried. 'Please?'

She didn't want the flowers—but she didn't want the girl to get the sack either. It wasn't *her* fault Sam was the biggest louse in history. 'OK. I'll sign,' she said. But the flowers were going to go straight into the bin.

Ten minutes later, she fished them out again. The hand-tied bouquet of roses and freesias was gorgeous, too beautiful to deserve dumping like that. She'd take it to the hospital for someone else to enjoy.

She wasn't curious about the card that came with them. Not a bit.

Not even the tiniest, tiniest bit...

She lasted nearly half an hour after putting the flowers in water before she opened the card. Two words, in Sam's black script. 'I'm sorry.'

Sorry for what? Walking out on her like that? Or sorry that it hadn't worked out? Well, she wasn't going to ask him. She didn't want to talk to him, other than on a professional basis. Though common courtesy dictated that she ought to write him a brief note of thanks.

As in just, 'Thanks for the flowers. Jodie.' She sealed it in an envelope and, just before she went on duty that afternoon, left it in his pigeonhole. The flowers went up to the geriatric ward—as Jodie told the sister in charge, 'To someone who'll enjoy them.'

Sam read the note and smiled. So communication was re-established. Grudging, but it was a start. She'd accepted his apology; now she might listen to the explanation. Or at least read it.

The next morning Jodie found a typed envelope with a Melbury postmark on her doormat. Junk mail? Or... Jodie frowned as she opened it to and found a photograph enclosed.

A photograph of an elderly woman she'd never seen before yet who looked familiar, particularly her grey eyes.

On the back, another note in Sam's handwriting. 'Mary Taylor.'

There was also a photocopy of a discharge sheet which also gave the date of Mary Taylor's admission for bacterial pneumonia. Jodie scanned it swiftly, worked out what Sam was trying to tell her and scowled. Well, now she knew where he'd been for those ten days—and why.

So why the hell hadn't he called her and told her what was happening? Why had he just left her in limbo like that?

She replaced the photograph and discharge sheet in the envelope and shoved it in a kitchen drawer. She wasn't even going to dignify this with a reply.

The next day, she had an email from Sam. *Patient recommendation.* Work, this time. OK, she could deal with that. Except the text of the message was blank—there was just an attachment. *Recommendation.doc.* Well, thanks, Sam, she fumed inwardly. That tells me a lot—I don't think. Who's the patient? What's the case?

She opened it and her eyes widened in shock. He'd sent her an article on the latest research about artificial insemination by donor.

Patient recommendation?

Enough was enough. She stomped down the corridor to his office.

'Is he in?' she asked Julianne.

'Yes, but—'

Jodie ignored Julianne's 'he's busy' and marched straight in, slamming the door shut behind her to forestall any interruptions. Dragon, beware, she thought—right now she could out-dragon anyone!

Sam looked up from his paperwork. 'Dr Price.'

She folded her arms. 'Stop playing games with me.'

'Games?'

'The flowers, the photograph, the email—just stop.'

He spread his hands. 'What else was I supposed to do? You weren't talking to me.'

'Are you surprised?'

He sighed. 'No. But give me five minutes to explain.'

'One.'

'Three.'

She wasn't in the mood for negotiating. 'Fifty-five seconds, starting now.'

'The hospital in Cornwall rang to say my mother had been admitted with pneumonia and was asking for me, so I didn't even stop to think—I just drove straight down there. I stopped on the way to ring you and explain but you were out and you don't have an answering machine.' He grimaced. 'Or if you do it wasn't switched on. I kept ringing and you didn't answer. I rang you at work and you were too busy to talk to me—with patients, with parents, away from the ward. I asked Julianne to tell you to ring me urgently. You didn't. I rang again and she said you were on leave.' He sighed again. 'I didn't know where you were or how to reach you. So I stayed with Mum, settled her in for a couple of days after she was discharged and came straight back to you.'

That explained why he'd looked so tired at Sarah Ellis's bedside. He'd just driven for eight hours or so—to come straight to her.

'And you made it clear you weren't going to discuss anything with me.'

'Do you blame me?' she snapped.

'I don't exactly have a good track record when it comes to talking things over,' he admitted wryly. 'But we need to talk, Jodie.'

'There's nothing to talk about.'

'Isn't there?'

'Your fifty-five seconds are up.'

'And?'

'And nothing!' She stomped out of the room again.

It was only when she was halfway down the corridor that Sam's words sank in. He'd asked Julianne to tell her to ring him yet Julianne hadn't passed on the message.

Her eyes narrowed. Why hadn't Julianne tried to find her to give her the message? Or she could have paged her or put a note with her post? Was she in love with Sam? Or was she just on some kind of power trip, trying to prove her importance to the team?

Not that it mattered. Because Jodie was not—definitely *not*—going to get involved with Sam Taylor ever again.

Though it nagged at her for the rest of the day. Patient recommendation. Was Sam trying to tell her that he'd come round to her way of thinking, that he was prepared to try AID if and when they decided they wanted children?

Stop, she told herself firmly. He's going away. And you're going to get over him. Not now, not tomorrow, not next year—but some day.

Later that evening, on his way out of the ward, Sam stopped dead in his tracks. He knew that voice. Except this time it wasn't singing a version of Incey Wincey Spider. This time it was singing an old-fashioned lullaby. 'Golden slumbers seal your eyes, Smiles awake you when you rise...'

He couldn't resist it. Even though he knew he should be dealing with the mountain of paperwork in his in-tray—and even though he knew he should keep away from Jodie—he walked as if spellbound towards that voice and leaned on the doorjamb.

She was cradling a small baby in her arms, one of the last bronchiolitis victims. Baby Madison had touched all their hearts because her fifteen-year-old mother had decided to give her up for adoption and refused to spend any time with the baby. Most of the nursing staff spent a few minutes each day talking to her and letting her hold their fingers, and some of them had gone as far as Jodie, cuddling her during feeds and generally making a fuss of her, giving her the affection her natural mother wasn't offering her.

Jodie was born to be a mother. The way she was cradling the sick infant, holding her so gently and stroking the soft little cheek... It was how she'd be with her own baby. The baby he desperately wanted with her.

And he'd left it too late. He'd thrown it all away.

He gave a choked sound and her head whipped up. She stared at him, eyes dilated, and he backed away.

'Sam?'

Her voice was clear and it echoed in the quiet of the evening ward—most visitors had left by now.

'I'm sorry. I know what you said. Just colleagues.'

'That's right.'

Was it his imagination, or was there a slight quiver in her voice?

Well, there was only one way to find out. And this, he knew, was definitely his last chance. 'Jodie. There's something I need to say to you.' he said softly. 'Please.'

'I'm on duty.' Her voice was steady as she put Baby Madison back in her cot, checked the monitor leads and tubes, and gently placed a sheet over her.

'It won't take long. Maybe it's too little, too late—but, please, hear me out.'

She faced him, unsmiling.

'We never talked in my family. I don't know why—it was just the way we were. I didn't get the chance to tell my father how much I loved him.' He bit his lip. 'Dad died of a heart attack when I was a student. I didn't get there in time for the end. So when I heard my mother was in hospital, I had to go. I didn't know how ill she was and I didn't want to make the same mistake again.'

She said nothing, but he could see the slight film of tears misting her green eyes.

'I thought my mother was asleep and I started talking to her—talking to her the way I'd always wanted to but never had. I told her about this woman I'd met. A woman with the eyes of an angel. How she was the most beautiful woman I'd ever seen. Everyone loved her and I wanted her more than anything in the world, but I couldn't give her the one thing she wanted. Babies.

'And then I found out my mother hadn't been asleep at all. She told me to tell you what I'd just said to her—pretend you were asleep if I had to.'

'Pretend I was asleep?' Jodie frowned, not following Sam's reasoning.

'So I could find the right words.' His mouth quirked wryly. 'I'm no good at talking. You know that. I just freeze and the words won't come out.'

There was nothing she could say to that.

'And she told me to follow my heart.' He spread his hands. 'You were right all along. There are lots of things we could do. If we had a baby with the help of a donor...' He took a deep breath. 'Look at Baby Madison here. She'll grow up with a mother who isn't her biological mother and a father who isn't her biological father—but they'll still be her parents and they'll still love her because she's *their* child. They'll have chose her, so she's special to them. Just as our child would be special to us.'

'Our child.' Jodie's throat worked convulsively. 'And that's the be-all and end-all, isn't it? A baby.'

He shook his head. 'If we're lucky enough to have children, that'd be the icing on the cake. But...' He raked a hand through his hair. 'Look, I don't want to finish this conversation in the middle of a hospital ward.'

'I'm on duty.'

'We need to talk,' Sam said. 'As from now, we're both off duty.'

'But—'

'But nothing. Your bike stays here, you come with me, and we're going somewhere a bit more private.'

'The ward's quiet enough tonight.'

'According to the duty roster, you should have left two hours ago and I'm supposedly several hundred miles away.' He smiled wryly. 'Though I know why you're still here. From what I've heard, I think everyone on the ward wants to adopt this little one.'

Was he suggesting…? Her green eyes were huge as she stared at him. 'Sam, I didn't—'

'There's only one way to stop you talking, Jodie Price,' he cut in. 'And that's this.' He curved one hand round her neck and touched his lips gently to hers.

After that first touch, the kiss turned explosive, and it was only when there was a loud cough behind them that they broke apart.

'Madison's monitor is going mad,' Fiona pointed out. 'And the two doctors in her room—consultant and registrar at that, I might add—are completely ignoring it, so I suppose the nursing staff will have to do something about it.'

'I…' Jodie flushed.

'Get her out of here, Sam Taylor, and sort it out. Pronto,' Fiona directed.

'Funny, I thought scary matrons who bossed doctors about died out years ago,' Sam muttered.

'I heard that,' Fiona said, checking the monitor resetting it and adjusting the cuff around the baby's foot. 'Go. The pair of you. And don't come back until you've got some good news for us, do you hear?'

'Yes, ma'am.' Sam took Jodie's hand and tugged her out of the room.

CHAPTER FOURTEEN

'WHERE are we going?'

'Somewhere quiet.'

Why had she even bothered asking? Sam was going frosty on her again. Or maybe… Hadn't he said something about the words not coming out, even though he wanted to say them? And he was still holding her hand. Holding it tightly, as if it were the only thing keeping him from drowning.

Jodie decided not to break the silence—when he was ready, Sam would talk.

Eventually, she realised where they were heading—through the cathedral close and down to the river, to the place where he'd first told her he couldn't have children and they had no future.

Her heart gave a sick lurch. Surely he wasn't going to do that again? Surely not, after the way he'd kissed her at the baby's bedside?

Make it be all right this time, she prayed silently. Please. Please. Don't let it all go wrong now.

At last they reached the bench where they'd parted so harshly before, now bathed in the glow from a streetlamp. Sam sat down and pulled her onto his lap.

'I find it so hard to talk—so hard to tell you how I really feel. So don't interrupt me now,' he warned, his face serious in the lamplight. 'Just hear me out.

'I love you. I love you more than anyone I've ever met. I think I've been in love with you since the day I met you, though I tried to keep away. After Angela, I swore I'd never get involved with anyone again, never give someone the chance to reject me because I'm not physically perfect.'

Not physically perfect? When he was the most gorgeous man she'd ever laid eyes on? Jodie was itching to jump in and tell him, but he'd asked her to hear him out. So she waited. Just.

'I didn't want to get hurt—but I couldn't stop thinking about you. When you asked me to Mario's, I wasn't going to turn up. But I found myself there, waiting for you. The Christmas party was even worse—I nearly kissed you in front of everyone.'

'And Christmas Day...' she said softly.

'I thought I'd died and gone to heaven. It felt so right, sleeping with you in my arms. I never wanted to let you go. I was on early the next morning. I thought you deserved your sleep, so I didn't wake you. I left you a note.'

'It fell down between the bed and my bedside cabinet. I didn't see it.'

He nodded. 'And you didn't answer the phone when I rang you from the ward.'

'I was on my way to Yorkshire.'

'I didn't know that then. I assumed you were already having second thoughts and had just ignored the phone. The more I thought about it, the more I was convinced it would never work out between us. It'd be unfair to raise your hopes of ever having your own children when I knew I couldn't give you a baby. I had to walk away, for your sake.' He smiled. 'Except I couldn't. When you kissed me in my office, I lost it completely. I couldn't help myself. The same thing happened at your house. Whenever you touch me, I go up in flames. I've never lost control like that with anyone in my life before, and it scares me,' he admitted frankly.

'I'd never hurt you, Sam,' she said softly.

'I know. I know *now*,' he amended. 'And then my mother was ill. She was asking for me, she's on her own, and I couldn't just abandon her, Jodie.'

'Of course not.' She'd have thought a great deal less of him if he had.

'I tried ringing you but I couldn't get hold of you. I asked Julianne to tell you to ring me, but you didn't.'

Jodie coughed. 'She, um, didn't pass on the message.'

'What?' Sam stared at her. 'But…she's normally so efficient.'

Not to mention being a dragon. Jodie shrugged. 'Maybe she was trying to protect you.'

'Protect me?' he echoed.

'Duncan calls her Cerberus,' she elaborated.

Sam's lips twitched. 'Which makes my office Hades.'

Jodie chuckled. 'I never thought of that. A snowflake's chance in hell, hmm?'

He smiled back, then suddenly sobered. 'These last few days I thought I'd left it too late. Being without you has been torture.'

'You don't have to be without me any more.'

'What about children? We can't just ignore the question and pretend it's not there. Infertility's a big thing, Jodie. If you—' he almost choked on the words '—you don't think you can handle it, I'll understand if you bow out now.'

'I don't have any answers. I don't know how I'm going to feel when my biological clock starts ticking.' She bit her lip. 'Ellen says I'm just ducking the issue. But we can face it when we come to it. Together. Whatever happens now, I want to be with you. That's what really matters, you and me.' She paused. 'Baby Madison…'

He stroked her cheek. 'Baby Madison is gorgeous—but she's already got a couple lined up to adopt her.'

Jodie blinked. 'Since when?'

'Yesterday morning.' He coughed. 'I, um, made a few enquiries.'

'You made enquiries?' she asked, surprised.

He nodded. 'It was just a crazy idea. Something that didn't work out.'

Was he saying he'd been prepared to adopt Baby Madison for her? He loved her that much? 'There'll be other Madisons,' Jodie said gently.

'I know.' He paused. 'I've applied to work abroad.'

'You've done *what*?' He'd told her he was going, but...*abroad*? Surely he couldn't mean it. Not when he'd just said he loved her and being without her was torture. He couldn't leave now. He *couldn't*.

'I couldn't handle working with you. Not when I wanted to hold you and kiss you and lose myself in your delectable body.' He laughed ruefully. 'You proved that to me in my office. Not to mention your house. I have no self-control when you're around.'

'You're not really going ahead with it, are you?'

'I don't know.'

A lump formed in her throat. 'What would make you change your mind and stay?' she asked carefully.

'You.' Sam shifted so that he was kneeling in front of her, completely disregarding the cold, wet, muddy grass surrounding the bench, or the fact that it had just started to snow. 'I didn't want to ask you in the middle of the ward, with an audience. Just in case you...' He stopped. 'I thought here—here, where I made the biggest mistake of my life—is the place to put things right between us again. I know I don't talk when I should do but I'll do my best to reform. I swear it.'

'How do you mean, reform?' she asked.

'Learn to discuss my feelings. It'll take time and I need someone—well, a certain someone—to take me in hand and teach me how. Jodie Price, will you please take pity on me and be my lawful wedded wife?'

She stared at him, not sure she'd heard him correctly.

The pause lengthened, and eventually he sighed and stood up. 'OK. I'm sorry. I blew it. I'll take you home.'

'Wait!' Jodie scrambled to her feet. 'Did you just ask me to…marry you?'

'Yes.' His voice was cracked.

'Whether we have children or not?' she tested.

He nodded. 'I want you, Jodie, more than I've ever wanted anyone in my whole life. And if you decide you want a baby, then we'll try whatever it takes to give us a child. Whether it's adoption, fostering, sperm donation—there are lots of things we could try. We'll find something that works for us, if and when *you're* ready. Because, babies or not, I don't want to spend the rest of my life without you. It wouldn't be living—it'd be just existing, in some grey and dull place. I want to be with you, Jodie. I want to wake up with you every morning. I want your face to be the last thing I see every night. The words don't even begin to say what I feel about you but…I love you, Jodie. I really, really love you.'

So he meant it, then. He really did feel the same way as she did.

'I'm not dreaming?' she questioned, still not quite sure she could believe her ears.

'Dreaming what?'

'You love me, and we're going to be together?'

Sam nodded. 'I love you. And we're going to be together—when you agree to marry me, that is.'

She chuckled. 'When, hmm?'

'Are you going to keep me in suspense for much longer?' he demanded.

'Ooh…' She pretended to consider it, still laughing, then sobered. 'Sam. You've been through all this before. You know, looking at ways to have a baby. With Angela.' She swallowed. 'I know it sounds as if I'm prying, and I really don't mean it to, but…what happened? And can you really bear to go through it all again? I mean, if it's going to just rip open old wounds for you, much as I want a baby, I'd rather not go down that route. It wouldn't be fair on you.'

He stroked her cheek. 'You're the one who's always reminding me you're not Angela.'

'I mean it, Sam. You've been hurt enough already. I don't want to add to that, stir up all the bad memories. I love you too much to put you through the mill again.'

He bit his lip. 'A lot of people who go through fertility treatment end up splitting up. The thing you both want most in the world ends up tearing you apart.'

'It doesn't have to be like that for us.'

'No. I know. Just because it happened before—'

'Doesn't mean it'll happen again,' she finished.

He sighed. 'It's not pleasant—though it's probably going to be worse for you than it is for me, being poked and prodded and asked never-ending and very, very intimate questions. You can forget about dignity—by the time all the investigations are over you don't have any left. And when you've done all that, the results seem to take for ever to arrive.'

She squeezed his hand. 'It must have been hard, seeing it written down in black and white that you couldn't have children.'

'I didn't actually see it,' Sam admitted.

Jodie frowned. 'What do you mean?'

'Angela opened the results. Then she shredded them. Well, she was upset,' he said. 'It was her way of dealing with it. I wasn't going to make it worse by ringing the lab to ask for another bit of paper.'

'So you didn't actually see what the results said?'

'Angela wasn't a medic, but she wouldn't have misread them, if that's what you're thinking,' Sam said.

Jodie's eyes narrowed. 'Does she have any children now?'

He shrugged. 'I've no idea. We didn't stay in touch. The divorce was handled by my solicitor. She didn't contest it and I...I didn't see her again.'

A tiny piece of hope sprang up in her heart. 'Are you really sure she told you the truth?'

Sam frowned. 'Why would she lie about something like that?'

'You said she left you for her boss. Maybe she used that as an excuse,' Jodie suggested.

He shook his head. 'Things were bad between us towards the end, but she wouldn't do something as horrible as that. But if I wasn't infertile, why didn't we...? Oh.' It suddenly dawned on him. 'You think she might have been the one with problems?'

'You might have reduced fertility, Sam, but if she had problems as well—problems she didn't tell you about, such as endometriosis or scarring of her tubes from an operation in her past—then that's why she didn't conceive.' Jodie bit her lip. 'It might not have been you. At least, not *just* you.' Which meant that she and Sam had more of a chance of having their own child. The hope flared brighter. 'Could your condition change, do you think?'

Sam shook his head. 'I don't see how. Besides, fertility decreases with age, doesn't it?'

'But neither of us are fertility specialists,' Jodie pointed out. 'Sam…I know it's a horrible thing to ask, but would you—would you check it out? Get a copy of the letter from your consultant so we know exactly what we're dealing with?'

He sighed. 'It's not going to change anything, but OK. If that's what you want, we'll do it.' He kissed the tip of her nose. 'Don't tell me you're going to be a reformed character yourself and keep a neat file on all this,' he teased.

She grinned back, not in the least offended. 'Well…'

'Jodie, the results might still be the same,' he said, 'which rules out IVF. AID might not work, and the authorities might hold my age against us when it comes to adoption.'

'You're only—what, thirty-five?'

'Yes, but there's a cut-off point somewhere,' he warned, 'and then there's all the admin and assessments to go through first to check if we're suitable. At the end of it all, we still might not have a baby. We might go through months and months of waiting and hoping and heartache for nothing.'

Jodie's eyes were huge as she looked at him. 'I know. Adoption's only one of the things we can look at.' She paused. 'But at the end of it all, if none of them work, we've still got each other. That's the important thing.'

'Have we?' he asked.

'Have we what?'

'Got each other? You still haven't actually said you'll marry me,' he reminded her.

She smiled. 'Yes.'

'Yes?' he prompted.

'OK, if you insist on being pedantic, yes, Sam Taylor, I love you and, yes, Sam Taylor, I will marry you.'

He pulled her into his arms and kissed her thoroughly. By the time he lifted his head, she was shaking.

'Cold?' He brushed a snowflake from her cheek.

'Yes—no—yes. I don't know.' She laughed. 'I can't think straight with you around.'

'I know the feeling. Good, isn't it?' He kissed her again. 'I think it's called happiness.'

'Happiness.' Jodie smiled. 'There was a point when I didn't think I'd ever be happy again—when I thought you'd left me.'

'I know, and I'm sorry. I've got a lot of making up to do to you,' he said.

She grinned. 'I'll hold you to that.'

She was quiet for a long time while he kissed her. When they resurfaced, her eyes were shining with tears—this time, tears of joy.

'I love you, Sam,' she said softly. 'Baby or no baby. I want to spend the rest of my life with you.'

'Nothing's ever going to part us again,' he promised.

'Ever,' she echoed. 'Let's go home. I thought coffee…or something.'

He smiled back. 'Define something.'

Her smile broadened and she traced his lower lip with her forefinger. 'I don't think I need to—do I?'

Two weeks later, Jodie finished dressing. 'Do I look all right?' she asked nervously, looking at herself in the long mirror.

'Yes!' came the chorus from her mother, Ellen, Annie and Fiona.

'I still can't believe you're getting married,' Ellen said. 'This quickly.'

'Not to mention beating Matt and me down the aisle,' Annie teased.

'There wasn't any point in waiting,' Jodie said. 'We wanted the rest of our lives to start right now. And hardly anyone gets married at this time of year, so it was easy to book the venue.' She smiled ruefully. 'I'm sorry about letting you down with the big church wedding, Mum. But Sam couldn't get married in church anyway, so this is the next best thing.'

'It's absolutely fine, as long as you're both happy. And you look beautiful,' her mother said, blinking away a tear.

Jodie had one eye on her watch. 'We'd better go downstairs.'

'Another first,' Fiona said. 'A doctor on time.'

'Oh, ha, ha,' Jodie said, but she was beaming from ear to ear. In only a few minutes she was going to walk into the hall of the beautiful old country house on her father's arm—and she was going to be married to Sam.

The last two weeks had been crazy. Her parents had been shocked and then delighted, especially when Sam had rung them later to ask formal permission for Jodie's hand in marriage. Matt, for once in his life, had been silenced. Ellen had simply stared and stared when Jodie had called round to ask if she fancied being a matron of honour, with Billy as page-boy. And Sam's mother's whoop of joy when they rung her with the news had been so loud that even Jodie, who'd been sitting on Sam's lap as he'd talked, had been able to hear it.

The morning after Sam's proposal, they'd gone into work together. Fiona had been there before them and had noted their arrival.

'Well?' she asked, hands on hips and her mouth compressed into a hard line.

'Well, what, Sister?' Sam asked coolly.

'Are you two finally seeing sense?'

'Probably not,' Sam said. 'But I need to see you later about something, Sister Ferguson. Something extremely important.' He gave her a sidelong look, then a huge grin and kissed Jodie soundly. 'And you, my love, have things to do this morning.'

'Mmm.' Jodie touched the tip of his nose with her finger. 'See you at lunchtime.'

He whispered something in her ear that made her laugh and blush. She gave Fiona a wink, then went home to make a few calls.

When Jodie returned to the ward at lunchtime to meet Sam, she caught various people whispering in huddles, but no one said a word to her. She found out what the whispers were about after lunch when Sam had whisked her into one of the most exclusive jewellers in Melbury to buy a simple solitaire diamond set in platinum. When they walked back onto the ward, there were congratulatory notices everywhere—drawn and decorated by the patients who could hold a pencil, with the handprints of various babies and those who were too sick to write. There was a huge table of canapés at the nurses' station, champagne for those about to go off duty and orange juice for those who weren't.

'I…' Jodie gave up, overwhelmed, and just beamed at everyone.

'Couldn't happen to a nicer couple,' Fiona said, hugging them both.

'But— When did all this…?'

'His credit card, my talent for organisation,' Fiona said with a wink, nodding at Sam. 'Come on, then, let's see the ring.'

They pulled a similar stunt the day before the wedding, decorating the ward with bows and papier-mâché bells, courtesy of the more active children on the ward. Jodie had changed the traditional bridal favours into goodie bags for the patients and boxes of Belgian chocolate sea-shells for her colleagues, and promised to bring in the photographs to show everyone.

And now she and Sam were about to take the final step… She shivered.

'Second thoughts?' her mother murmured.

'Never,' Jodie said softly. 'Just nervous.'

'You'll be fine.' Her mother hugged her. 'Now, stop it, or you'll *really* make me cry!'

As the string quartet began to play 'The Arrival of the Queen of Sheba', Sam turned to face his bride. Stunning barely began to describe her. She wore a slim-fitting ivory raw silk dress with a kick-pleat at the back, and her hair was pinned up in a way that reminded him of the young Grace Kelly. As she came closer, he realised that there were pearls in her hair—presumably some sort of posh hairpins. Her bouquet was a very simple arrange-ment of ivory roses and gypsophila, and walking behind her he saw Ellen in a simple lavender raw silk shift dress, Billy in a sailor suit and little Amy Simcox toddling along next to him in a smaller version of Ellen's dress, slightly unsteady and clutching Billy's hand.

Tears pricked at the backs of his eyes. Amy Simcox, the toddler Jodie had sung to and played with while she'd been in traction. Jodie had gone round to see her after the splints had been taken off, taking a couple of toys to help encourage her to walk. Amy, the sick child who'd started this whole thing off. It was fitting that she should be their bridesmaid. Trust Jodie to think of that.

Everyone in the rows of seats in the ballroom stood up as Jodie approached, then sat down again as the reg-istrar began his speech. By the time he informed Sam they were man and wife and the string quartet played Pachelbel's 'Canon', there was hardly a dry eye in the room.

'And now,' Sam said, 'I'm going to kiss the bride.' And he did.

'I don't think I've ever seen a more radiant bride,' Ellen said.

Jodie just grinned broadly at her best friend.

Ellen tipped her head on one side. 'I recognise that look. Is there something else you're not telling me? Like…you're going to make me a godmother?'

Jodie shook her head. 'Not quite. We're working on it, though. Sam's written to the clinic that treated him, asking for copies of all the test results and his records. He's going to have another test, too—what seemed impossible a few years ago might be something we can work with now. You know how quickly medicine advances.' Her eyes sparkled. 'But for the moment I'm just enjoying having Sam all to myself.'

Ellen chuckled. 'From the look on his face, he's having similar thoughts.'

Jodie glanced towards her new husband, who was in earnest conversation with her father. As if he knew she was looking at him, he lifted his head to catch her gaze and smiled at her. The sheer love in his face made her feel as if she were walking on air. Happiness, she thought. Even if they never managed to have a baby, they'd still have this. Always.

Several hours later, when Sam and Jodie were dancing cheek to cheek, he turned to whisper in her ear. 'Happy?'

'Very. You?'

'Uh-huh. I'd rate this as the second-best day of my life.'

'Second-best?' Did that mean his first wedding day had been better? Jodie tensed.

He dropped a kiss on the end of her nose. 'It's going to take a lot to beat Melbury cathedral on a winter night, with snow falling and you accepting my proposal of marriage.'

'Oh.' She relaxed.

'Mum agrees with me about you,' he told her. 'You're the most beautiful woman in the world and you have the eyes of an angel.'

'Flatterer!' She grinned. 'I'm sorry Dad and Matt gave you a grilling.'

'Only natural. They love you very much.' He paused. 'They were a bit easier than your mum and Ellen.'

'Ah.'

'I think they all just wanted to be sure of my intentions.'

'Which are?'

'To make this the best and happiest marriage in history,' he said simply. 'I love you, Jodie.' He kissed the curve of her neck. 'Do you reckon anyone would notice if we slipped away?'

'Only your mum, my parents, Matt and Annie, Ellen, Fiona and the rest of the ward,' she retorted, laughing.

'Worth a try, though,' he said, edging her towards the door. 'Because, right now, I can't wait to have you all to myself...'

CHAPTER FIFTEEN

'I CAN'T be.' Jodie stared at her GP in a mixture of shock and delight just over two months later. 'I can't be.' It was impossible—wasn't it?

'All your symptoms add up. Have you done a test?'

Jodie shook her head.

'We can do one here, but you might just as well use a home testing kit. They're as accurate as the ones we use and you'll get the confirmation now instead of to-morrow morning.'

'So, how pregnant am I?' she asked.

'About ten weeks, I'd say,' the doctor said sagely. 'We'll send you for a scan to check.'

'But…' Sam didn't think his condition could have changed. How could she possibly be pregnant? And to be ten weeks pregnant—that meant she'd conceived on their honeymoon. In Venice, the most gorgeous city in the world. Not that they'd explored many of the sights. They'd taken advantage of the dark evenings to have early nights. Not to mention afternoon naps… Her lips curved at the memory.

They'd never once used protection, assuming they hadn't had to. And she'd had a period since they'd come home. A very light one. Earlier than she'd expected. Her next one had been missing altogether, but she'd put that down to rushing about—that and the occasional bit of nausea. And she'd put that down to nerves about some forthcoming exams. It was the stuff of family legend that Jodie was sick when she was nervous, and she'd actually thrown up over her examiner's feet on the morning of her driving test. Had she been wrong and it had been morning sickness instead?

She'd been feeling tired lately, too. She'd just assumed she was a bit run-down, so she'd come to her GP to check her iron levels. And now he was telling her she wasn't anaemic or run-down, she was expecting a baby—the baby they'd thought they'd never have.

She couldn't quite take it in.

They were going to have a baby—a baby of their own?

'Is anything wrong, Jodie?'

Jodie shook her head. 'I'm just a bit stunned, that's all.'

'A happy accident, hmm?'

'Yes.' Yes, yes, yes! She smiled. 'Something like that.' But before she could tell Sam, there were a couple of things she needed to do. On impulse, she reached over and kissed her GP. 'This is better than, oh, all my birthdays and Christmases and everything rolled into one.'

'Well, congratulations,' her GP said warmly. 'And before you go, we'll book you in for your antenatal appointments.'

Antenatal appointments. Jodie hugged herself. Just wait until Sam heard the news—he was going to be a dad! This would really knock him for six.

'So, did the GP say you've been overdoing it and you need iron tablets, then?' Sam asked as he walked into the kitchen, later that evening, to find his wife sitting with her feet up on a chair.

'No. I'm OK.'

'Hmm. I still think you're studying too hard.'

'I'll slow down,' Jodie promised. She had a feeling that, once Sam knew, she wouldn't have a choice in the matter! 'Stop worrying. Everything's fine.' More than fine, but there was something else she wanted him to see before she told him her news. Something she'd found lying on the doormat when she'd returned from the doctor's.

Fed up with the endless wait for the paperwork to come back from Sam's previous specialist—who'd retired and the results had apparently been archived, so it would take a long time to retrieve them—she'd persuaded Sam to go for another test. A test whose results now lay in the brown envelope she was holding. Had she not already guessed what it had to say, she'd have probably taken the envelope straight to Sam's office and made him open it. As it was, she'd been confident enough to wait for him to come off duty. 'Um, this came for you in the second post.' She waved the envelope at him. 'Open it.'

He heard the impatient note in her voice and frowned. 'What?'

'It's from the clinic. Look at the franking,' Jodie said. 'Come on, open it! Let's see what they have to tell us.'

'You could have opened it,' he said.

'Not on your life.' Someone had read his results once before—and Jodie knew for certain now that Angela had got it wrong. This time there would be no mistake. She wanted Sam to see it himself in black and white.

The truth.

'Are you going to open that envelope or not?'

He nodded. 'In a minute.'

'Sam? Don't freeze on me now. *Talk* to me. I'm your wife, remember? And you promised to reform,' she pointed out.

'Yes.' He sighed. 'Sorry. It's— I suppose it's a bit like opening your exam results. Except I always had a pretty good idea how I'd done in my exams, whereas this...

I don't know. I've got no control over it. And it scares me, Jodie. What if…?' His voice tailed off.

'Whatever it says, I love you,' she informed him firmly. 'Now and always. That's not going to change, whether you can have babies or not. I love you, Sam Taylor, for keeps. OK?'

'OK.' He gave her a nervous smile, then slit the envelope. He read the short letter in silence. Then he read it again. Then he read it a third time, just in case he'd got it wrong. And then he dropped the letter on the table, picked Jodie up and whirled her round in his arms.

'Good news, I take it?' she asked in amusement when he'd put her down.

'The best! Jodie, either something's changed or Angela got it wrong. Maybe she thought subfertile meant infertile—I don't know. Apparently, I've a very low sperm count, but the motility's fine.' He whirled her round again and laughed. 'Which means that if we want to try it, ICSI should work for us.'

'That's fantastic news.' She kissed him.

'All this time… All this time I thought I couldn't have children, and I've put you through hell over it. I'm so sorry.'

'That's in the past,' she said firmly. 'I think we need some champagne. To celebrate.' Well, *he* could have the champagne. She would have just a tiny sip.

'Definitely.' Sam rubbed his nose against hers. 'We're going to be parents, Jodie. We really, really are.'

If she didn't tell him soon she'd burst! But she'd promised herself this. She wanted to see his face as he worked it out for himself—that she already knew the results of his tests before she'd even seen them. 'Oh, before I forget, I've got a present for you.'

'Present?' His eyes widened. 'I haven't forgotten an anniversary or anything, have I?'

'No.' Sam bought her flowers every month to celebrate the day she'd agreed to marry him, a gesture which still delighted her. And there were one or two more private dates they celebrated in other ways. 'It's— I suppose you could call it a late wedding present,' she said. 'A late honeymoon present even.'

He frowned. 'I'm not with you.'

She handed him a small package. 'Here.'

His frown deepened. 'What is it?'

'Open it,' she said mysteriously.

Sam did so—and gazed in surprise at the paintbrush. 'What's this for?'

'There's something else with it.' She turned the brush round in his hands so he could see the plain brown envelope taped to the bristles.

He opened it and just stared at the narrow white stick. 'Jodie?'

'Turn it the other way round and read it,' she said.

With shaking hands, he did so—and noted the blue line in the two windows. 'Jodie...' He lifted stunned eyes to hers. 'Is this—is this what I think it is?'

'Yep.'

'You're pregnant.' He looked as stunned as she'd felt when her GP had told her the news.

'Which is why I've been feeling so tired. Not because I've been studying too hard. And that's why I've been feeling sick, too—morning sickness, not exam nerves.' She smiled. 'The GP examined me, but I did the test just to make sure. We've got a scan booked for the week after next.'

'How—how long?'

'Ten weeks, apparently—which makes this a Venetian

baby.' She grinned broadly. 'If you weren't so heavy, I think I'd spin *you* round the kitchen!'

'We're going to have a baby.' He stared at the test stick, then at his wife. 'Jodie—we're going to have a *baby*!' His eyes glistened with tears. 'I can't believe it. We're actually going to have a baby. You're carrying—' his voice was hushed with awe '—my child.'

'Hence the brush. You've got some decorating to do. Our baby's nursery,' she clarified with a grin. 'Lemon yellow. Though we could use blue as we're obviously having a boy.'

'Who says? It's definitely a girl,' he retorted. 'A girl as beautiful as her mother.'

'Ha.' She hugged him. 'It's been killing me, keeping this quiet since lunchtime. I nearly rang you about twenty times to tell you—only I didn't dare ask Julianne to put me through.'

'As if you're scared of anyone.' He kissed her again. 'I can't quite take this in. We're having a baby... Oh, heavens. You haven't been rushing around on your bike, have you?'

Jodie looked slightly evasive. 'Not since lunchtime.'

'I'm locking it up. I know what you're like. From now on, I'm going to be your taxi service. No cycling, no rushing round, no overdoing things. And why are you standing up? You should be resting!' He sat down at the table and pulled her onto his lap.

'Stop fussing. I'm perfectly healthy.' She tangled one hand in his hair. 'Just...pregnant.'

'Pregnant.' He savoured the word and stroked her still flat abdomen. 'Pregnant with our baby.'

'Are you...pleased?' she asked diffidently.

'*Pleased?*' Sam swallowed hard. 'That doesn't even begin to cover it. I thought—I thought we'd have to wait for months. The results of my test today…well, that gave us an extra option—IVF. But it all takes so long. I never dreamed we'd have a child of our own so soon.' He shook his head. 'I'm shocked, I'm excited, I'm scared, I…I want to climb up on the roof and tell the whole world I'm going to be a dad!' Words he'd never thought he'd ever, ever be able to say. Six little words. *We're going to have a baby.*

'Not a good idea,' Jodie said, taking the pregnancy test and paintbrush from his hand and putting them on top of the letter from the clinic.

He stared at her, his skin prickling. 'Why not? Everything's all right, isn't it? I mean, you're not— Our baby— I…' Fear bubbled up through his words.

'Stop worrying. You'll drive me insane if you're like this for the next thirty weeks.' She kissed the tip of his nose. 'All I meant was, if you fell off the roof, you'd be in plaster for months, and I want you at antenatal classes with me.'

'Just you try stopping me! I'll be there at every single appointment. I'll learn how to give you a proper back rub, I'll do all the breathing with you, and you can swear at me all you like while you're in transition. I love you, Dr Taylor.' His eyes turned silver. 'You *and* our baby.'

'And I love you.' She nuzzled his cheek. 'Though I'd kill for a Margherita pizza with avocado.'

He grinned. 'In anyone else, that'd be a craving. In you, that's normal.'

'Actually, I do have a craving.' Her lips twitched. 'Two.'

'Name them,' he said instantly. 'They're yours.'

'A bowl of cornflakes with ice-cold milk, no sugar.'

'And the second?'

She pursed her lips. 'I want to eat them in bed. Next to a certain dark-haired, grey-eyed doctor.'

He gave her a sidelong look. 'How about a rain check on the cornflakes?'

'And a very, very private celebration before we tell the rest of the world?' she suggested.

'It's a deal.' He kissed her, then swung her into his arms and carried her out of the kitchen.

EPILOGUE

SAM sat on his wife's bed and cradled their sleeping baby in his arms. 'I can hardly believe he's ours—he's really here,' he said, his voice hushed.

'How did we create something so perfect?' Jodie asked with a smile, reaching out to hold the baby's tiny fingers. 'I could watch him for hours. He's the spitting image of you. He's definitely got your nose, the same shape face as you. Oh, and your mouth. You look like him when you're sleeping.'

'His eyes might not be the same,' Sam pointed out.

'Well, you know all babies have blue eyes. They'll change—they'll turn the same beautiful silver-grey as his dad's,' she said confidently.

'Our baby boy.' Sam gently kissed the top of his son's head. 'Look, his hair's curly already. And he's fair, like you.'

'He's *perfect*,' she said proudly. And he was. Sam had done the paediatrician's check himself, no doubt haunted by what had happened to him as a baby, and he'd actually been in tears when he'd told Jodie everything was fine.

Her smile broadened. 'You know, Matt's going to be unbearably smug about the fact he shares our son's name, but I couldn't think of anything more appropriate. Matthew, gift of God. Our little boy.'

Sam met her gaze and smiled. 'We've been so lucky.'

'Haven't we just?'

Matthew Taylor gazed sleepily up at his father, moved his head to nuzzle Sam's chest, then realised that no milk was forthcoming. He opened his mouth and let out a loud howl of protest.

Sam chuckled. 'I'll change all the nappies you like, bath him and cuddle him and mop up any posseting—but this is definitely something he wants from his mum.' Gently, he handed the baby back to his wife, who leaned back against the pillow and adjusted Matthew's position until he could latch onto her breast. Sam watched them for a moment. 'You look like one of those Renaissance paintings,' he said, his lips curving. 'You know, Madonna and child.'

'They're supposed to be serene,' Jodie pointed out. 'Our son already knows his own mind—and he makes sure you know about it, too.'

'Just like his mum,' Sam teased, laughing.

'Huh. Aren't you supposed to be on ward rounds?'

'Uh-huh.'

'As in paediatric, not maternity?' she enunciated, amused.

'Detour,' he said simply. 'I was missing my wife—and my son.' He glanced at his watch and sighed. 'Actually, although I could stay here with you for ever, I'd better go. But I'll be back as soon as I've finished the ward rounds.' He leaned over to kiss her. 'I love you.'

'I love you, too.'

'And as for you, scrap, don't exhaust your mum too much.' He stroked the baby's cheek. 'I can't wait to take the pair of you home tomorrow. And show you off to everyone on the ward—Julianne's made a schedule of who's visiting and when.'

Jodie tried to keep a straight face but couldn't stop the giggles. 'A schedule?'

'To make sure you don't get overtired.' Sam's lips twitched.

'That's very sweet of her.' Jodie's smile broadened. 'But I don't give much for her chances. Most of them have already beaten her to it. Fi was the first one down, Mick babysat Charlie in the corridor while Shelley nipped in for a quick cuddle, then they swapped over, and Madge brought me a whole plate of lemon-curd tarts.'

'Where?' Sam demanded, looking round.

'Um, you've been beaten to them.'

'By half our ward?' he asked resignedly.

'Mmm. Duncan, Stuart, Megan and Sheila all had their fair share. Oh, and Lyn and Richard.' She smiled at him as Matthew decided he'd had enough milk and fell asleep again, clutching her finger tightly in one tiny fist. 'Life doesn't get any better than this, does it?'

'You wanted one of each,' he reminded her. 'We might need ICSI next time.'

'I'm happy right now,' Jodie said softly. 'Being here with the two men I love most in the world. A little girl, yes, that'd be the icing on the cake—to have one of each. But as long as I've got you, Sam, all's well with my world. And it always will be.'

He kissed her tenderly. 'Always,' he promised.

Make your Christmas wish list – and check it twice!

Watch out for these very special holiday stories – all featuring the incomparable charm and romance of the Christmas season.

By Jasmine Cresswell, Tara Taylor
Quinn and Kate Hoffmann
On sale 21st October 2005

By Lynnette Kent and
Sherry Lewis
On sale 21st October 2005

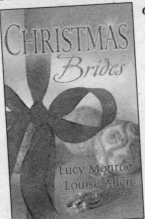

By Lucy Monroe and
Louise Allen
On sale 4th November 2005

By Heather Graham,
Lindsay McKenna, Marilyn
Pappano and Annette Broadrick
On sale 18th November 2005

By Marion Lennox, Josie Metcalfe
and Kate Hardy
On sale 2nd December 2005

By Margaret Moore, Terri Brisbin
and Gail Ranstrom
On sale 2nd December 2005

By Lisa Jackson, Barbara Boswell
and Linda Turner
On sale 18th November 2005

Celebrate
the charm of
Christmases
past in
three new
heartwarming
holiday tales!

COMFORT AND JOY by Margaret Moore
1860 Llanwyllan, Wales

After a terrible accident, Griffin Branwynne gives up on the joys of Christmas—until the indomitable Gwendolyn Davies arrives on his doorstep and turns his world upside-down. Can the earl resist a woman who won't take no for an answer?

LOVE AT FIRST STEP by Terri Brisbin
1199 England

While visiting friends in England for the holidays, Lord Gavin MacLeod casts his eye upon the mysterious Elizabeth. She is more noble beauty than serving wench, and Gavin vows to uncover her past—at any cost!

A CHRISTMAS SECRET by Gail Ranstrom
1819 Oxfordshire, England

Miss Charity Wardlow expects a marriage proposal from her intended while attending a Christmas wedding. But when Sir Andrew MacGregor arrives at the manor, Charity realises that she prefers this Scotsman with the sensual smile…

On sale 2nd December 2005

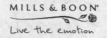

MILLS & BOON®

Live the emotion

Medical romance™

A CHILD TO CALL HER OWN by *Gill Sanderson*

Dr Tom Ramsey is enchanted by the clinic's new midwife – she rekindles emotions Tom thought he'd never feel again. But midwife Maria Wyatt is haunted by memories – memories that come flooding back when she meets Tom's adorable son James...

DELL OWEN MATERNITY: Midwives, doctors, babies – at the heart of a Liverpool hospital

COMING HOME FOR CHRISTMAS
by *Meredith Webber*

A&E specialist Nash McLaren has come home for Christmas, and is surprised to hear GP Ella Marsden is back. He thought no one in the town would trust a Marsden again. But, working with Ella, Nash starts to remember how good it feels to be with her...

EMERGENCY AT PELICAN BEACH
by *Emily Forbes*

Dr Tom Edwards has come to Pelican Beach to escape city life – meeting Dr Lexi Patterson after five years wasn't part of his plan! But, working together, they save lives, share memories and become close. The career-driven Lexi of the past has changed – she can't let Tom go again...

Don't miss out!
On sale 4th November 2005

Available at most branches of WHSmith, Tesco, ASDA, Borders, Eason, Sainsbury's and most bookshops

Visit www.millsandboon.co.uk

MILLS & BOON®

Live the emotion

Tender
romance™

HER ITALIAN BOSS'S AGENDA *by Lucy Gordon*
(The Rinucci Brothers)

Olympia Lincoln is so relieved when her new assistant shows up – she sets him to work immediately. What she doesn't realise is that he's actually Primo Rinucci, her new Italian boss! Primo can't resist playing along – this way he can get really close to the beautiful Olympia…!

A BRIDE WORTH WAITING FOR *by Caroline Anderson*

Annie Shaw believes her boyfriend, Michael Harding, died in a brutal attack nine years ago. But he's actually been forced to live undercover… Now Michael is free to pick up his life and reveal himself to the woman he loves. He can only hope that Annie will fall in love with the man he has become…

A FATHER IN THE MAKING *by Ally Blake*

After waiting so long to hear from the Gaspers, Laura thought they couldn't care less about her – or her daughter, Chloe. So when Ryan Gasper turned up at her Outback home she was understandably suspicious. Ryan's career – his life – was back in the city, but something about Laura made him want to stay…

THE WEDDING SURPRISE *by Trish Wylie*

Desperate to save her father's business, Caitlin Rourke enters a reality TV contest with the prize money in mind! To win she must convince her family that she's marrying a stranger – but as she gets to know her fake fiancé, Aiden Flynn, she finds it impossible to keep her feelings for him a secret…!

On sale 6th January 2006

Available at most branches of WHSmith, Tesco, ASDA, Borders, Eason, Sainsbury's and most bookshops

Visit www.millsandboon.co.uk